W9-BAZ-997

THERE WAS TROUBLE IN AFRICA,
BUT THEN, THERE WAS ALWAYS
TROUBLE IN AFRICA. AND THAT
CONTINENT, BECAUSE OF ITS SAVAGERY
AND NUMBERLESS CONFLICTS WAS A
NATURAL BATTLEGROUND FOR
THE MERCENARIES.
WHEN ALL ELSE FAILED THESE WERE
THE MEN THEY SENT FOR.

THE MERCENARIES

Though this book is a novel, much of
what is described here has happened. All
the political and military conditions described
here are true, as I have reason to know.
—Giles Tippette

"AN ADVENTURE STORY . . . WELL
PLOTTED, BELIEVABLE AND
FAST-PACED."
—*Houston Chronicle*

OTHER TITLES BY GILES TIPPETTE

Fiction
THE SURVIVALIST
THE TROJAN COW
THE BANK ROBBER

Nonfiction
SATURDAY'S CHILDREN
THE BRAVE MEN

Giles Tippette
THE MERCENARIES

A DELL BOOK

To Mary Grace.
Thanks for the loan of the
typewriter.

Published by
DELL PUBLISHING CO., INC.
1 Dag Hammarskjold Plaza
New York, N.Y. 10017

Copyright © 1976 by Giles Tippette

All rights reserved. No part of this book
may be reproduced in any form or by any
means without the prior written permission
of Delacorte Press/Eleanor Friede, New York,
N.Y. 10017, excepting brief quotes used in
connection with reviews written specifically
for inclusion in a magazine or newspaper.

Dell ® TM 681510, Dell Publishing Co., Inc.

ISBN: 0-440-15174-0

Reprinted by arrangement with
Delacorte Press/Eleanor Friede

Printed in the United States of America

First Dell printing—June 1977

Though this book is a novel, much of what is described here has happened. All the political and military conditions described here are true, as I have reason to know.

—Giles Tippette

ACKNOWLEDGMENTS

To Peter Hawthorne, without whose help this book would not have been possible. A good friend.

To James R. Booth, Lt. Colonel, U.S. Army (retired), for his help on the military matters.

And to the Kraut. And Gerry. And Reg Brett and South African Airways. And Howard Watson. And Les Gould. And Peter Van Rensburg.

And about a ton to Bob Cornell. And to two great people I can't name here for their own sakes, but who were maybe the most timely friends I ever made, and as loving as any I've ever known for caring about a stranger.

To Faye and Lavern Harris.

And Doug Garner of the Rhodesian diplomatic mission and his wonderful wife.

Finally, to my wife and two children, who survived.

THE MERCENARIES WERE GATHERING IN JOHANNESBURG. RUMOR SAID THAT ANOTHER BIG OPERATION WAS ON. THERE WAS TROUBLE IN AFRICA, BUT THEN, THERE WAS ALWAYS TROUBLE IN AFRICA. AND THAT CONTINENT, BECAUSE OF ITS SAVAGERY AND NUMBERLESS CONFLICTS, WAS THE NATURAL BATTLEGROUND FOR THE MERCENARIES. WHEN ALL ELSE HAD FAILED, THEN YOU WANTED THE COLD, EFFICIENT KILLERS WHO COULD COME IN AND DO A JOB AND GO AWAY LEAVING NONE OF THE RESIDUE OF MEN WHO FIGHT FOR A CAUSE.

THERE WAS ONE IMPORTANT DIFFERENCE THIS TIME, FROM ALL THE PAST CAMPAIGNS. THIS TIME NO ONE KNEW, OR COULD GUESS, WHY THEY WERE GATHERING OR FOR WHAT OBJECTIVE. THERE WAS A GREAT DEAL OF TALK IN THE BARS AND ON THE STREET, FOR THE FEELING WAS THERE. BUT THAT WAS ALL IT WAS, JUST TALK. IN A LAND WHERE EVERY HOTEL MAID COULD TELL YOU THE LATEST BATTLE PLAN, A SUDDEN SILENCE HAD COME. THERE WERE GUESSES, BUT NO ONE KNEW ANYTHING FOR SURE. THEY TALKED OF MOZAMBIQUE AND ANGOLA AND RHODESIA, AND EVEN OF SOUTH AFRICA. BUT IT WAS ALL JUST TALK. A VERY FEW MEN KNEW WHAT WAS ACTUALLY TO HAPPEN.

1

Johannesburg

The note had been waiting for him at the hotel when he arrived after the long flight. It had been hand delivered, for there was no stamp and nothing on the front except his name: Cody Ravel. The desk clerk had handed it to him as he checked in.

> Mr. Ravel:
>
> If you are not too fatigued from your long journey, I'd be obliged if you'd come around to my place this evening at half past eight. Only give the address to any cabdriver and he'll know the way. Let yourself in through the front gate and ring the doorbell.

It was unsigned, but he knew whom it was from: the same man who'd recruited him, the same man who'd sent him the airline ticket, the same man he'd come 7,000 miles to see. Someone named Jerome Weston.

He took time for a hot bath, to soak some of the tiredness out of his bones, and then lay down for a forty-five-minute nap before he went downstairs and hailed a cab.

They went out of the city over the expressway and then

turned off onto dark streets lined with Jacaranda trees that were dropping their blossoms. The address they stopped at was surrounded by a high palisade fence. Over its top, Cody could just make out the eaves of a high-roofed house against the night sky.

The driver said, "Mind the dogs, sir."

He stopped and turned, edgy because of all the security Weston's letters had impressed him with. "What dogs? How do you know they've got dogs here?"

"Everybody out here's got dogs, sir. Big dogs." The cab pulled away.

He let himself through the gate and walked up the dark approach to the house, half-expecting a sudden, fierce rush. But none came. He walked up on the porch and stopped in front of the massive door, put out his hand to ring the bell, and then dropped it. Instead, he turned away and walked to the edge of the porch, looking out at the black night. He got out a cigarette and lit it.

Well, he thought, another strange door. Another look, another try, another test. You kept moving, you kept hopping, from one person to another, one job to another, one door to another.

And what, he asked himself wryly, did he hope to find behind this one? His immortal soul? Happiness? Satisfaction? A new thrill?

He flicked the cigarette out through the night, watching its glow arc across the dark lawn and die in a burst of sparks. "Crashed," he said half-aloud. "Crashed and burned. Shot down in flames."

He turned and rang the bell. The door was opened immediately by a black maid with tribal markings on her high cheekbones. He said, "I'm expected."

She said, bowing back, "You come, please, sah. Master waiting."

He followed her down a long hall, its sides lined with

hunting trophies: sable buck, Cape buffalo, lion, kongoni. Everything was dark, heavy wood.

Ahead of him, the maid opened a double set of doors into a large, paneled library.

From a huge mahogany desk in a far corner, a stooped middle-aged man suddenly came rolling out in a wheelchair. He coasted up to Cody, his hand out. "Come in, Mr. Ravel. I'm Jerome Weston. Come in and sit down."

They sat down across from each other. Weston produced a bottle of Scotch and poured them both a drink of neat whiskey. Cody sipped his.

"How was your flight?" Weston asked him politely.

"It was long," Cody said.

"You came on South African Airways?"

"That was the ticket you sent me."

"Oh, yes, of course."

Then they sat there for a moment, studying each other.

At length, Weston said, "Well, what are your impressions?"

"Of what?"

Weston waved his glass vaguely. "Why the whole thing, I should imagine."

"What makes you think I know enough to have any impressions?"

"You are rather abrupt, aren't you?"

"I'm waiting," Cody said.

Weston threw back his head and laughed. "And quite aware that I'm sizing you up."

"I've been looked over before."

"Tell me, weren't you surprised? At my first letter? It must have come to you like a bolt out of the blue, so to speak."

Cody took a small sip of his drink. "It's happened before."

"Indeed?"

"People hear about you. Word gets around. I've been

3

doing this a long time so I'm not much surprised by anything anymore. Your letter came at a good time."

"Well, we can be thankful for that," Weston said. He raised his glass.

Over in the corner, Cody could see the dogs. Two of them. Big, with tufts of hair running down their backs. They seemed asleep, but Cody noticed that if he so much as shifted in his chair each would flick up an ear.

He said, "So there are the dogs."

Weston looked up sharply. "What's that?"

"The cabdriver. When I got out, he told me to be careful of the dogs."

"What an extraordinary thing to say. Had you given him some reason?" Weston had his head cocked slightly to the side. His eyes were narrowed.

"No. I didn't say a word to him the whole way out. He said everybody out here's got dogs. Big dogs, he said."

"Ahh." Weston smiled slightly. "Quite so."

Cody said, "That's a little strong, isn't it? Is this place that dangerous?"

"It could be," Weston said. Though he was small, his face seemed large, even for his head, and there was a mobility about his features that caused his expression to change with the pattern of what he was saying. He spoke rapidly, but with only a moderate British accent. Now he cocked an eyebrow and drew down one corner of his mouth. "This is an unhappy continent, Mr. Ravel. There are many forces at work, even in this city. And who knows . . ." He shrugged and his face went bland. "But it's the haves who keep the dogs. The have-nots don't need them. I don't suppose that's much different from the rest of the world, eh?"

"I wouldn't know," Cody said. "I never stayed in one place long enough to need a dog."

Weston's eyebrow went up, but he reached out for the bottle of Scotch. "Let's have the other half, shall we?"

Books lined the sides of the room they were in. It was a big room, high-ceilinged and long. Around the top of each wall, more trophy heads were mounted: kongoni and antelope, wildebeest and kudu, and, on each side of the massive fireplace, lion and leopard. Overhead, two circular fans turned slowly. It was a dark room, heavy with massive mahogany and teak. It was an old house, Cody guessed, old and built to last. He'd felt, as the maid had brought him down the hall, as if he were entering another century.

"Tell me, Mr. Ravel, about your combat experiences."

Cody lowered his drink. "What's that got to do with anything?"

"We're interested in everything about you. You can understand that, I'm sure."

"I wasn't a military pilot."

"We know that."

"So what does my combat experience have to do with it?"

Weston ignored the question. "You were, I believe, a platoon commander with an American special forces group in the early days of the Vietnam war."

"How do you know that? That wasn't on my resumé."

Weston pulled at his ear and looked across the room. "We're a small operation, as you can imagine, Mr. Ravel. But we're not totally without resources. I'm merely interested in why you left your country's army with such an obviously brilliant career in front of you."

Cody took a drink, shuddering slightly at the taste of the Scotch, and set the glass on the small table beside his chair. "I didn't like it."

"Why not?"

"Listen," Cody said. He ran a hand across his face. He could feel the effects of the flight from New York begin to sink in as the Scotch relaxed him. "Listen," he said, "you hired me to come over here as a pilot. Flying transport and recon. You've got my flight records and ratings."

"And quite impressive," Weston said.

"So what's this talk about combat experience? You're not talking gunship work to me because I've got no gunship experience. And even if you were fool enough to expect me to try it, I wouldn't be fool enough."

Weston stopped a moment to open a box of cigars. He held the box toward Cody.

"I'll smoke a cigarette," Cody said.

Weston lit his cigar, holding the flame long against the end while he puffed slowly. Then he put the cigar in an ashtray. "You've no past experience as a mercenary, Mr. Ravel."

"You know that."

"Then I suggest that it's presumptuous of you to interpret what my questions might mean."

Cody lit a cigarette. He was feeling more tired. The nap at the hotel hadn't helped much. And he was hungry. He tried to think when he'd eaten last. Sometime on the plane, but his hours were so turned around by the seven-hour time difference that he didn't know exactly when that was.

"You're thirty-six," Weston said. He looked at Cody. "You got out of the service at twenty-two. What have you done with the other fourteen years?"

"Listen," Cody said, "I don't want to seem *presumptuous* again." He let the words drawl out with a bite in them. He'd expected it to be straightforward and quick. He thought it had all been settled by mail. He would fly for them; they would pay him so much money. And that was it. Outside the odd chance of getting shot at. But now there were these questions that he couldn't see had much to do with the job. And he didn't want to answer them.

Weston said, as if reading his mind, "You mustn't be impatient with me, Mr. Ravel. Indulge me, please."

"It's all there in the resumé," Cody said. He pointed at Weston's desk.

The cripple waved a hand depreciatingly. "Facts and figures, Mr. Ravel, facts and figures. I need something a bit more than that."

Cody looked down at his hands and didn't answer. They were long, slender hands, deceptively slim as was the rest of his body. Part of the deception came because he was tall, over six feet, but that didn't hide the sudden flare of his back muscles as they rose to his shoulders. He was heavily tanned and his hair was bleached to an almost blond from the years of waiting around this or that little field for whatever illicit cargo or passenger. He looked young except for the wrinkles around his eyes and the tiredness in his face.

The cripple noticed Cody looking at the trophy heads and said, depreciatingly, "Afraid they're a bit moth-eaten now."

"Who killed 'em?"

"Why, I did, lad." He suddenly slapped the arm of his wheelchair. "My legs weren't always pneumatic tires, you know. As a matter of fact, I used to be something of a rounder in my own right." He smiled faintly at distant memories. "Even used to be a slaver."

"Yeah?"

Weston made a face. "Well, not to the letter of the word. Used to get my truck and go down in Mekorekore land and get a mob of the bushmen blokes drunked up on mealie beer, then haul them down into Rhodesia and contract them off to the farmers for 10 quid each." He pulled at his ear. "Of course, it wasn't really slavery. The farmers paid the blokes and they done bloody well better than they'd done starving in the flaming bush. Proper food and proper lodging. Of course, that was thirty odd years ago." He looked away, frowning slightly. "I'm from Rhodesia, actually. All the family's still back there."

Cody didn't respond. He knew very little about Africa. Names like Mozambique and Angola and Rhodesia and Zambia were only words to him, having no place or form or identity.

Weston came back to him. "You're not married?"

"No."

"You've no dependents?"

"No." He refrained from pointing out, again, that it was all there on the resumé.

Weston said, "No country, no family, no wife. Tell me, Mr. Ravel, where do your loyalties lie?"

Cody said shortly, "With me."

"What is that supposed to mean?"

He gave the cripple a level look. "Whatever in the hell you want it to mean."

"That's no answer."

"It wasn't much of a question, either."

They stared at each other for a moment. Weston broke the tension by picking up his cigar. He puffed at it meditatively for a moment, laid it back in the tray, and asked casually, "Tell me, do you think of yourself as a man who can be trusted?"

"With what?"

Weston sighed. "You will spar, won't you?" He looked at Cody a long time. The pilot stared back out of his brown eyes. Weston suddenly laughed shortly. "You're not exactly spoiling for this job, are you?"

"I can take it or leave it," Cody said. He ran his hand over his face again. "So far, I don't know enough about it to be interested one way or another. So far, we're playing your ground rules. You made it clear in your letters that this was a clandestine operation, and I was going to have to go a ways on faith. Okay. I accepted that. And I'm still accepting it. But you're running a lot of bullshit in on me that I don't think's got a goddamn thing to do with me flying airplanes for you or whoever's running this show." He suddenly stood up. "Look, I'm tired and I'm hungry. Let's take this up tomorrow. Maybe I'll be a little more receptive."

"Oh, I'm sorry," Weston said. He stretched out his hand for a buzzer on his desk. "I should have thought. I'll have something prepared."

Cody shook his head. "No. No, thanks. I want to go to a restaurant and eat by myself and have about six bourbons and then crash for about twelve hours. After that, we'll see." He turned toward the door.

Weston said sharply, "One moment, please."

Cody paused.

"I'm afraid," Weston said, "that that won't be possible. It's absolutely necessary that you and I come to some agreement this very night."

"Why?" Cody asked, still halfway across the room.

"Let's just say it's in the order of things. Now will you please sit down?"

Cody studied him.

Weston said, "Of course, if you don't want the job . . ."

Cody said, "I'm not at all convinced there's a job, anyway. This doesn't look much like a military operation to me. You, this house. For all I know, you're some madman who likes to send people airline tickets."

The cripple smiled thinly. "Let me assure you that we are about some very serious business. And we are only interested in serious-minded people. Now will you please retake your seat?"

Cody looked at him for a moment longer. "All right," he finally said. "But let's quit playing games with those goddamn ring-around-the-rosy questions of yours."

"Will you have something to eat?"

"No. Not until this is over. I'll eat back at the hotel. Where I can relax."

"As you will."

Weston leaned back in his chair and regarded Cody thoughtfully. "So you think perhaps this is a game. You think perhaps that I'm some grandiose fool in a wheelchair with too much money and too little to spend it on, who sends off letters and airplane tickets to well-known venture pilots."

Cody glanced up at him sharply.

Weston said hastily, "Oh, well-known only in certain circles, of course." He half-smiled. "Well, let's see just how haphazard and casual this operation really is. Let's examine a few facts about you. And as you listen, you may come to see that the accumulation of these facts would be well beyond the resources of a demented cripple in a wheelchair. Eh?"

Cody looked at him steadily.

Without consulting the papers on his desk, Weston said, "You've flown in Canada, Mr. Ravel. You've flown in Mexico and Cuba and South America. You have flown in the Mideast. You have smuggled gold and you have run guns. You have been involved in many illegal activities. What impresses us, Mr. Ravel, is that you have also acted clandestinely for, shall we say, the side of law and order? Do I need to mention any names here?"

Cody said, "You're telling it."

"Yes, indeed. And I can see that you're impressed."

Cody shrugged. "Anybody can make guesses."

"Oh, you want specifics?" Weston leaned back and looked at the ceiling. "All right. Let's consider the time your government wanted a particular defector back. Scientific chap. And they had him trussed up and ready for you. In that little field in Mexico. Does that bring back any memories, Mr. Ravel?"

Cody looked down at the floor.

"Or the other side of the coin. The two bank robbers. Of course, I will give you that you didn't know what they were hiring you for. And they were later caught. I use it only to illustrate our research."

"All right," Cody said. "I'm impressed. You're big time. Hurray. What else?"

"You're a very cocksure young man, Mr. Ravel. Very capable. *We're* impressed. You have the amazing facility to enjoin trust from all your associates."

"Okay," Cody said. "Okay. Now what does it all come down to?"

"It comes down to that we're very eager to hire you."

"I thought that was all settled."

Weston pulled at his ear. "Well, the fact is, you're being considered for more of a job than the normal transport pilot one I originally contacted you about."

"What sort of a job?"

Weston laughed dryly. "Well, we're back to that enigma we began with. Unfortunately, all I can tell you is that it's an important job. In point of fact, it will put you in possession of highly confidential information. Dangerous information. You might begin to see, then, why I've had to be so diabolically clever."

"Why me?" Cody asked bluntly. He was watching Weston, his eyes narrowed.

"Oh, come now, Mr. Ravel. That should be obvious to you. What is the saying? Your reputation has preceded you. Of course, none of this is up to me. Not the selection. It happens that the man you'll be working for is one of your own countrymen. A fact that he likes. But we are still determining how much to trust you, while you decide if you trust us. Your kind doesn't grow on trees. This search has gone on much too long and time is running out. I hope that you can fill this rather special function for us. And that you'll want to. Of course, that will have to be decided in time. And it can't be decided by me. But it at least explains some of the questions I've felt rather silly about asking you."

"And how do we go about figuring out if you'll want me?"

Weston shrugged. "I rather imagine we take it a step at a time, feeling you out along the way."

"That doesn't tell me much."

"Of course not," Weston said intently. "It wasn't intended to. It may be decided that we don't want you for the job without your ever knowing. We may simply choose to keep you as one of our regular pilots. As I say, you've always got a job." He shrugged.

"This other. Who decides?"

"You're not expecting a name."

"Look, goddammit. Somebody's running this show. And it ain't you."

"Oh yes," Weston said, nodding rapidly. "Someone *is* running this show. A very special someone."

"When do I meet him?"

"I don't know," Weston said honestly.

"Christ," Cody said disgustedly. He snubbed his cigarette out in an ashtray. "What makes you think I'll want this goddamn special job, as you call it?"

"Well," Weston said carefully. "We can't know for sure. But your background, your experiences, the type of man you seem to be led us to believe that you would like it very much."

"You know a hell of a lot about me."

Weston shrugged.

"I'm not sure I like that," Cody said in a hard voice.

"Well," Weston said carefully, "you must understand we've got a bit at stake here."

Cody looked at him, considering. "You're crazy as hell. You know that?"

Weston didn't smile. "Be that as it may."

"You don't ask much, do you? That's like playing poker where the other guy doesn't let you see his cards. Just tells you when you've won or lost."

"I'm not making the rules, Mr. Ravel. I'm only following orders." Weston picked up a fountain pen and looked at it carefully. Then he looked back up at Cody. "Well?"

After a moment, Cody shrugged. "I'll stick around."

Weston suddenly smiled. "Welcome aboard, Captain Ravel."

"What do I do now?"

"You wait," the cripple said. "You go to your hotel and you stay there. You talk to no one, you call no one, you write no one."

"How long do I wait?"

"I don't know," Weston said quite honestly. "As you've gathered, I'm only the go-between. The procurer, as it were."

He put out his hand and pushed the buzzer. "I'll have my man Joseph drive you back to your hotel." He leaned back in his wheelchair and locked his hands behind his head. "Joseph is of the Matabelle tribe. When my ancestors arrived here a hundred years ago, Joseph's ancestors were busily involved with exterminating the Mineshona, who were another tribe of this area. Joseph now knows how to drive a car and to wait table and even to give me my insulin shot. But he would still kill a Mineshona out of hand if he didn't fear the white man putting him in jail. A situation, by the way, he finds utterly incomprehensible."

Cody looked at him curiously. "I have a feeling you had some reason for telling me that."

Weston smiled thinly. "Perhaps the moral is that everyone in Africa has enemies. And now that you've joined our tribe you too have enemies. And they'll kill you just as quick as Joseph would a Mineshona if they get onto you."

"I didn't need the explanation," Cody said.

"One further point. In a few days, you'll be going to

our regular headquarters for processing. Pay and records and official documents and all that sort of thing. And you'll see and be around our ground chaps that are in training. Once they learn that you're a pilot, they'll be all over you to see what you know. Say nothing. None of them knows aught about the operation. They haven't the first clue as to what they're actually training for. And even though you think you know nothing now, you might be surprised what they could piece together."

"All right," Cody said. He could feel the tiredness coming down on him again like a cloak. He wondered if he'd be able to hold out long enough to eat.

They shook hands and Weston went to the library door with Cody. The dogs raised their muzzles and watched them all the way.

"Another warning," Weston said. "You'll find this place different from any you've ever been in before. Everyone will be curious about you. Everyone will be asking questions. Everyone will be suspicious. Make no mistake, you're in a country at war."

They shook hands again and Weston said, "Good night, Captain. I'll be in touch with you shortly."

When Cody was gone, Weston went back to his desk and dialed a downtown hotel. He gave a suite number. A voice came on. Weston said, without preamble, "Colonel, I think he's your man." He listened for a moment, then said, "Actually, I'm rather pleased. He gives nothing away and doesn't like questions. Gets downright rude about it." He laughed and listened. "Yes, you've explained that and now I understand." He listened again. "All right. I'll set up a meeting on your signal. And go ahead and have him processed. Oh, really? That, already. Very well. Whatever you say." He listened again. "You're off again, then. Yes, I understand. Whenever you get back. Yes. Well, good night."

He sat back and smiled. The smile was brief, for his

mind had turned to another problem. He ran his hand through his thinning hair and then left it resting on top of his head. "Now," he said aloud, "if I could just locate those blasted AK-47s."

2

Johannesburg

Dougie Lord lived a Spartan, solitary existence in a furnished room in a pensioners' hotel on the outskirts of downtown. He was fifty now, a wiry little man who felt lost without the military. Each day when he came home from his work in an electronics firm, he dressed in khaki drill shorts and shirt, with his service ribbon carefully pinned over the pocket, proper shoes and khaki-colored heavy socks, folded correctly just below the knee. His room looked much like a noncom's in a barracks might, furnished with bare necessities. Each morning, he still made his bed with military corners, and three times a week he went to the gym and put himself through a set of calisthenics he'd learned in the British army. The pensioners' hotel suited him exactly. It was a drab building, its antiseptic halls and rooms unenlivened by color or even enough deterioration to give it character.

Lord had been recruited for his first mercenary operation, the Congo, right out of England, ten years ago. At the time, he'd been laboring away with a trucking firm and grieving over the intense military cutback that had cost him his army career. Then he'd read an amazing ad in the *Manchester Guardian* that asked for military veterans with combat experience, a limited number of dependents, and a willingness to travel. It promised good pay and adventure in return. Since Dougie had had combat experience from Dunkirk on through the Suez Canal and Korea, he felt he was certainly what they were looking for. He had no dependents. The army had been his only wife and he was ready to travel. He didn't care so much about the pay, though a man did need a certain amount of brass; what he wanted was back in the military. He sent off a letter and got a cable in return telling him to report to Johannesburg. He quit his job the day he got the cable and was gone on an economy flight the next, kit bag in hand. In Johannesburg, he was chosen on the spot and immediately given the rank of sergeant and put in charge of the military police.

Those first mercenaries were a random group, hurriedly picked from the assortment of drunks and adventurers and crooks that had answered the ads. Dougie and his squad were in charge of maintaining order and discipline, while the other noncoms and officers tried to form the disparate group into something like a cohesive fighting force. Lord's only regret was that there wasn't time to do the job properly. It was all very rushed and only partly organized. Yet it was necessary, in such a situation, that the troops quickly learn the dangers of violating military discipline. Dougie and his squad taught this lesson with fist and boot and club. He was much appreciated by his superiors, for he was a man who could be made to believe in the gods chosen for him and who was ready to serve with unquestioning zeal.

Ever since the Congo, his life had been very flat. There had been no mercenary operations, no military, nothing but the dullness of his job and the pensioners' hotel. But Dougie had kept himself in shape, never drinking, never smoking, doing the manual of arms in his room with an old Enfield rifle he'd kept. Then, three months ago, had come the call from his old company commander in the Congo, Carlton-Brooks. He wouldn't be a proper part of the mission, but at least he was on the training side and it was the military.

Coming in from training, he'd found a BBC correspondent waiting to see him. Afterward, he'd dutifully called in a report to the adjutant.

Carlton-Brooks hadn't seemed too concerned when Dougie told him. "Ah, well," he'd said, "they will nose about, won't they?"

"He got aught off me, Major. Chap I knew from the old days, bloke named Landon. He's got onto the Wild Geese Club for some'res and he's keen on it. I told him it was just a boozin' club for all the old blokes. Seemed to satisfy him well enough."

"Well, we've got to expect that. Right enough, Dougie."

"Then he wanted to know if Drakes was still the hangout for all the blokes."

"What'd you say to that?"

"I give him the big laugh. Said all the old boys still went down there to tell their lies, but if there was a do that mob would be too drunk to get on the plane. You know me, Jack. Chap ought to keep fit."

Of course, it was such a different crowd these days. Dougie was puzzled by where all the new, young faces had come from. So many Americans, so many British and Aussies he'd never seen before. He wondered who'd found them and how they'd come over. But he didn't wonder long, for it wasn't his business to wonder about such things, and if there was one thing Sergeant Major Dougie Lord knew, it was to tend to his business and leave the proper areas to the proper officers. Of course, there were still a few of the old boys around. Them that had been young enough in the Congo campaign that, ten years later, they were still under the age limit.

Gerry Ruger and Wilf Schneider were arguing. The training was over for the evening, and they were standing in the auditorium of the old armory that had once been used by the South African Police, but had since been turned over to the Wild Geese Club. Most of the mercenaries had either left or were taking showers. A few were still sitting around on the mats that had been used for the hand-to-hand drills, drinking the two bottle allotment of beer. Ruger and Schneider were still both in the camouflage fatigues that they'd been issued for training.

Ruger was angry. "Fuck it all," he said to Schneider. "I'm bloody well going to have some answers. Else I'm going up to Oman, old sport. The Sheik is paying damn fine and I've the papers at home. All it takes is my signing and shooting them in and I'm off. Fuck this bloody boy scout foolishness. All their bloody secrets. All the bloody drill. Who the hell they think they're jacking with, Ned in the first primer?"

Schneider was a short, solidly built German. He had a placid, assured way about him, tinged with a kind of gentleness that made it difficult to believe that he was what he was, a very capable killer. He and Ruger had served in the Congo campaign, and they had been friends ever since. Schneider said, "Gerry, please, you'll only make trouble for yourself."

"With Jack Carlton-Brooks? Are you daft, man?" Ruger was Scotch, but, like Schneider, most of his accent had eroded away in his travels. Only when he was very angry did his voice go down in his throat and words slide out like they were coming through a saw blade.

"It's not Carlton-Brooks," Schneider said carefully. "We are being examined. I don't understand why, but we are on inspection. And it's not what you say to the adjutant, it's what he'll report to the people who are actually important, who are actually in charge of this operation."

"Aaaah," Ruger said. He looked away. There was

sweat on his forehead that he wiped off with a vicious swipe of his finger. "Ah, screw it all."

"Gerry," Schneider said, "sometimes you make me very angry. You will please stop talking like this. The campaign is important to me. The money is very important to me. I don't want to hark back to past obligations, but since you took the knife out of the Spaniard's hand in Buna, I'm in your debt."

"Ah, fuck you, Kraut. You don't owe me bloody aught."

"Yes. I owe you the sense you don't always display. Now, you will calm down."

"Fuck you," Ruger said.

Wilf Schneider looked at him a long moment. By profession, he was a photographer. He had come out of the Congo with 20,000 rand. Some of it had gone into building his home. Some of it had gone into the half-finished sailing yacht that was moored in Cape Town. He cared nothing for the fighting, but only for the money that would give him the release he sought. He had a wife and two children, and he had resolved that this would be his last campaign. He had been five years old when the Nazis were defeated in Germany, and he had spent four years in displaced persons camps. The rest of his life he had very carefully amassed as much security as he could. He was not at all like Gerry Ruger.

"You will leave now, with me. We will go to Drakes and have a beer. Okay?"

"No, it is not okay," Ruger said.

"Ah, Gerry. You must act the fool."

He stood back, looking at Ruger. At his home, in his files, was an 8 x 10 black and white photograph of his friend. It had been taken ten years before, during the Congo campaign. Gerry had been standing alone in the back of a transport truck firing off to his left, his rifle at his shoulder, his helmet tilted back off his forehead just enough not to interfere with his aim. The camera had caught the smudges on his fatigues and the bulges of the grenades in his pockets. They'd been on a road in the Congo, going into a village they'd thought was secure. Then, just a mile out of the village, had come an ambush from both sides of the jungle. They'd all piled out and dived into the weeds that lined the road. All except Gerry. He'd stood there, very casually, firing into the bush first on one side and then the other. In the weeds, Wilf had come to one knee and shot the photo. Later he'd asked Gerry what he'd been thinking about. His reply had been typical. "Buggers can't shoot anyway. If they hit you, it's by chance. Better to give them a target to aim at. That way you can be sure they'll be wide." Then he'd smiled. "Besides, I didn't want to go piling off into that bloody dust and filth. Too bloody hot."

A man passed them, turning down the hall. "What's up, chaps?"

Ruger whirled, his face going furious. "Bloody aught!" he shouted. "Bloody, fucking aught."

"All right, Gerry," Schneider said. "I can see that you're determined to have your say. I want no part of it. Go on, then. I've given you my advice."

"Then what else?" Ruger said. He put his hands out, palms upward. "Sit around this bloody hole and rot?"

"It's coming. But you won't be patient. Now perhaps you'll make such a noise with your mouth that you'll ruin your own chances." Schneider shrugged. "But then, you will do what you will do."

"You won't see him with me?"

"Of course not."

"You coming down to Drakes later for a beer?"

"I'm going home and eat my supper. Perhaps I'll come in later. If you want to go to Drakes, I'll go now."

"No," Ruger said. He shook his head and grinned. "You know me better than that, Wilf."

GILES TIPPETTE

"Suit yourself," Schneider said. He turned and walked down the hall and out of the building.

At the front of the armory were several small offices, one in use by the senior officer in charge, Jack Carlton-Brooks.

Carlton-Brooks called himself the adjutant though he could have been the executive officer or the commander for all any of them knew. He was the only organization officer any of them had seen so far. And that, along with a lot of other questions, was on Ruger's mind.

He was, as he'd told Wilf, going to bloody well have some answers.

The door to Carlton-Brooks' office was closed, but Ruger didn't bother to knock.

The adjutant was working over some papers. He looked up and tried to smile as he saw Ruger.

"Ah, Gerry! How's the lad? Come in, come in."

Carlton-Brooks had been Ruger's company commander in the Congo. But he was now a fat, graying man who drank too much whiskey and who was hard to visualize as the charger who'd once barreled into a rebel stronghold firing a hand-held machine gun over the windshield of a jeep. But he still had one valuable asset. He had a soft, persuasive way that made the men believe he was sympathetic to their problems—even though nothing was ever done. He could tell from the look on Ruger's face that he was in for a few hard moments.

"Well, Gerry," Carlton-Brooks said affably, "how's the lad? How's it going?"

"Don't talk that bloody cock to me, Jack," Ruger said savagely. "You know me." He hesitated a beat and then said abruptly, "The Sheik of Oman is recruiting. I've been offered a commission. I've got the medical OK and the application filled out at home. All I bloody got to do is post it and back will come a ticket for transport."

Carlton-Brooks frowned. "We'd hate to lose you, Gerry."

"Then come across with something," Ruger said violently. "Are we going to muck around here the rest of our bloody lives?"

Carlton-Brooks looked away. "You know I can't tell you anything, Gerry. It embarrasses me to admit I don't know much myself. You lads, especially you old Congo hands, are going to have to recognize something different is laid on here. We've got to carry on under the conditions, that's all. We are professionals and we mustn't forget that." He had a towel wrapped around his neck, and he took a moment to use one end to mop at the perspiration on his face and at the V of his shirt front. It was hot in the armory, even that late at night. He asked, "What is the Sheik offering?"

"A lieutenancy," Ruger said. "A thousand rand a month."

Carlton-Brooks shook his head. "That's not a lot, Gerry. Not for a man of your background and capabilities."

"No," Ruger flung back, "but it's a bloody lot more than I'm getting here. It's something at least. Not a bloody lot of recruit training!"

"I appreciate that," Carlton-Brooks said sympathetically, "and I can understand how some of you chaps must be feeling. But, I tell you, lad, this is a big one. And when the ranks are given out you're assured of at least a sergeancy, if not more. And the money will be a damn sight better than any thousand rand the Sheik is paying. I know right now all you're getting is subsistence pay . . ." He trailed off.

"Yes, and that's rotten, too," Ruger said. "I tell you, Jack, this whole bloody fuck-all is bloody cock and somebody had better get something laid on!"

Ruger was a business-forms salesman, but he was no more suited for that than he would have been for any other civilian occupation. He could function for a time, but then his thin veneer of civilization would begin to wear and he'd have to break out. His third marriage had just gone on the rocks, which was a symptom rather than a cause. He attracted women easily and casually, but he had never found any sort of lasting comfort with one.

Carlton-Brooks knew the best course was just to let Ruger blow off steam. He wasn't the only one frustrated by the boring treatment and the lack of information about their mission. There were others finding their way to his office. Fortunately, a large number of the men were first-time mercenaries, recently discharged veterans, still used to the seemingly pointless routine and the, at this point, low pay.

He had lied to Ruger in one sense. He did know a few things, but he knew embarrassingly little. He had been hired directly by Weston to form the cover organization of the Wild Geese Club and then to process the recruits and lay out their training. There was nothing to the training; it was simple boot camp routine, not really intended as training at all. Its only purpose was to assemble a likely crowd of prospects from whom final selection would be made. Carlton-Brooks had been told to make evaluations for the best seventy men based on conditioning, discipline, and general levels of combat skills. It was really too broad a description, but he was told bluntly that no further details would be available. Nothing about the target, or its terrain or climate. Nothing about the enemy. Nothing about the type of combat to be encountered. Nothing. Just find the best seventy men and don't bother to ask any more questions.

Which was a little demeaning to an old soldier of his rank and stature. But, then, he supposed he was lucky to be on the inside.

Ruger's harsh voice broke in on his thoughts. "Ah, the hell with it. I think I'll go up to Oman."

Carlton-Brooks looked at him sympathetically. The adjutant said, "Ah, lad, that's no good. You go up to

Oman and it's going to be all training. That's a barracks life, lad. The Sheik hasn't got anything on, you'd be nothing but a bloody palace guard."

He watched the shot go home. He knew his man pretty well.

Gerry looked down at his hands and shook his head. "Jack, you bastard. Why don't you tell us a little something. Just a clue."

"I know no more than you, lad. Believe me on that. I'm just the mother hen and you well know it I probably won't even be going along when you chaps hit the field. Surely you'll be told something when the commander comes on post. Why not just hang on till then."

Gerry looked up, another flash of anger in his black eyes. "Who is this high mucky muck and what's his game? Is he too good to come around the common soldiers?"

The adjutant shook his head again. "That I don't know, lad. I've never laid eyes on the man."

Ruger stared at him in astonishment. "You mean, you don't know who the bloke is?"

"Not a clue."

"Christ!" Ruger said in disgust. He stood up. "I'm going and get bloody drunk."

"I'd watch that, Gerry," Carlton-Brooks advised. "It'll make the training that much harder tomorrow night." He leaned forward confidentially. "I want you to know, lad, that you're in the running for a gong. How would you like that?"

Ruger gave him a sour look for a moment and then began to smile. "Jack, you old whore, don't you come that bloody shit on me. D'you think it's not the joke of the outfit that you promise a gong to all the bitchers? Christ, we'll all be bloody officers." He started to laugh and then stopped. "But mark me on this, Jack, I'm bloody tired of waiting and all your blarney isn't going to change that."

* * *

Cody was getting tired of waiting. His orders had been to stay at the hotel and that meant too much time in the hotel bar, too much of the hotel food, but mostly too much time in his room, just thinking. And thinking was no good for a man who no longer had any of the questions, much less the answers. Mostly he just lay on his bed, naked, and smoked and thought, letting old times run through his mind. There had been some good ones and some not so good, but it hadn't seemed to matter either way. Sometimes he wondered what he was doing in Africa. Africa, he would think. What the fuck was Africa? He didn't know a goddamn thing about the place, nor much care. Looking out the window, he'd thought that Johannesburg looked about like a hundred other cities he could name. Concrete was concrete and people were people, and in the end it always came down to the same realities no matter what bullshit they tried to cover it with. Except he wasn't having any of the bullshit and hadn't been for a long time.

Then, finally, the message had come. Another cryptic note from Weston, left in his box at the desk and delivered, no doubt, by the enigmatic Matabelle in his off-hours from killing Mineshona. The note had instructed him to report to Major Carlton-Brooks at a certain address. A cab had taken him to the outskirts of the city and left him in front of a large, blockish building set in the middle of a paved lot.

Through the front door was a sort of lobby. It was eight o'clock, but there were still several men lounging around. There was a sameness about them that didn't come just from the camouflage fatigues and the combat boots. They were uniformly young and uniformly tough and hard-looking. Cody asked one of them for Major Carlton-Brooks.

"That way, mate," the man said, gesturing casually toward a hall. He watched Cody out of flat, curious eyes.

There was a door and he knocked. A voice said, "Come!" He swung it back. There was a man seated at a desk; red-faced, perspiring. Another man, angry-looking, was standing near the door. They both glanced up.

"I'm looking for Major Carlton-Brooks."

"I'm he."

"My name is Ravel. I'm a pilot."

"Ah!" the adjutant rose hurriedly to his feet. "Come in, come in."

Cody looked at the other man. "Am I interrupting anything?"

"No, no, no," the adjutant said. He looked toward Ruger. "The, uh, sergeant was just leaving. Eh, Gerry lad?"

Ruger gave him a black look for a second and turned. But at the door he said, "Mind you, Jack, I'm not kidding."

When Ruger was gone the adjutant sighed and said, "Please come in, Captain Ravel. Just close the door behind you, if you will."

Cody sat down and lit a cigarette. The adjutant smiled, his face pinking. "Well," he said, and put both of his fat hands flat on the desk top. "You're here for processing, but I suppose you already know that."

"No," Cody said flatly. "I don't know a goddamn thing."

Carlton-Brooks colored slightly more. Then he half-laughed. "Well, you are here for processing. And we're very happy to have you. Our work won't take long. Would you like a drink, by the way?" He started to open a desk drawer.

"No," Cody said. He sat back in the chair, watching the major, waiting.

Carlton-Brooks looked a little disappointed. He slid the drawer closed. "Well," he said again, "then I suppose we should get on with it. Quite simple, of course. First let me put you straight about me. I'm the adjutant, supposedly, but I'm really nothing more than a glorified housekeeper, as it were. I process you lads, and see to your training and records and that sort of hash. Of course," he said, "in your case, Captain, your training will be up to someone other than me. You have your application filled out?"

"Yes," Cody said. He took it out of his jacket pocket and laid it on the desk. It was an application to the Wild Geese Club—a sporting and recreational organization for ex-military and ex-police. Or so it said. Cody laughed dryly. "Some club," he said. "Name and address and number of dependents and then twenty questions on military and combat experience."

"Yes," Carlton-Brooks said, "quite. But it suffices." He picked up a paper and handed it across to Cody. "Here's the real goods. This is your contract. It exists between you and a Society Anonymous that has funds in escrow to take care of you and all the other chaps. It's the usual bundle. As you know, you're to have the rank and pay of a captain. Twenty-four hundred U.S. dollars each month and unspecified bonuses. You can draw the pay in whatever currency you like. You'll want to look it over."

"No," Cody said. "Gimmee something to sign it with."

"Quite," Carlton-Brooks said, relieved that it was going off so smoothly. He handed a pen across. "You'll be given a copy which we ask you to safeguard. Perhaps in your hotel safe for the time being. Most of the chaps give their copy to the wife or next of kin. The terms are quite simple and about what you'd expect. In training, in barracks, you can receive half your pay in cash here, the other half being paid in deposit to the bank of your choice. Once in operation the total each month is paid into that bank."

"All right," Cody said. He signed, put the name and address of his bank in the States, and passed the contract back across to Carlton-Brooks.

"Now here," the major said, "is the insurance form. You'll need to put in the name and address of your beneficiary and . . ."

"You can forget that," Cody said roughly.

"I say, what?"

"I said you could forget that. The insurance."

The adjutant looked confused. "But it's, uh, for the protection of your family, your dependents."

"Don't have any," Cody said.

Carlton-Brooks shrugged. "Well, just as you say, old chap. Still, I wish you'd take it along with you. You might think of some charity you'd like to help out by getting killed." He tried a smile, which didn't work.

Cody folded the form and put it in his jacket pocket.

The adjutant said, "There's one other bit of nonsense to be got through. The oath." He looked embarrassed. "Are you a religious man, by chance?"

"No."

"Then we'll dispense with the Bible. If you will, please raise your right hand and repeat after me. Just stay in your seat."

Cody intoned, as the major read off a card, something about swearing on his life and his honor not to desert his comrades and to faithfully execute all orders.

"Silly," Carlton-Brooks said, looking embarrassed, "but I'm told it impresses some of the less cynical chaps. Cover all ports, eh?" He put out his hand. "Welcome aboard, officially, Captain Ravel."

Cody asked, "Look, is there a chief pilot on this operation? Someone I'm responsible to?"

Carlton-Brooks looked shocked. "Why," he said, "it was my understanding that you were." He saw the surprise on Cody's face and said, in confusion, lamely, "I had a call this afternoon. I'm sorry."

"What's the equipment?" Cody asked, showing nothing on his face now.

"You don't know?"

"No," Cody said.

"Then, old chap, I damn sure don't know."

"Then you wouldn't know about the maintenance."

"No."

Cody got up. "Am I all through?"

"Of course."

"Free to leave?"

"Certainly."

They shook hands, each wondering about the other. "Thank you, Major," Cody said carefully.

"And thank you, Captain."

There was a disparity in their ranks. For Cody was in charge of an active function and Carlton-Brooks was not. They both recognized the difference.

Cody stood up. "Do I ever actually meet the commander of this operation? I keep meeting people who seem damn interested in letting me know how unimportant they are. I assume there is a commander?"

"Oh, yes," Carlton-Brooks said.

"That's handy," Cody said. "Especially for a military operation." He leaned slightly forward. "But, of course, you don't know him."

"No," Carlton-Brooks said, "I don't." He looked away.

"Well, thanks."

"I'm afraid," the adjutant answered, "that you'll just have to prepare yourself for some eccentricities in this do. You'll find it a bit different from past operations."

"Oh, it's all the same to me," Cody said. "I don't give a shit either way. Good night, Major."

When Cody was safely out of the room, the major

quickly opened the desk drawer and took out a half bottle of Scotch. He sighted it against the light and then turned it up and took a long pull, taking it away from his mouth only when the bite of the whiskey forced him to.

He was glad to have the business of the pilot over with. It had been made clear that he wasn't to bollix this one. "Damn nonsense," he muttered to himself, and had another drink out of the bottle. Then he sighted it against the light again and regretfully put it back in his desk drawer. He'd said he didn't know the commander, which wasn't true. He did know him and he was afraid of him, the American colonel. He fervently hoped the man hadn't returned to Johannesburg yet, for that would mean meetings and questions and being under the gun from those hard eyes. "Ah, well," he said to himself. "Just be a soldier, Jack. Do your job." He opened the desk drawer again.

The lobby was now deserted. Cody stepped through the front door and walked into the dark parking lot, suddenly conscious that he didn't have a way back to town. He knew he was quite a ways out, but he thought that if he started walking toward town he'd surely come across a cabstand or some place he could use a phone. He could always, he knew, go back in and have the major call, but he didn't particularly want to do that. Besides, it was a nice night, cool now with some of the dryness gone out of the air.

As he began to walk, he thought, So all of a sudden I'm the chief pilot. And how the hell did that happen? What did they decide about me that made me, suddenly, one of the big cheeses?

Behind him, he heard a car suddenly start up. He kept walking and then the car was alongside him.

"Hey, mate!"

The car was idling beside him. He turned his head slowly, but it was too dark to see the face of the driver.

"It's me, Ruger, the sergeant from Carlton-Brooks' office."

"Oh." Cody stopped.

"You'd be needing a lift to town from the looks of it."

"Yeah, thanks."

He opened the passenger door and got in the front seat.

"My name's Gerry. Gerry Ruger."

Cody said his.

"You'd be the pilot, then."

"I'm *a* pilot," Cody said.

In the darkness, he could see Ruger shrug. "You're the first we've seen."

"That's interesting," Cody said.

They rode now in silence. Finally Ruger said, "Look, I'm on my way to Drakes to meet my mate for a beer. That's the place all us chaps in our line of work hang out. Come along."

"Why not?" Cody said. He'd had enough of the hotel.

"You'll like it," Ruger said cheerfully. "Nearly always a fight going on."

Cody said, "Lucky for me you were still here. Looks like I'd of had a long walk."

"Oh, no," Ruger said. He turned and grinned, his teeth very white against his tanned face. "I waited for you. I took it you wouldn't be too long. Not just for processing."

"Why'd you do that? Wait for me?"

"Why, simple, old chap. I wanted to pick your brains. I'm going nuts to find out what's up and you'd know. The pilots have to know."

Cody suddenly laughed. "So that's what you thought, huh?"

"Sure. Christ, you're an officer. Where's it to be, chap? Eh? Angola? Nearly has to be Angola."

Cody just shook his head. "You got a hell of a shock coming, buddy."

3

Johannesburg

Drakes was, as Ruger had said beforehand, a seedy joint. The first thing Cody noticed when they walked in was the bright lights and the peanut shells on the floor. They covered it, crunching with every step.

They stood a moment at the front while Ruger looked around for his friend. "Not here yet, I guess," he said. They sat down and Cody immediately noted how heavy the furniture was. He grinned sardonically at Ruger.

"Oh, yes," he said, "I been in places like this before. All over the world."

"How's that, sport?"

"Like you said, a lot of fights." He swiveled his head slowly. "Not a woman in the place. Nobody wearing a suit. And they keep the lights up and they make the furniture good and heavy so you can't break it. And I'll bet you they don't bring you the beer in a mug. A mug makes a damn handy weapon."

"Ah," Ruger said, showing his teeth, "a man who's been around. You're all right, pilot." He turned and yelled at the waiter. "Hey, Jack! A little service." He rapped on the top of the table with his knuckles.

The waiter came over, a beefy, red-faced man holding a tray on his hip. "All right, then, belay the noise. What's it to be? I ain't got all night.

"No need to snarl, Jack," Ruger said in a hurt voice. "Here we've got a new customer and what's he to think?"

"Com'on with it," the waiter growled. "Is it to be a pitcher of pilsner?"

"Right enough. And three glasses."

There was a bowl of unshelled peanuts on the table. Ruger took one, throwing the shells over his shoulder as he ate. "Supposed to be good luck," he said to Cody. "I think it's just an excuse so they don't have to sweep up."

The waiter returned and slammed down a pitcher of beer and three glasses. With a piece of chalk, he wrote the amount of the bill on the table top. "Don't muck with that," he told Cody and went away sourly.

"Who's the friend you're waiting for?" Cody asked.

"Ah, a no-good German. A Kraut name of Wilf Schneider. I doubt he'll show up. But we always stop off here for a beer on the way home." He nodded his head into the room. "'Bout half this job is from the armory. See that table with the four young ones at it? That's Hunter and Smyth and Lauffler and Coleman. First-timers, just out of their own services. But good ones, I think. All of the new blokes have had commando or ranger training." He slipped his beer, his black eyes continuing to rove the room. "That far table back yonder is a bad lot. Two of 'em old boys. See that one little shrimp sitting sort of sideways to us? That's Peters, John Peters. Wilf and I were in the same commando with him in the Congo." Ruger shook his head. "Whoever's running this do was a damn fool to let Peters in."

"How come?"

Ruger tapped his head. "He's psycho. A bloody psychopath. We lost eight men in our commando when we were rolling up the east side of the Congo, and I swear John Peters did for four of 'em. Pop in the back, that sort of job."

Cody studied the man's profile. His face had sharp, definite features. "He have a reason?"

Ruger shrugged. "For a sane man to understand it, you'd have to say it was for the swag, the loot we'd picked up. We'd get in a dustup and a chap would buy it and Peters would show up with his loot. You couldn't argue that, that's war, but Peters was always in the right place and the chaps were always shot oddly, never properly from the front."

"Why didn't somebody fix Peters?"

Ruger shrugged again. "We could never really be sure. And then Peters isn't an easy man to do for." He looked over at Cody. "Besides the rest of us weren't psycho." He suddenly looked toward where Peters was sitting and called across the room, "Hey, Peters! John Peters!" The little man turned their way and Ruger said to Cody, "Look at his eyes. Like flaming mirrors. Cold as bloody ice." He called out again to Peters, "How's your back shot, John? Had any practice lately?"

Peters stared at him for a moment. "Bugger you, Gerry Ruger."

Ruger laughed. "Not bloody likely, John. For I'll never let you behind me." Then he lounged back in his chair and took a drink of beer. He said to Cody, "I'd do for the bastard if I could ever provoke him. But he don't provoke, not straight-up-like."

"You're not afraid of him, then?"

Ruger turned and gave him a flat look. "I'm not afraid of anything, old sport."

"That's handy."

"Uh oh," Ruger suddenly said. "Here's a case." He nodded at a man who'd just come in. The man was smallish and blond and wearing a carefully-cut business suit. He walked by their table and took one in the middle of the room. "That's a chap named Landon. He's a journalist. With the BBC. He's been nosing about trying to get onto what's up. He can't believe don't none of us know aught." He looked carefully at Cody. "You're not having me on, then? You don't know what's up?"

"I just got here," Cody said. He poured them both another glass of beer.

"Is this your first time, then? In a do?"

Cody made circles with his beer glass. "Yes, this kind."

"How'd they find you, then? You a Yank."

Cody shook his head. "I don't know."

"It's a wonder," Ruger said, "what's on. Nothing like the old days where they advertised in the papers and dragged in any warm body off the street that would come. All of a sudden, all these hard boys show up and everything's laid out all proper, like the Black Watch regiment. My mate, the square head, is very approving. It does his German heart good to see such organization. Me?" Ruger ran a hand through his dark, curly hair. "Me, it's driving bananas. So." He came back to Cody. "What'd you come in as, then? Rank."

"Captain, I guess," Cody said.

"Ooooh. Captain! That'll be a nice bit of brass. Of course," he added, "that ain't where the real money is. That's in the swag."

"Swag?"

"Looting." He gave Cody a wink. "We done all right in the Congo, I can tell you that. Not so well in Nigeria, bloody poor place, but it was all right. Now," he said, looking around and leaning toward Cody, "if it's Angola, and it just about has to be, we ought to come out rich as kings." He suddenly laughed. "I was just thinking on something. Happened in Bunda. I wish the little Kraut was here to tell it. We blew up a flaming bank, only we done it too well." He laughed again. "Ah well, I'll save it for him." He looked around. "I wonder where he is."

Cody looked at his watch. "Look, I haven't had any dinner yet, and I been eating in that goddamn hotel for three days. You want to go get something to eat?"

Ruger shook his head. "No, I'll hang on here a bit."

"Where's a good place to eat?"

Ruger half-smiled. "Try the Lourenço Marques. You'll find that interesting. I've got the bill here. And one thing." He stopped Cody as he got up.

"What?"

"I don't want to sound like an old maid, but watch yourself out on the street alone."

"Why?"

Ruger shrugged. "Just do, that's all."

He found a cab outside. As they drove away, he was unaware that the man in the business suit had hurried out after him, going quickly to his car. The man had no trouble following the cab in the deserted streets.

The cafe was crowded and very dark. The headwaiter didn't seem to speak much English, and Cody finally resorted to Spanish which worked well enough to get him a table. When his eyes became accustomed to the gloom, he noticed the black crepe. It was strung in streamers across the ceiling, and each table was bordered by a band of it. And there was the quiet, an unnatural kind of quiet for a busy restaurant. Cody could hear a woman sobbing.

The waiter came and he ordered a drink. "What the hell's going on?" he asked. But the waiter only shrugged and went away. At the table next to his, Cody noticed a man sitting with his face buried in his hands. A woman and three small children were with him, and the woman spoke to him in a language Cody couldn't understand.

The waiter came with the drink and a menu. The menu was written in something like Spanish, but not quite. Cody couldn't make out any of it.

Then, suddenly, a man was standing at his elbow. "Do you mind if I join you, old chap?"

Cody looked up. It was the correspondent Ruger had pointed out to him in Drakes.

"What?"

"I said do you mind if I sit down?"

"Yes," Cody said, "I do."

"I'm sorry about that, old chap," the man said, sitting down. "But there's no other place left in the house. Besides, I see you're having trouble with the menu. It's in Portuguese, by the way."

"Who the hell are you and what do you want?"

The correspondent lit a cigarette. "You know who I am. I saw our friend Ruger point me out to you in Drakes. I followed you here. I want to talk to you."

"What about?"

But the waiter was there and Landon said, "Let's order first, eh? Let me recommend the broiled lobster tails. They're very good here."

They had two drinks and then dinner came. Landon asked a lot of questions, but Cody answered only in monosyllables. Finally he said, "Look, buddy, you invited yourself to sit down here. I don't know what you're after, but I'm tired and getting a little short of temper. You keep trying to find out my life history, and I'm liable to write you some right up to date."

"Why are you being so defensive? I wish I knew your name. You haven't offered it and I've been too polite to ask."

"The name is Ravel," Cody said. "Cody Ravel. I'm an American and I'm on vacation. Anything else?"

"Yes," Landon said, chewing, "I'd like to know what you can tell me about your mercenary operation."

"What the hell makes you think I'm a mercenary? What do you do, stop people out on the street and pop the question?"

Landon smiled. "Old chap, you were in the wrong place with the wrong crowd for me to believe you. And, oh, do you have the look about you!" The correspondent sat back, smiling. He looked pleased with himself.

"Look," Cody said, "if you know so goddamn much, tell me one thing. What the hell's the deal with this place, this cafe? Why all the black crepe? And why are all the customers sitting around like they're at a wake?"

"You don't know? How long have you been in Africa?"

"That's none of your business."

"What do you know of what's happening in Africa?"

"Oh, I don't know. What do you know about what's happening in Nova Scotia?"

Landon smiled again. "This is the cafe Lourenço Marques. Lourenço Marques is the capital of Mozambique, and Mozambique is, or was, a Portuguese colony on the east coast of Africa. Several weeks ago, it was taken over by a black nationalist movement." He nodded around the room. "These people you see here are refugees, white settlers. They are somber because they have lost everything. Their homes, their farms, their factories. Everything. And these are the lucky ones. They got out alive."

Landon buttered a piece of bread. "It was understood before the Portuguese colonial government pulled out that the white settlers were not to be disenfranchised. That was part of the agreement. But I went in on the story, frantically waving my press card over my head for what little protection it afforded. It was quite a mess, I must say."

"Too bad," Cody said shortly. He looked around at the people. He could still hear the sound of the woman sobbing.

Landon said calmly, "I think, actually, only one incident bothered me. And I don't know why it should have. I had been in Lourenço Marques often before and around the corner from my hotel was a little kiosk run by an old man who'd been there forty years, I expect. I used to stop in for an odd item now and then. When the mob came for him, I understand he tried to hold them off with an old single shot rifle. The last I saw of him, he was lying on the sidewalk in front of the kiosk with his head chopped off. They said he'd been there for three days. But then," Landon said, pausing to take a sip of coffee, "there were so many bodies lying about that one shouldn't have noticed the odd lot, eh."

Cody didn't say anything.

"I expect some of these are just freshly out. I understand lately it's been harder and harder for some of them to get out. Alive, that is. Some of them, of course, were back in the bush on plantations, and it was a time before news of what had happened reached them. But then," he said, smiling cheerily at Cody, "that's Africa."

Cody looked at him steadily, flatly. "Are you for real, Landon?"

"Of course. A little neurotic, perhaps. But Africa can do that to you. They keep trying to rotate me home, but I won't go. I prefer to remain here and go crazy with the rest of the continent. But tell me," he said, breaking off to pursue another subject, "is it to be Angola next?"

"What's Angola?"

Landon smiled. "All right, I'll play. Angola is the Portuguese colony on the west coast. The black nationalist movement that knocked over Mozambique is just as busy in Angola, and the Portuguese government is making noises like they're going to pull out. Except I understand the settlers there don't intend to go down quite so easily. After all, they've had the example of Mozambique to profit by. But if the Portuguese military pulls out, that leaves only one alternative, doesn't it?"

"What's that?"

Landon laughed out loud. "Why, the mercenaries, old chap. You and the rest of the lads. Do you think something this obvious can be hidden? We're all prepared to wink at it, officially of course, but, my god, lad! There it is. Now, why don't you give me a break? When's the jump off to be? Soon I'd say, judging from all I've heard."

Cody just shook his head. "You're starting to bother me. I wanted a quiet dinner and some drinks and then, finally, some sleep. And I got to run into a cracker box like you. I'm grateful for the guided tour, but I'm tired of playing cowboys and Indians."

Landon said, cocking his head to one side, "Let's see. . . . What would you be? Bazooka your specialty? Perhaps an explosives man." He shook his head. "No, I think not. I rather expect you're an officer. Perhaps fairly high up. At least a section commander. Am I close?"

Cody laughed in spite of himself. "Don't you ever give up?"

"Not when I know what I'm talking about."

"Well, this time you don't." Cody looked at his watch. "I got to get out of here. You seem to speak the lingo. Call the man for the bill."

"Good," Landon said, "I'll drive you back to your hotel."

"Oh, no you won't."

Landon laughed. "Try and get a cab this time of night, old chap. You might accomplish it in an hour's time. And I certainly don't recommend your walking."

Cody finally shrugged. "Hell, I don't care. A ride's a

ride. I guess I can listen to you for fifteen minutes more."

Landon tried to pay for the whole bill, but Cody insisted on paying his part.

"I'm not trying to buy you, old man."

"That's all right," Cody said. "I come a little higher than a meal."

They walked to Landon's car and got in. But just before he started the engine, Landon snapped his fingers. "Listen, you're not really in a rush to get to your hotel, are you?"

"Why not?"

"Because I've just remembered there's someone I'm supposed to see tonight. An old friend. Why don't you come along?"

"No thanks. Now start the goddamn car and take me to my hotel."

"Don't be in such a rush, old lad. This is a very special someone. An exceedingly beautiful girl."

"Why should you want to take me to see your girl?"

"She's not my girl. She's a friend. I think you two would get along." He looked over at Cody. "You're not averse to a bit of crumpet, are you?"

"What's a bit of crumpet?"

"Oh. A piece of ass, as you Yanks say."

Cody stared at him a long moment. "You're out of your goddamn mind, Landon."

"Why should you care?" the correspondent asked him. "Remember? You're an American tourist on vacation. An American tourist on vacation wouldn't turn down something like this, would he?"

Cody could see Landon looking at him, waiting, his hand on the starter key. He was suddenly tired. And he didn't want to go back to his hotel and wait. "That's right," he said, "I'm an American tourist on vacation.

43

So take me to see this exceedingly beautiful piece of ass. But—" He put his hand on Landon's outstretched arm. "—one piece of advice, buddy. You get me in any kind of a box, and I'm going to break your fucking neck. You understand?"

"Never you fear," Landon said cheerfully as he started the car. "I'm only trying to bribe you with a common coin. I want your cooperation, my friend."

"Well, that's all right," Cody said. "It's your loss."

But as they went down the dark street Landon said, almost to himself, "It is Angola, isn't it? It has to be."

4

Longhaven Farm, Rhodesia

The hard times should have been behind them. Bill Long-hurst was forty now, his wife Ruth was five years younger. They farmed in the Shamva area, in northern Rhodesia, fifteen miles south of the Zambian border. They had come there twelve years earlier, before it was a farm, when it was raw, rough land that had never been touched. It was still remote, but then it had been eighty miles to the nearest town, Bindura. There had been no electricity, no telephone, no gas or water or refrigeration; no house, no fences, no barns, no roads, no mail service, no stores or clubs or restaurants; no doctors or newspapers or dentists or hospitals. They had gone there with two small children, and their first house had been a tent and board shack that Bill had hastily erected. In the twelve years, their children had increased to four and they had built a second and then a third house and a good farm. They were still without many of the things that would have made life easier. There was still no electricity, except for the generator that powered the lights and radios in the operations shack and provided current for the alarm fence. The government had provided that, but it wasn't large enough to power the house, and, even if it had been, there wouldn't have been enough petrol to run it much.

There were phones now, but they were undependable, hastily installed after the government had recognized the national emergency. The most reliable means of communication was the big radio in the operations shack and the Argi-Alert battery-powered wireless system that connected the eight farms now in the valley.

And roads had come, but because of the mines, you drove on these with your heart in your mouth until you got to tar, which didn't occur until the police station at Shamva, thirty miles away.

There were still no stores or newspapers or doctors or dentists or school. But, without the emergency, it wouldn't have been a bad life at all. It was the kind of life they'd wanted, the kind they'd worked so hard to build through all those years, and Bill, looking at Ruth, thought how unfair it really was. By now, all the hard work should have been over, the strain, the worry. She should have been free to enjoy their life; visit with the neighbors, go into Shamva to their little club, even organize the school she'd wanted to have for so many years.

But, of course, none of that could be, for while they still lacked many things, they now had something they didn't want.

The terrorists.

They came down from Zambia, from the staging and training camps just over the border. Their own particular brand was of ZANU, the Zimbabwe African Nationalist Union. The intention was to drive the white farmer from his land, either by killing him and his family, or by scaring him away, or by bankrupting him through the destruction of his fields and his equipment and livestock. To do this, the terrorists came equipped with AK-47s, Chinese-made light mortars, Chinese bazookas, Chinese personnel equipment, Chinese- and Russian-made land mines, and Chinese radios with fixed crystals.

In 1972, Bill had been given a medal as the outstanding farmer in the country on Rhodesia's Independence Day honors list. Two years later, he was again given a medal: this one for valorous and meritorious service, under fire, as the leader of a police reserve antiterrorist unit. Both awards were won in the same place, on his farm. It was well he'd won the combat medal, for he wasn't likely to win a farming award for some time.

It was, Bill sometimes thought, amazing that they had held on as long as they had. But hold on they would, and be buried here if necessary. That is, he thought, if Ruth held up. And, sometimes, he wondered how she and the other women stood it. It was easier for him and the men. They, at least, could sometimes fight back, sometimes get the bastards in the sights of a rifle. But for the women it was constant, unrelenting strain and worry.

But there was no help for it. Everything they had was in the farm. Even most of the money from the good years was gone now, eaten up in losses and the destruction the terrorists had made. And no one to sell to, even if they'd been willing to surrender and give up. Their farm was on the main route the terrorists took to come into the country. Other parts of the north might get brief rests as the invaders concentrated somewhere else, but they never did.

Except for the latter part of the dry season. But the relief was so bittersweet short, and so uncertain, that you never really rested at all.

He stood there, a smallish man in safari shorts and knee-length socks. He still had the big calf muscles and the upper development of an athlete. The only change that had come with the forty years was a little graying in his red hair and the beginning of a faint potbelly.

He was dirty from a day in the fields, and he thought he ought to go and have a wash, but he was too tired just yet. Ruth was sitting behind him, across the room. He looked at her admiringly for a moment, watching her bent over her work. She was hand sewing a dress for one of their daughters.

He said, "D'you know what I think I miss the most of all of it? From the old days?"

"What's that, Bill?" she asked him without looking up from her work. She pronounced "Bill" almost as if it were "Bull," only not quite using all of the "u." Her accent was Rhodesian: British worn down at the edges by colloquialisms and contact with other nationalities.

"The evenings," he said, looking around at her. "You can't enjoy an evening properly indoors. And I used to enjoy more than anything else coming in from the lands and sitting out on my porch, drinking a few beers, and watching it get dark."

She bent her head and bit off a piece of thread at the end of a seam. Then she shook the dress out to see how it was coming, holding it up in front of her by the shoulders. "And I used to enjoy sitting out with you. Those rare evenings I'd got supper organized and safely in the oven early enough."

Now they could no longer sit out on their porch in the evenings, because some sharpshooter terrorist might be lurking just inside the forest. They'd killed Marry Marsh that way a year ago at his farm.

"Rather childish, I suppose." He laughed sheepishly.

"I should think not," she said.

"Used to be," he said, still at the window, "I could sit out there and see the farm growing in my mind's eye. Know the fields we'd try and get cleared next, and

practically be able to see them in wheat or tobacco."
He made a gesture with his hand. "Can't see them in
here. But then it's no loss. Hard enough to keep what
we've got going without thinking about new fields."

"Aw, com'on, Bill. None of that now."

He turned and looked at her, smiling sheepishly.
"You're right," he said. "I'm sorry. Sometimes the farmer
in me forgets."

"Why don't you go and have a wash," she said.
"You've got time for a long, lovely bath before dinner."

"The new troops are just settling in," he said. "I
really should go and meet the officers."

"Not tonight." There was a firm note in her voice.

"You don't want to invite them in for dinner, then?"

"No," she said, "no." It came out stronger than she'd
meant. She looked at him for a second. "Just tonight,"
she finally said. "Just tonight let them settle in, and
we'll have them tomorrow night."

He shrugged, understanding. "All right, love. I'll just
go and have that bath then."

When he was gone, she got up and crossed to the
window he'd been looking out. Her view was marred
by the grenade screen. And beyond that was the ten-foot-
high alarm fence that circled the house and the outbuildings. But a fence wouldn't stop the mortar shells.
For that, they had the roof covered with sandbags. And
for the roof to sustain the extra weight, they'd had to
take the ceilings out of all the rooms and stage support
timbers under the rafters. The walls in each room went
up eight feet and then ended in nothing. Above was the
underside of the roof and the raw lumber of the rafters.
There was no privacy in it. Sound from one room carried
up and over the walls and all over the house. Even
now she could hear clearly the sound of Bill's bath water
from the back of the house.

She suddenly crossed her arms and hugged herself,

not from a chill in the air, but the desperate tiresomeness of it all.

In her teens and early twenties, she'd been a celebrated beauty and much of it still remained, though the times of hard work on the farm had taken their toll. But the element of strain, compounded by fear and danger and frustration and anger at the injustice of it, threatened to do more harm than all the other ravages.

She had been a schoolteacher in Bulawayo when she met Bill. He was just out of the university, where he had been a famous soccer player. He'd carried on with the game, playing for Rhodesia on the World Cup team. They'd come to Bulawayo for a match, and a meeting had been arranged between the athlete and the local beauty. Now they had been married fifteen years, and Bill was no longer the cocky athlete with the springy walk and the perpetual grin. He was forty and tired all the time, his face creased with strain and his eyes red weary.

It had been enough before, trying to work a farm from the wilderness, but now, with the terrorists, it was more than a man should have to live with. Regularly, two nights a week, he and the police antiterrorist unit he commanded were out on ambush and checkpoint patrol all night. And two or three times a week, likely as not, there'd be a contact or a sighting, and then Bill and the others would go slipping off into the night, not to return, usually, until dawn, dead-tired, dirty, and aching, mostly with frustration of chasing the quicksilver enemy half the night only to have him fade into nothing. And then a day of work still ahead on the farm. But Rhodesia needed her farms, they were her lifeblood, and farmers such as Bill had to carry on; there was no one to replace them. But it was the strain, she thought, that brought Bill down the most: the strain of being ever watchful, ever alert, reading danger into the slightest sign. He was always, as they said, switched on. Even in bed with her. Nights, with his body tight against hers, she'd feel him suddenly stiffen at a distant sound, the chance of danger interrupting even his lovemaking.

Strangely, she had gotten to where the danger no longer bothered her. She was afraid at the odd moment, and she was always afraid for Bill, but the one thing she longed for, relished, hoped for in the future, was privacy.

Just plain, simple, everyday privacy. She felt guilty about resenting the intrusions of the friendly soldiers, for they were there for the obvious good of the Longhursts, but she resented the necessity, the wrongness that should cause her yard and house to be filled constantly with strangers. And there was the matter of the bathroom. They had only the one, and no way to get another, not with the labor and material shortage. But the soldiers, because they were bivouacked inside the fence, obviously could not dig a latrine, and so they were forced to use her bathroom. It embarrassed them, but they came trooping through her house all day when they were in camp and far into the evening.

And there was always a mob for dinner. Or the officers would be in for drinks in the evening. Or Bill would be out with them in the operations shack planning some mission. She never saw her husband alone, except at night in bed, and moments in bed had become too precious for him to do much except sleep. So many nights he'd come in at three or four in the morning, filthy from chasing through the bush, too tired to bathe, too tired to do anything but stumble out of his clothes and fall into bed. Some nights he would fall asleep before he'd even finished undressing, sitting there with a sock or shoe still in his hand. She'd get up and undress him and pull and shove him under the covers.

They didn't talk about the fighting, about what happened on the patrols, but she knew from his sleep that it was often bad. He'd begin thrashing about, grinding his teeth, and muttering unintelligible phrases and curses. Sometimes he would cry softly like a hurt animal. She would lie quietly by his side trying to soothe and calm him without his awakening. Nights like that, she thought how bloody hard it was to be a man with all the pretense and bravery and trouble that seemed so necessary.

Behind her, she heard a step and turned quickly. It was one of the two Bright Lights. He said, "Oh, hullo, I was just looking for Bill."

"He's bathing."

"Ah, I'll catch him later then."

"Yes." She watched him leave. The Bright Lights were another matter. They were the personal guard sent down from Salisbury and rotated each week. Every able-bodied man in Rhodesia between the ages of seventeen and fifty-five was required to give thirty days of national service either in the Police Reserve or the Army Reserve. The Bright Lights were mostly businessmen or professional people, in nonessential jobs, given the special training of bodyguards. They were called Bright Lights because they came from Salisbury, and Bright Lights was the nickname for Rhodesia's biggest city. The Longhursts had two—though they could have had more—one for Bill and one for her. Neither he nor she ever stepped foot outside the compound without a Bright Light. When Bill went to the fields, there was a Bright Light walking a step behind him, FN rifle in hand, safety off, switched to automatic-fire, his eyes watching for any movement in the surrounding forest. And if she went out, so did a Bright Light, even for the half-mile trip down the road to the laborers' compound.

Of course, no one went out casually anymore. They didn't go to the store; supplies were trucked in. They didn't visit a neighbor. There was no social life. They didn't go down to the club in Shamva for a drink or a set of tennis. They didn't go anywhere except out of necessity. They stayed home and did their work and tried to hang on. And meanwhile, there were always strange men in the house. And the army outside.

And before that the laager. In the American west, it had been called circling the wagons. When the trouble had first started, and before the government had been able to institute measures like the fences and the Bright Lights and the standard issue of FNs to the farmer and the farmer's wife, all the families from the farms in the valley would come to their house an hour before dark each night and stay until the morning. Their house was the biggest and Bill was the leader, so it had been natural that the others come to them. But for six months, it had meant fifty people in the house every night. Supper in shifts, babies crying all night long, an endless line in the bathroom. The men had tried to organize themselves outside and in the outbuildings, but there had been more than enough women and children to take up every bed and pallet that could be arranged. Ruth had never before taken much stock in talk about "nerves," but she'd felt hers very often to the breaking point before the laagering had ended. Of course, how could she complain; the people who were there by necessity hated it every bit as much as she did. The women who were sleeping with her in her bed missed their husbands as much as she missed Bill. They would have preferred to have been getting breakfast in their own kitchens instead of fumbling around in some neighbor's. It was just a hell of a situation. But there'd been no help for it.

She turned at a noise from the kitchen and swiftly crossed the living room and the dining area to go through the heavy swinging door to the large cook room. Her cook and houseboy were at the sink shouting at each other.

"Now what's all this?" she asked sharply in Shona.

"This new boy, Missy," her cook said. "He is doing his work wrong."

"Let's have no domestic crisis this evening," she ordered crisply in English. Then, back in Shona so the new boy would understand, she asked her cook, "Now, exactly what is the trouble, Emma?"

His name was Emgukura, but she'd called him Emma for the two years he'd been with them. He'd been the Anderson's cook before Anderson was murdered and his wife moved away. He was a good cook, used to European ways, but he was getting on for an old man and he had an old man's cranky ways. He was peeved now about the new boy. Their old houseboy had been abducted from his kraal by the terrorists and taken back over the border to one of the press-gang training camps. Presumably, he would come back one day bearing an AK-47 to shoot his former employers.

Emma was still glowering. He flung out an accusing finger. "Look, Missy. Look at what a mess he is making of the potatoes. Why must I be burdened with him, Missy? He is very stupid and will not learn."

"You must teach him, Emma," she said soothingly. "He is not stupid, and he will learn your ways if only you will be patient."

Emma flung a pot peevishly into the sink. "He will not learn. He is only a worthless Karanga. Let's be rid of him, Missy. Let me bring up one of my relatives from my kraal."

"No," she said sharply. They had been over this all before. "You will do as the bwana orders. Now get back to your work."

They had imported the boy from a tribe to the south

of Salisbury. The theory was that he would have no local ties and would be less susceptible to the extortions of the terrorists. Even the most loyal boy could be made to turn traitor if the terrorists threatened his family. So far, none of the families in the valley had been harmed by their personal servants in the way that the Mau Mau had worked in Kenya. But one had to be constantly on guard and take nothing for granted.

She looked in the oven to see how the meat was coming. They were having a roast joint. Praise God they might conceivably have a quiet dinner for a change without the men being called away before the cheese could be brought out.

She became conscious that she was still holding the dress she'd been working on. She left the kitchen, went down the long hall to one of the children's rooms, and hung the dress in a closet. It was almost finished and Lord knows she had plenty of time left before she could get it in her daughter's hands.

She stood in the room looking around. The room had the clean, closed-in smell of a room that isn't often used.

Their four children were away at school in Salisbury, even the five year old. When the valley had begun to populate, there'd been wonderful plans of starting a school there for the younger children. The older ones would still have to go into Salisbury to finish, but there were Ruth and two other women who'd been schoolteachers, and they could have seen the children on their way through the first few forms. But then had come the terrorists, and the valley was no place for children. So even the younger ones had to be sent away to boarding school. They saw their kids twice a year on the farm: at Christmas and for the brief summer vacation. But it was such a strain having them there, fearing what might happen, that it was almost a relief when they were back safely in Salisbury. But it wasn't right that you couldn't raise your children in their own home, that you couldn't have them with you. She wondered what they thought, if they considered it normal that everyone who farmed had terrorists as they had locusts or rinderpests. What a warped upbringing they were getting. Of course, the older two knew it was all out of kilter, because they'd had the farm and a family life for several years before the terrorists came. But they had their scars. Poor Todd, their oldest. He'd had the bad luck to be with his father at the little native store just after the terrorists had killed the Dutchman. Todd had seen a man cut almost in half by a machine gun, his wife and children screaming hysterically, the gangsters only just moments gone.

Thinking about it made her so angry she wanted to scream. The hell of it was you could never catch the bastards. They hit and then slipped away into the bush, buried their weapons, and became innocent tribesmen. Or went back across the border to rearm and get their ardor reinforced by the instructors at the training camps.

She came out of the children's room and walked to the back bedroom. Bill was standing in the middle of it, a towel around his middle, deep in thought.

"Bill?"

"What? Oh." He turned, running his hand through his still damp hair.

"What's bothering you? Something special?"

"No," he said.

"Bill. You've been at something all evening."

He walked over and sat down on the bed.

"What it is, Bill?"

"Dammit," he finally said, "I think we're going to lose Woodward. I saw him this afternoon. He offered me his farm. On any terms."

"Not Don! Don pulling out? I don't believe it."

Don Woodward was the only bachelor in the valley. His farm adjoined theirs to the south.

"Yes." He sighed. "Dammit."

"What's the reason? Don should be the last to go."

He looked up, hesitated, and then said, "Got a cig?"

She crossed to a bureau, took out a box of cigarettes, and lit him one.

"Thanks." He smoked a moment. "Well," he said, "looks like old Don has finally caught it." He laughed shortly. "He says he's in love and wants to get married. Seems this girl in Salisbury has finally wrapped him up in the old matrimonial net. To be soon, I understand."

She crossed her arms. "So?"

He tried a smile, but it didn't work. Finally he said, "Well, it seems the prospective bride don't fancy this kind of farm life."

He'd hated to tell her and now he watched the reaction. She put her arms slowly down to her sides and knotted her fists. "Goddamn," she said lowly.

"I know, love," he said. He got up and put his arms around her. She buried her face in his chest. "I know, it ain't fair. Everybody can run, but us. We've got the bad luck to have to stick it out. It's a rotten deal." He held her, felt her trembling just a little. He wished sometimes she'd break down and cry. Or scream. Or throw something.

"Dammit," she said, her voice muffled.

"I know, love. Look, isn't it about time you went into Salisbury for a little vacation? Just a week? I can make do."

But she was over it now. She shook her head, withdrawing from his arms. "Don't try that on me, Bill. Just tell Don Woodward, and his bride, that I said they could go to hell. No, I'll tell him myself."

He smiled at her. "Poor old Don."

But, going out of the room, she turned back to him for a moment. "Bill?"

"What, love?"

"Is it ever going to end?"

"I don't know," he said. "I truly don't know."

5

Salisbury

Neal Hall, the Deputy Minister of Defense, slipped a standard issue .45 caliber automatic in his waistband, put on his coat, and then called to his wife, Winsome, "Dear, I'm going out a bit. Don't wait up, I might be late."

She answered something back, but he didn't hear what as he went out the door and got his car out of the garage. Since the emergency, she'd become used to his erratic comings and goings. But then, in forty-five years, there'd been a lot of it.

He was sixty-seven years old and tired and too fat and feeling the heavy weight of a frightening responsibility. As the minister in charge of internal security, he was one of the few men in Africa who knew specifically why and for what the mercenaries were training in Johannesburg. The prime minister and the minister of defense knew the concept and had ordered the operation. But they knew nothing else. By choice. It was his show and his alone. And he was on his way to a meeting with the man who had to make it work: the American colonel who'd been discharged from the Marine Corps for the good of the service. The commander of the mercenaries, the commander no one had seen.

He drove toward the center of town, down a broad avenue lined with Jacaranda trees that were throwing their blossoms as the African summer came to an end. Off in the black sky, he could see distant flashes of sheet lightning, but he knew it was just heat energy being dissipated; there was no rain in it. Not that the rains would be long in coming. They were going to have to hurry, he thought.

He was an anachronism now and he knew it, an old fighter who'd seen Rhodesia change with the years and who'd given most of his life in her service. He should have been retired, raising mangoes and roses and going on an occasional safari, but Rhodesia couldn't afford for him to retire. He, as much as any man in the government, knew the country inside out. He knew the people, especially the black tribesmen; he knew the terrain, the logistics, the cities, the countryside. He had been a civilian administrator and he had been a soldier. He even, though he would not admit it, understood the political problems facing Rhodesia. In his younger days, he had been a district commissioner, administering large areas and many diverse peoples when the tribes were still savage, and he had lived in areas where he and his wife were the only white skins for hundreds of miles. He had ruled with courage and, he thought, with justice and a fair amount of luck. He had become virtually a legend among the tribes. They had learned that he was a man who understood them. They had also learned that he wouldn't put up with any nonsense.

It was late, almost eleven o'clock, and the streets were virtually deserted. He could feel the weight of the .45 in his waistband, and he shifted in the seat to position it more comfortably. He carried the weapon because he, like all other important government officials, was on the assassination lists of the several revolutionary groups. Though he never thought of them as revolutionaries.

He was nearing the downtown section, and he could see the squat, imposing front of Government House. Passing it, he felt again that surprised, stunning sense of satisfaction he'd had when John Tyron, the Defense Minister, had called him into that secret meeting so many weeks ago and had given him the job—the job of wiping out the terrorist bases in Zambia.

As a straightforward military operation, it wasn't particularly difficult. But it couldn't be done as a straightforward military mission. It couldn't be done in force. It couldn't be done with planes or tanks. It couldn't be done openly.

It had to be done in the utmost secrecy, and Rhodesia could never be connected to the operation. Not to the point of proof, anyway.

That was the political aspect. Neal understood it, though it inflamed him almost to the point of uncontrollable anger. They'd lived with it now for almost seven years. Zambia said, in the U.N., that there weren't any terrorist bases within her borders. Therefore, there weren't any bases. And if they went openly and wiped out the bases, it would be innocent villages they would be said to have attacked. And that would be an act of aggression by bloody old racist Rhodesia against a black neighbor.

He'd always thought the hell with the rest of the world. Let them send in their bloody U.N. troops; he'd prefer to be shot down fighting the bastards than to pussyfoot around like some skulking bushman. But that couldn't be, and he knew it well. Cooler heads than his were needed to keep poor old crippled Rhodesia alive. All the buggers wanted was an excuse, any excuse, and in would come the U.N. troops, and when they left, the white settlers might as well go with them for they'd have nothing left.

But, God, how he hated them all, especially the turncoat, fornicating British. On the bookshelf at home was a picture Winsome insisted on keeping out. It was of him in a British uniform when he'd been a tank commander in the desert campaign. He reflected bitterly how many men Rhodesia had given, men who'd fought to volunteer to help save the mother country. Oh yes, they'd helped pull the old bitch's bacon out of the fire, and she'd repaid by disowning them.

But he shouldn't be bitter, he told himself. Because now, by God, he had something he'd never dreamed he'd get. He had his chance at the murdering bastards in their nests, and he'd never ask for more. For years, he'd raised his bull voice in the ministers' meetings, insisting something be done about the terrorist bases before the northern farm country was lost. A loss they couldn't afford, couldn't sustain and go on. He had instituted all the domestic defenses, but the only real defense, he'd said, was to go in and wipe them out at the source. Rhodesia couldn't win a war of attrition, not with the sanctions, not with the shortages, not with their outmoded equipment. The fact that they were using FN assault rifles was indicative enough. The weapon was twenty years old and hopelessly behind such newer models as the Russian-made and Chinese-copied AK-47. Pistols. Common handguns were at a premium in the country. They didn't even have enough to equip all the military officers for whom the weapon was regulation. Their air power was almost nonexistent. They had twelve old Aloutte helicopters that had been used by the French when they were in Vietnam. And those were so valuable that they dare not get them too close to combat. The terrorists mined the roads, but Rhodesia had no proper mineproof vehicles. They had to take old Land Rovers and jeeps and modify them with sandbags and conveyor belting to collect the exploding shrapnel. In Rhodesia, you made do with whatever you could.

And then had come that surprising call from John Tyron. For that, he supposed, he had to thank Mozambique. They had known for years that if Mozambique fell to the Frelimoists they would have the same situation on their eastern flank they were now sustaining to the north. And that would be intolerable. John Tyron had sat there that morning, smoking quietly. He'd said, "Well, Neal, I've got a job for you. One to your liking, I think."

And then he'd told him.

But there'd been conditions. Tyron had said, "You are to begin making preparations immediately, but you are not to go forward unless Mozambique actually falls. That will be your signal. I say signal because from the time you leave this office, you will be completely on your own. If this action gets laid on, there will be one hell of an uproar from Zambia and then one hell of an uproar from the rest of the world. The prime minister is going to have to lie with a straight face, and the less he knows, the easier it will be for him to lie. In short, you've got to make absolutely bloody certain that, even though everyone knows we did it, there'll be no way for them to prove it."

Neal remembered his voice rising as he'd asked, "Do you mean the military is not to know?"

"No one is to know. There may be logistical problems, but you have enough authority in your office to be able to handle them."

He'd asked, his voice still louder than necessary, "Well, if the military is not to know, who the bloody hell am I supposed to use, phantoms?"

The minister had given him his thin smile. "I suggest a small force of international, paid fighters."

"Mercenaries."

"Mercenaries. And the more international, the better. You may set up a forward strike camp in Rhodesia, but I don't want your chaps loose in this country at any time. I don't even want them to know what country they're in."

He'd asked about money.

"You're to have hell's own kind of money. By next week, two million Rhodesian dollars will have been deposited for you in a bank in Johannesburg. The money is coming from the Friends of Rhodesia Trust. They've scraped it up somewhere, God knows how. You are to work through the Trust's man in Johannesburg. I think you know him, Jerome Weston. He's been working in the guise of an import-exporter, but in reality he's been one of our most successful sanction busters. Obviously, you're not to be directly connected to this matter, so Weston will have to front it."

And that had been that. With one last condition. Tyron had risen and come around the desk. He'd hesitated before he'd said, "Look, Neal, I know what a bitch of a job I'm handing you. But we need this, we need it badly. We understand that you can't get all those bases. There's no time for that. You've got to hit and get out. You can't be caught. Maybe this is no more than a gesture, but it's a vital one. Morale is very low in the north. We've got to get these people some rest, some relief."

It had taken the minister less than half an hour to give him the job; since then, he'd been working for months to bring it into reality. The fall of Mozambique had given them a fresh sense of urgency.

In those months, Neal Hall had undergone many changes of mood. At first, elation; then, bewilderment as he began to understand the scope of the operation; then, despair as he began to fear it could not be done under the terms set. And then they had found the American colonel, Matthew Brady, and Neal had begun to hope again.

He parked two blocks away from the hotel where Brady was staying. It was the Miekles, an old safari hotel that was beginning to fall behind the modern construction that was going up in downtown Salisbury. But it was still a first-rate place to stay. Walking toward it, Hall thought nostalgically of the times when he and Winsome had come in from a long tour of duty in the bush: how grand the hotel had seemed, how good that first long soak in a real bathtub, that first Scotch and water in the lounge, dinner upstairs.

He went through the lobby and took an elevator to the fifth floor, then walked quickly down the hall and knocked on Brady's door. It opened immediately.

"Matthew."

"Hello, Neal."

They had found Matthew Brady working as a military advisor to an Arab sheik. He had come dearly, and he had come with some conditions of his own, but he had taken charge from the first day. Indeed, it had been Brady who had devised and arranged the Angola diversion which would make possible two strikes against the terrorist bases. They had had disagreement over the method and the operational approach, because of Hall's intense fear that something might go wrong. But, in the end, he had recognized Brady's superior military mind, and he had withdrawn from active participation in the actual planning. He'd had only one specific instruction for Brady: "Colonel, you may wipe out the objectives. Obliterate them. But if proof gets out that we've had a hand in it, then you've failed in what we've asked you to do. And you may have condemned a nation to extinction."

Brady had looked into the old fighter's face and said

simply, "Minister, I understand the conditions. Don't worry."

Except Hall could never quite stop worrying.

Now they sat in Brady's hotel room and talked. Brady had brought Scotch in from South Africa.

"Aaaah," Neal Hall said, "God bless you, Matthew. The cruelest cut of all in the sanctions has been the Scotch. I'm still British enough to crave it, hate to admit it as I do."

"I brought you two bottles extra. They're in my suitcase."

Brady was a large man, larger than he looked because of the heavy shoulders and the short, thick neck. Though he'd been in Equatorial Africa for some time, he wasn't tanned. His skin was burned a deep red. He wore his hair in the traditional Marine crew cut, but it was even shorter because he was going bald: a growing circle of pink skin showed clearly on top of his head. He was relaxed now, leaning back and dangling his glass from a big, hairy hand. But even relaxed, his face was ugly—cold and impassive. Looked at from the front, it was flat. He had high cheekbones, but they fell off to flat planes. His chin was broad and square, and his brow was wide and flat. His nose had been broken often enough so that the top part looked mashed back into his face.

He had left the Marine Corps under unusual circumstances. While serving in Vietnam as a division commander, he had shot and killed a South Vietnamese general. Against orders and during a firefight, the general had pulled his troops back, and one of Brady's companies had been chewed to pieces through the opening. Brady had asked for charges against the general and had been told that was not politically expedient. The next day, Brady had sought out the general in a forward camp and shot him. The affair was never made public, but in order to hush it up and to placate the South Vietnamese government, Brady had been asked to resign. He had refused and been discharged for the good of the service. He was not bitter at the Marine Corps, or anyone for that matter. He'd done what he felt he had to and supposed the Corps had also. Anyway, it was all past, and he no longer even thought about it. All he wanted out of the rest of his life was to go on being what he was, a soldier.

Neal Hall said, "Matthew, I'm not going to pretend I like this. I don't like it one damn bit."

"That's too bad, Neal," Brady said. He didn't smile.

"I think the idea of your going up in that north country is foolhardy. It's dangerous. Anything could happen to you."

"Well, I'm going," Brady said.

The minister shook his head and poured himself another inch of Scotch. "You are totally and fundamentally indispensable to this mission. It's too late to replace you, and if something were to happen to you we'd be in one hell of a mess. Goddammit, Matthew, I'm serious!"

"I understand that."

"You could be hit by a sniper. You could run over a land mine. Your airplane could be shot down."

"You just get the arrangements made."

"Dammit, Matthew," Hall said, his voice rising, "I'm telling you, you are not to go."

Brady put his glass down. "Listen, Neal, we've had this out. If you think I'm going to run a combat operation based on nothing more than aerial photographs and maps and reports other people have written, you're out of your goddamn mind. I want a feel for the terrain and a feel for my enemy and a feel for the situation, and I can't do that in Johannesburg. So just cut the bullshit."

"Christ!" Hall stood up and then sat back down.

"Nothing is going to happen to me," Brady said. "Now, have you got the arrangements made?"

"Yes," Hall said grudgingly. "Or they will be. You're to stay with a farm family up there, some people name of Longhurst. Their farm is right in the hottest zone, and if there's anyone who knows the terrorists, it's those chaps up there. They've been living with them for quite some years. Also, one of the best experts on tribal lore and the spirit medium business is the D.C. for the area. Chap named Jim Leslie. I'll arrange for him to brief you."

"That sounds all right," Brady said.

"On the face of it, you're to be an American general who's come over unofficially to get a firsthand look at the situation. Of course, everyone will be falling down to help you because half this country still labors under the silly hope that the United States will come charging over the hill to save us." Hall made a grimace of distaste and took another drink of Scotch. He went on. "You'll be met at the airport, and your pilot will be briefed and all that sort of rot. By the way, who is the pilot?"

"A man name of Cody Ravel. An American, a Texan."

Hall shook his head. "I don't like that part one bit. He's going to learn an awful lot."

Brady said, "Just how the hell do you expect your lead pilot not to know everything?"

"But what do you know of this fellow?"

"On paper he looks perfect."

"On paper!" Hall's voice rose. "You mean, you haven't met him?"

"Not yet. But I will as soon as I'm back in Johannesburg."

"Oh, my bleeding ass!" Hall said. Now he did stand up. "What in God's name makes you think you can trust him?"

"I'll know after I see him," Brady said.

"Good lord!"

Brady grinned, the effect making his face uglier. "I like his type. He's a man who doesn't give a goddamn about anything."

"That's hardly a recommendation."

"It is if you know the breed," Brady said. "Now listen, Neal, you're going to have a heart attack if you don't quit worrying about every little detail. And that wouldn't be good, because you're the man who's got to keep putting money in the bank account. So how about you just relaxing and leaving all this to me."

Hall got up and went to the window. Far off to the north, he could see the heat lightning still brightening the black sky. He turned around. "Matthew, you do realize time is growing short."

"I know that, Neal."

"The rainy season is very close."

"Look, we're almost ready. We've just about got the men picked. Weston should have the weapons in the warehouse any day now. We'll make it. In seven days, we'll move to the forward training camp."

Hall came back and slumped in the chair and sighed. "I know it, Matt," he said finally. "It's just—"

He stopped, letting the thought trail off.

Brady looked at him. "We're going to kick the shit out of them for you, Neal. We're going to get the bastards off your back."

"Christ, I hope so," Hall said. He left not long after, taking his two bottles of Scotch.

Brady sat in his chair for a time longer, slowly drinking one last whiskey and water. As he sat, he began to smile to himself. This was the way he liked it. No politics. No extenuating factors. No intercessions. No concessions. Just go and wipe out the fucking objective. Pure war. Pure soldiering. He threw back his head and laughed.

6

Johannesburg

It was an ordinary looking house in the suburbs. Light showed dimly through a front window.

"You sure it's not too late?" Cody asked. He was beginning to regret his careless decision. Not that he was worried about Landon; he knew what the correspondent was after. But his orders had been to stay near the hotel. Which, he thought to himself, was probably the reason he'd come.

Landon said, "Oh, no, lad. It's never too late to visit Flic. That's her name, by the way. Not her real name, more like a nickname, or a professional name."

"Well, what makes you think this Flic will want to see us? Or me, anyway?"

"Oh, Flic's like that. She enjoys interesting people. I rather think she's going to be fascinated by you."

They were at the door. "Me? An American tourist?"

"She loves American tourists."

"By the way, what did you mean her professional name? Is she an actress or something?"

"Sort of."

"What does that mean? Either she's an actress or she's not."

"Well, let's just say that in her particular profession she's called upon, from time to time, to simulate various emotions. You'd call that acting, wouldn't you?"

Landon reached his hand out for the bell, but Cody grabbed his arm.

"Listen, Landon, what is all this bullshit? Is she what I think she is?"

"Probably."

Cody tried to see his face in the dim light. "What do you do, pimp a little on the side?"

"No, this is purely a social call. Any arrangements you make with Miss Flic will be on a noncommercial basis."

"A whore," Cody said flatly, "I haven't been to a whore since I was sixteen. Landon, you are the craziest bastard I ever saw in my life. What makes you think I won't knock your fucking head off?"

Landon gave him a bland look. "What, you an American tourist? Just for showing you around town?" He put out his hand and rang the bell. "Now, don't be too crude, old boy. You'll find this a rather high-class lady. The word 'whore' hardly applies."

"If she fucks for money, she's a whore."

Landon suddenly gave him a grin. "And what is it you do for money?"

They sat in her living room. Cody was sunk down in an overstuffed armchair and she was across from him, curled up on a small sofa. Landon had left, had been there one moment and gone the next. The girl was wearing a pair of silk lounging pajamas so sheer that he could see the form of her body when she moved. Her nipples pushed out against the material so that it hung down as if from a point. She was beautiful, as Landon had said. She was dark and her hair was dark. Her fingers were long and slim, and her nails were glossed a deep crimson. She could be French, he thought, or Eurasian. There was a hint of Oriental about her eyes, but that could have been makeup.

They sat there watching each other. He was drinking bourbon that she'd brought him, and she was smoking. They had talked very little. Landon had carried the conversation, and now that he was gone, they sat and looked at each other.

"This is silly," Cody said finally.

"How is that, silly?"

"Well, Landon has gone, leaving me out here somewhere in the goddamn boondocks. He's got some wild idea that I'm a mercenary, and I assume he's dropped me off here so you could work me for all the details. Is that about it?"

"I don't know," she said. "This is the first I've heard of it."

"Yeah, I'll bet."

"Are you? Are you a mercenary soldier?" She cocked her head at him.

He laughed.

"No, really. I think that would be very exciting. Tell me about it, if you will."

"Oh, it's just loads of fun," he said. "We're heroes, you know. Dashing around the country. Thrill a minute. Bang, bang, bang. You've got no idea."

"You're making fun of me."

"I don't see why not," he said. "You ought to feel like a damn fool. I know I do."

She took a long pull on her cigarette, tilting her head as she blew out the smoke. "Why should you feel like a fool? We're here, you're having a drink. It's very pleasant."

"Maybe I'm just tired," he said. He yawned. "It's not

the company; I've just never got my hours straightened out."

"Ah, jet lag. The best thing for that is to stay up twenty-four hours straight, and then you will have a good sleep and be back on schedule."

"You recommend I stay up all night tonight?"

"If you like."

"How shall we pass the time? You got any ideas?"

She shrugged, smoking her cigarette and looking at him.

He laughed, still without much humor in his voice. "Well, thanks anyway, but I think I'll go back to the hotel. How do I get a cab out here?"

"Cabs are very difficult at this time of night. Why don't you stay here and go back to your hotel in the morning?"

"Is that what I'm supposed to do? You mean, it's supposed to take you all night to get the story out of me? My god, I'd thought you'd be better than that."

"You seem angry. What do you have to be angry about?"

He didn't answer, just finished his drink. He held out the glass. "Can I get another one of these?"

"Of course." She came across and took the glass. He watched her walking away, admiring the tightness of the silk across her buttocks and thighs. She crossed the room to the bar, and he said, "Well, I'll hand it to Landon for one thing. You are a damn good-looking woman."

"That's nice to hear," she said, bringing his drink.

"But you've heard it before."

"Yes, just as you've heard that you're a handsome man before." She curled back up on the couch. "Now, tell me about yourself. Are you married?"

"Sure. Want to see the pictures of the kids? Got a swell shot of us all down at the beach building sand castles."

"Why must you be unpleasant?"

"Let me ask you one instead. Is Landon paying for this party? Or are you doing it for him for old times' sake?"

"Look," she said, "if you are going to continue to be rude, I will not mind if you leave. Landon is an old friend of mine. He brought you by because he thought we would enjoy each other's company."

"Sure," he said. He sank back in the chair, sipping at his drink. He was beginning to relax. It was fun in a way, he thought. What the hell was wrong with drinking whiskey with a beautiful girl, no matter how screwy the setup. Maybe he'd even go to bed with her. He looked around the room. It was very well furnished, obviously expensive. "You do pretty well here. Business must be good."

"Yes," she said. "And how is yours?"

"Great," he said. "I'm in the hardware business back home. Doing so well I can afford to take vacations in Africa."

She snubbed her cigarette out in the ashtray. "Why don't you leave now?"

He grinned at her, his face hard. "No. I'm just beginning to enjoy myself. Besides, like you said, cabs are hard to get at this time of night."

"Perhaps I can find one."

"Don't bother. I said I was beginning to enjoy myself."

"Then act like it. Be pleasant. You've been angry from the first moment."

"Funny about that," he said. "I've got this thing about being played for a fool. Landon must think I'm the sap of all time. If I was a mercenary, it's a goddamn cinch I wouldn't come here and spill my guts just for a piece of ass. Or maybe I would. You may be fantastic. Landon may be right; you might be so good that I'd babble my head off. If," he added, "I had anything to babble."

"Let's stop this. Landon knows you're a mercenary.

There's nothing dangerous in admitting that. He doesn't expect you to give him any secrets; he only wants your cooperation when the time is right. Nothing more."

"Is a story that important? *This* important?"

"He thinks so. I don't know."

"What's your connection to Landon? Why are you doing this?"

"Landon is a good friend."

"Don't give me that."

She tossed her head and frowned. But then she answered, "Landon helped me. In the beginning. He helped me make contact with the right people."

Cody slowly grinned. "The rich ones, uh? The ones that could afford you."

"If you like."

"Enough of this," he said. He suddenly got up and crossed to her. "Come on."

She looked away. "I'm not sure I want to sleep with you now."

"Sure you do." He took her hand and pulled her to her feet. "Just pretend I'm one of the paying customers."

Her eyes suddenly flared and she drew her hand back as if to slap him. He caught it by the wrist, grinning. "Com'on, let's see how much you can get out of me. If you're good enough, I'll even make up some stuff."

He came awake suddenly. He was on his back, and for a moment he stared up at the ceiling. Then he rolled over and looked at his watch. It was one P.M. For a second, he lay staring at the dial, trying to think. Then he remembered and raised himself to a sitting position. The bedroom was bright and cheerful, sunlit from a pair of large open windows on either side of the bed. It was a large bed and the sheets felt cool and satiny. He looked over at the other side. The girl was not there. Then he looked for his clothes. His jacket was hung over the back of a chair. His pants were folded over the seat. He threw back the covers and stepped to the floor.

He went first to his pants and took out his wallet. He had $2,000 cash in it. He took a rapid count. It was all there, but there was something wrong with his wallet; it looked rearranged. Tucked in a pocket were his pilot's license and his airman's medical certificate. He always kept the license first because he needed it oftener. Now their order was reversed. And some of his other cards looked out of order. He'd put the note from Weston in the money compartment. Now he took it out and unfolded it carefully. It looked to have been refolded and not along the original lines.

"Son of a bitch," he said tightly.

The worst was in his jacket, the copy of his contract and the insurance papers. They'd been put in an envelope by Carlton-Brooks, and Cody could still see him tucking the flap inside. Now the flap was out.

"That stupid bitch," he said.

He looked for her first in the bathroom. She wasn't there. His head was hurting and he took a moment to wash his face and then to brush his teeth with a toothbrush, hers he supposed, that was hanging over the sink. He went back in the bedroom and dressed slowly, conscious that he'd had too much to drink the night before. When he was finished, he went looking for her. He found her in the kitchen by following the sound of eggs frying. She was at the stove. She turned and smiled as he came in. "Sit over there," she said, pointing at a breakfast table. "I'll bring you some coffee."

He sat and watched her silently. She gave him a glass of orange juice and then the coffee. He drank the cold juice down rapidly, grateful for its feel in his stomach. As he drank the coffee, she brought him a plate with eggs and a small steak and broiled tomatoes.

"You're not going to eat?" he asked.

"I never eat breakfast," she said.

She was wearing a robe, half-buttoned so that he could see most of her breasts. He studied them. "You look very pretty this morning," he said. "A woman who can look beautiful at night and pretty in the morning has got a lock on it."

"That's a nice thing to say." She was sitting across from him. "You were very sweet last night. Afterwards."

He rubbed his head. "I was very drunk."

"Is that an apology for being so unpleasant at first?"

"It might be an excuse for being sweet."

He picked at his breakfast for a moment and then pushed it away.

"You'd feel better if you ate," she said.

"Oh, I doubt it." He leaned back in his chair and lit a cigarette. "Landon call yet?"

"Please don't start that again."

"I wasn't starting anything. I just thought he'd be curious as to how we got along. Old matchmaker Landon."

She looked down at her hands.

Cody said, "He told me you were an actress. Or you had to be an actress in your business. Is that hard, I mean simulating all those groans and moans?"

"As soon as you're ready, I'll drive you to your hotel."

"Look, you're taking me all wrong. Maybe it's my tone of voice. That's the way I sound all the time. People think I'm mean and I'm really not. I'm really a sweetheart." He was watching her carefully. "I wasn't saying you couldn't enjoy your work. What the hell, I fly airplanes for a living, but sometimes I like to take one up and wring it out just for pure pleasure."

She studied his face. "You're a pilot, then?"

"Sure," he said. He took a sip of coffee. "By the way, what's your real name?"

"Flic," she said.

"No, no, no. I mean your legal name. Flic's nice for its purpose, but I feel I know you well enough to know the real you."

She looked hard into his eyes. "It's unimportant," she said, and looked away.

"Oh, I don't know about that." He got to his feet. His hand suddenly shot out and grabbed her by the throat of her robe. He jerked her to her feet and started for the bedroom, dragging her behind. She had been too surprised to react at first, but now she was clawing at his arm, jerking back. He plodded steadily ahead.

Once through the door, he whirled and threw her toward the bed. She landed in a tumble.

"All right," he said. He stood at the foot of the bed, breathing heavily. "Where are your papers? You had a look at mine, so let me see yours."

She stared at him, her face blank.

"Listen," he said, leaning toward her, "I'm told there are people in this city and in this country who would kill me if they knew I was a mercenary. Do you understand me?" He reached out and took her face by the jaws, shaking her head back and forth. "Do you?"

"You're hurting me," she said, feeling the strength of his fingers on her jaw.

"Hurting you? Listen, little girl, I'll break your fucking neck. Now, you done got yourself into something a little more serious than you understand. Your good buddy Landon has put your sweet little ass in a box. Now, you tell me all about yourself, because I'm going to tell some people about you and if anything happens to me they'll know who to come looking for."

"You sonofabitch!" she said. She tried to slap him, but he caught her arm with his free hand.

"Okay," he said. He let go her jaw and then slapped her hard with his free hand. Her head snapped sideways and she stared at him, shocked.

"Your name," he said. "Your papers." He drew his hand back again. "Baby, I ain't playing. You give me some information or I'm going to put enough knots on your face that you won't be worth two dollars a trick."

When she didn't speak, he slapped her again, this time backhanded on the other side of her face. "Next, I break your nose."

She burst out crying and flung herself across the bed, clawing at the drawer of a small table. "Here!" she said. "Here, here, here!" She took something out of the drawer and flung it at him. "You bastard!"

It hit him in the chest and fell to the floor. He picked it up. It was her passport. Her name was Louisa Durier. She was thirty years old and had been born in Algiers. It was a French passport.

He tossed it back on the bed. She was lying back now, an arm over her face, crying quietly. One leg was pulled up, throwing her robe open. Even with the anger still hot in him, she was very desirable. He turned away. "All right. Now I know enough about you also."

She didn't speak.

"Where's the phone? I need a cab."

When she didn't answer, he turned and went out, finding the phone in the front room. He was looking through the directory when he heard a sound behind him.

"Please."

He looked around. She was standing there. Both sides of her face were red.

"I'm sorry," she said.

"Go to hell," he said.

She took a step nearer him and held out her hand. "Here are the keys. I have a car just out back. Please take it, and come back tomorrow so that we may talk."

"That's a laugh," he said.

She was calm now. "I meant you no harm, I swear it. I thought it was an innocent favor for Landon. I can understand how you feel. We lived in Algiers," she said, "as French. My father and mother went there many years ago to settle. I was there through much of the trouble. When the French left. I understand about here. It is the same as Algiers."

She was still holding out the keys. "Please take the automobile. By the time you return tomorrow, you will have told someone about me and then you will feel safe, and perhaps we can talk and I can make you understand that I meant you no harm."

"I feel safe," he said.

"Then take the automobile. And come back."

"What the hell do you care if I come back or not?"

"Please," she said. She put her hand to her cheek. It was already beginning to swell. "It's a better bargain than you offered me."

He still didn't move.

"It's a little thing for you to do. You can see there's no risk in it for you."

He suddenly shrugged. "Sure. It's your car." He put out his hand and she dropped the keys in his palm. "I won't be back," he said. "I'll leave your car parked somewhere and you'll have to find it."

"I don't care about the car."

He laughed. "That's a strange attitude for a whore." Then he wheeled around and went out the door.

She waited until she heard the car start, then moved to the window and watched him back out and drive off. She stood there until he was out of sight. Then she went to the phone and dialed a number.

"Landon," she said, "I'm afraid that I cannot help you."

She listened for a moment. Then she said, "Yes, that is true. Unfortunately. But I'm very much afraid that I lunch over when I get there and be ready for business." Then he hung up.

He walked out on the balcony and sat down in a metal chair, propping his elbows on his knees and letting his hands hang loosely between his legs.

At the meeting would be Weston and Carlton-Brooks and the Portuguese colonel, Sancho Cardeones. It was a very important meeting because it was the first step in the carefully planned deception. Today, he would instigate a classic leak.

He glanced at his watch. It was later than he'd expected, but he still didn't move, just sat there thinking.

Back in the States, he had a wife and two sons. The sons grown now. A wife he saw very seldom. He supposed, he hoped, that she had made a life for herself. He knew that she'd expected him to retire from the military when the Marine Corps had let him out, and he knew how bitter she'd been when he hadn't. But that was just more of what she'd never understood about him. But, at least, he kept her well provided for. He had been paid a $50,000 advance when he'd taken the contract. If he succeeded, fully, in his mission, he'd be given a bonus of $100,000. In addition, he had been given a quarter-of-a-million-dollar life insurance policy, paid up, with his wife as beneficiary. At least, he could give her money.

It was not often that he gave in to reflection. He was a man who lived in the time and place that he was, seldom interested in the past. It did not strike him as unusual to find himself in this city and in this time with this unique mission at hand.

But it was, he thought, a long way from Oklahoma.

"Hell," he said aloud. His voice was country, still touched by the Southwest accent after all the years of the military and all the years of traveling.

He thought about it, how long he'd been a soldier.

may never see him again. He's very angry with me just now."

She hung up the phone and went to stand at the window again, looking out.

7

Johannesburg

Matthew Brady was back in Johannesburg, in his suite in a luxurious downtown hotel. He had been up since five A.M., working steadily. Beside him was a waiter's tray with a large pot of coffee and a half-filled cup. It was the second pot of the day, and what remained had long since grown cold. Spread out on the table in front of him were topographical maps and aerial photographs and personnel records and a master roster. He was working on the master roster.

After a moment, he leaned back and stretched, rolling his shoulders to ease the nagging pain in his back. He rubbed his eyes and then lit a cigarette, grimacing at the stale taste. Then, he stared out the balcony window, letting his mind go restfully blank.

He had almost three hundred men in training. Of these seventy would be picked for the primary mission. The others would be used in the diversionary campaign. Up to now, none of the troops had seen him, even knew of his existence. The personnel not chosen would never see him. Nor would one group ever know of the other's mission. It was an intricate and workable plan, fulfilling

Neal Hall's primary requirement of secrecy. Brady didn't know how they could have made it much more clandestine. Only three men knew the actual details. Of course, his lead pilot would have to know. Thinking about that, he picked up Cody Ravel's personnel file and studied it through a haze of blue cigarette smoke.

This one had to turn out. The time was running short and they were about out of the right kind of applicants. A great deal of the success of the operation depended on the lead pilot, and Cody Ravel's kind of pilot wasn't easy to find. He had pinned Weston down hard on the man.

"That pilot. Have you changed your mind?"

"I think he's the one."

"That's not good enough."

"Well, as I've said, he's a spot different. He's hostile I'd say he's a pretty hard boy. You've seen the file o him."

"Goddammit, Weston," he'd said flatly, "that's n what I mean. I'm running out of time. Is he the one Are you sure of him?"

But Weston had shook his head. "No thanks, Colone I'm not making that decision. You've asked me to giv you a judgment and I've done that. That's as far as go."

"Have you got a meeting set up yet?"

Weston looked at him calmly. "I'd like to remind yo Colonel, that you only got back this morning. And y don't let me in on your comings and goings."

"Then set one up, quick."

But first, there was this other meeting, set for lunc Brady suddenly didn't want to have to sit down and through the opening small talk. He was tired and i patient. He got up and walked to the desk telephone a dialed Weston's private number. When the cripple ca on, he said, without preamble, "I'll be an hour late. Ha

From the time he was seventeen and had enlisted in the Marine Corps as a buckass private. That made thirty-four years, twenty-nine of them in the Corps. Bird colonel wasn't a lot to show for twenty-nine years, but then he'd never done too well with the internal politics. They liked him when there was a fight, when it was straight combat, but he hadn't been too popular when it came down to the game playing and the ass kissing. He could have retired with twenty-seven years: the pay and retirement benefits would have been the same, no matter how much longer he'd stayed. He would never have made general. That was a cinch. But he'd stayed anyway. And no one had understood why. Certainly not his wife. But then, how did you explain what it felt like to be good at something and to enjoy doing it?

"Aw, fuck it," he said. He got up and went back into the room, closing and locking the balcony doors behind him. Then, he gathered up all the maps and photographs and other papers, put them in a briefcase, and locked the briefcase in a closet. He put the key in his pocket, took an automatic pistol out of a drawer, shoved it deep in his waistband, and then put on a sports coat, buttoning it so that the gun wouldn't show. He called the desk to order his car and went out the door.

They had finished lunch and moved into the library by the time he arrived. They were seated around a low table in the middle of the room. A side table had been pulled up for glasses and liquor.

All except Weston rose as he entered. He shook hands with each man in turn, accepted a Scotch and water, then sat down.

"Well, Colonel," he said to Cardeones. They had been together twice before, but the involvement of the Angolese was so delicate that their meetings had been handled with an almost impersonal caution.

"I am happy to see you, my Colonel," Cardeones said formally.

The Portuguese colonel was a short, dark man, dressed in a blue double-breasted business suit. Until a few months ago, he had been a member of the Portuguese army on active duty in Angola. He was now under the command of Matthew Brady with orders to lead a mercenary army in guerrilla warfare against the Frelimo terrorists in Angola. Other than that, he knew almost nothing about what was to come. Certainly not that his was to be a diversionary tactic for political purposes.

Weston and Carlton-Brooks watched and listened as the two commanders talked. They had been told to expect Cardeones, but nothing else, and lunch had been a polite, awkward affair with a great deal of meaningless talk and a number of silences.

Abruptly, Brady turned to his adjutant. "Major, at his convenience, Colonel Cardeones will present himself at headquarters. You are to provide him with office space and all amenities commensurate with his rank. He is to be introduced to the troops under your training as the commander of this mission." He looked at Cardeones. "Is that satisfactory, Colonel?"

"Of course."

"You'll make any further arrangements once you take command."

"My thanks, Colonel."

Brady gave Carlton-Brooks a bare glance as he and the Portuguese colonel arose. "My thanks for coming," Brady said. He escorted the colonel to the door.

When he'd returned and sat down, he said brusquely to Carlton-Brooks, "All right, Major. Let's have your report."

But the adjutant was not over his astonishment. He asked, "Am I to understand, Colonel, that Colonel Cardeones is the commander of this mission?"

"I said he was to be introduced as the commander. You know damn well who the commander of this mission is." He gave the adjutant a flat stare.

Carlton-Brooks colored, embarrassment rising across his face. He said in a controlled voice, "Thank you, Colonel. I apologize for the breach."

Brady said simply, dryly, "Report."

The adjutant replied formally, "As per your orders, we have been concentrating on physical fitness with special emphasis on individual reaction to discipline and routine."

"Don't give me that shit, Major."

Carlton-Brooks glanced unhappily at Weston. The cripple was carefully looking away.

"Very well, Colonel. I can pick the men you want right now. If you insist. At this moment, I would say that I'm sure of at least sixty and I could make a calculated guess on the others." He stirred in his chair. "However, I want to point out, sir, that you've given me very limited criteria to work with."

Brady narrowed his eyes. "You were told to find the best seventy fighters. The seventy men who would best respond to tight discipline and a bastard of a combat campaign." He suddenly leaned forward. "The meanest seventy sonofabitches you've got. Why the fuck do you need criteria for that?"

Carlton-Brooks sat upright in his chair. He said stiffly, "Nevertheless."

Brady said, "Pack that shit in, Major. This ain't Sandhurst."

Carlton-Brooks was trying to control himself. "Colonel, there is one situation you had best be aware of. A great many of the men are complaining. A few have quit, though none that I have notched for selection. But a good many others, some good men, are threatening to quit." He stopped, suddenly fearful. He was afraid of Matthew Brady, though he couldn't say why.

He went on. "The main problem, sir, seems to be what it's all about. And when. And where. The men don't know, of course, that they're being looked over for selection, so they don't understand the purpose of the basic type of training that they're being given." He hesitated and then said, a tremor of nervousness in his voice, "Also, there's the looting. You've got to remember, sir, that these are mercenary soldiers and given to a bit more freedom in their conduct and thinking than your regular soldier of the line. In my past experience in the Congo and the other campaigns I've—"

He ceased speaking as Brady cut a hand sharply through the air.

But Brady only looked at him curiously and then got out a cigarette and lit it. He took a long moment and then sat even longer, studying the glowing end. Finally, he asked, almost in an offhand voice, "What would they think of Angola?"

"Angola?" Carlton-Brooks smiled. "They would think very well of it, sir. Angola is quite a rich country and I'm sure the lads would consider the opportunities endless."

Brady yawned. "Well," he said carefully, "I don't see where you have any problems, Major."

"How is that, sir?"

"You've just met Colonel Cardeones, haven't you?"

"Yes, sir."

"Well, Colonel Cardeones was an officer in the Portuguese regulars, recently detached. He's served in Angola for the last ten years."

"Are you telling me the job is Angola?"

"I'm not telling you anything, Major," Brady said harshly. "Nor are you to tell anyone anything. But I can't conceal what Cardeones is or where he's served. Nor

can I keep you or anyone else from drawing inferences."
He rose abruptly. "That will be all, Major." He gave
Carlton-Brooks a brief handshake. "I will want your
roster any day now. Be ready. You're excused."

He did not show the adjutant out.

When he sat back down, Brady looked at Weston.
The cripple smiled cheerfully.

"My turn, I suppose."

"Correct."

Weston shifted slightly in his wheelchair. "I'm having
no difficulty with most of the weaponry. The FNs and
the mortars and the light machine guns are all in the
warehouse. But, frankly, Colonel, I'm in a spot of difficulty on the AK-47s."

"Why?"

Weston shifted again and laughed. "Well, Colonel,
you must realize that a Russian-made assault rifle is not
the most likely item to find on the open market."

"If they were on the open market, I'd buy them myself and wouldn't need you. I was told that you are a
man who can get anything if the money's there."

"Fundamentally, that's true. But—"

"No buts, Weston. Get them and get them quickly.
You may have less time than you think."

"I've come to expect that," Weston said. "Actually
though, I'm guilty of pulling the poor mouth a bit.
Possibly to pad my part."

"Oh, I appreciate you," Brady said, his voice dry.

"Well, the impossible, Colonel. Now that the lines
are open again to Mozambique, I think I'll have my hands
on your goods in fairly short order."

"Mozambique?" Brady raised his thin eyebrows.

Weston smiled slightly. "Where else would you expect
to find a good quantity of AK-47s outside Russia or
China?"

"You are actually dealing with someone in Mozambique?"

"Of course. There's an engaging rogue there named M'butta who is much like myself, a trader. He had the foresight to aid the Frelimoists in the early days, and now he's got a fairly free hand."

"And he'll sell you AK-47s?"

"Of course. After all, he's a businessman first. Now, we're just engaging in a bit of last minute haggling. Purely for the sport of the thing."

"Jesus Christ," Brady said. He slumped back in his chair and ran a hand tiredly over his face. "What a hell of a game."

Weston watched him. He asked, "Matt, how's it going? How does it really look right now?"

Brady shrugged. "I wish I knew. It's a guess. A calculated guess from one end to the other. I'm nine hundred miles from my enemy. I've never seen his terrain except in pictures. I know nothing about his ability or his nature. I'm taking seventy men to do a job I might well need seven hundred for. Who knows? Who the fuck knows?"

"I imagine you do," Weston said.

"Yeah," Brady said. "I damn well better." He stood up. "I got to go. When do I look this pilot over?"

"I thought tomorrow night."

But Brady shook his head. "No. Tonight. We'll be leaving for Rhodesia in thirty-six hours. Make it about eight for dinner. I want a chance to get to know him."

The phone was ringing as Cody let himself into his hotel room. When he picked it up, Weston said, "You have been out of touch most of this day."

"What?" It was a second before Cody recognized the voice.

"I have been calling you since eight this morning. You were told to stay in reach."

"Listen," Cody said, "knock it off." His mood was bad.

"All right. We'll table this for the moment. Present yourself at my house this evening for dinner. It is not a social engagement."

"What time?"

"Eight sharp. Be on time."

"I usually am," Cody said. "Anything else?"

But there was a click and the phone went dead. He put it back on the cradle and sat down on the side of the bed and lit a cigarette. After a moment, he looked up the BBC bureau in the directory and dialed the number. Landon answered.

"Listen," Cody said, "your playmate struck out."

"Yes," Landon said, "I've talked with her."

"I took her car. It's in the parking lot of the Carlton Hotel. The keys are in it."

"I think she expects you to return it to her."

"Oh, I don't think I will. She makes me uncomfortable, she's so well-read. Especially papers in my billfold."

"Look, old boy," Landon said, "you're taking this matter all wrong. I don't want any of your bloody military secrets. All I'm asking of you is a little cooperation. There's a hell of a story in this and I want it. I ask only that you give it to me first when the time is right."

"Listen, Landon, get off my case. I'm going to tell you once and once only."

"Oh, don't get belligerent. I'm doing you no harm. And neither is the girl." There was a pause. "She liked you. She liked you very much. Of course, that was before you got a trifle nasty."

"Gosh, that's swell," Cody said.

"Why not go see her again?"

"Don't have time. It might interfere with my sightseeing. You know where her car is." He hung up.

8

Johannesburg

He stayed in his room the rest of the afternoon, reading and smoking. From time to time, he'd lay the book on his chest and stare up at the ceiling, thinking. Not that there was a lot of any value to think about, and thinking was something he'd decided to give up a long time ago, anyway. Maybe there was somebody somewhere who knew what it was all about, but he was goddamned if he did.

Sometimes he was a little surprised at time. All of a sudden, he was thirty-six, and he didn't know how he'd got there so fast. It seemed that he'd been waiting all his life; waiting to find the right place, the right people, the right interests. And the time had just gone while he'd skated along on the surface, not particularly happy, not particularly unhappy. Just coasting.

Lying there, he recalled images from the past. Sudden, isolated images. The time they were going to steal the gold statue out of the little church high up on a plateau in the Andes. And all they'd had to use was a worn-out 1956 Cessna Skyhawk. There they were up there, trying to get through the last pass, and the engine starving out, even with the mixture full lean. And then the downdraft and the wall of the mountain coming up, and he was kicking hard left rudder with the controls getting musky and the stall warning light flashing red and Travers beside him, white-faced and sweating, "Oh, Jesus, oh, Jesus." And then the other rock face and no control left and the engine weaker and weaker, then catching just the tiny updraft off the windward face and then enough flying speed and room to turn and going back down.

And for what? For the gold statue? Hell, he hadn't given a damn about that. To see if he could get a worn-out airplane up to that plateau? To impress the four shoddy crooks who'd hired him?

Hell, he didn't know.

And another image. When the man had hired him to fly the twin Beech on a smuggling run into Canada, and he'd got to the airplane and found it loaded with golf clubs and he'd said, "You're kidding," and the man had said, no, he wasn't. That there was some kind of heavy duty on American-made golf clubs.

But that had been one of the funny ones.

And the twinkling light of the machine guns on the takeoff roll after he'd landed on the beach to pick up the three Cubans that the guy from Miami had hired him for. Hearing once again the tiny plop plop plop as the bullets went through the Plexiglas window just behind him, the motor roaring as he shoved the throttle in. And the one Cuban hit and bleeding all over the back of the airplane and thanking God whoever was shooting at them hadn't led them more or he'd still be on that beach. Or wherever they'd have buried him.

For what? For the $2,000 the man had paid him?

Or ferrying single engine airplanes to Europe, the long hours over the cold ocean with the rear seats full of gasoline drums, listening to the engine.

Or crop dusting.

Or running guns into Mexico for those crazy students who'd tried not to pay him because the money had to go for the cause. What cause? Who the fuck cared about the cause? Give me the money, José, or me and the guns is both leaving. And then the knife and having to break the kid's wrist.

And all the women. And he was damned if he could remember much except that he'd never understood any of them. Which was, one of them had said, because he never gave anything of himself. Well, he hadn't told her, but he'd have liked to give something if he'd just known what.

And all the time just coasting. Just waiting. Never consciously saying that there was someday, somewhere going to be a place and time and reason for him. But always having it in the back of his mind.

He'd always been restless. He couldn't remember a time he hadn't been. His folks had died and he'd lived with his uncle, ranching on a semifailure of a spread in Texas. Cutting out of there when he was seventeen. Getting just enough college to get in OCS. But feeling restless immediately in the army and taking every special course they had until he was almost a charter member of the special forces group. And being sent to Vietnam back before the U.S. was supposed to be there. But being there and leading a platoon of commando people, supposedly for reconnaissance reasons, but getting in plenty of fire-fights. In the dark, the steamy feel of the country smothering him, the sound of the small arms, the flash of a phosphorous grenade. Somebody getting shot; lying there, bleeding.

For what?

Getting out. Finding flying. Becoming the sort of pilot who made the right kind of people say, "You need something in or out of a bad place, get Cody Ravel. Good man. Got a tight asshole and a tight mouth."

And all the time waiting. And looking. Except he didn't know for what. And finally deciding that didn't any of it make a shit, so maybe there really wasn't that place he was finally going to come to.

Now he was in Africa. In a hotel room. Waiting to see a man. Waiting for orders. Waiting to fly somebody or something someplace, and that wouldn't be the place either.

He suddenly sat up and swung around on the bed and lit a cigarette.

Maybe he asked too much, he thought. Or expected too much. Except he didn't know what he was expecting. What was a man supposed to do? Get a wife and have kids and live in the same house all the time? And go to church and believe in the government and rightness of all things? And have friends and play poker every Monday night for a quarter limit? And have a little flying business and fly people to appointments and business deals? And vote for the senator of his choice, and buy a new car every two years, and believe in either capitalism or communism or the monarch, or become a yogi and live on a mountain, or raise show dogs, or marry a woman eight years older who had a lot of money, or adopt Korean orphans, or read a lot and become intelligent on some subject? Or bum around the world flying airplanes and get the shit scared out of him often enough to feel alive?

Then come to Africa and fly airplanes for the mercenaries, whatever it was they were going to do?

He got up and went into the bathroom and brushed his teeth and shaved.

On the way to Weston's, he stopped in at Drakes because he had an hour to kill and couldn't stand to stay around the hotel any longer.

"Here he is," he heard someone say.

Gerry was at a table in a corner, grinning and beckoning. Cody walked over and sat down.

"This is the Kraut," Ruger said. "Wilf Schneider. Bloody good you've come along. I'm trying to get drunk and the bastard is about to put me to sleep with his flaming theories."

"Hello," Schneider said, smiling slightly. "Gerry has told me about you."

They poured him a glass of beer.

Cody said, "What are you doing here? I thought you trained in the evenings."

"Five nights a week," Schneider said. "This is an off night."

"And bloody about time," Ruger put in. He sounded drunk. "Some of the lads is had about all they can take. And I'm one of 'em."

"Gerry," Schneider said, "please go and move your car. They will impound it."

"Fuck 'em all," Ruger said.

The German looked at Cody. "He's parked his car in a no parking zone and it will be taken away. He's got the keys and I can't make him move it."

"Fuck 'em all!" Ruger said loudly.

"Why don't you move the car?" he asked Gerry.

The Scotsman's face suddenly cleared. He looked at Cody. "Because I don't want to," he said. "Do you know a better reason, lad?" His voice was quiet and flat.

"I guess not," Cody said.

They drank. On their second pitcher, Gerry asked, "Going to tell us now, pilot? What's it all about, Alfie? We got to know."

"What difference does it make?"

"Because I'm fucking curious, that's what!"

"Gerry," Schneider said. He put his hand on his friend's shoulder. "Don't be so loud. We don't want to be thrown out."

"They throw me out," Ruger said, "they'll have some dead bodies to go along as color guard."

Then he laughed. He looked at Cody. "I'm getting drunk, pilot. Can you tell it?"

"Yeah, I noticed."

"Or should I call you Captain?" He looked over at Schneider. "We got to get our licks in on the brass here while the gettin's good, Kraut. Once the operation starts, we'll have to sir him and salute and all that bullshit. This is going to be a proper boy scout operation, you can bet."

"How are you getting this drunk on beer?" Cody asked.

"On beer? Fuck, I'm drunk on insanity, mate. On frustration. On waiting. On the itch, if you read me. Is that the way you pilots talk—do you read me? And over and roger and all that bullshit? Tell us, pilot."

"Gerry," Schneider said quietly.

"Let him alone," Cody said. "Yeah," he said to Ruger, "we say all that. We say over and under and roger and fuck you, Jack, and stick it up your ass and all that kind of talk. You like pilot's talk? You want to hear some more?"

Ruger looked at him a long moment, his eyes seeming to dilate. Then he suddenly laughed. "A hard boy," he said to Schneider. "We got us a hard boy here. And a Yank, no less. Except he won't tell us what the fuck is going on or where we're going. And we know he knows. So that don't make him no mate, does it?"

"What do you care?" Cody asked him, looking straight into his face. "One place's the same as another, isn't it? You say you want to go so bad. What do you care where it is? Or who it is? Or what it is?"

"Ah!" Schneider said. He pointed his finger at Ruger. "Do you hear what he said? It's the same as I've been telling you. You want a proper attitude, Gerry. And here's a Yank pilot to teach it to you. What difference *does* it make?"

"Ah, fuck you both." Ruger came back to Cody. "You better be good, Yank. You hear me? You better be bloody good. Times we was most scared in the Congo was when 'em flaming pilots the CIA had laid on was takin' us from one action to another. We used to cheer and clap when one of them bastards got the plane on the ground in one piece."

"He is not joking," Schneider said.

"And are you brave, pilot?" Ruger pulled his head back to look at him from a long way off. "We went out in a relief column to save one of the blokes who'd gone down in an observation plane. But we got there too late. And guess what?"

Cody took a drink of beer.

"The rebels had already got him," Ruger said. "Fixed him proper. Drove a bloody stake up his ass till it come out his mouth. What do you think of that, pilot?"

Cody looked at him, his beer glass in one hand. "I think you run your mouth," he said.

Ruger laughed. "Ha ha. Oh, pilot. Come, tell us. What brings you here?"

"What brings you here?"

"Us? It's different for us." Ruger jerked a thumb at Schneider. "The Kraut here, all he wants to do is take pictures. And make money." He laughed harshly. "This, lad, is your true mercenary. He don't give balls shit for nothing else except the bloody money. And them bloody fucking photographs he clicks that camera off at. He's insecure, see? Money, that's what the chap wants."

Schneider was shaking his head, a quiet smile on his face. "Gerry" was all he said.

"But me?" Ruger pointed a thumb at his chest. "You want to know about me, pilot?" He leaned quickly toward Cody and his voice went down to a raspy whisper. "Me, pilot? I tell you, lad. I don't believe the mother-fuckers can kill me. Other blokes die. Not me. I'm immortal. I think I'm bloody Jesus Christ. I want to see if they can kill me. That's why I want to know where and who. You got to keep score, lad. You got to keep score." Then he suddenly drew back and looked away. Under his tan, his face looked thin and drawn.

Cody didn't say anything.

Schneider said, "Gerry, you talk such bloody cock."

Ruger flared back. "Oh, is it now?" His voice was sneering. "You want to know what's bloody cock? It's hearing a fucking Kraut with a British accent. Now *that's* bloody cock for you!"

"Don't mind him," Schneider said to Cody. "He gets like this."

"Don't you apologize for me, you bastard!" Ruger's voice was furious.

"Shut up, Gerry," Schneider said.

Ruger laughed. "The Kraut," he said. "I could kill the bastard, but I won't. And he knows it. So he bosses me. That's the laugh, boys. The laugh."

Cody left not long afterward.

Matthew Brady was standing when Cody came through the door of the library. He came forward from a far corner. "Captain Ravel," he said.

Cody turned instinctively at the voice. And instinctively he said, "Sir?"

Brady put out his hand. "My name is Matthew Brady. I'm the colonel commanding this operation."

They stood there for a long moment, facing each other. Cody could feel Brady's hard hand. At length, he said, "My pleasure, Colonel."

They sat down and a maid came in with drinks.

When she was gone, there was another silence. Then Brady said, "We'll pass over the bullshit. How do you like it so far?"

Cody looked over at Weston, then back to Brady. "Like what?"

"The operation."

"What operation?"

"That's what we're coming to."

They sat there. At length, Brady began to talk. "I already know quite a bit about you, Captain Ravel, from your flying records and your service jacket and some investigation we've done. And also what Weston here has thought. I've got a hard decision to make and I've just made it. I'm going to put my marbles on you. We'll be using two pilots, you and another that you'll have a hand in selecting. But you'll be the pilot in command. Let me assure you that the maintenance and the equipment will be the best. We've got a lot riding on this operation, and we don't intend to lose it through faulty flying equipment. Are you satisfied on that point?"

Cody nodded slowly, studying the colonel, thinking that this finally was it. Brady looked, Cody thought, like an ex-prize fighter or an over-the-hill pro football player. Or a tough-ass professional soldier. Even his civilian clothes looked temporary, like a man who'd put on a bathrobe before dressing for the day.

Brady was going on. He said, "But there's a hell of a lot more to it than that, where you're concerned. First, you and I are going to be doing a little recon flying in the target zone area."

"All right," Cody said. He took a sip of his drink, beginning to be tired now of sitting around places, talking too much, drinking too much. It had been a long week and the restlessness was rising strongly.

Brady took a cigarette out of the box he had in his

jacket pocket. He did not take his eyes off Cody's face. "But there's a catch to all this. And I want you straight in your mind what flying for me is going to involve."

"What's that?"

"Right now, you've still got an option. But if you take this job, you're going to be on the inside like only a very few men are. It'll be necessary that you know practically every damn detail. And that's a hell of a dangerous cargo to be carrying around." He stared hard at Cody.

"So?"

"There'll be some hazard connected to the actual flying on this job." Brady leaned forward. "But that ain't nothing to having the information you'll have and making a slip and letting it get out. Then I become the enemy."

"All right," Cody said. He took a sip of his drink.

"I want you to understand that it's your right to refuse this part of the job. You can refuse and still stay on as backup pilot. You've signed a contract, and it's your right to take only what was originally offered you. But I need you. Now, you want to think about it for a moment?"

Weston shifted uneasily in his chair.

"I don't have to think," Cody said. He put his drink down. "I'll take the job."

Brady's eyes were narrowed. He was leaning toward Cody intently. "You understand the conditions? Because I've got to have a guarantee. And the only kind I can get is to tell you that the security of this operation is more important to me than your life. If you breach it, in any way, I'll have you shot. Or I'll shoot you myself." He leaned back in his chair. "Now. Do you still want the job?"

"Yes," Cody said steadily.

Brady looked over at Weston. He laughed, a bare chuckle. "Shit," he said. He looked very pleased. To

Cody he said, "Then you're my man. But I got some bad news for you. I got a three room suite in a downtown hotel. You'll move in with me tonight. I want you where I can lay my hands on you day or night. You and I are going to be getting out of here pretty damn quick. You can give your heart to God, Captain Ravel, but from now on your ass belongs to me."

"Yes," Cody said. Then, after a pause, he added, "sir."

"That's not necessary."

"I know that," Cody said. He felt good. "What do I do now?"

"We're leaving day after tomorrow morning. We've bought a light civilian aircraft. A Mooney. Do you know anything about it?"

"Enough."

"All right. Get your ass out to the airport tomorrow morning and get what maps and charts you need to get us where we're going."

"Where?"

Brady looked at him, then at Weston, and then back to Cody.

"Rhodesia," he said.

So now he knew. Except it didn't matter. The only thing he thought of was to laugh. Landon had been wrong. The others, Ruger and Schneider had been wrong. But it was just another name. He looked at Weston, remembering that the cripple was from Rhodesia. "Tally ho," he said.

Weston laughed.

Brady said, "All right. Now, let's have a stiff drink and see if Weston has got something for us to eat." He looked at Cody. Even relaxed, his eyes were flat and penetrating. "What did they call the evening meal where you grew up in Texas?"

"Supper," Cody said. He understood the question and its intention. "Dinner was what you had at noon."

"Captain Ravel," Brady said, "me and you is going to get along."

Toward the end of the dinner, Weston tried to stand up out of his wheelchair. "Joseph," he said over his shoulder, "help me." The black man came and with his help, Weston was able to stand up. He raised his glass. "I have to do this," he said. There were tears in his eyes. "Think me a bloody fool, an old trader like myself. But Christ," he raised his glass higher. "To Rhodesia. Goddammit!"

They stood.

Cody thought, It's as good a fight as any other.

9

Longhaven Farm

Bill Longhurst walked into their bedroom with a slight frown on his face. He was carrying a piece of paper in his hand. Ruth was at her dressing table, brushing her hair.

"Here's a surprise," he said, looking down at the paper.

"God," she said, brushing hard at her hair, "what it must feel like to have your hair properly done. Honestly, Bill, the next trip to Salisbury I'm treating myself to the works. And damn the expense."

"Sure, love," he said. He came up behind her, looking at her face in the mirror. He gestured with the paper. "We're to have houseguests."

"What!" Ruth slammed the brush down and wheeled to face him. "Good God, Bill, what is it this time? Half the government house coming down?"

"No," he said, grinning slightly. "But it's interesting. Seems we're to have two Americans. Yanks. A general and his pilot."

"A Yank general?"

"Yeah. Have a note here from Jim Leslie. Says they'll

be arriving in forty-eight hours to have a look around. All very unofficial and hush-hush. We're to give them complete cooperation and ask no questions. How's that, no questions?"

Ruth turned back to the mirror. "I hope to God they don't stay long. That'll be just marvelous having some bloody Yank general poking about and asking asinine questions." Her voice turned bitter. "Why don't they send us a couple of mine proof trucks instead?"

Bill sat down on the bed, still looking at the note. "I wonder if it can mean anything. You don't suppose they're finally interested in a realistic look at the thing, do you? It couldn't be that, could it?"

"Oh, who knows, Bill." Ruth's voice sounded tired and impatient. "The bloody Yanks are always sending people about to look things over. And then doing bloody naught about it. Don't get your hopes up."

"Still, it's curious. Him coming up here. By the way, we're to take every precaution. Mustn't get an American general killed up here. Be bad for international relations."

"Of course not," Ruth said. She was working at her eyes with mascara, but wondering all the time what the use was. "International relations are so good now, we must be very careful not to disturb them. But it's all right. Americans don't get killed, you know. It's not in their constitution."

"You're on a fair tear today. Something special come up?"

"Something special?" She wheeled on her bench. "No, Bill, nothing special. It's a wonderful calm life when nothing special is having your backyard occupied by a full company of infantry and your roof sandbagged and your roads mined and some bastard ready to take a shot at you. And your cook agitating for another kitchen boy, so that you're certain he's been got to and wanting to bring in another gentleman to put arsenic in your food. Of course not. Nothing special." Her face was drawn and tense, and the hand holding the mascara was trembling.

Longhurst looked down at the floor. "Ah, Ruth," he said. He was trying to think of something encouraging to say, but there didn't seem to be anything. It was the same every year. As the dry season neared its end, they began to tense up from the knowledge of what was to come. He'd seen it in Ruth in the past few weeks, and he'd felt it in himself. All of a sudden something popped out that they'd never said before. He said, "Ruth, do you want to give it up?"

She had picked up her hairbrush again. Now she put it down. "Give what up?"

"This," he said, gesturing with his hand. "All of it. The farm. The whole lot. Sell out or abandon it. Take what we can get for the equipment and move to Salisbury or Johannesburg or somewheres." He wouldn't look at her, but kept his eyes on the floor.

"Are you daft, Bill?"

He sighed and stood up. "No. But I've been thinking. It's on us again. Or nearly so and I don't know if I can stand to put you through it for another year. It's been on my mind, Ruth."

She turned back to the mirror and began to brush her hair. "Bill Longhurst, get out of here." She was brushing furiously. "This is my farm too and don't you forget it. And I'd bloody rot before I'd walk away and give it up. You ever say anything like that to me again and I'll begin to wonder if you're the man I thought you were."

He came up behind her and touched her softly on the shoulder. "I'm sorry, love."

"Get out of here," she said. She wouldn't look at him in the mirror. "Go and see about your bloody soldiers."

He stood a second longer, awkward, feeling he should

say something, but not knowing what. "Right," he said.
He wheeled. "I'll see if they're settling in all right." At
the door, he stopped, hesitating for a moment. "Sorry,
love."

"Don't be sorry, Bill," she said. "About anything."

There was a platoon of Territorials, Rhodesian Army
Reservists, camped in the backyard. Before them had
been a section of Continentals. And before them had
been others.

"Hullo," Bill said, walking into the bivouac area and
up to where the lieutenant was sitting on a campstool before a makeshift desk formed from supply boxes.

"Good evening, Mr. Longhurst," the lieutenant said.
He was a young man of twenty-five or twenty-six, slimly
built with red hair and freckles. In civilian clothes, he
would have looked boyish; in combat fatigues and boots,
he looked capable.

"Settling in all right?"

"Quite so, sir." The officer glanced at the confusion
and litter of thirty men, two trucks, and enough gear
and supplies to sustain them for a month. "We're trying
to hold the uproar down to a minimum, sir."

"Not to worry," Bill said. "By the way, Mrs. Longhurst says you're to come to supper." They were be-
neath a mbasa tree. Bill leaned up against the trunk
and looked around. The platoon had dug in a machine
gun nest so that its line of fire commanded the lowlands
that fell away to the south from the high point the house
sat on. The field of fire, however, was interrupted some
thirty yards distant by the ten-foot-high, close mesh,
electrified fence that completely encircled the house
and workshop and operations shack. Longhurst looked
at it. He both hated and was grateful for the fence. He
hated it because it made him feel like a prisoner on his
own land. But he was grateful for the simple reason that

he could remember what nights were like before it went up. It was not electrified to shock because there wasn't enough electricity. But it was devised so that if it were jostled, the alarm would go off. It was almost personnel proof, as long as an attack didn't come in such strength that the attackers cared nothing about the element of alarm.

After the lieutenant had accepted the invitation to dinner and returned to checking his supplies, Bill wandered off toward the front of his house. He was feeling almost rested, having got sleep two nights straight. They had gone almost two weeks now without an incident, and the respite would make it that much harder to take it when it started up again. Bill glanced at the sky. It was deep blue, clear as far as he could see. But the rains would come, and that would create the foliage for the terrorists to hide in and would bring the game back for them to eat, and they'd come again, thick as ever. Of course, there were still small groups operating within a few miles of where he was standing. But they wouldn't make the big raids, the murderous strikes on the well-fortified farms until their numbers were larger.

Bill looked at the front of his house. In the plaster around the windows were the numerous pockmarks from the bullets, and here and there the bigger scars where an odd bazooka shell had hit.

But the direct attacks at the farms were fairly rare. They were too costly. The terrorists liked to shoot, but they didn't like being shot back at. What they liked was the easier mark; the farmer in his fields, the solitary car on the road, the shot from ambush.

Or the unprotected natives that worked for the farmer.

That was where the bastards were at their best. Against their own people.

The natives used to live all over the place in their little kraals, family groups. There'd be seven or eight of their little kias, their mud-wattled thatched huts, grouped together, a man sleeping in one with his favorite wife of the moment; other wives in the other huts; and perhaps a father or an old mother or an aunt or uncle or two in the rest. Then it'd be another hundred yards, perhaps two, to the next kraal. That's the way they liked it; that's the way they had lived for centuries. But along had come the terrorist, and even though he said he was their brother and their liberator, they'd moved out of their old kias, the women dismantling the forming sticks; they had rebuilt close to each other, in great groups, as if there were some protection in the numbers. But it didn't do much good. When the terrorists came among them, they came ten or twenty strong, fingering AK-47s, and the peasant knew what could happen to him if he didn't look sharp. The terrorists would come in and squat down and take their ease on the ground and say, "You, munt, bring us food. The best you have. The best in the village." Or they would say, "Here, I want a woman. Give me yours." And the munt did as he was ordered because if he didn't, he would soon be dead, and perhaps not as soon as he wished.

Or they would come in and call a man out and say, "You, brother, you're going with us. We're going to take you back to Zambeziland and teach you to be a liberator." And if the man didn't want to go and said he didn't, the terrorists said, "Good. Then we will kill your family one by one until you decide to go." Even if the man then said yes, yes, he would go, that might not be good enough, and the terrorists would kill one of his children or one of his wives to teach him that he should be more ready with his heart for the movement. Sometimes they would say to a peasant, "You are to kill the farmer you work for. Yes, and his wife also. And when we win, you will have his farm and his house and his

he great and famous spirit medium, and the people
truly awed. For they knew what it meant to have
happy spirit staying on to bring them bad luck.

of this, and many other things as well, should
turned the peasant laborer and farmer into the
ated foe of the white farmer. But it did not have that
. It did not make the native the farmer's ally, ex-
in a few cases, but it did not make him the terror-
willing ally either. Their mistake was in thinking
the native wanted to be a part of a cause. All he
ed was to drink his beer and have his wives and do
work could not be avoided and live the happy,
eful life. He'd been doing it for centuries and he
ed to go on doing it.

ll Longhurst employed a hundred men, all of whom
l with their families in the compound they'd erected
across the north field from the headquarters. They
e fencing it, at the natives' request, with the same
cing as that around the house. Bill had already seg-
ated his boss boys and his tractor drivers and mechan-
and other skilled laborers and put them behind a
otective fence. T   special targets of the ter-
rists because the   because they
ere doing well   In the
t two years, Bi
cted. Of cours
ucted. Some
to join the
they'd been
th for fear
bad his
. He'd
le to
hat
o

in h
and he
backward
mess, and the
spirit would stay
he got his face back.
the liberators. The terro

fat cattle and all the grain in his ba
man did not believe this, did not
were going to win, and sometimes h
did, they would kill him, slowly so
watch and they'd say, "He was a tra
not believe in the movement. This v
if you don't believe."

But they had many methods. Often
into a village and call a man out alon
of the people and say, "This man ha
formation to the white police about
liberators. He is to die." Now, it didn
the man had been giving information
far as that went, there was no way for
know. All that mattered was to make tl
they knew all that was happening, and t
were tempted to talk, they'd get the sa

They'd kill the man ritually. First they'd
hand and foot, laying him on the groun
Then they'd squat around him and beat h
with slender sticks no more than half an in
It took a long time to kill him like that a
it took, the better the lesson it was for the
was a most awful way for a man to die a
could see that. The victim never quite lost
ness, because no blow could be delivered ha
to stun him. Consequently, he was consci
e last moment. The rhythmic beating
s nose and his sinus cavities a
sually died from strangul
own his throat. By
villagers we
around

shown. Clever Mobanzo he'd been called. Bill was sure they'd love to get their hands on him in one of those training camps. They'd teach him how to be a section leader and operate an AK-47 in no time. Or mine roads. He knew all the roads intimately. And since it was part of terrorist strategy to send a man back to his home area, where he could receive aid from his people and encourage others to join up, Bill confidently expected to run across Mobanzo on a patrol some night or other. He fervently hoped it would be with Mobanzo grinning up at him from the ground, a bloody hole through him.

"Freedom!" they'd shouted in Kenya. "Uhuru!" Here the cry was self-determination. Which was a laugh. It didn't even translate into Shona. There was no such word or phrase in the whole language because they had never had it themselves, even centuries before the white man had set foot in Africa. It was something taught them by outsiders who were using the poor bloody blacks for their own purposes. The ones who could say it had to say it in English. Some smashing nationalism when the ideal they were supposedly fighting for was so alien to their culture that they couldn't even say it in their own language. But it was a very complicated business, and there was no use in a man thinking of why his enemies were wrong and he was right. Both sides could do that. The point was they were the enemy and they were that for one good and simple reason: they wanted to take something that belonged to him. The land he stood on and worked and loved was his land. He'd bought it and he was paying for it and he'd dragged it into productivity from nothing. That gave him claim, and no one or nothing was going to drive him from it. They might kill him, but they'd have a bloody awful time doing so, and that would be the only way they'd remove him.

It was that simple.

He walked around his house to the little operations shack in the back. It was connected to the house by a breezeway with a protecting wall and was made out of plastered-over concrete blocks. The government had built it.

At the door, Bill paused. There was a sign: ALL WEAPONS SAFETIED BEYOND THIS POINT. He pulled out the automatic pistol he wore in a canvas holster at his side and made sure the snap was on safety. He opened the door, but didn't go in. The two Bright Lights were inside, one manning the big UHF-VHF radio and the other lounging on a bunk.

"Have you seen Chris?" Bill said, asking after his farm manager.

"Not lately," the man at the radio said.

"Likely he's down at the pump house," Bill said. "I'll go and collect him, and we'll have the evening beer."

He closed the door.

The Bright Lights were silent for a moment after he'd gone. They'd been talking about another Bright Light, a man nicknamed the Ram because he always tried to seduce the wives of the farmers to whom he was assigned.

The room was dominated by the big radio that sat on a table by the door. It had both ground to ground and ground to air capabilities, because the headquarters was sometimes used to coordinate air and ground operations. The Bright Light relaxing at it was Mike Carr. The other was Richard Denton. Carr glanced at his watch. "About five minutes to security check." Every six hours all the farmers in the area reported in on their Agri-Alert phones, and then an hour later, a security check would come in from the police station at Shamva.

By the door was a rack of FN automatic rifles, and in a corner were other weapons, including a bazooka they'd captured from a terrorist group. Most of the walls of the shack were covered with information pamphlets on the different types of land mines and personnel weapons used by the terrorists. Some of them were beginning to yellow with age. On the back of the door was a map with different colored pins stuck in it. One color showed sightings of terrorists, another where a contact had been made, and a third where contact had resulted in kills or captures. There were black pins to indicate where farmers or their workers had been killed or abducted. There were one hundred and sixteen black pins in the map.

There was another map on the wall that showed the valley in detail. Longhaven Farm was just at the bottom of a large, green-shaded area. That was the Tribal Trust Lands of Chief Madziwa. It was from here that the trouble came. The terrorists crossed the Zambezi River, came over the escarpment, and then down through the Trust Lands. The Lands belonged to the tribes, and no white man could go in there to conduct permanent business, not even the army. It was a very sore point with the farmers in the valley.

There was a knock on the door, and the houseboy put his head in. "Beer?"

"Yes," Carr said. "You might as well bring it along." He left and Carr yawned. "Two more days of this."

From the bunk, Denton said, "That Longhurst is a right enough chap."

"Yes," Carr said. "But for my money he's crazy like the rest of them. I'm damned if I'd live this kind of life for a bloody farm. A week of it is more than I can stand. How the hell do they put up with it for years?" Carr was an insurance adjustor in Salisbury.

Denton said, "The Ram told me that was the secret of his success. He says the wives are so starved for any kind of change, any excitement that they're pushovers. And he says that some of the wives tell him that their husbands stay so switched on all the time that they get impotent. From nerves, I guess."

Carr yawned. "The Ram is a bastard. Imagine doing that to a guy you've been sent out to bloody help."

"Oh, I don't know," Denton said. "What's the harm in it? If the woman wants it and the old man don't find out, who's been hurt? Some of those old girls lead a pretty bad life."

Carr looked around at him. "Do you think the Ram could succeed with Ruth?"

Denton grinned. "I know he'd be bloody well-tempted. And who wouldn't."

"Why don't you try, then?"

"No, thanks. If our girl Ruth didn't go for the idea, she might just take an FN and cut you in two."

The door suddenly opened, and Bill and Chris Bantes came in. It had been only in the last year that Bill had been able to afford the luxury of a farm manager, though the title was misleading. Bill was still the manager, but Chris was able to relieve him of some of the details. It wasn't a particularly good living for a young man, but it was the only way he could learn farming, unless his family owned lands.

Chris was boyishly handsome, though it wasn't obvious at the moment. One whole side of his face was covered with thick, healing scabs. The upper part of his left arm was the same and, underneath his shirt, his back was covered with more scabs. Two weeks before, riding in the back of an army truck, he'd been blown up by a mine. He was in one of the new Rhino's or he'd have been killed. The rear wheels had detonated the mine, and the blast had pitched the back end up like a bucking horse. Chris and another man had been thrown out. The other man had been lucky enough to land in a clump of bushes. But Chris had gone straight forward, skidding along the hard, rocky ground, the abrasive surface of the road peeling off hide and flesh a quarter of an inch deep. He'd been a mess, but he'd only missed one day of work, and most of that at the infirmary in Shamva.

"How's the new skin?" Bill asked him.

Chris grinned as well as he could with one side of his face. "Itchy," he said.

Bill looked over at Mike Carr. "Well, are we not to have our evening beer then?"

"The boy was just out. We've sent him to fetch it."

"Well done," Bill said.

Chris and Robin, his wife, lived in the second house Bill had built, the one he and Ruth had lived in before their present house. It was down by the tobacco-curing barns and was surrounded by the same type of fence as around Bill's house. It had been a fine house for just Chris and Robin, but now they had a one-year-old baby and a Bright Light, and four rooms weren't enough. Bill had commissioned a local African builder to add an extra sleeping room. The builder had been a good man, energetic and ambitious, a good worker. The terrorists had killed him shortly after he'd started. The half-finished room was as he'd left it; they hadn't been able to find another man.

The houseboy came in with the tray of beer and said he was ready to leave.

"I'll go," Chris said. He took his FN out of the rack and followed the boy out. With the door open, Bill could see it turning dark. It was painful to send them out in that black, but there was no help for it. The terrorists could get to the best and most trusted servants.

The door opened, and the lieutenant and his sergeant came in.

"Ah," Bill said, "there you are. I was about to come and fetch you. Dinner will be ready shortly, I expect. In the meantime, the beer's arrived."

They took bottles and there was a round of cheers.

"I didn't ask," Bill said to the lieutenant. "Is this your first bivouac in this part of the country?"

"Yes, quite," the lieutenant answered. "I've just come on the security side."

"I say, you were with the Rhodesian Light Infantry previously, weren't you? Jim Leslie, our D.C., knows of you."

The lieutenant blushed. He had been a commando tracker and was famous in such circles. After fourteen months in the bush, he'd gone on reserve duty. His nerves had been very bad toward the last. He looked like a boy unless you looked closely into his eyes.

They drank in silence for a moment. They'd all been to war, and they knew what it was like without talking about it.

Chris came in. He racked his FN and took a beer. "Hullo," he said to the soldier and went forward to shake hands.

"I say," he told the lieutenant, "I spotted a patrol of your blokes sloping along today. Out for a look see?"

The lieutenant looked startled. "Not us. We haven't had a patrol out today. Been settling into bivouac."

There was a sudden silence.

Chris asked urgently, "Are you sure?"

The lieutenant looked over at his sergeant. "Any patrols out?"

The sergeant shook his head. "No, sir. All the men been in and accounted for."

"When, Chris?" Bill asked calmly.

"'Bout ha' past five. Hour and half ago." He was looking distressed. "Up toward that new field we've been planning. Up to the hummock on the north. I was up on it, and I saw this file of men. I hadn't got any glasses with me so I didn't have a close look." He turned to the lieutenant. "They came out of the bush and went cutting across the edge of the clearing. Single file. Trail arms." He stopped and then went on. "It was so close to the farm. I never for a moment doubted. I knew you chaps were due in today."

For emphasis, the lieutenant shook his head again, slowly.

"Oh my God," Chris said, "I am so frightfully sorry. What a stupid assumption."

Bill got up. "Not to worry, Chris. Go along now and get your kit." He turned to the lieutenant, trying to keep his voice cheerful. "Well, shall we see some of that famous tracking I've heard so much about?"

The lieutenant rose. He drained his bottle of beer, then turned to his company sergeant. "Alert the men. I'll want four patrols of five. And you and the platoon sergeants. Water and rations for twenty-four hours."

Bill said, "I'll just step along and tell Ruth. Perhaps she hasn't laid out supper yet." He went out the door thinking how disappointed she'd be. Not that she'd say a word. He called back over his shoulder. "With you in a moment."

10

Longhaven Farm

They came slipping into the kraal just at dark, just as the women were lighting their cooking fires. There were six of them, dirty, fierce-looking men in combat fatigues carrying AK-47s. The leader was the terrorist Mobanzo. It was familiar ground for Mobanzo, this kraal of Emgukura, for he was a distant kinsman of the old cook and had once lived there. Though that had been before the kraal had been moved closer to the others, making a sort of haphazard compound. But he'd been back since, and he slipped without hesitation through the low opening of the old cook's mud-wattled kia.

Outside, his men squatted in the dark, watching and holding their automatic rifles. The women who were cooking and the few men out of their kias averted their eyes, going on with their business, trying to be as unnoticeable as possible. One of the women got up and started toward the darkness outside the circle of the twenty odd huts, but a low grunt from one of the terrorists brought her back to her fire. Another motioned at one of the kraal kinsmen who was standing and he immediately sat down. It had got very quiet.

Inside Emgukura's kia which was larger than the others, a kerosene pressure lamp hissed from a ridge-pole, throwing shadows into the distant corners. The cook was seated cross-legged in the middle of the hut, drinking mealie beer from an aluminum cooking pot he'd stolen from the Longhurst's kitchen. Mobanzo was in and seated across from him before he even noticed. He saw him over the rim of the pot he had at his mouth, and his eyes suddenly rounded in fear.

Mobanzo looked steadily at him, his rifle across his knees. For a moment, the old man didn't move, only his lips kept working, sucking at the thick, gruel-like beer. Finally, he lowered the pot. "Aaaahhhee," he said, the sound escaping in a long sigh.

"Well, old man," Mobanzo said, "I see that you are still living very well." He looked slowly around the hut. In a corner, Emma's youngest wife was squatting, waiting to bring him his supper. She drew back as Mobanzo's eyes passed over her. "Yes," Mobanzo said, "you do very well." He rubbed the back of one hand over the wiry whiskers on his sharp-pointed chin. He had a long face, his kinky hair started far back from his forehead and then grew straight out from the back of his narrow skull, so that in profile he looked as if his head were always just slightly tilted back. His eyes were very white with hard black centers. There was amusement in them now. He swept his hand slowly around the room. "A plump young wife. Much too young for a worthless old man like you, but then you can afford the bride price for such a one because you suck for the white man. Look, a proper white man's bed. You have a mechanical lamp. You sit there drinking beer from the white man's cooking pot. And look at how well-kept your garments are and how plump and fat you are."

The old cook shifted, not speaking.

Mobanzo set his rifle down by his right knee, on

the butt. His finger played idly with the safety catch, snapping it back and forth, while he grinned at the old man.

"Yet," he finally said, "your comrades, the true people's freedom fighters sleep out in the bush like animals, getting our food like bush niggers. We have no plump young wives. We have no beer. And yet you sit there swilling your beer in front of me, flaunting your riches."

"Aaaah," Emma finally gasped. "It is little and of poor quality."

"We will see," Mobanzo said. He reached out and jerked the pot out of the old man's hand. Then, he sat there sipping it, watching over the rim. "Beer is for men," he said, "not old eunuchs who work in the white man's kitchen." He drank for a moment longer and then lowered the pot. "Why don't you speak, old man? What has happened to your tongue? Has the white man cut that out just as he's cut off your testicles?"

Emma opened his mouth and then shut it soundlessly. He glanced helplessly over at his wife and then quickly back to the terrorist.

"You have learned bad manners, old man. You have not yet bid me welcome nor made me gifts of food or drink. The drink I had to take for myself."

"I will see," Emma said. He started to scramble to his feet, but Mobanzo let the barrel of his rifle tip toward him.

"No, old man, it's too late. I see your true heart in your eyes. This way you treat your own kinsman."

"I was not thinking," the old man began to babble. He passed a hand over his gray, woolly hair, running it from the back to the front. "I was weary. I had much on my mind. I am truly ashamed."

"I think you were surprised, old man," Mobanzo said. He laughed, a brittle sound. "I think you did not expect to see me again. I think so much time had passed that hope had sprung in your heart that I was gone. Even perhaps that I was dead. Or that I had forgotten."

"No, no," the old man said, "no, no."

"But I have not forgotten," Mobanzo said softly, his voice caressing the Shona words.

"Aaahhheee," the old cook said. He looked away.

"Why have you not done as you were told, old man? Do you want to die? Do you want to lose your soft life in the white man's belly?"

"Aaaheee," Emma said. He ran his hand over his head again, nervously. "That is very difficult, kinsman. Very hard."

"Do you know what happens to those who don't aid the cause, old man? Do you know what happens to those of the people who suck for the white man? Only my voice has kept you alive, old man. There have been orders that you were to die if you could not do this thing. And yet that worthless Karanga is still in your white man's kitchen." The soft cruelty went out of his voice. Now it was hard, harsh. "You were told! Ordered. That one of our people would replace him! We know you are too weak and worthless to do the proper job on the *bwana* and *Missy*." He bore down sarcastically on the names. "That is why we must have a true comrade in the kitchen. Oh yes," he said, "I have pleaded for you, but now even I can speak no more. Am I to suffer *masimba* over you, old man?"

Emma wrung his hands. His voice was almost hysterical. "But it is impossible. Missy, she say no. She say no, Emma. She say I don't speak her that no more. Bwana say no. They will not let me have the one you have chosen. They say they put me out I speak that to them."

Mobanzo stared at him a long moment, his eyes glittering. Then, he turned the pot up and drank for a long time. When it was empty, he wiped his mouth and then belched. He threw the pot into a corner. "Old man," he said, letting the rifle point at the cook, "this is your last warning. Soon we will be leaving, but we will be back. Do you understand me, old man?"

"Yessss," Emma said waveringly.

"And I will not kill you with this rifle. This is too good for a worthless old man like you. You understand how you will die, don't you?"

The cook wrung his hands, twisting them up to his face. "Please, kinsman. I will try again. I will succeed. Only a little more time."

"You'll have more time. Watch for the rain, old man. When it comes, you will see us also. Very quickly." He looked at the cook, studying him gravely. Then he suddenly grinned, his teeth crooked in his mouth. "But you have cost me much *simba* with my leaders, old man. This is my kraal, my tribe, and yet I can accomplish nothing. I must have a show of faith. A juju." He grinned again. "I think I will have your two eldest nephews. Stephen and Lodi."

The old man's mouth dropped open.

"You don't mind that, do you, old man?"

"They are so young," Emma barely whispered.

"That is for the better. That way they can be taught the proper way. We will make soldiers out of them. They will return with me and my men, and then this kraal will have someone else to be proud of beside me." He smiled cruelly again. "Now, go and get them, old man. Get all the people."

The old cook slowly rose. He stood there.

Mobanzo looked up at him. "Are we to have difficulty over this?"

"No," Emma almost shouted. "No, no, I will get them." He scrambled for the door.

"And old man," Mobanzo stopped him. "Return with them. Do not come back and say you can't find them, for I have already seen that they are here. My men are outside and they will help you. And while I wait, I will have this food that has been prepared for you."

"Oh, yes," Emma said. "Of course."

Mobanzo smiled. "And I will use your woman also. You don't mind that, do you?"

The cook stared at him, glancing quickly toward his wife in the corner.

Mobanzo said softly, "After all, it will be a favor from a kinsman. Your balls have been cut off, old man."

"Yes," the cook said. "You are a kinsman." He ducked quickly through the low entrance.

Mobanzo looked into the shadows, toward the woman. He smiled, rubbing his hand over his crotch. "I will take you first," he said, "even before the food. For I am that hungry. Come here."

She shrank back further, and he suddenly got to his feet and dragged her out of the corner and threw her down. Then, he pushed her long dress up until it was past her breasts.

"Ah," he said. "Ah."

But just as he started to mount her, he heard a sound at the door. He whirled, bringing up his AK-47. It was one of his own men.

"Comrade," the man said, his eyes drifting toward the woman.

"What is it, you fool? Speak."

The man came back to Mobanzo. "There are soldiers on the road. Patrols. They say they are very near."

Mobanzo got up, buttoning his pants. "Have you got the two boys?"

"Yes. They are bringing food also."

"All right," Mobanzo said. He gave the woman a look, nudged her with his foot and then stooped through the door. Outside, a knot of people was assembled. From some of the women, there came a low keening. In the middle were the rest of the terrorists with the two boys and the old cook. Mobanzo grinned at them. "Soldiers for the cause," he said. He looked at the youngest, who only came up to his shoulder. The boy's face was slack with fear. "You want to be a freedom fighter, don't you, munt? You're a man now."

The boy's eyes rolled in his head. On the outside of the group, his mother was making low whimpering sounds, stretching forth both of her hands.

Mobanzo laughed and looked at the other boy. "And this one. Lodi. Do you know what to call me?"

The boy opened his mouth, then closed it. No sound came.

"Comrade," Mobanzo said. "You will call me comrade." He laughed and tapped the boy's chest with the end of his rifle. "And I will call for your spirit if you fail in the people's cause."

He looked around at the circle of peasants. He brought his rifle up and pulled the chamber back so that a shell clicked menacingly. "If there are those here who would aid the white man with information, we will know." The people stood there, looking at the ground. "We will know. If you make a mistake about that, it will be too bad." Then he turned and pointed his rifle at the cook. "Don't forget, worthless old man, that I will be back."

Then, they turned and melted into the darkness. The man just behind Mobanzo whispered, "Which way shall we go? The patrols, they say, are on the road."

"We will go east and hide," Mobanzo said. "We will cross tomorrow night. Or the next. Keep those boys in the middle."

They moved swiftly in the dark, stumbling only occasionally over the hard, rocky ground.

The man behind whispered, "Do you think the old man will report us? About the two boys?"

Mobanzo laughed softly. "Not that old man. Not

any of his people. Not until I'm dead and he's seen my body."

Down the line, there was a muffled thud and then a whimper of pain. Mobanzo knew what it meant. One of their unwilling recruits had tried to run. Well, he thought, they would learn soon enough. It gave him real pleasure to steal men from the Longhurst farm. It would give him more pleasure if they could get a man inside who could give them poison.

Still, he was troubled by a thought. It was not often that there were patrols out during the dry season. And for a time, they had been careful to keep the area quiet around Longhaven Farm so that they would have no trouble crossing back into the Tribal Trust Lands. He doubted that they had been spotted. Still, he was uneasy. It was time to leave, anyway. Only a night or two more. When it was safe.

11

Johannesburg—Rhodesia

They turned off the freeway short of the main airport terminal and took a feeder street into the general aviation section back down the field. It was early in the morning, just past sunrise, and the air and the sky still had that golden haze of a clear morning when the air is thin and bright. Cody looked up at the sky through the windshield. It was blue as far as he could see. The forecast was for CAVU over the southern half of Africa through the rest of the day. Flying in Africa, during the dry season, was a simple affair. There wasn't any weather to worry about except dew point haze at the higher elevations.

The airplane was there, gassed up, inspected, and ready to go. For Cody, it held no surprises except for the high quality modifications. It was a Mooney Chaparral, a single engine, four place, retractable gear, U.S.-made civilian airplane. It was relatively fast for its type. But it had been made faster by the installation of a turbo super charger and power boost unit. At altitude, it would do 240 miles an hour ground speed.

It was a solid, airworthy ship that would take a lot of mishandling without coming unglued. It had the P-51

air foil wing and an extremely high glide ra
could be important over rough country if the
and he had to find that one flat spot for an
landing. And with the big, barn door flaps
could land or take off in an amazingly short s
runway.

While Brady stowed their gear in the luggag
partment, Cody did a walk-around preflight.

"Ready?"

"Let's go," Brady said.

The airport was empty. Out on the flight line,
could see a big South African 727 jet waiting to
off, but other than that, there was no traffic. Cody flip
on the master switch, the boost pump, adjusted the m
ture and prop levers, and hit the starter. The engin
roared into life. He pulled back on the rpm and le
the engine settle down while it warmed up. Waiting, he
turned on his radio, tuning it to ground control, put
the transponder on standby, and tuned in his mute radio
to departure control.

But before he released the brakes, he pulled the throttle
down until the engine was quiet enough to talk and
looked at Brady. "Buckle your seat belt," he said.

Brady gave him the barest flicker of a glance, noting
the tone, and connected the belt over his flat stomach.

Cody was still looking at him. "One thing we better
get clear. I've never been in this situation before so I
want it understood. You're the military commander and
I work for you. But in this airplane, I'm boss. I'll take
you where you say to go and get you there healthy, but
when we're in the air, I decide how we get there. Is that
clear?"

A smile almost quirked Brady's face. But he only
nodded shortly and growled, "Understood."

"Fine," Cody said.

They climbed straight out. Cody got the gear up, pulled

prop rpm back to climb power, and then settled wn for the long ride to altitude. When they were forty iles out, the radio crackled with the voice of departure ontrol: "Mooney five-five-eight-one Foxtrot, Johannesurg Control. Radar surveillance terminated, frequency hange approved. Cheerio."

Cody pressed the button on his mike. "Five-five-eight-one Foxtrot understood. Thank you and good day." He hung the mike up and looked around at Brady. "Okay. Nine hundred miles to go."

When they passed through 10,000 feet, Cody reached over and unhooked the oxygen mask hanging on the cabin wall by Brady. He handed it to the colonel. "Put it on."

He put his own on. They'd be flying at 17,000 feet, which was the optimum for the super blown engine.

Below them, the ground was hard and brown looking.

Cody glanced over at Matthew Brady. They'd taken off their jackets. The colonel's chest and shoulder were bisected by the straps of a shoulder holster which hung just under his left armpit, the butt of the service automatic black against the light blue of his sports shirt. Cody could feel the weight of his own gun sagging against his chest.

The evening before, they had gone out to dinner and then back to the suite. Brady had sat him down in the drawing room before a table. Then, he'd got his briefcase and spilled the contents on the table. He had proceeded to brief Cody on every detail of the mission. Cody had sat listening impassively as the colonel had talked. When he was finished, Brady had leaned back and lit a cigarette. "Now, you know everything and I know you know it. Do I make myself clear?"

Cody had lit a cigarette. He'd waited a moment, staring back at Brady through the smoke. Then he'd said, "You hired me because you'd already decided you could

trust me. Don't waste any more of our time by warning me again."

That had been another time Brady had almost smiled. Instead, he had begun gathering up the papers and stuffing them back in his briefcase. "You're in charge of the flying on this operation. Which means it's your responsibility. You've also been promoted to major, with whatever increase in pay that means. I forget the pay schedule."

Cody had lifted his eyebrows slightly. He said easily, "Hell, this outfit is easy. Come in as a captain, make major five days later. When do I make colonel? Next week?"

Then Brady had smiled sardonically. "That's it for you, fly-boy," he said. "Unless," he added, "you'd like to lead a combat team for me? You got the experience."

"No, thanks," Cody had answered dryly, "I don't like to walk. Or train. Or get shot at."

Brady still had the amused look about his mouth. "What makes you think you ain't going to get shot at in an airplane?"

All Cody could do was shrug.

Brady had been true to his word; he'd kept Cody in close contact. They had stayed in the hotel, even taking their meals there. Brady was occupied working over the maps and photos and reports. Occasionally, he was on the phone to Weston or Carlton-Brooks. He had not shared any of the work with Cody until the night he'd given him the briefing. Cody had spent his time familiarizing himself with the air charts and navigation aids in Rhodesia. The words that had passed between them had been largely impersonal. Only once had Brady broken the conversation away from the present, and that had been to ask Cody details about his tour of duty in Vietnam. But Cody hadn't wanted to talk about that and he'd answered shortly and vaguely.

A few times, he thought of the girl, Flic, but it was mainly with curiosity. She was good-looking and she was great in bed, but then, he thought, you could say that of a lot of women.

They passed over the Messina VOR and then they were over Rhodesia. There was no change in the terrain below. The colonel was still absorbed in the papers on his lap.

When they were forty miles outside Salisbury, Cody called approach control. "Salisbury control, this is Mooney five-five-eight-one Foxtrot inbound for a landing. Forty DME South on a heading of zero one zero degrees. Fifteen thousand feet and descending. Squawking appropriate VFR code."

Salisbury control came back to him with radar contact and instructions to descend to 7,000 feet and continue inbound and to squawk 1150. He complied and then called in, "Five-five-eight-one Foxtrot Salisbury control. Identing one one five zero. Eight thousand feet descending to seven thousand. Request you notify Salisbury operations that United States committee is inbound and will be landing in approximately fifteen minutes. Parking at Rhodesia Air-Tech. Please advise you copied."

The radio crackled. "Mooney five-five-eight-one Foxtrot."

Cody depressed the mike button. "Go ahead Salisbury approach, Mooney five-five-eight-one Foxtrot."

"Understood your last transmission. Have notified operations. Appropriate personnel standing by Rhodesia Air-Tech."

"Roger," Cody said into the mike, "five-five-eight-one Foxtrot." He put the mike back in place. "Looks like they're waiting for us."

They were vectored straight in. The airport spread out

in front of them as they made their final descent, the silver of the runway clearly outlined against the dry brown of the land surrounding it. He landed and taxied to the Air-Tech parking space. A line boy signaled them into place, and Cody pulled out the mixture control. As the engine fanned down and died, a quiet descended. It was suddenly very warm in the cabin.

They got out stiffly, tired from the trip. An olive drab station wagon suddenly came swooping up. A young officer in military tunic and hat and knee-length shorts jumped out. He marched up to Brady and touched the baton he was carrying to his forehead. "Brady? Lieutenant Holly. I'm to provide you ground transport, sir."

As they drove into the city, Cody stared out the window. There were more Jacaranda trees here, still in blossom, than there had been in Johannesburg. There were other tropical-looking trees that Cody had never seen before. The buildings had that old colonial look to them and, as they neared downtown, there were black policemen at each intersection in shorts and white pith helmets directing traffic.

Though Salisbury was a fairly large city, it didn't have the look of a metropolis about it. It had no imposing skyline and the buildings seemed to be restricted to eight or ten stories. The downtown section was built around a large park that took up several blocks.

"Miekles, isn't it, sir?" the young officer asked, looking back at them.

Brady nodded. "And then, I won't need you anymore. Appreciate your help in avoiding customs."

"Right, sir."

They pulled up in front of an old-fashioned-looking hotel. Cody and the colonel got out, and their baggage was brought in by a swarm of porters.

While Brady registered, Cody looked around him. The

Miekles had once been the safari headquarters. It was famous all over Africa for its food and hospitality. Heads were mounted all around the lobby: Cape buffalo, kudu, kongoni, sable. It had a very solid feel about it, given by the mahogany and exposed beams and the solid wood paneling and the heavy furniture. It reminded Cody of Weston's house.

Brady turned away from the desk. "Let's go up."

He'd taken a suite. "You sleep in there," he said, pointing to one of the bedrooms. "Get settled down and wait. I'm going out and I don't know how long I'll be gone. But be here when I get back. Don't leave the hotel. You'll be given a flight briefing sometime this afternoon."

The first thing Cody did was take a bath. The bathtubs in Africa had been a pleasant surprise. He had never found an American bathtub he could properly stretch out in, but every bathtub in Africa thus far had been seven feet long.

He lay soaking for a half hour, letting the slight tiredness from the trip fade away in the hot water. Then he got out, dressed in clean clothes, and went downstairs. Just off the lobby was the Jacaranda Lounge. At its entrance was a sign, old by the look of it. It said COAT AND TIE PLEASE EXCEPT THOSE JUST IN OFF SAFARI. It was a large room, filled with low tables and comfortable armchairs. Two walls opened up to long rows of large windows that had been propped out to let in the morning breeze. Cody took a seat at one of the tables and a waiter arrived instantly, serving tray at parade rest on his hip. The costume of the waiters showed the Arab influence. They wore long, white knee-length coats and white breeches with a wide red sash at their waists.

Cody ordered a beer.

"Off the shelf, sah, or refrigerated?"

"Cold," he said.

A few tables were occupied by colonial-looking old gentlemen having their late morning tea or the eleven o'clock whiskeys. They all looked very *pukka sahib* in safari suits and long mustaches.

Cody settled back to wait. He had no idea how long Brady would be gone.

He was in his room that afternoon when the Rhodesian army pilot arrived. "Carstairs," the officer said, shaking hands. "Hope I'm not disturbing you, lad. I was told to come around this afternoon and give you a flight briefing. Are you up to it just now?"

"Yes," Cody said, "come in." He let the pilot in and settled down in the drawing room. The officer had a briefcase full of maps and charts with him.

"I must say," the officer noted, taking the material out of his briefcase, "this seems a bit unorthodox. Fancy them bringing an American pilot all this way. Our chaps not good enough, eh?"

But he said it laughingly, so Cody didn't mind. "I think," he said, "the big idea is to keep it all quiet. Unofficial, sort of. So far as it goes, the general and I are just two American tourists on vacation." He lit a cigarette.

"Well, here's the scam," the officer said. Using a pencil as a pointer, he said, "Here we are in Salisbury. You're going up to the Longhurst farm. I've flown over most of that country and there's no big trick to it. Of course, it's all pilotage, the navigation, no radio aids. I'd recommend you follow the highway which ends right at Shamva North. No mistaking that. Then, you take a westerly heading on the only little dirt road going west out of the place and look for Bill's big reservoir."

"I'll probably just take a direct heading out of here," Cody said.

The Rhodesian frowned slightly. "Well, that's all right, of course, but it's awfully easy to get off in that country if you don't know it well. Could get a bit hairy. Bill's place is only fifteen miles south of the Zambian border. If you missed it you could be over Zambia before you knew it. You wouldn't want that."

"Isn't the border defined? I thought a river was the dividing line."

"It is, but the old Zambezi River this time of year is not much. Dried up in spots. There's no real landmarks in that part of the country. Pretty desolate. And each hummock or every little native village looks pretty much the same." He paused. "On both sides of the river."

Cody asked, "What kind of landing strip does this farmer have?"

"It's all right," the flyer said. "We use it at odd times. Twenty-four hundred feet, sod of course. I imagine old Bill will have mowed it fresh, knowing you're coming. Now, one point that's important." With his pencil, he outlined a big green section of the map just above the point he'd marked the Longhurst farm. "On your approach. This is Bill's place. Here's the landing strip, just northeast of his big reservoir, which you'll have no trouble spotting. This green area is the Tribal Trust Lands and that's where our friends hang out mostly. Don't, under any circumstances, make your approach out over the Trust Lands. It would be no trick for one of the blokes to be laying out here with the safety off his AK-47 rifle. You'd be a nice fat target hanging up there on approach with your flaps down at about eighty miles an hour."

"I see," Cody said. He rubbed his chin.

"Which brings us to lesson two," the lieutenant said. He smiled. "You'll climb out to about one thousand feet AGL. But as soon as you get near Shamva, you've got to take it right down on the deck. And I mean down on the deck. That's the only way to fly in that country."

"How low? A hundred feet?"

"Not near that. More like ten. Right down on the tops of the trees and the taller ones you hedgehop over. Down low, going fast, you're on a terrorist and gone before he can get his rifle up. Up high, he's got time to see you coming. The AK-47 will fire to a height of thirty-five hundred feet, old boy."

"I see," Cody said again. He put his cigarette out slowly.

"Landing, I recommend you get it on the ground fast. That's your most vulnerable time. Don't, for God's sake, use a long, slow approach. I'd recommend a three hundred sixty overhead from right off the deck."

Cody nodded.

"One more thing. The rockets. I'm seeing to the modification on your aircraft. They're cutting a storm port on the passenger side to match the one on the pilot's side. And I'll see to the flare pistols and plenty of cartridges."

Cody looked up. "What are you talking about, storm ports and flare pistols?"

"For the rockets."

Cody looked puzzled.

"Oh, I see. You didn't know about that. The terrorists have a delightful little shoulder-fired rocket. Heat seeking. Goes for the manifold. It was developed by the Chinese for use in Vietnam against your recon and spotter planes. Devilish because it's so small that every bloke in the field can be equipped with one. Fortunately, it's awfully slow. You can see it coming if you keep a sharp lookout. The countermeasure is quite simple. One of our chaps hit on it, out of desperation I suppose. You fire a flare out the window and the fool rocket goes for that instead of you because the flare's hotter. Nice, eh?"

"Oh, sure," Cody said. "Sure."

They got off at dawn the next morning. He climbed out, picking up the highway north without much trouble. There weren't that many highways in Rhodesia. He'd put one flare pistol in Colonel Brady's lap before they'd taken off and made the other ready in his own hand. Brady had smiled thinly. He knew what it was for.

It was only a hundred sixty miles to Shamva and he was starting his descent a half hour out of Salisbury. The country was not mountainous, but there were rolling hills, some that rose a thousand feet above the flatter terrain. He stayed directly above the highway, holding at five hundred feet above the ground. In places, the roadbed wound tightly through the hills, and Cody was forced to bank and turn the airplane like a sports car. He glanced over once at the colonel, but Brady looked steadfast, staring straight ahead.

Then they were into Shamva. Cody swooped low over the little handful of whitewashed buildings, banking as he angled to the west looking for the little dirt road. He decreased altitude until they were just over the tree-tops. The country turned rougher, with sharp peaks and ridges on what had been rolling hills. Cody held the nose of the airplane just below the horizon, the downward sweep of the cowling making it look as if they were flying into the ground. As they roared swiftly through the traces of the hills, the rising contours of the ground rose abruptly to meet them, the ridges and jagged edges of the cliffs flashing by each wing tip at two hundred miles an hour. Cody was trying to hold over the little dirt road, but the road wound and ducked too sharply at times, and he was forced to take it as it came, trying to smoothly anticipate the rises and falls ahead of him.

It was rough-looking land, dry and brown. Fortunately, there weren't many tall trees. Cody had a chart in his lap and he flung it over to Brady. "Watch for Longhurst's farm. The reservoir. It's marked. I'm too fucking busy to look."

With his peripheral vision, he saw Brady take up the map, glance ahead. Then, as a tree suddenly reared up in front of them, he saw Brady's hand sneak out instinctively toward the yoke. "Careful, Colonel," he said.

"Is this really necessary?" Brady asked him tightly.

"What they told me back in Salisbury," Cody said. "Don't want a rocket up your ass, do you? And watch that map, goddammit."

But he saw the reservoir before Brady did. It appeared as just a glint of water off to his left as they flashed between two hills. He immediately pulled the airplane up in a climbing turn to the left. It was an abrupt maneuver, and he could feel the G forces building. He topped the turn out, flipping the airplane upright in a quick move, and roared ahead straight and level. They flashed over the water and then over the farm at fifty feet. The landing strip was where they'd said it would be. Below him, Cody could see the buildings of the farm, blurring past, then the conical huts of the Africans' compound. There were figures in the yard of the farm, looking up and waving. And black and white cattle in the fields. He hadn't touched the power, and they were flashing by at two hundred miles an hour. Then they were past, and he kicked the airplane over into a hard left bank, turning at a sixty-five degree angle. He heard Brady say, "Goddammit!" Then he was coming back, swooping over the landing strip for a look. It didn't appear from the look of the bushes on the ground that there was any wind to speak of. He decided to land south to north, a maneuver that would keep him well clear of the Tribal Trust Lands. He pulled the airplane around to the right in a long sweeping turn, coming back on the runway. He was still carrying full cruise power.

He came rushing in toward the end of the runway. In the turn, he'd gained altitude and now he depressed the nose. The runway rushed nearer and nearer. The land around the strip was cleared for farming and he was down right on the deck. The air-speed indicator crept up to 220, then 240 and began to edge into the red.

"What the hell!" Brady exclaimed. "You're not going to land!"

"Not yet," Cody said. And, as they flashed over the end of the runway, he suddenly pulled the airplane straight up in the classic 360 degree overhead landing pattern, pulling the power at the same time. The nose was pointed straight up, and through the windshield was nothing but blue sky. Cody watched the airspeed fall off, 200, 160, 140. Then, just at the top, as the airplane was about to enter a loop that it was not designed for, he let it fall off slightly to the left, hitting the gear down switch as he did. They were falling over and swooping back toward level. Cody could suddenly see brown terrain drop into position and felt the airplane shudder slightly at the wind drag. They were in an eighty degree bank, swooping back toward the end of the runway. He hit the flap switch, holding it down until he felt it come to the full down position. And then, perfectly, the end of the strip was there again and their air speed was down to eighty miles an hour and they were ten feet off the ground. They soared in and Cody flared out like an eagle coming to rest; the wheels of the little airplane touched the sod, and then they were rolling smoothly. He taxied to the end nearest the farmhouse, swiveled the plane around off the strip, and then pulled out the mixture control and let the engine die.

In the quiet, he reached across the colonel and opened his door. Brady didn't move for a second.

"We're here," Cody said.

Brady turned and looked at him, giving him a flat, appraising stare. He said, "You're either a fucking genius or you're crazy."

"Let me know when you figure it out."

"I will," Brady grunted.

12

Longhaven Farm—Rhodesia

Ruth showed Cody down the long hallway and into one of the smaller bedrooms. "We'll put you here, I think," she said. He put his suitcase on the bed and looked around. "It's one of the children's rooms," she said, in answer to his unasked question. "They're away at school. In Salisbury. We've put the general in the room across. And the bathroom's down the hall."

"It looks fine," Cody said. He looked thoughtfully at the grenade screens over the windows.

"I hope," Ruth said doubtfully, comparing him to the small beds, "that you'll be comfortable. The children's beds . . ."

"No problem," Cody said quickly. He turned to look at her. She was standing by the door, her hands in the pockets of some sort of smock. He had been surprised to see her, but then he expected a farmer would have a wife. Though the place didn't look as much like a farm as it did an armed camp. He wondered what a woman like her was doing in such a place. She was pretty and he could see through the drawn strain in her face that she had once been prettier. She was small, but there was a womanliness about her that gave him an unexpected, out of place catch in his throat. He didn't realize he'd been staring at her so openly until she suddenly blushed.

"Well," she said, a little rapidly, "you've got everything you need, then?"

"Yes," he said. "I'll be just fine."

"Good. Come out whenever you're ready. Tea will be shortly. I think your general is out in the operations shack with Dill."

"Thanks," he said.

She started through the door, then looked back. He was still watching her.

Brady was talking with Bill Longhurst. The last shift of Bright Lights had rotated, and now two new ones were on duty. They stared curiously at Brady.

Longhurst was saying, "So we'll just probably have a quiet evening. Let you settle in. Perhaps go and visit one or two of the other farmers this afternoon. Best to do it before night, you know. Then our D.C., Jim Leslie, will drop in later."

"Sounds fine," Brady said. His flat eyes had already taken in every detail of the operations shack, as well as the outside defenses. Most of the army company that had been camped there had moved out temporarily to outposts and checkpoints, but Brady had recognized the signs of their presence.

Longhurst looked at the American, wondering. He didn't quite understand it all, what an American general could be after. He must though, Bill thought, be some sort of toff with the way the orders had come from on high and the way it had been impressed on all of them that he must be safeguarded. Though it really wasn't the best time for him to have come, not to have a quiet look around. They were all on standby alert, which was the reason the army was out in ambush patrol.

Chris' report of the terrorist stick had been reinforced by a number of sightings, and that indicated there was more than one section working the vicinity. Even at that moment, they were being tracked and searched for.

"Well," Longhurst said, "shall we go in and have some tea? I want a good wash for myself, first. And you might want to freshen up."

"Fine," Brady said. He gave the Bright Lights an automatic flat stare.

Mobanzo, the terrorist, and his men were laid up during the afternoon heat. They were about eight miles southeast of the Longhurst farm, in a little wadi with an overhanging kopje that gave them some measure of security from detection. During the night, they had joined up with another six-man section led by an experienced terrorist nicknamed Mau Mau. Mau Mau's section also had some recruits, three of whom had been press-ganged.

Mobanzo felt uneasy. It was nothing specific, and he thought they were safe enough from detection where they were, but he was anxious to be out of Rhodesia and back into Zambia. That evening, they would slip through the valley farms and make their way into Madziwa's Tribal Trust Lands, rest there, and then continue up on the desolate Zambezi escarpment and from there into Zambia. It was time for all the sections who'd been operating in Rhodesia to make their way back to the bases across the river to rest and rearm, and to allow their political leaders at the camp to see that they were still motivated in the people's cause. Some of the regulars, the more intelligent and experienced ones, would be held over at the camp as instructors. Mobanzo was secretly hoping he might be chosen for such duty. It was true he hadn't had the elite training in China or Cuba, but he'd made several successful missions into Rhodesia, including this one. He'd had almost a year in the bush and, he thought, it was time he was given better duty. He kept it to himself, of course, but he hadn't joined the party to go on living like a bush nigger. He wanted some of the easy life at the bases, kicking the trainees around. He looked over at the recruits they were taking back, grinning slightly at the memory of how frightened they'd been. Of course, they were still frightened. He called over Lodi, old Emma's nephew. "Hey, munt!"

The boy looked up at him sullenly. Mobanzo grinned. "You going to be a brave freedom fighter for the people's cause?" When the boy didn't answer, Mobanzo laughed. None of them was worth much, he thought. They'd spend all of their time at the training base trying to desert and, once they were brought back into Rhodesia, by whichever section leader was unlucky enough to draw them, they'd fight only out of fear of being shot by their own leaders. Munts like these, Mobanzo thought, deserved the white man. Never, on their own, would they lift a hand to remove his heel from their neck. Well, willingly or not, they were going to serve a purpose. They'd be given a month's training, perhaps two months' at the most, and then be sent back over as cannon fodder. And in any engagements, they would be put in the front of the fighting. It didn't matter if they got killed, in fact it was better for the recruiting, because then you could point to such reluctant patriots and say, "See, even they, once they learned the righteousness of the cause, came willingly to die for it." Though it was doubtful if any of the people really believed such talk.

Mobanzo didn't care whether they believed it or not. He knew that some of the freedom fighters, as they called themselves, were troubled that the people did not support them and had to be forced to give food and aid and concealment. It didn't bother Mobanzo. He wasn't in the party for the people's sake; he had joined because it offered him a better life and more power and money than he'd had working on the white man's farm. Of course, he never said this. With his innate cunning, he'd seen that it was very important to parrot the slogans and sayings they'd been taught. The political commissars and the commanders liked it, and that was helpful to a man in getting on.

Mobanzo wished the day would hurry by. They had grown careless these last few days, going into villages and doing an occasional murder and then kidnapping these two boys. They were certain to be reported as being in the area, and Mobanzo had no doubt that government troops and trackers were searching for them. The commissars at the training camps made light of the government troops, called them running dogs and cowards, but Mobanzo did not believe this. He knew how many faces would be missing when they got back to the camps. He'd heard from the villagers about this group and that group who'd been wiped out. He supposed, if they were dutiful, they should take a few of the big mines from were they'd been cached long ago and mine some roads. But Mobanzo didn't like to mine roads. It was hard work and dangerous, and a man was never there to see the damage he'd done. Besides, that wasn't part of his job this mission. They were on orders to flit quickly about the country and give the impression to the Rhodesian police of increased terrorist activity. During this lull before the rainy season, almost all of the terrorists would return across the Zambezi, and it was important that the white government not be allowed to relax.

Mau Mau got up from where he was sitting and hunkered down by Mobanzo. He was called Mau Mau after the Kenya terrorists because he liked to kill so well with his bare hands. He had attempted to file his teeth to a point, in the old tradition, to make himself look more fierce, but he'd botched the job. He would have looked ridiculous rather than fierce had it not been for the insane light that shone in his eyes.

It was hot, even in the shade of the stunted mbasa trees. Mobanzo made some comment about it, but Mau Mau was looking off into the distance.

The other men were ranged against the wall of the wadi, most of them sleeping. The recruits had been given arms out of the hidden caches, but that was just for show and to make them easier to herd back across the river. They had not been given ammunition.

Now Mau Mau said, "I think we should have one more raid before we go back." He looked around at Mobanzo and grinned.

Mobanzo was alarmed. "What sort of raid?" he asked cautiously. He had to be very careful not to sound uninterested in the party's work. But he wasn't interested in anything this crazy Mau Mau could propose.

"A raid on a farm," Mau Mau said.

Mobanzo gave a short bark of laughter. "On a farm? Haven't you seen the troops that are in the area? That would be senseless."

"I have information," Mau Mau said, nodding wisely. "There is the farm of Thompson, the one we should have killed before now. I have information that tho soldiers who were there have gone away. I was told this morning by a worker on his farm."

Mobanzo was even more troubled. Thompson's farm lay off to the east. Such a raid would take them further from their sanctuary in the Trust Lands. He said, "That is impossible. It is ten miles across to Thompson's farm, and already the sun is beginning to drop. We could never be in position and have a plan of attack."

Mau Mau said, "I was not speaking of tonight. We would move close tonight and hide out and then raid him tomorrow night."

Mobanzo was liking the idea less and less. It was time they were back over the border. They could be detected at any time. He shook his head, still arguing cautiously because it would ruin a man to be branded a coward or unwilling. "No," he said, "we have these new men." He pointed toward the recruits. "It is our duty to get them back to Zambia, so they may receive the proper training and indoctrination." He said the last with the proper touch of righteousness.

Mau Mau grinned, a hideous sight. "It is because of them that I want to do it. We will make them charge the house. It will be excellent training for them." He laughed.

Mobanzo knew that wasn't so. Mau Mau would make the new recruits charge the house, all right, but not as a training exercise. He just wanted to see them cut down.

"We are twenty," Mau Mau said. "That is a big number. The party leaders would not be pleased if we didn't make use of so large an army." He grinned slyly. "And if we make the new boys charge the house, then we can do a lot of damage elsewhere. Perhaps we can kill the bwana Thompson. Then we would get a medal and a large cash bonus."

Mobanzo looked away, studying a far-off hill. He was frightened. He had to think of some reason that would deter this madman. Finally, he just shook his head and said slowly, "I don't think it's a good idea. You take your men and do it if you want to, but I'm the leader of my section and I'm going to take them back to Zambia."

Now, Mau Mau also squinted off into the distance. "I will tell the political leaders back at the camps that you're a traitor to the cause. They will believe me," he said softly.

That was true, Mobanzo thought. They were always willing to believe a denouncement. It didn't matter if it were true or not; it gave them a chance to make an example. His mind tumbled in panic, trying to think of a way out.

Longhurst was taking Brady and Cody to visit some of the other farmers. They were in the Land Rover the government had provided. It was built like a short pickup with benches in the open back for four men. Only two were back there now, the Bright Lights. Longhurst was driving, and Brady and Cody were in the front with him. They drove out the little dusty road through the farm and then turned on what was called the main road, though like all the other roads in the area it was just a rutted track. Driving with one hand, Longhurst took the two-way mike off the dashboard and flicked the button. "Alpha Sierra, this is Alpha Sierra One. Come in, please."

There was a crackle and then a voice came over, not very clearly, "Alpha Sierra, go ahead One." It was Robin, Chris' wife, standing her tour at the radio desk in the operations shack.

Bill said, "Proceeding pre dest. Be that loc ten to twelve. Will report by A A."

Brady was sitting on the outside. Looking across Cody at Longhurst, he said, "You people take enough precautions."

Longhurst shrugged again. "Could be," he said. "Then you never know." He pointed to the road ahead. "Notice how we've cleared away from both sides of the road. Back a distance of fifty yards each side. Took a lot of work and a lot of machinery could have been busy on something else. But we haven't had a road ambush that did any harm in six months now. Still, I don't know." He fell silent for a moment. Then he said, as if quietly and calmly going on with a point, "But, of course, you never know what will do any good. The WOG's not awfully good as a sharpshooter, or so we thought. It's rise up out of the side of the road and fire a burst out of an AK-47 for him. So we cleared the side of the road. Then, a couple of months back, I was riding along a road just like this 'un. Had an agricultural chap with me, down from Salisbury. Middle of the day. We were going off to visit one of the farmers in the north end of the valley. We were riding along talking and then he got silent. Didn't say anything. I finally looked over him, and he was just sitting there, his chin down on his chest. Then I hit a bump square on and he pitched over in my lap." Longhurst took one hand away from the wheel and tapped his left temple with a forefinger. "Had a little hole right here. Shot. Don't know where it come from, I didn't hear any gun." He waved a hand out the window. "But there's enough places for a sharpshooter up there. We just didn't think the terrorists could shoot." He shrugged again. "I sometimes think we take too many precautions. Other times, they don't seem enough. Point is Gen—uh, I'm supposed to call you mister. Point is, Mr. Brady, we're damn few. We can't afford to lose even one man, especially not if he's a good one.

"Some things," Longhurst went on, "you can't do bloody aught about. The mines in the road, for instance. They don't mine the tar roads, of course, but they stay steady on after our dirt ones. I think we all hate the mines more than anything else. And there's not a damn thing to be done about them."

Cody asked, "Could this road be mined?"

"Oh, quite," Longhurst said easily. "Several have been exploded on this stretch we're on right now."

"I thought you said this vehicle was mine proofed."

Brady laughed shortly, but Longhurst answered, "Well, after a fashion. The seats have been raised as you'll notice and sandbags put underneath. And there's conveyor belting under the frame that's supposed to collect the shrapnel, but I don't know how much good it would all do."

"Why not?" Cody asked, suddenly gluing his eyes on the road ahead, as if he might spot a detonator sticking out of the red dust.

Longhurst looked over at him. "Well, these're fairly large mines. Hundred pounders. You run over one of those and you're going to get blown up a bit." He tapped his knuckles on the steel overhead of the cabin. "We'd likely break our heads on this."

"Can't something be done? Some protection?"

Longhurst nodded. "Too right. We wear seat belts." At Cody's look, he laughed shortly. "But there's three of us in here and only two seat belts. Wouldn't be fair play to leave one chap out, would it?"

"My God," Cody exclaimed. "Why don't they sweep these roads?"

Longhurst was thoughtful for a second. Then he said, "I rather think we're doing it now."

All his life, Cody had heard men say they were so scared their ass was puckering. He suddenly understood the expression.

"Speaking of precautions," Longhurst said across to Brady, "this chap we're going to see is all the way around the bend at one extreme. His name is Percy Bice. You'll see what I mean when we get there."

After a while, they turned off the main road, rattled over a cattle guard, and then wound their way through fields lined with trees until a house came into view. It was set up on the high ground with a rocky cliff at its back. Longhurst stopped ten yards short of the fence. It surrounded the house, though it was much closer in than Bill's. Inside this fence, there was another fence just around the house. Bill pointed this out. "Also," he said, "around the outside of the fence, he's got trip wires that are raised at night. They're wired to vertical charges that go off, sounding the alarm. One night, Bice tripped one himself and then nearly got shot when his Bright Lights cut down on the area with their FNs."

He drove up to the gate. Before he could honk his horn, men suddenly appeared in the yard carrying FNs. "He's got four Bright Lights," Longhurst said.

They got out of the Land Rover, their two Bright Lights jumping down from the back. The gate was opened and they went inside just as Bice came out. He was a tall, thin man in his forties who didn't look strong or well. He was carrying a shotgun and had a pistol at his hip.

"Hullo, Percy," Longhurst said. "Meet a couple of American chaps." He introduced Brady and Cody. Then he said casually, "I've been telling them about your defenses."

Bice was like an eager, nervous child. He pulled Brady toward his fences, explaining about the alarm system of each and how they were connected. Then, he explained about his trip wires. "And also," he said, pointing to the rocky cliffs above, "I've got charges mounted all up there. If the bastards have a go at me, I can sit in the house and fire the charges off and mortar the buggers to death with rocks. And here—" He pulled Brady over to the fence and pointed to one-inch pipes that were pointed down each side of the inner fence to enfilade the approach. "Those are shotguns—same as. Loaded with nails and bolts and nuts. Scrap iron. I can fire them from inside the house, and they'd clean up the sides of the fences in a swoop. Isn't that ingenious?"

Brady admitted it was, looking over at Longhurst.

They went into the house. Bice's wife, a plump little housewife named Nancy, came out of the kitchen to meet them. There were a couple of small children, two or three years old, scurrying about. Bice led them into the den. As they walked through, Longhurst whispered to Brady. "He's got trip wires running about the house. Watch what happens."

Bice's house, like Longhurst's, didn't have ceilings. But up under the main eaves, Brady could see some sort of square structure. Bice explained proudly. "It's a little sandbag house we've got up there," he said. "We could hold out up there till help came if the bloody terrorists got in the house."

"He's also got a siren," Longhurst said pointedly. "You can hear it all over the valley."

"And look here," Bice said. He led the way over to a trapdoor and opened it for their inspection. "Leads right straight under the fence," he said. "In a pinch, we could get away."

Brady leaned over, looking into the black hole. It smelled of loam. "Took a packet of work," Bice said. "Had to take two dozen hands out of the fields, but it's worth it."

They sat down, Bice perching nervously on a chair with the shotgun across his knees. "Would you care for an orange squash or some such?" He looked over at Brady. "Sorry I can't offer you liquor. The bloody terrorists have made a teetotaler out of me. I'm afraid to take a drink. That's when they'd come." He suddenly looked miserable.

They talked on for a few minutes, about crops, the weather, the sort of things all farmers talked about. Then, all of a sudden, a loud bell went off. They all jumped, but Bice sprang to his feet, losing his grip on the shotgun. It clattered to the floor, but didn't go off. "Goddamn, Nancy!" Bice swore. He went out of the room shouting at his wife. "You've got to teach the kid about the wires, dammit!"

Longhurst said quietly, "Those are the trip wires in the house. The kids hit 'em and the bell goes off and Bice nearly has a heart attack."

They left not long after that. As they drove away, Brady said, "Yeah, he's gone. He's either gonna go crazy or kill himself with that shotgun. He'll break."

"The hell of it is," Longhurst said, "Percy's a damn good farmer. He's not cut out to be a soldier. Not the type. He's a farmer, and he ought to be able to farm in peace." He shook his head. "We'll lose him, I suppose, but it'll be a loss for Rhodesia. Won't be easy to get someone else to come in and take his farm. We've already got three vacant. I suppose they'll stay vacant."

"Maybe not," Brady said shortly. He lit a cigarette and looked out the window.

Jim Leslie was there for dinner that evening. He came driving up in a Land Rover with two black policemen as guards.

Leslie was a surprisingly young man. He was tall and sandy-haired and boyishly handsome. But a close look showed the lines of care in his face and the tiredness in his eyes. He wore the D.C. uniform of white shorts and white tunic with red shoulder bands. His two askaris were in starched khaki with polished Sam Browne belts and scarlet tarbooshes on their heads, and brown leather leggings polished to such a sheen that they looked like patent leather.

Before dinner, Brady and Longhurst and Leslie and Cody settled down on lawn chairs behind the wall connecting the house to the operations shack.

"About the only place you can sit outside," Longhurst commented, "and still collect a breeze without the odd bullet flipping by."

The houseboy brought them a tray with gin and a syphon and a bowl of sliced limes. They talked for a time about general situations, world conditions, farming, the United States' involvement in international affairs. Cody watched Brady, noting that, even when he seemed relaxed with a drink in his hand, his eyes were constantly shifting, taking it all in.

Longhurst finally asked, "Well, what do you think of it all, General?"

Brady put his head back and took a long drink. "Haven't seen that much," he said, "You seem to have things in pretty good shape here. At least around the house."

Longhurst smiled over at Leslie. "Unfortunately, we can't grow that much wheat or tobacco within the fence."

Brady asked, almost casually, "Tell me about your enemy. Is he any good?"

Leslie frowned. "That depends. Some of them have had pretty first-class training and they tend to be fair fighters. You must realize that this movement is not brand-new. A lot of these revolutionaries—"

"Don't call them that, Jim," Longhurst broke in bitterly. "Call the bastards what they are—gangsters."

"Well," the D.C. said, "whatever." He turned back to Brady, going on in his calm, measured voice. "But some of them were recruited as early as the mid-sixties and have had training in many of the communist countries, even Russia and China. These are pretty hard fellows, well-indoctrinated. Not," he said, "that they're in the majority. Far from it. The majority of the chaps have had a dash of training in Zambia, and then the more promising ones have been sent on to Tanzania to be turned into section leaders." He got out a cigarette and lit it. "Of course, it's difficult for us to say how good they really are, for we very seldom get them in a straight punch-up. Their tactics are pure Maoist, the same they used in Vietnam: take the farmlands, and the cities will

155

fall by themselves. Of course, it's all out from Peking. We know that there are at least a half million Chinese in Zambia alone. God knows what the numbers are in the closed states. You see," he said, leaning forward, "the terrorist isn't after the army. He's after chaps like Bill and the rest and their workers. If he can make them throw up their hands and believe, he's got the battle won because meanwhile his political allies are putting God's own kind of economic pressure on us from the outside. That's where the bloody rest of the world is making such a mistake. They think it's a racist matter, and of course, that's what the African bloc preaches in the U.N. But it's no such thing. It's bloody property and it's communism."

"Spare me the propaganda," Brady growled.

Leslie smiled and looked over at Longhurst and shook his head. "Why?" he finally said. "The other side makes damn good use of it."

"But I'm interested in the caliber of the man on the line, that guy out there with an AK-47 or a mortar waiting to bust your ass. What does he believe in and how hard will he fight for it?"

Leslie pursed his lips in thought. Finally, he said, "Well, that's a hard one. And the answer is yes and no."

They all laughed.

Leslie said, "I'm not at all sure I can explain it to you, because I'm not sure you can understand the effect the spirit craft has on the tribal African."

"Spirit craft?"

"Witchcraft if you like, though it's not that."

"What's that got to do with how good a soldier a man might be?"

Leslie leaned forward to the low table between them and began to mix himself another drink. "It's got to do with that because it has to do with everything that makes the tribal African act as he does. The terrorists, of course, make very good use of spirit craft, both in their recruiting and in motivating the chaps for an attack. Get them to believe they're invincible to bullets and all that."

Cody looked over at Brady. "We had some of that in the U.S.," he said. "Remember the Ghost Dancers and their medicine shirts bullets wouldn't go through?"

"I've heard of that," Leslie said. "It's much the same. Actually, I think the most difficult aspect of the spirit craft for the white man to understand is the native's attitude toward it. We think in terms of believing. It's not a matter of belief on his part. It's a fact. The spirits are a fact." He pointed at the wall. "Like that wall over there. We don't sit here and discuss whether we all believe that wall is there because we know it is."

He sat back with his drink, swirling it slowly. "For the tribal African, the spirits are as much a part of his daily life as food and drink are to ours. He doesn't make a move without consulting the appropriate spirit. If something goes wrong, he doesn't look for external causes; he knows that a distressed spirit has got hold of the situation and the way to make it right is to placate the spirit. If something goes wrong with one of Bill's tractors for instance, his mechanic, who is black and who is African, knows that a muti, a bad spirit, has entered the machine. He will go ahead, by rote, and make the adjustments he's been taught to do as a mechanic. But he knows that the machine will never be right until the spirit has been placated. You couldn't, in a thousand years, get the chap to understand that the dirt in the carburetor is what caused the engine to quit and that alone. You must remember," he said, "that this has been part of his culture for five hundred centuries. It's only in the last fifty years that we've been assimilating him into the white man's culture and telling him this is wrong. It's going to take a bit longer before he begins to believe it. Which is what upsets the missionary chaps. They come along and preach about Jesus, and the African who believes—there, I'm using that white man's word again, 'believe.' Never mind—but the African believes in all the spirits so he's quite willing to take on the missionary's also. So the missionary goes away happy that he's made a convert until he comes back the next day and finds the African slaying a goat as a sacrifice to some long-dead uncle. This upsets the missionary no end, and he jumps on the WOG who doesn't understand what the big fuss is all about. Just because you take on a new spirit doesn't mean you ought to neglect the old. He deals, every day, with dozens and hundreds of spirits. And he's mortally afraid of every one and damn anxious that they should all stay pleased and happy."

The houseboy came in to light the pressure lamps over the back door. Cody watched him and asked, "Why don't you have electricity up here?"

Leslie looked amused, but Longhurst answered, "Mainly, Cody, because it would take ten thousand men just to guard the lines. The terrorists would delight in having something like that to cut and tear down."

When the houseboy was gone, Leslie went on. "Actually, there's an order to the whole muddle. To the African, at least. Some spirits are more important than others, though he's afraid of all of them. First off, there's Mwari. He's the main spirit. One of the reasons why the missionaries are misled into thinking they're making progress is that the African very easily assimilates the idea of a universal God. He's already got one, Mwari, and as far as he's concerned, he and the missionary are talking about the same thing. But then, they come to cross-patches over the matter of the lesser spirits. The missionary says there aren't any and gets angry with the African, and the African bugger is astonished that the missionary should think that the main spirit, just like a king or chief, wouldn't have subordinate spirits to look after things on the local level." Leslie smiled. "Makes perfect sense I should think, but the missionary dismisses it as heathen rot, and everything falls into a muddle. So much for theological understanding between the races."

He looked at Brady. "Is anything I'm telling you of interest? We've lived with this sort of thing so long, it's old hat to me and Bill."

"Go on," Brady said.

"On a day-to-day level, there are two main spirits that the African is involved with. These are Mhondoro, the tribal spirit, and Mudzimu, the family spirit. There are others, but just for purposes of a general discussion, we can say these are the most important. Normally, these spirits are considered benign by the African, and he can keep them happy with sacrifices of goats and mealie meal and beer and that lot. But when anything goes wrong, the African is convinced that one of the spirits is unhappy, and he immediately gets busy trying to appease it. If his cows go sick, for instance, it's more than likely the family spirit. If it doesn't rain, then it's the tribal spirit. These spirits have various homes. A family spirit might be in a piece of ground or a tree. A tribal spirit in the body of an animal. All the tribes have totems, such as the lion or the snake or whatever. The spirit is considered to reside in that animal until it wishes to make itself known. Then, it enters the spirit medium and speaks through him or her."

Brady said, "Spirit medium? Like a witch doctor?"

"Exactly. When an African needs to make a decision, he goes to the proper spirit medium. The medium tells him what the spirit says to do."

Brady looked thoughtful, "That makes the spirit medium a pretty important boy, doesn't it."

"That," Leslie said with a little smile, "is an understatement."

"Well, what about your average medium? Is he pretty ethical?"

"He's as ethical as any other African," Leslie explained, "which doesn't answer your question, since the African lives by his own state of morality, and that in most cases doesn't agree with the white or European version. Remember that the medium himself is an African, and the spirits are for him a fact also. But he can be persuaded, by outside forces, into believing that the spirits want such and such. Presents, for instance, or money, are to him a direct indication of the spirit being in agreement with the man who's giving him the gifts."

"Tell me more about how the terrorists make use of the spirits."

"Oh, well, that's really quite simple. Say you've got a recruit you want to join up and he won't. You could threaten his family, but you'd prefer to have him a more willing soldier, so you go to the appropriate spirit medium. If you give the medium the proper presents, and he wants to, then he'll tell the boy what the spirit said to do. And in most cases, off he goes. It's just an additional pressure the terrorist recruiter can bring if he's got the time and the money. And, of course, they usually have a spirit medium in some of the training camps. These fill the boys up with all sorts of mumbo jumbo and make them believe they're impervious to the white man's bullets and that sort of rot. It does all right for stirring them up at the start, but I rather think it wears off after a few weeks in the bush dodging government patrols.

"But," Leslie said, looking down at his drink, "make no mistake. We'd be in a hell of a mess if the terrorists could get all the spirit mediums on their side."

"Why don't they do it then?" Brady asked.

"D'you want to know the real reason? Because the spirit mediums are generally pretty intelligent and pretty logical fellows, and they don't believe the terrorists are going to win in the end. And no African cares to be on the losing side." Leslie smiled, just slightly. "We also do a bit of politicking ourselves among the spirit folk."

Dinner was a quiet affair, just the Longhursts and Brady and Cody and Jim Leslie. They had mutton, which Cody wasn't particularly fond of, but it came with a rice curry that he liked. Bill Longhurst, in the colonial tradition, carved and served their plates from his end of the table, the houseboy passing the warmed plates down to each of them. Later, there was a great wedge of domestic cheese and then coffee. The houseboy put a decanter of brandy beside the cheese, but no one touched it.

Bill Longhurst grinned. "You don't want any of that," he said, indicating the brandy. "That's the local stuff we call Cane. Awful, but we set it out before any unsuspecting strangers in case they're not wise and will help us get it drunk up."

A little later, Leslie asked Brady if he'd like to take a trip with him the next morning. "I'm going up in the Tribal Trust Lands to see old Chief Madziwa. Nothing important. How'd you like to come alone? About twenty-five miles up there. Not too dicey, I should think."

Brady nodded. "Fine with me."

As they were leaving the table, one of the Bright Lights came hurrying in. "Bice's seen a flare, he claims. He just rang on the Agri-Alert."

"Oh, damn," Longhurst swore. "Let's go and see, but knowing that fool, he's seen a star."

They rushed out back, scanning the sky. It was dark blue, a half-moon the only light. Below, the small hills made black masses against the night.

The Bright Light said, "He said it looked to be coming from the direction of Don Thompson's farm."

Longhurst bit his lip. "Go and ring Thompson. See if he's let off a flare, though God knows why he should."

"Already have. He answered and just laughed. Said Bice was a fool."

"Nothing new there," Longhurst said. "But then, so is Thompson." He looked around at Brady who was squinting up at the night. "Thompson lives down southeast of here about eight miles. Won't have a Bright Light. Forgets to turn on the alarm on his fence about half the time. Runs around the country like he'd never heard of a terrorist. They've ambushed him a half dozen times, but he's leading the old charmed life." He shook his head. "It's just a matter of time."

As they started back to the house, Longhurst said to Brady and Cody, "By the way, you'll be hearing firing all night. The army chaps are out in ambush patrol, and they're planning on giving the bush a good spraying tonight. It impresses the local WOGs no end."

They went to bed not long afterward. Ruth gave Cody a pressure lamp and showed him how to operate it. Bill offered him a pistol, but Cody held up his hand. "Already got one."

"Good. Well, then, I'll be saying good night."

They shook hands with Leslie, and then Cody and Brady went off down the hall to their rooms. At his door, Brady growled, "Com'on in here a minute."

Cody followed him into the room, and the colonel went to his suitcase and brought out a bottle of Scotch. There were glasses on the dresser and he poured them each a drink.

"Health," he said.

"Salud."

They drank and then Brady said, "Remind me when we get back to Johannesburg to bring these people back a case of Scotch."

"We coming back?"

"Very near here," Brady said. He turned away and walked to the window, looking out, seeing nothing in the dark. "Goddammit," he said. Then, after a moment, "I like these people."

"So do I," Cody said. He set his empty glass on the dresser top.

The colonel turned from the window and looked at him. Finally, he nodded, a brief gesture. "All right. Get out of here. Good night."

"Good night," Cody said.

In his room, he set the lamp on the bedside table and then undressed. He saw to his pistol, checking the load and making sure that the safety was off. Then, he crawled into bed and turned off the lamp. The room was immediately very dark. He lay on his back, hearing the night sounds of a house settling down. He was deep in the middle of Africa and he half-expected to hear a hyena howling or a lion roaring. But Longhurst had told him the game was mostly gone out of the area, driven to the game preserves by the advance of civilization. There were heavy curtains over the windows, and Cody had been told to keep them pulled. In the quiet, he could hear the sound of springs as someone got into bed.

He was just about to doze off when he heard the sound of firing. It came from far off, but it was unmistakably the sound of automatic weaponry. Occasionally, there was the faint sound of an explosion. Then more chattering of machine guns. Cody lay listening to it. When he finally slept, it was still sounding.

The terrorists had been badly frightened. They'd been approaching Don Thompson's farm the night before when the firing had begun. Some of it had been so close that, at first, they'd thought it was directed their way. It was luck that some of the more nervous men had not given their position away by firing their weapons.

All night, they'd lain under cover and watched the flashes in the hills around them.

Mobanzo had been worried. It looked like a big operation; the area seemed to be crawling with troops. Now, in the daylight, he was having an argument with Mau Mau.

"It is obvious," Mobanzo said, "that the troops are still here. It would be foolhardy to risk an attack now. We must make our way into the Tribal Lands and cross the river."

But Mau Mau was still adamant. "It is clear to me," he said, "from the scattered fighting that there are many of our people in the area. If we begin an attack on the farm, no doubt we will draw much help from the others who are near. They will rally to us."

Mau Mau was so stupid, Mobanzo thought. But he still had to be handled carefully. "Listen to me," he said urgently, "if there were other of our people here they would have left the area by now. It is clear to me that this is our duty now. We must leave and take these new recruits back. Some of them almost deserted in the dark last night. If we wait further, they will be gone and then who is to answer to the commissars? You will have to answer."

It was a powerful argument, but Mau Mau still clung to his interest in attacking the farm.

"Listen to me," Mobanzo insisted angrily, "your stupidity has already brought us many miles away from the Trust Lands. Forget the bwana Thompson's farm. The troops would ambush us before we could make our escape. Our only chance is to leave very soon." Very casually, he took his AK-47 down from the rock it was leaning against and laid it across his lap, the muzzle pointing toward Mau Mau.

Mau Mau saw the move. He said, "Perhaps you are right. Of course, I want to do what our leaders would

think right. But would it be wise to travel during the light?"

"It would be as wise," Mobanzo told him, "as waiting here to be discovered. Even a fool such as yourself should know that the troops are watching this area. Perhaps a patrol of the RLI is coming near us even now. It would be better to be moving."

He stood up and looked at the sun. It was almost noon. "My men are moving out. We will move very cautiously until dark. By then, we should be near the Trust Lands and we can go forward boldly. If you wish to come, you may." He lifted his rifle.

Mau Mau nodded. "Perhaps what you say is right."

Mobanzo smiled. He was clearly the leader now, another token of his advancing power. He said roughly, "Tell the men to see to their supplies and water. It will be a long march."

After Brady and Leslie had left the next morning, Cody went out to see about his airplane. Three of the African farm laborers were there. They stood watching him as he went around the plane, checking the control surfaces and the engine and the landing gear. Then he got in, started the engine, and checked the mags and the other systems. Everything appeared to be all right. As he started the engine and the propeller caught, making the big roar, the men had fallen back in fright. Now, they crept back closer, watching carefully. Cody killed the engine, then turned off the mags and the key and crawled out, locking the cabin door behind him. As he jumped to the ground, he glanced at the men, wondering what they were thinking. They couldn't know much about an airplane. It must be a strange sensation for them, almost like watching magic. He gave them a nod and walked away, back to the house. As he walked, he glanced up at the sky. It was clear blue. He wondered how much longer they'd be at the farm. Not much longer he hoped. But as he thought about that, the image of Ruth came into his mind. He knew enough about the farmer's life now to wonder how she stood it. Or why she stood it.

Bill had gone to the fields, and Cody went into the house. He found Ruth sitting at the dining table sewing, a cup of coffee in front of her. She was wearing rimless glasses and she looked up with a quick smile as he came in.

"Oh, hello. Like some coffee?"

"Sure," he said. He pulled out a chair opposite and sat down. She clapped her hands and the kitchen boy came in with another cup and poured Cody his coffee.

"You didn't go with your general and Jim?"

Cody smiled. "No, I only go when we're in the air. Driving around on roads I understand have big fire-crackers under them doesn't really turn me on."

She laid her sewing aside and took off her glasses. She was wearing a yellow starched blouse with the collar laid back so that he could see her tanned throat and the top of her chest. She looked demure, almost girlish, but there was something about her that kept bothering him. He looked down at her hands on the table.

"I'm sorry I missed you at breakfast," she said. "But I chose a long bath instead. Sometimes it's the only possible time of day."

"I don't blame you." He looked down to keep from looking at her so directly.

"You're an army officer in America? Or a flight officer, I should say."

"Something like that," he answered. He stirred his coffee.

She suddenly laughed and Cody thought how good it sounded. "We're all terribly curious about you two, you know."

"You are?" He laughed also.

"Yes. We can't imagine what two American officers are doing going around up here. Especially when so far as the United States is concerned, we don't even exist."

He picked his coffee up and sipped it. "I couldn't tell you that," he said carefully. "I'm just the airplane driver. All I do is point it in the direction the general says."

"But you can't blame us for being curious. Or for hoping." She picked up the material she'd been working on and then put it back down again.

"Hoping what?"

She shrugged. "Oh, I don't know. I really shouldn't say that. Probably you're here to study our methods of guerrilla fighting. That's what Jim Leslie says. But you can't blame us for at least the hope that it could be something more substantial. Like aid. Or even understanding." She stopped and then said, "I'm sorry. That's rude of me. I make it sound as if you're not welcome unless you've come to help us."

Cody was uncomfortable. "Like I said," he began.

But she cut him off. "I know. You're just the airplane driver." She suddenly laughed again. "But probably that's all rot too. You're probably a CIA agent and the general actually works for you."

Cody grinned. "Do I look the CIA type?"

She cocked her head at him, studying his face. "Well . . ." Then she said, "Actually, never having seen a CIA agent, I don't have the slightest idea what one looks like."

He said, carefully because he was not sure how he meant it, "You don't look much like what you are either."

"What do I look like?"

"Like you don't belong here. Not in all this."

It brought a strain between them for a moment.

She said, "I really don't know what you mean."

"Walking around here with a pistol on. Living in an armed camp. Looking as tired as you do."

He hadn't meant to say it, not quite so openly. He had made it a talk between a man and a woman and he hadn't meant to do that; he had no right to do that.

She put her glasses on and took up her sewing. "You Yanks are very direct, aren't you?"

"It just seems a waste."

"A waste?" she looked up sharply.

"Yes." He pushed his coffee cup away. "This farm. This kind of life. Is it worth it to you? Does it mean that much?"

"It's our farm," she said, "and we won't be driven off it."

"It's just property. You could get another farm. How many years of this have you had? What fun can you have? Your children gone. Listen, I lay in that room last night and I didn't sleep so well. I kept waiting for the mortar shell to hit or the room to fill up with terrorists. How the hell can anything be worth that?"

"First off," she said steadily, looking at him, "it's not just property. We've made this place and we intend to keep it. We don't do it for the money, if that's what you're implying. We—"

"Look, Ruth, this is none of my business. I really shouldn't have brought it up."

"No, no, now you have." She took her glasses off again and gave him a fierce look. "When you said that it was a waste, did you mean that I was wasting myself as a woman out here?"

"I don't know what I meant," Cody said.

"You certainly meant something."

"Okay." He held her eyes with his. "Then, yes that's what I meant. I know if you were my wife I wouldn't keep you here under these conditions."

"Captain Ravel," she said coolly, "there's no danger

of that. Any man that was my husband wouldn't be one to walk away just because there was a spot of trouble."

He stood up. "Thanks for the coffee, Mrs. Longhurst. Excuse me for calling you Ruth a moment ago. Guess it's my Yank directness."

"Think nothing of it," she said.

And then, as he started out of the room, she called to him, "You'd be surprised, Captain Ravel, what a woman doesn't think of as a waste."

"I might," he said. "Maybe you'll teach me."

"I probably could," she said, looking at him steadily. He grinned, crookedly. "But there won't be the chance."

"No," she said. She took up her needle.

Brady and Leslie were on their way back, traveling down a rutted path in the Trust Lands a few miles before the turnoff back to the farm. Leslie asked, "Well, 'id you think of the old boy, old Chief Madziwa? regal, eh?"

.dy nodded. "Knows how to command men."

He should. He's a twenty-eighth-generation chief in . direct line. Like to see European royalty match that. Did you notice the gold plaque around his neck? The government gives him that, that's his badge of office from us. Which is a good point, I think. We have done our dead level best to cooperate with the customs of the African and not to interfere with them. While at the same time trying to improve his conditions. You look around Africa and you won't find a higher standard of living for the black anyplace else. But what's got to be understood is that this is a damned complicated place and the tribal system is damned complicated and the spirit craft is complicated and the customs are complicated. The whole damned business is complicated. Yet chaps six thousand miles away who've had two months in Africa, and some who've never set foot on the bloody continent, set themselves up to tell us what to do!" He hit the steering wheel with his palm. Then he looked over at Brady and shook his head and smiled. "Sorry."

It was four in the afternoon, dry and hot. The dust rose from the tires of the Land Rover and trailed out behind them in a thin, billowing plume. Now and then, they passed an African woman herding goats or a solitary tribesman sitting by the path. Each time, Leslie raised his hand in greeting.

Brady said, "You ought not to have pissed the British off. They're the ones who got the rest of the world down on you."

"Bugger the British," Leslie said with feeling. "And I've still got relatives over there. So bugger them too."

"It was the unilateral Declaration of Independence. That's illegal. Or at least that's what they say."

Leslie gave him a quick, knowing smile. "Ah, doesn't it seem a bit familiar to you? Didn't you chaps do something similar in about 1776, wasn't it?"

Brady laughed. "Yeah, but we got away with it. Besides, the Indians didn't outnumber us."

Leslie didn't laugh. "That's one war we'll never win," he said. "The population war. You see, that's what I mean about respecting the tribal customs. A black African can have five wives. A white only one. So we're never going—"

At that instant, the two-way radio crackled. "Alpha Alpha, do you read? Alpha Alpha, do you read?"

Leslie quickly picked up the mike and thumbed the button. "Go ahead, Alpha Sierra. Go ahead, Alpha Sierra; Alpha Alpha ready to copy."

There was another crackle and then a voice came through clearly. It was Ruth. She said, "Contact three miles north this loc. Contact closing. Advise your ETA."

Leslie replied, "ETA your loc thirty minutes. Is it possible to go direct contact?"

"Negative, Alpha Alpha. Proceed direct Alpha Sierra. Twenty mutineers. All elements alerted and converging. Alpha Sierra out."

"Roger," Leslie said into the mike. Then, he stuck his head out the window and yelled to the two askaris in back, "Hang on!" His foot hit the gas pedal and they pounded ahead, jumping and bumping over the rough road.

13

Longhaven Farm—Rhodesia

The contact had been established easily, almost casually. The twenty men in Mobanzo's group were seen by a worker on Don Thompson's farm, almost as soon as they'd broken camp to head for the Trust Lands. But is wasn't until a couple of hours later that he reported it to the boss boy, who in turn reported it to Don Thompson. He'd contacted the police, who'd alerted all elements. Even on what sketchy information they had, it was easy to see the band was heading for the Trust Lands. Subsequently, about noon, an army spotter plane had seen them just as they'd crossed an opening and disappeared into the bush. A six-man RLI tracker section had been put down a few miles to their rear, with orders to close gradually, though not to make contact, and to cut off any retreat to the southeast. Meanwhile, other elements were gathering to encircle them before the attack was made. They were then only a few miles from Longhurst's farm and would have to pass just to its northeast corner to enter the Trust Lands. The operations shack had become the center of activity. Unfortunately, most of the army units were scattered in ambush outposts. They could be reached by radio, but only one, a six-man unit to the direct north was in a position to help. They were converging on foot, hoping to reach a flanking position before the terrorists could arrive. Another six-man stick of RLI had come in by helicopter. They were clustered in the operations room while the helicopter sat in the front yard, its rotors idly turning. The lieutenant of the RLI unit had taken charge of the overall planning.

The lieutenant and Bill Longhurst bent over a relief map of the immediate area. They had x'd the several sightings that had been made of the terrorists and were fairly sure of their direction.

"They're heading perfect," Bill said. "If they keep on coming, they ought to approach the main road just about here." He made a mark on the map at a point three miles north of his farm.

"If nothing spooks the buggers," the lieutenant said. He studied the map. "If Army Baker arrives in time to the north, we ought to have the blokes penned. I want you to take your chaps up the road to the point you've indicated there. Then move into the bush here." He made an arrow on the map aimed straight at the line the terrorists were taking. "Take up positions on this ridge here. See it?"

"Too right," Bill said. The ridge ran parallel to the road, about a half mile into the bush. Bill knew the place. It would be ideal for an ambush. There shouldn't be much cover below, and the terrorists would come out of a long, wide draw that would throw them up to the ridge. He looked around the room, counting heads. "I'll have seven men. We'll take wide spacing, and even if they go off course a bit, we ought to keep them from slipping through. Still—" He looked down, studying the map. "The country is a bit easier to the north. They just might drift up that way. And if Army Baker doesn't get in position in time, they could slip through. You're coming in from the south I take it?"

"Right," the lieutenant said. "We'll put down a couple of miles north of here and then come flanking in below your ridge. If the other RLI chaps are close behind, we ought to have them bottled up. If, as you say, they don't do a bunk in some other direction."

Bill asked, "Couldn't you put that helicopter over them? If they've strayed, we could move our line, in time, I should think."

The lieutenant shook his head. "Afraid not. You want to see them scatter, just put a military aircraft in over them. They'd know what was up and go off in twenty directions. Besides," and he grinned slightly, "the damned thing's so slow they'd be sure to shoot it down, and I'm afraid we can't be losing a helicopter for twenty terrorists. Not good economics, you know."

Cody had been leaning against the wall by the table, listening to them talk. "Say," he said, touching Bill's shoulder, "let me ask you something."

Bill looked up, a little annoyed. "What?"

"Why can't I fly reconnaissance in my airplane? It's civilian so they probably wouldn't be spooked by it. And I could circle right over the top of them, and you'd be able to see me from your positions and you could adjust accordingly."

The lieutenant looked questioningly at Longhurst.

Longhurst said briefly, "Oh, I shouldn't think so, old chap. But thanks for the offer."

"No, listen," Cody insisted, "I mean it. I want to do it. And I don't see why it wouldn't help."

Bill grimaced. "The last thing we need, lad, is an American flyer shot up over here. Relations are none the best now."

"The hell with that," Cody said. "Listen, they're not going to shoot at me. You think they'd give away their positions when they couldn't know for sure who I was? Hell, the airplane hasn't even got Rhodesian markings. They wouldn't take that chance."

They stood there staring at each other intently for a second. Then, Longhurst turned and looked at the lieutenant. "What do you think?" he asked. Then added, "I rather imagine he'd know what he's about. He's a military pilot."

The lieutenant looked at Cody, then shrugged. "Why not? I don't see how it could hurt. Except you understand, you're not to flush the buggers. You're not going to do anything foolish like buzzing them, are you?"

"Don't worry about it," Cody said. "They're going to think I'm the agricultural commissioner. As long as they're coming your way, they'll never notice me. When do I go?"

"As far as that goes," the lieutenant said, "we'd all better get cracking. Bill, why don't you move out with your men? We'll just be off ourselves."

At that moment, the radio crackled. Ruth, who was manning it, turned to Longhurst. "It's Jim Leslie. He's just turned onto the main road. Wants to know if he's to proceed on in."

Bill said, "No. Hang on a second." He thought. "He'll be just a couple of miles to the north. Tell him to proceed inbound two miles and wait for us. We'll rendezvous on the road. That'll give us three more men, not counting Brady. We can leave him at the Land Rover."

Cody heard the last as he started through the door. He had a big picture of Brady staying with the Land Rover.

Leslie replaced the mike on the dashboard. They were racing along at fifty miles an hour, a ferocious pace on the dirt road. In the back, the two policemen were holding on with both hands. Leslie shouted, "I hope you won't mind if we leave you by the side of the road. We're going to stop just a bit further on for a rendezvous with Bill and his chaps. Then I expect we'll be taking a little walk in the bush. You should be quite all right here. Of course, I can leave one of my boys with you."

"That's your happy ass," Brady said. He picked up the FN they'd loaned him, sticking the muzzle out the window while he checked the load and the safety switch. "You got any extra clips?"

Leslie looked troubled. "Oh, I'm afraid we couldn't have that. This could be a bit risky."

"Look," Brady yelled flatly, "let's get it straight and not have any argument. I been listening to that radio and I know what's going on. I came up here to get a look at these people and I'm going to do it if I have to go on my own. Is that clear?"

Leslie frowned. "This, uh, puts me in a bit of a tight place. Especially if you get yourself killed. Tell me, how long has it been since you've seen combat?"

"Shit," Brady said. He spit out the window. "I ain't never stopped seeing combat. Now, let's get this show on the road."

As he ran toward the airplane, Cody mentally reviewed the picture of the map. He had a pilot's instinct for locations, and he knew exactly where he was and where the terrorists were supposed to be and what the terrain looked like.

There was one African left on guard. He was sleeping under the wing and jumped up in alarm as Cody leaped on the wing and opened the door. "Get clear," Cody yelled at him.

He was taking off as soon as he started taxiing. There didn't seem to be any wind, but he wasn't going to worry about that. He just rammed the throttle home and headed it down the middle.

They were at the interception point and waiting when Bill's section got there. Longhurst quickly filled Jim Leslie in.

"Right," Leslie said. "Bill, you carry on. You're more familiar with the situation and the terrain than I am. By the way, Brady is going in with us."

Longhurst gave Leslie a questioning look. "Is that wise?"

Leslie shrugged and looked at Brady who was standing at his shoulder. "You argue with him. I've tried."

"Save your breath," Brady told them shortly. Then, "How we going in, column or skirmish line?"

"The terrorists should still be a couple of miles south. We'll move up to the ridge in column and then deploy down the line."

They plunged into the bush, moving openly and walking rapidly to get into position.

There were twelve of them. Brady and Leslie and Longhurst were in front. Next came the seven farmers in Bill's stick and then Leslie's two policemen and one Bright Light. They were armed with FNs except for Bill's stick, who also had grenades. As they walked, they distributed the explosives so that each man had two.

They scrambled up the gentle incline of the ridge. It fell away much sharper on the other side. At the top, they concealed themselves among the brush and rocks. Bill fanned the men out. He sent the first man down two hundred yards, spacing the rest at thirty-yard intervals. Lastly, he said to Brady, "Stay with me, if you will, sir. You and I will take the north flank point."

They crept now, moving slowly and cautiously down the back of the ridge until it began to slope away toward flat ground. There, they went down and took up positions behind a thin growth of low bushes.

Before them was the swale of the gully floor. It ran level for three hundred yards and then began to climb toward another ridge. The opening to the floor came just off to their right, where another, higher, ridge crested. If the terrorists came through the opening and proceeded on a logical line, they'd climb right into the ambush.

The terrain before them was bushy and broken, interspersed with rocks and boulders. Their elevated position, however, gave them a relatively clear field of fire.

It was very quiet and hot. Lying there, Bill was conscious

of being thirsty. He had a water bottle back in the Land
Rover but he'd forgotten to bring it. He glanced sideways
at Brady. The American looked incongruous in his slacks
and sport shirt, staring intently at the terrain before them.

In the quiet, there came a faint buzzing from overhead.
He looked up and could just make out the little plane
against the bright background of the cloudless sky. He
nudged Brady and gestured upward with his head. "That's
your pilot," he whispered. "Up there."

"What?" Brady frowned.

"Your pilot. He's going to keep the buggers spotted for
us if he can."

"Shit," Brady said. He swore softly.

Cody climbed to 1500 feet and then idled back to cut
down on engine noise.

He hoped to see them quickly, rather than arousing sus-
picion by having to circle too long over the area. He was
taking a line a little to the south of where he thought they'd
be, so he could spot them out the window on his side. He
held the air speed at eighty miles an hour, slow flying with
twenty degrees of flaps.

The ground slipped by below him, rocky and brown. Suddenly, he caught sight of a movement just ahead and slightly
off to his left. He put the airplane into a gentle bank,
straining to see. There was more movement, and figures. He
banked, slowly losing altitude. Then he recognized the dress
of the RLI: the patrol trailing the terrorists from the east.
He was too far south. The terrorists were moving faster
than he had anticipated. In between the rounded humps of
the trees, he could see the road in patches. He pushed in a
little power and climbed, starting to circle back, knowing
he'd gone past the path. Heading back to the southwest, he
thought he could recognize the ridge that Longhurst and
his people were supposed to be occupying. On the road, he

could see the vehicles they'd left standing. He peered intently out the window, the ground slipping by empty.

Then he saw them. They were out in the open, almost, moving in single file. The leaders had stopped and were staring up at him as he swept over them.

He climbed now, going for altitude. At 2500 feet, he reduced the power and then came back into a sharp 180 degree turn.

With the altitude, knowing where to look, he spotted them immediately. They were moving rapidly, their heads down, jogging, carrying their rifles at trail arms.

And now, he could see the RLI patrol that was following from the east. They were a half mile back and losing ground because they appeared to be proceeding cautiously. He couldn't see the group converging from the south. He assumed they were right below him. Nor could he make out the army patrol that should have been coming in from the north. As he passed over the terrorists again, he looked directly to the left, searching for Bill and his people. He could see the ridge he thought they must be occupying, but he couldn't be sure.

There was no point now in hiding his intentions. He jerked the airplane around in a hard bank and turned for another look. The terrorists were still moving fast. He saw them come up behind the low ridge that formed the southern wall of the swale they were supposed to enter. But, even as he watched, they veered to their right, to the north, going along behind the back of the protecting ridge. "Oh, hell!" Cody said aloud as he swooped past. He climbed and turned with the picture of the terrain in his mind. The ridge they were proceeding along ran toward the end of Bill's ridge at an angle. When they came out from behind its protection, they'd be exposed only briefly unless Bill and his men were deployed much further north than Cody thought they were. He grabbed the mike and dialed in the frequency of the radio set in the operations shack. "Alpha Sierra, this is five-five-eight-one Foxtrot. Do you read?"

"Go ahead five-five-eight-one Foxtrot. Alpha Sierra." It was the cool voice of Ruth.

"Listen, I don't know what to do. Bandits not heading into the ambush. They've got a ridge between Bill's party and themselves. By the time Bill sees them, they're going to be past. Is there any possible radio communication?"

"Negative, five-five-eight-one Foxtrot. I can transmit to Army Baker through Shamva, but I don't know their position. Shall I relay?"

"Goddammit," Cody swore. He hung up the mike without answering, knowing there wasn't time, and immediately put the nose of the airplane down, pulling the power. He headed, in a long dive, right for the file of terrorists. As he neared, he could see them look back, then duck their heads and continue jogging. He swooped over their heads at two hundred feet. As he leveled out, he looked to his left, looking for some sign from the ridge Bill was occupying. He saw nothing.

"Goddammit!" he swore again. The terrorists were halfway down the ridge and would be past the end and gone. He peeled the airplane around in a hard bank, reaching into the back seat as he did. His hand found the flare pistol. He dropped it in his lap and aimed the airplane for the guerrillas. He pulled the power completely and thumbed open the storm port. The ground was rising to meet him.

The terrorists stopped, staring up at him. He could see their black, upturned faces. Then he was over them and he suddenly kicked in full left rudder and lay the airplane over on its side in an almost ninety degree bank. He could feel the G forces pulling at the flesh of his face as he heeled the plane around in an abrupt, shuddering turn. The airspeed indicator dropped suddenly. He hit the flap switch, putting it down fully, then grabbed the flare gun and aimed it out the port. The sharp, banking turn had brought him right over the guerrillas. He knew he didn't have but an instant. They were straight down from him, two hundred feet out the window.

He aimed the flare gun and fired. For a second, the scene was frozen except for the line of orange fire blazing swiftly toward the ground. Then it all began to happen. He felt the airplane shudder as it began to stall in the low-speed, high-angle bank. He didn't bother to put the gun down. He just let go of it, kicked right rudder and jammed the throttle to the wall. He had a glimpse of the air-speed indicator. It was down to sixty and he could feel the airplane buffeting and jumping as it lost flying speed. The low trees were rushing up, even as the air-speed indicator began to rise.

Then, just as he began to get flying speed, he felt a series of odd bumps and jolts. For a second, he thought the airplane was breaking up from the strain, and then he realized he was being shot at. A tuft of upholstery out of the seat beside him floated into the air. He heard a whang and a thump, and the windshield turned into a spider's web. Then he heard a whack and something hit his feet. It was a numbing jolt. It felt as if he'd been slammed in the arch with a baseball bat. He wanted to look, to see if his foot was gone, but the ground was very close, and it was taking all his attention to keep the airplane flying.

Gradually, he was regaining flying speed. He got the nose up and began to climb, carefully holding it straight and level. Some of the control surfaces could have been shot up and he didn't want to make any sudden moves until he could assess the damage. He glanced quickly down at his feet. His right one was hurting, badly, and even as he looked he could see blood pouring out of the top of his shoe.

He kept the airplane ahead straight and level until he got a thousand feet of altitude. Then, he very gingerly began to test the controls. They all seemed to be working, and he turned back in a long, gentle bank to see what had become of the battle.

It was all over by the time he arrived over the scene. He had missed the effect his flare had had on the terrorists. As it hit the ground, they'd turned, in headlong flight, and rushed straight toward the point to which Longhurst's group was hurrying to intercept them.

Brady realized, before Longhurst, what the flare meant. He jumped to his feet. "Let's go!" he commanded. "They're behind that ridge." He went running, bent at the waist, through the rocks and scrub bushes, bounding off the point of the ridge and then sprinting as he hit the flat ground. Behind him, he could hear Longhurst yelling for the others. When he was fifty yards short of the end of the ridge, he felt rather than saw the sudden movement as a figure came bursting through the brush. He skidded to a stop and dropped to one knee, throwing the FN to his shoulder and sighting at a cleared space just beyond a little clump of mbasa saplings. The bushes quivered violently and a man burst into view, running headlong toward the road. Brady sighted and squeezed off three evenly spaced shots. The man went down, disappearing into the ground growth. Without hesitation, Brady jumped up and sprinted forward another ten yards, falling behind a rocky ledge. He got his rifle up just as a group of terrorists popped out of the bushes. He fired a short burst of automatic fire. One of the men dropped, the other three cast a wild look in his direction and then turned off to the north. One of them fired a random blast at him. The AK-47 went TUUUUUURRRRRAP, but the man was running, running backward, while he fired and the burst went wild. Brady cut him down with ten shots of automatic fire, the high velocity shells twisting and pummeling him before he could fall. Then, the others were there, kneeling and firing. Behind the ridge, they could hear other firing as the RLI troops closed. Bill's group dashed forward and threw grenades over the low hump of the ridge end. Their blasts mixed in with the firing of the FNs and the answering fire from the terrorists until the noise pounded back at them like shock waves.

It was done quickly. They continued firing for a full minute after resistance had ceased and then moved in. Fourteen of the terrorists had been killed. Four were wounded and two had got away in the confusion. All four of the converging group met just at the center of the battle. The smell of gunpowder and cordite from the grenades hung heavily in the air. Here and there wisps of smoke drifted. The trees and underbrush in the little area were torn and broken from the bullets and the explosives.

The sudden quiet was eerie. Without saying much, they moved slowly through the bodies, making sure those that were dead stayed dead and searching the wounded for concealed weapons. Longhurst stopped by one young terrorist he thought he recognized, noticing how new his AK-47 looked. He picked it up. There was still Cosmoline in the barrel and the clip was empty. He grimaced and showed it to Brady. "Wasn't even loaded. Some of these lads I reckon had just been press-ganged. They were being taken back for training. Damn pity."

"Pity, hell," Brady said flatly. "Kill them now."

He turned away, stepping through the underbrush to study the bodies. They were, he thought, a pretty sorry-looking lot. But then, a terrorist, by the nature of his job, didn't have to stand parade inspection. He stopped and looked at one. It was Mau Mau, dead, his chest blown apart by a grenade. His features skinned back in a hideous grin, exposing his ridiculous-looking teeth.

Mobanzo had been wounded. A burst from an FN caught him in the right knee, and the lower part of his leg was shot away. One of the RLI commandos was kneeling by him, putting a tourniquet on his thigh. "Got to save this 'un," he said cheerfully. "I think we've got papers on him. He ought to be able to tell us bloody plenty."

Brady looked down curiously. "What'll you do with him?"

"Oh, the heli will be along directly. I imagine we'll airlift him and the other blokes into the little hospital in Shamva. Then, when he's well enough to travel, we'll take him into Salisbury and give him a bit of a party."

Mobanzo had his teeth set against the pain. But he turned his head slightly and stared at Brady, hate radiating from his eyes. "You might as well kill that one," Brady said casually. "He's not going to tell you much."

"Ah, that's what he thinks," the young commando said. He finished his work and patted Mobanzo cheerfully on the thigh. "We like his kind. A bloody lot of fun."

Overhead, Cody flew by slowly. He could see it was all over. He cautiously wigwagged a salute with his wings and turned for the landing strip.

Brady and the commando watched the plane disappear. Then Brady gestured at Mobanzo. "Think he'll live?"

"Oh, of course. For a while. He'll lose part of that leg, I expect." He laughed. "Don't suppose he'll ever play soccer again."

Brady looked curiously at the young RLI commando. He was wearing shorts and rubber sneakers and a sleeveless camouflage shirt. Neal Hall had described their work: "These blokes take their kit in one hand and their FN in the other and off they go into the bush. They can track at a run for thirty miles a day. Your terrorists don't like these chaps at all." Brady could see that this one couldn't be over twenty years old. He had a laughing, cheerful face, but there was purpose enough in his eyes and in the way he hefted his rifle. "Well, cheerio, I'm sure we'll be off in a moment to have a scout around the area for those other two blokes."

Brady turned away. He could hear the sound of a helicopter in the distance, its rotor blades going whupwhup-whupwhup.

They sat up in the operations shack that night celebrating and drinking beer.

Cody was a hero to the extent that the Rhodesians ever made much over anyone. He'd been an outsider and he'd taken risks and performed well, and they went out of their way, casually, to let him know they appreciated it. His wound had been very slight. One of the shells had come through the bottom of the fuselage and hit the rudder pedal. The impact had been what had given his foot such a jolt. The bullet hadn't penetrated, but a piece had splintered off and torn through his shoe. It had cut a groove in the side of his foot and nicked a vein in his ankle. That was where all the blood had come from. It was too slight to go into Shamva, so Ruth had bandaged it and given him a tetanus shot, and now he was seated on the wall bench by Brady, laughing and drinking beer.

There had been one other casualty, a soldier in Army Baker squad. He'd caught an AK-47 round in the shoulder and been taken to Shamva.

Brady looked at Cody. There was a slight, amused smile on his face. "Our first wounded hero," he said under his breath. "I don't know the indemnity pay scale. Do you get money for a scratched foot?"

"Four thousand dollars," Cody said in the same low tone, "and a promotion to major."

"You're already a major."

"Goddammit," Cody said, "I forgot. I don't guess you'd make me a colonel, would you, Colonel?"

"I don't think so," Brady said dryly, but he gave Cody a lingering, appraising look and nodded, just slightly.

The room was becoming smoky and hot. Someone, against procedure, had opened the door, but there wasn't much breeze stirring. Cody sat there, drinking beer and listening. Across the room, Ruth was sitting between Bill and Chris' wife, Robin. He thought that sometimes he could feel her eyes on him, but he couldn't catch her looking. After a time, he got up and went out the door, out into the yard almost to the fence. Off to his left, he could see the lights from the soldiers' bivouac and hear the low murmur of their voices. He lit a cigarette, carefully shielding the flame with his hand. Then he stood there, breathing deeply and looking up at the sky and far out into the black night. He felt, rather than heard, someone come softly up to his side. He didn't look around.

"Why did you do that?" It was Ruth.

"Do what?" He dropped the cigarette and ground it out with his shoe. She was standing, staring out as he was, not looking at him. She had her arms folded and a light sweater over her shoulders.

"What you did in your airplane."

"I don't know. Does it matter?"

"Yes."

"Why?"

"Because you seem to think we're such bloody fools for staying here. And then you did that to help us. That's not very consistent, is it?"

"That's me," he said, "Mr. Inconsistency." He was suddenly angry, angry at her, angry at himself, angry at the whole mess.

"The chaps are impressed," she said, still not looking at him. "They think it was a rather brave thing to do. A little plane like that."

"Yes," he said, a savage tint in his voice, "well, maybe the *chaps* don't know what's dangerous and what's not. What do you think?"

"I don't know," she said.

He suddenly turned and took her by the shoulders and kissed her hard on the mouth. She didn't move, either to respond or to draw away. After a second, he stepped back. "Well," he said, "that's more waste."

She didn't say anything.

His voice flared. "Well, goddammit, don't just stand there. Say something. Do something. I just kissed you. React, dammit."

Her voice was low. "So you kissed me. What difference does it make?"

He stared at her for a second and then turned away. "Yeah, you're right. What difference does it make. What the fuck difference does any of it make." He was aching inside to talk to this woman, to tell her about himself, to ask her questions, to listen to her opinions. But he knew he wouldn't, just as he never did, just as he never could. He wanted to turn to her and say, "Look, I'm blowing the whole show. I'm thirty-six and not a goddamn year of it has stood for anything. I've got nothing, nobody, except a few bucks in the bank and the ability to handle an airship. *And that's it*! That's fucking all I've got to show for it! All the years. Nothing in my head, nothing in my heart, nothing in my soul. Escapades, thrills, cheap challenges, cheaper women. If I believe in something, it turns to shit. If I care about something, it ends up cheap and I feel like a fool. All I know how to do is keep my mouth shut and fly an airplane and drink whiskey and live in hotel rooms and look like I'm all together. Look at *For Whom the Bell Tolls*. Hemingway had it easy. All anybody had to do was say, 'I'm for the Republic' and that settled it. Here they say, 'Africa for the blacks.' The communists say, 'Workers, throw off your chains.' The preachers say, 'Give your life to Christ!' The businessmen say, 'An honest day's work for an honest day's pay!' They all got something to say. They all got a way for you to live. But what do I do? How do I figure what I want and what's worth wanting? Tell me that, Ruth. Tell me that."

And what he most would have liked to say to her then was, "You want to know why I got in that airplane and did what I did? I did it for you. Because you seemed so sure of what you wanted. And I could help just a little bit. That made it easy. And if I knew, it would always be easy."

But he didn't say any of that. Instead, he turned away from her and lit another cigarette. He said, "I hope I didn't embarrass you."

"Why should it have embarrassed me?"

He turned on her, then, savagely. "Don't ask me questions back, goddammit! Give me answers." He threw his cigarette down and went striding away.

The next day, Cody and Brady flew reconnaissance along the escarpment above the Zambezi River, studying the terrain. They located the roughed out, cleared off strip that Hall had arranged for, and Cody took coordinates from local landmarks so that he could find it when the time came. It would be their forward jumping-off point. All that day, he was angry and withdrawn. At one point, Brady looked over at him. "What's the matter with you, cowboy? You act like you got a burr under your tail."

"Nothing," Cody had answered savagely.

Brady had laughed.

The next day, Bill took them into the infirmary at Shamva to see Mobanzo. As they drove, he said, "This one, this Mobanzo, was one of my chaps. Used to work for me. I'd rather been expecting to see him sooner or later. Chris has been checking and two other boys were abducted. I rather thought I recognized one of them."

Cody said, "You don't act very surprised."

Longhurst shrugged. "It's not the first time. Nor will it be the last." He laughed. "Some good has come of it, however. Our old cook came in very shamefaced to Ruth and confessed that Mobanzo had been putting pressure on him to change the kitchen boy. As if they thought that sort of nonsense would succeed."

They had Mobanzo in a little wire enclosure off the main ward of the infirmary. They had amputated his leg at the knee. He looked up as they entered.

Bill stood at the end of the bed and said cheerfully, "Well, home again, heh, Mobanzo?"

The terrorist stared back sullenly.

Brady said to him, "You lost your leg. Was it worth it?"

Mobanzo continued to stare.

Brady asked, "Why didn't you and your men fight better? You were running away rather than fighting. Are you cowards?"

Mobanzo would not answer.

"Did you know how to fire the weapons you were given? Why didn't you fire more? You had some men with you. Black men. You didn't give them ammunition. Their rifles were empty. Why was that? Didn't you trust your own people?"

Slowly, Mobanzo turned his eyes away and looked at the wall.

"You won't get anything out of him," Bill Longhurst said.

Cody stood there, looking at the inert figure on the mattress.

"Shit," Brady said, "let's go. We're talking to a mummy."

Cody had a chance for a moment alone with Ruth on the morning they left. He said to her, "You asked me why I did what I did. Brady did a little something himself. Why didn't you ask him? Or did you?"

She shook her head.

They were standing in the hallway. He had just come out of his room with his suitcase.

"Why not?"

She looked up in his face. "I don't know. It seemed somehow natural for him."

He stared at her intently. "I'm afraid I'm going to be thinking about you a lot, Ruth."

She said, "That would be a waste, Captain Ravel."

"We use the word 'waste' a lot, don't we?"

There was a little ceremony at the airplane when they were ready to leave. They'd shaken hands and Ruth had kissed them both on the cheek. Then Bill Longhurst said, "Just a second, if you will." He came forward, looking self-conscious. "We won't charge you for these." He swiftly hung the talisman of the antiterrorist regulars around each of their necks. It was an FN bullet suspended on a black lanyard.

Brady looked down at it on his chest. "Thanks," he said. "We appreciate it."

Then they shook hands again. Cody did not look at Ruth. As they took off and circled, they could see the little group, still standing there waving.

That night, Bill and Ruth lay in bed. It was still early and, for a change, Bill wasn't exhausted.

"Do you suppose," Bill asked, "they got what they came for?"

Ruth was facing away from him. "I suppose so," she said.

"Imagine that Yank pilot. Bloody swooping that airplane around and firing down that flare. That was a good show, don't you think?"

She was silent for a moment. "It was all right," she said finally.

He put his arm lightly across her waist. "That's the kind of chap all the girls have eyes for, isn't it?"

"Don't be a bloody fool, Bill. How would I know that?" She was still turned away from him.

There was a long silence and then he said, "A chap like that—he wouldn't keep you penned up in this bloody war." He had not meant to say it, even lightly. He threw his arm across his face. "Oh, hell!" he said.

She turned then, putting her arm around him. "Bill, you damned old fool. Stop that. I won't have that sort of talk from a man like you."

"Ah, Ruth," he said, "what would I do without you. What would any of us."

14

Johannesburg

It was late on a hot afternoon. Major Carlton-Brooks sat in his office, a towel around his neck to soak up some of the perspiration, working over the master roster. The calls would go out the next morning at four A.M. The majority of the men were already selected; now he was down to the borderline cases.

He pondered over Lavel Horstmann, a Belgian with commando experience, familiarity with most modern weapons. The man had a good attendance record at the training sessions and no worse than average marks on attitude from the instructors. By all means, he should be selected, but Carlton-Brooks still hesitated. Perhaps, he thought, it was because he didn't like Belgians from the old days of the Congo campaign. Which, he told himself, was a damn unprofessional attitude. He carefully added Horstmann's name.

But the real shocker for him had come that morning when Matthew Brady had marched into his office. The word was go, and right now. They'd be loading up the next night. Brady had said, "Add your name to the list, Major. You're coming to the forward camp as adjutant, directly in charge of the support personnel."

He'd fully expected to be left behind. He'd asked   le
little stunned, "And who's going exec, sir?"   s

"Major Ravel."

So it was Major Ravel now. They'd gone off somew
Ravel had left a captain and come back a major. An
shocker.

"Let's see," Carlton-Brooks said half-aloud to hims
pondering over the list of names. He stopped at that
Simon García, a Mexican national. The major had nev
even seen a Mexican before and couldn't imagine what or
was doing in Africa as a mercenary. But he was a goo
soldier and spoke good English. He marked down García's
name.

And then there was John Peters. Well, everyone knew
about John Peters. But he was a hell of a fighter. And that
was what Brady had asked him for. With a touch of mali-
ciousness, he added Peters' name.

It was growing late and Carlton-Brooks was tired. And
they still, he thought, had hell's own kind of work left to do
all the rest of that night. He had sixty-nine names. The last
one he put in was Dougie Lord. It was a direct breach of
the age limit, but Carlton-Brooks was feeling defiant. Besides, he thought, seven of the seventy would act as support
personnel, to be used only as a backup to the other combat
teams. Lord was an excellent training officer and, Carlton-
Brooks decided, deserved one last go.

And so did he, he thought to himself, leaning back in
his chair. He got out the bottle of Scotch in his desk drawer
and sighted it against the light. It was two-thirds down.
He'd been nipping a little heavily that day. But he'd have
one more in celebration. "Cheers," he said to himself, turning the bottle up.

Brady and Cody spent the afternoon sitting around the
hotel suite. For once, the colonel was not busy with the end-

ss papers and maps. Neither was drinking, but they were
moking cigarette after cigarette.

"Planes ready?" Brady asked for the third time.

"Yes, Matt. The condition of airplanes tied down on a
ramp doesn't change from hour to hour."

"And Edge? He's got his full instructions?"

"Matt, Art Edge and I have been practicing all week. The
man is a good pilot. He knows his job. Now, will you go
look at your maps or something?"

Brady lit a cigarette, grimacing as he always did at the
taste of tobacco. "Why does the goddamn tobacco in foreign countries always taste so shitty? Answer me that, if
you know so goddamn much."

"The hell with this," Cody said. He got up and put on a
sports coat.

"Where the hell you think you're going?"

"Out."

"Out where?"

Cody turned at the door. "To get a piece of ass, if it's
any of your fucking business."

"Oh, no you're not."

"You just watch me."

Brady suddenly chuckled. "Well, cowboy, let me give you
some advice. You better get you enough to last you a long
time, because where we're going there ain't going to be
any."

"Go fuck yourself, Colonel."

"I've tried," Brady said, "but it ain't no substitute for the
real thing."

Cody closed the door over the sound of Brady's chuckle.

He called Landon from a pay phone in the lobby.

Landon laughed dryly when Cody identified himself.
"The tourist," he said.

"Cut the shit. I want Flic's address. I could maybe find
the place on my own but you can save me some time."

"I'll give you the address, old sport, but I rather doubt she'll be glad to see you. You'll perhaps remember that you were a bit rough your last visit."

"You going to give me the address?"

"And, of course, I can't intercede for you now. You'll be on your own. Fact is, I don't need you now."

"What are you talking about?"

Landon sounded pleased with himself. "Oh, it's no good going on with the charade. The story's out. It's Angola, as we thought all along."

"I wouldn't know about that. I'm just a tourist, remember."

"Of course, of course. By the way, I saw that you checked out of the Carlton Hotel. Been off sight-seeing?"

"Sure. That's it."

"You could," Landon said, "perhaps give me some color background. I'd appreciate that. In return, I might put in a good word with Flic for you. Of course, I don't expect anything big. I've got my man for that."

"Flic handle that little service for you?"

"What? Jealous?"

"Oh, go to hell, Landon."

He gave Cody the address, and just before they hung up, he asked, "By the way, does the name Colonel Cardeones mean anything to you?"

Cody deliberately let a pause build up. Then he said, "No."

Landon laughed. "You are rich, old sport. Perfect. Well, good luck with Flic. And give her my best. No, change that. Better give her your best."

Cody was smiling as he hung up the phone. "Stupid sonofabitch," he said.

She answered the door immediately. For a second, she stood staring at him and he thought she was going to close it.

"Hello," he said.

"I was expecting someone else." Her voice was unemotional.

"Can I come in?"

"I have very little time."

"You got a customer coming?"

"Yes." Her stare was cold.

"For a few minutes?"

There was a pause and then she opened the door and shrugged. "All right."

They sat down in the living room. She was wearing another pair of silk lounging pajamas. They were gray and set off her dark features.

After a moment, Cody said, "Look, I'm sorry I slapped you. I don't normally do that to women."

She looked directly at him. "That wasn't all I minded. I minded that you called Landon. I minded that you did not bring my car back. I minded that you went off without a word."

"Well, look," he said, "you'll remember you weren't exactly playing it straight yourself."

She shrugged. "So what? You came here to fuck me. You fucked me. I looked through papers as a favor to a friend. If you had been willing to tell me the truth I wouldn't have had to do that."

"Jesus," he said. He looked down at the floor and shook his head. "You got it all worked out. Except, it's all bullshit."

"So what?" she said again. She was smoking a cigarette, looking very cool.

He got up and crossed to the couch and sat down beside her. She watched as he unbuttoned her blouse and then threw it back over her shoulders. He cupped one of her heavy nippled breasts in his hand, feeling its firmness, kneading it gently. "I want," he said, "a ride like no man ever had before. I want you to send me to the moon. I want you to get every drop out of me I got."

She took a long draw of her cigarette and blew the smoke out. "Why should I do that?" she asked him.

He looked up into her face. "Because it matters to you with me."

They stared at each other for a long time. Then she punched her cigarette out in an ashtray and stood up. "Just a moment."

She went into the other room and he could hear her telephoning, but he couldn't understand the words.

When she came back, she said, "All right. But understand that this time there are no obligations." Then she knelt in front of him and unbuckled his pants, sinking her soft face into his stomach as she slid them over his hips.

A long time later, Cody looked at his watch. They were lying on the bed now, staring up at the ceiling. He saw there wasn't much time left.

"I got to go," he said.

She put her hand on his stomach. "You have a very nice body," she said.

"Coming from you, that's quite a compliment. But I still got to go."

"Will you make a lot of money out of this fight? This mercenary business?"

"What's a lot of money? And who cares about money?"

"I do."

"Then, I probably won't make enough."

"Maybe we'll have enough together." She turned her face to him, her hair dark on the pillow. "Perhaps you'll come back and we can go off together."

"Sure," he said.

"No. I mean it." She gave her head a quick shake. "I'm so tired of Johannesburg. I'm so tired of old, rich men with fat bellies who want to talk to me about their wives. I hate their hands on me." She reached up and stroked his face. "Perhaps you'll come back and we'll go off together. Perhaps that could be. No?"

He laughed and pulled away from her hand. "Sure, why not?" He sat up on the side of the bed and yawned and stretched.

"Are you going far?"

He looked around at her and grinned. "Still working for Landon?"

"Oh, I was never working for Landon," she said angrily. "He's a friend and he asked me for a favor. But that was before I had met you. It's all different now."

He went to a chair and sat down and began pulling on his pants. "Let's see, how many times have I heard that line before?"

"Oh, Cody, you are such a bastard. Do you know that Landon said he was frightened to death of you. He'd followed you over from some other place, and he said he was terrified to go up to your table. He said you looked so unapproachable."

"Well, it sure didn't stop him."

"Landon has a lot of brass."

"Say, he's queer, isn't he?"

"Queer?"

"Homo. A fairy."

"Oh, of course." She laughed.

Cody said, "Well, I'm glad he brought me to you instead of trying something else."

"He's not a fool," she said. She was lying on her side, curled up like a cat. She watched him put on his socks. "Will you come back?"

"What the hell difference does that make to you?" he asked her. He stopped dressing, sitting in just his slacks and socks, and got out a cigarette and lit it. "What the hell do you know about me? You've seen me twice. And why should I want anything more to do with you? You're a fucking whore."

Her eyes flashed. "I am getting very tired of hearing you say that." She opened her legs and put her hand between them. "What makes this so sacred, so holy? Men work with their brains and get paid for it. What is the difference? It's just another part of the body."

"Well, I think—" he began.

"But, no. You fly airplanes. Why don't you fly airplanes for love? Why shouldn't I come to you and say, 'Please, Cody, fly the airplane for me for love.' Eh? How about that?"

He laughed. "Baby, for you I'd do it."

"No! All the time."

"I got to eat."

"So? Is it different for me?"

"Yeah," he said, "but you're going to get old and ugly and nobody will want to fuck you anymore. But they'll still want me to fly the airplanes."

She gave him a roguish smile. "Perhaps that's what I'm thinking about."

He laughed out loud.

"Now what is so damned funny?"

"I just had a thought," he said. "It's perfect. I'll fix you up for your old age."

"What?"

"My insurance," he said. He gave her a sarcastic look. "One of those papers you prowled through in my pockets. I'm going to put you down as beneficiary."

"Why should you do that?" She looked at him curiously, not sure if he were teasing or not.

He shrugged. "Hell, there's nobody else."

"No one? No family?"

"Not that I know of. None that I've seen in fifteen years. I think an old uncle that raised me died about five years back. He was the only one I ever cared about anyway."

"But where do you live? Where is your home?"

"That's a damn good question. I guess I don't have one."

"But you have to have some permanent place. You must."

He thought a moment. "I guess I'd have to say it's a little bank in Texas. A place where I send whatever extra money I've got. I never thought about it before, but that would be it, I guess."

"But what do you have? Don't you have an apartment somewhere?"

"I've had apartments. Always on short-term lease depending on the job I was on."

"Do you have a car? How do you get your mail? How do people find you? Do you just drift?"

"I don't know how to answer all this, Louisa. I've never really sat down and thought about it, if you want to know the truth. I've just been drifting. One year ran into another. You know how it goes. The flying business, especially my kind of flying, is a pretty small club. You get into some airport and they know you and some guy says so and so is trying to get hold of you. And you call him and he says can you do such and such and you say okay, or you say 'Your plane' and he may say, 'No, charter one in your name.' And one job leads to another." He stood up and began putting on his shirt. "For Christ's sake, quit asking me so many goddamn questions."

"But I'm interested."

He walked over to the bed and sat down on the edge of it. "But I'm not interested in talking."

She put her hand on his arm. "Are you happy?"

"Happy? Now don't start that shit. Next you'll be asking me what my sign is. Com'on, let's keep it clean."

"Are you afraid to answer me?"

"Happy? What the hell is happy? I live, I exist, I fly airplanes, I drink a little whiskey, occasionally I get to fuck a woman as beautiful as you, I eat, I sleep. What else is there? Now cut this out."

"Why do you hop around so? Always going somewhere else. I think perhaps you're very unhappy."

He slapped her, a sudden stinging blow on the buttock. "I said cut it out. Are *you* happy? See how easy that is to answer."

"It's easy. No."

"Then do something about it," he said. He stood up. "I got to go." He tried another laugh, but it didn't come off very well. "Usually I don't have anyone to tell good-bye, but you got a fifteen thousand dollar stake in me. That'll at least give you a rooting interest."

"Cody, please stop that."

"Why? Wouldn't it make you happy for the postman to drop you off a little check for fifteen grand?"

"No," she said.

"Anyway," he told her, "it makes me feel less like a free-loader. This way, I feel I'm paying like the rest."

"Please come back," she said. "Please."

He stood looking down at her. "Why?"

"Because I want you to. Very much."

He leaned down and kissed her swiftly. "I might." Then he was gone out the door.

15

Johannesburg

The seventy men who had been selected were sitting in a small meeting room waiting for Colonel Brady, whom they'd never seen and didn't expect, to come in and tell them what it was all about.

The calls had gone out early that morning. The message had been simple and direct.

"You have been selected for a special force. You have been warned to have your affairs in order to be gone for at least three months. You will have until ten P.M. tonight to report."

They were told to bring nothing, not even a change of clothing.

All seventy had reported.

Sitting there, the men were quiet. As they'd reported to the armory, they'd been stripped of their civilian clothing and given a new issue of green khaki fatigues and black berets and field boots. All of their personal possessions, including billfolds, watches, rings, civilian clothes, whatever, had been taken from them, and now they sat there, unidentifiable from the skin out. A few had protested the loss of their more private possessions, wanting to keep pictures of their wives, for instance. But it had been explained that everything they were leaving would be sealed in individual packets and kept awaiting their return.

Even their cigarettes and lighters had been taken. Each man, as he'd filed into the meeting room, had been issued two packages of a standard brand, along with matches.

At first, as they'd filtered in, there'd been curious and excited talk of what it was all about. Each man had questioned his neighbor until he was finally satisfied that no one knew any more than he did. In the end, there had been nothing more to talk about and they had subsided into silence.

Then, from the back of the room, there came a sudden hum of excitement as the rear door opened. Matthew Brady marched down the center aisle of the room followed by Jack Carlton-Brooks. The hum followed him until he reached the raised platform at the front of the room and then wheeled to face them. The noise died almost instantly as his eyes swept the room.

"You men have never seen me," Brady said distinctly and flatly, "but I'm your commanding officer."

He paused, his eyes traveling slowly over the faces.

"You've already been told you were selected for a special force. That is true. You were the best of the men we could recruit. You have probably gathered that the mission of this special force is highly secret. That is true. Let me now tell you that you're facing two to three weeks of hard, rigorous training. I'll personally supervise that training."

From a few who were slow enough not to recognize the new feeling in the room there came a suggestion of a moan. Carlton-Brooks instantly snapped to attention. "SILENCE!" he roared in a voice he had not used for some years.

There was a startled quiet.

Brady continued. "After that training, you will be going on a series of strike missions. They are not suicidal, but they will be dangerous. During the entire period of this operation, you will be totally isolated, totally incommunicado. You will neither make nor receive phone calls. You will neither write nor receive mail. Such recreation as you're allowed will be totally restricted to your training base."

He paused.

Then, "As of this moment, your pay is doubled. And no man will receive less than twice the base of a sergeant."

Brady went on, "However, if there are any among you who wish to withdraw, now is the time to do it. Get up and walk out."

His eyes swept the room.

"Beyond this point, the choice will no longer be yours to make. Outside, there are two buses waiting to take you to the airport. Beyond here, you will not be allowed to leave or to resign this mission for any reason. Is that clear."

It was not a question, but a statement of fact.

Brady gave them another moment, then he said grimly, "All right. You are all now volunteers. We leave tonight for a forward base camp for training. You will not be told where this base camp is. Nor will you be told who your mission is against or in what country."

He paused then to let the last sink in. A few heads jerked up at his words; a few men got worried frowns.

"Let me say," he added, "that your mission will not violate the personal or national patriotism of any of you. Nor will it be in direct conflict with the interests of your nations of origin."

In the audience, Ruger whispered, not to anyone, but to himself, "It's a game. It's all a bloody game."

"There is one further point," Brady said grimly, "that you need to know right now. Any man who attempts to communicate with anyone except those in this room, those who supervise the training, or any other members of this mission will be considered to have jeopardized the success of this mission and he will be shot. Is that clear."

Again, it was not a question.

"This operation," Brady said, "will be conducted at all times as a military mission and you will be considered to be under military law with myself as the final judge and arbiter. Failure to comply with the military code will be dealt with accordingly. That's all."

As Brady stepped from the platform, Carlton-Brooks snapped to. "ATTENTION!" he roared. The men scrambled to their feet as Brady walked down the center aisle and out the back door.

Carlton-Brooks said loudly, "As your name is called, you will stand down and board the bus at the side door. File out smartly." He swung up the clipboard by his side and called out, "Aggagin, George! Bocca, Leodro! Bottoms, Timothy! . . ."

The men filed slowly out of the meeting room. Some of them were apprehensive, some puzzled and curious; Gerry Ruger was insane with delight. Even at attention he couldn't keep the grin off his face or keep from whispering, "Here we go! Oh, here we go! No more business forms, no more rotting in that fucking city! Ho, ho, ho, ho!"

And then they were trotting out into the starry night. Before them were two chartered buses, their engines turning over with a throttled hum. As they came up to the door of the second bus, Ruger halted in surprise. "Why look, chaps! Here's Dougie Lord."

Lord was standing by the door of the bus, his sergeant's baton tucked up under his arm. Business-like, he said, "In you go, lads. No loitering. In quickly! Snap it! Snap it!"

He wore a side arm, as did the six men under his command. It was like the old days in the Congo.

Inside, the bus was lighted, but there were blackout curtains over the windows. Schneider was looking down, though it took a man who knew him very well to spot it. But Ruger could read it, and he slapped the German on the shoulder. "Com'on now, Wilf. None of it, lad! It's a game," he said, for the innumerable time since the call had come, "all a bloody game. So what if you get your bleeding head shot off and your wife and kids are husbandless and father-less. Forget it! It don't mean bloody aught! It's all a game, lad! It's all bloody rot!"

Schneider said, heaving himself up, "This is a very serious operation, I think. I believe we will earn our money."

"And did you hear that?" Ruger said excitedly. "Doubled the old pay bag. And no man below a sergeant. Which ain't all that big for us because we were already bloody ser-geants, but what about it? Hey? What's up, I say? Big doings, hey?"

But they got no further, for the buses were loaded and Dougie Lord was climbing aboard theirs, followed by three other military policemen. He stood stiffly at the front. "We are now pulling out. Remain in your seats and do not, I repeat, do not pull back the blackout curtains or in any other way try to see out or permit this bus to be seen into. Smoking will be permitted!"

Matthew Brady stood by his car until he'd seen the buses loaded and their doors shut. Then he climbed in and set out. He paid no attention to the buses that were following, but drove rapidly toward his destination. They were not depart-ing from the main airport, were instead using a small, vir-tually deserted landing strip far out of town that had once been a military base but was now in rare use by general aviation. Brady drove automatically, his mind on details of the operation. There were so many loose ends, so many strings floating in the water. Some of them were worrying him, even at that late date.

Damn it, he thought angrily as he drove. That's unpro-fessional. You do the job a step at a time, and you do it the best you can and don't walk around sweating the out-come like some fucking amateur.

Out on the lonely airstrip, Cody stood in the night, smoking. Behind him was the silhouette of a DC-3. Down the line a hundred yards, another stood, all rounded outline against the light sky, its big vertical stabilizer sticking up like a misshapen pie wedge. The pilot of the other plane was beside him, a Canadian named Arthur Edge. He was older than Cody, 45; a bulky man with thinning hair, dressed in a flight suit and a nylon jacket against the night chill. Cody looked at his watch. It was ten after eleven.

"Ought to be here soon," he said.

"Yeah," Edge answered. He glanced up to the sky. "It's clear as a fucking bell," he said. "Thank God."

"Yes," Cody said.

He didn't know a great deal about the pilot. Weston had procured him, and he'd been there waiting when they'd returned from Rhodesia. He had been a military pilot and then had knocked around all over the world. His last job had been for an Israeli nonsked cargo operation. But while Weston had brought him in, Cody had had the last word on the man's ability. And after a short time in the right seat beside Edge, he'd recognized a touch almost as subtle as his own. To Weston's relief, he'd given his OK.

They'd spent the last week checking out the two DC-3s that had suddenly appeared. The planes were of 1946 manufacture, but they were in sound shape, the big engines recently given a major overhaul. Inside, they'd been fitted with thirty-five narrow canvas seats. The little chairs almost filled the cargo hull, barely leaving room for a narrow aisle down one side.

Cody had told Brady he was flirting with the thin edge of the possible. A load of thirty-five men, not to mention their gear, seriously overloaded the airplanes. It meant flying with half tanks, with very little reserve.

Some genius of a maintenance man had installed modified STOL kits on the leading edges of the wings that improved the bird's short takeoff and landing characteristics. That was what made the flying barely possible.

"How do you feel about it, Art?" Cody asked, flipping his cigarette away in the night and watching it hit the concrete and burst into a thousand sparks.

"Hell," Edge said, "I feel tip-top. Why not?"

"Why not indeed," Cody said.

He wondered, standing there, if he would have taken Edge's job. In the final analysis, Edge was not going to be a pilot but an airplane chauffeur. The magnetic compass and the directional gyro and all the radio navigational aids had been taken out of the second airplane. All that was left were the primary group of instruments for maintaining the airplane in flight and a single two-way VHF radio. The pilot of the second airplane had only one job—to follow Cody and land where he did. Cody had argued with Brady about this, but it hadn't done any good.

"Listen," Brady had told him, "you're thinking like a fucking fly-boy, worrying about your brother airman. Get that shit out of your mind. This is a military operation and you're my second officer. That comes first. Is that clear? You object to this because you would feel that way if it were being done to you. But it's not. And the guy's happy. And we don't have to worry about him knowing too much. All he's got to do is keep that airplane on your tail, and if he's the pilot you say he is, he ought to be able to do that."

"Yeah," he said now, for no reason, "it's going to be all right."

"What, Major?"

Cody shook his head. "Nothing. Just thinking out loud." He swung around. "Don't you wonder what you're getting into?"

Art shrugged. "Hell, do you ever really know, anyway? No matter what you're doing? It's all the same. And the pay's good, so screw it."

Which is a hell of a good attitude, Cody thought.

Art said, "I been flying them for twenty-five years for first this guy and then that. It gets to where it makes less difference every year who it's for. You just point the nose in the right direction and keep the wings level. That's all it ever comes down to. Anything else is just excess weight and balance to worry about. So I say to hell with it."

He walked away from Edge, walking toward the runway until he was in front of the airplanes. He turned and looked back at them. The breeze was freshening, and he could feel just a hint of moisture in it. He looked at the two airplanes standing there, and it made him think of one day in a little town in Texas. It had been maybe six or seven years ago. He had been flying somewhere and put down at dusk into Conroe. As he'd made his approach, he'd noticed a line of old planes sitting off the runway, back on a deserted ramp. Big airplanes, old Convairs and DC-3s. While his plane was being refueled, he'd asked the man about them. The man had just shrugged and said they'd been there a couple of years. Belonged to some guy who'd bought them at an auction. They'd been flyable then and he'd brought them there because the parking space was cheap. Since then, they'd just sat there.

Cody had walked out the ramp. He'd walked out there among those old, obsolete airplanes, eight or nine of them in a row. He'd walked out there and just stood looking at them. The paint was fading, but he could still see OZARK AIRWAYS along the fuselage of one and LAKEWAY AIRLINES on another. They'd been cannibalized. All of the props were gone and here and there an engine was missing, leaving the wing looking somehow crippled and embarrassed.

A bay door was standing half-opened on a DC-3, the short stairs still in place. He'd gone up the stairs into the airplane and into the passenger cabin. He'd stood there for a moment, in the back of the plane, beside the stripped steward's compartment. Nothing but the bare aluminum frame remaining, all the trays gone, all the storage compartments gone.

He'd walked forward, going up the slanted aisle. The upholstered seats were still in place, though they were starting to mold. Up forward, there was the lounge, with a table. He looked in one of the recessed ashtrays. It was full of old cigarette butts. He picked up one and broke it between his fingers. It was brittle. He turned and looked back, thinking of the people who'd sat in those seats. Some of the overhead had broken loose from the ceiling and the insulation was drooping down.

He passed into the flight deck, stopping in the little aisle behind the cockpit where the big electrical equipment and the cabin heaters were installed. There was an aircraft log on the floor. He'd picked it up and read a few of the entries: "Directional finder erratic" or "One hundred rpm drop number one engine." Each entry was signed with the scribble of some long gone pilot. Long gone and his airplane forgotten.

He'd gone further forward and eased himself into the command pilot's seat. Sitting there, he'd taken the control yoke in his hands and pulled. It was stiff but it came back. He looked out the port window as he turned it left and right, watching the ailerons react. They still worked.

The instrument panel had been cannibalized of all the radios. But everything else was still there. He'd reached up and flicked the mag switches for the engines, number one and number two. Then he'd punched the buttons for the boost pumps.

"Switches on," he'd said, feeling very bad. The wind was whistling through the broken windshield, and he could smell the mustiness of the old, forgotten airplane.

"Ah, the hell with it," he'd suddenly said. He'd let go of the yoke and turned out of the seat and made his way down.

He hadn't looked back as he'd walked toward the little terminal.

He'd paid the man for the gas and the man had said that he thought the guy was coming pretty soon to cut the old airplanes up into scrap metal. "They're just junk and we're going to have to raise the rent pretty soon. But they ought to bring a pretty good price for scrap."

Flying away in his modern plane, he had felt very bad. Those airplanes, he'd thought, had been the best at one time. When they were new, there'd been nothing better and the pilots who'd flown them had been proud. And now they were done, and they just sat there on that ramp with the wind whistling through their dying members.

He stood there in the night in Africa looking at the two old DC-3s. These were a couple of old war-horses, he thought, but they could still go. They still had a purpose.

Well, that was the purpose. Don't ever let them cut you up into scrap. Make it count, whatever it was for.

Well, he thought, any place I can fly into I'm going to fly out of.

He turned and walked back to where Edge was standing. His mood was starting to lift. "Hell, Captain," he said, "we got a nice night for a flight."

"I agree," Edge said.

A pair of headlights suddenly pitted the dark. They came on, growing larger. The car stopped a few yards away, and Brady got out. He came toward them, carrying a military canvas suitcase. Without a word, he walked by, pitched the suitcase in the open door of the airplane, then turned back. "I'll ride with you," he said to Cody. He looked them over in silence for a moment. "You both ready?"

Cody nodded, but Edge said, "Yeah, if that overloaded craft will get off the ground."

Brady swung on him. He said, "Captain, I didn't ask you for conditions."

Edge said, as evenly as Brady, "Colonel, if I didn't think I could fly that thing, I wouldn't be standing here in a flight suit."

Cody turned away to suppress a slight smile.

Then, they all three just stood waiting until the buses arrived. Under orders of silence, the men filed off the buses and into the planes. The military policemen stood at the doors urging them on and warning, "No smoking, no smoking."

When they were all in, Cody wished Edge luck and then climbed aboard. Brady was right behind him, and they made their way up the narrow aisle of the slanted fuselage. It was totally dark inside, with blackout curtains over all the passenger compartment windows. Cody squeezed past the last row of seats and slipped into the cockpit. It was lighter there, moonlight streaming in through the windows. He waited until Brady was in the copilot's seat, then closed the cockpit door and started flicking on switches.

Moments later, they were booming down the dark runway, the landing lights throwing beams far out into the darkness. The airplane lifted off smoothly, better than Cody had expected, and then they were climbing. The radio suddenly said, "Coco one this is Coco two. Right behind you. Believe it or not, this thing is flying."

They circled for altitude over the airport, turning through the compass twice. With that and the blacked out windows, none of the men would have any idea in which direction they were heading. Or, when they landed, what country they were in.

They flew five hundred miles almost due north and landed on a little sod strip outside a former British South African Police training depot. Convoy trucks were there waiting, parked by the side of the strip. Once again, the transfer was made and then, with the military police driving, they made the short trek into the camp. In the dark moonlight, the camp did not look nearly as drab and featureless as it would under the hot sun. They drove into the compound; the gate was shut and locked behind them. For their purposes, it was ideal. It was fifty miles from anything and there was a ten-foot-high barbed wire fence around the whole enclosure.

Brady watched as the men got out. Carlton-Brooks came up and stood by. Brady said, "Get them bedded down. Reveille at six." Carlton-Brooks said, "Well, we're off. We've begun at last."

16

Forward Camp, South Africa

The camp was at the northern tip of South Africa, a few miles from the Rhodesia border. The nearest town was Messina, but there was no way to get there. No roads ran near the camp, except the ruts that led three miles to the little dirt airstrip. It was set in the midst of a sea of little rolling hills with nothing to break the force of the sun that burned down fourteen hours a day except the hills that were scantily covered with thin underbrush and thorn trees; that and rocks and hot, baking rust-stained soil. The location and its hardships had been deliberately selected as a training ground for antiterrorist commandos of the British South African Police. It had been turned over intact and empty to Brady and his men.

Inside the forbidding fence, the compound consisted of eight barracks, a small headquarters shack, and a larger mess hall that doubled as an assembly room. The buildings were low, flat topped, plastered and whitewashed to a whiteness that was almost blinding in the sun and against the red dirt background. The walls of the buildings were thick, with little square windows.

There would be no outside communication. The only

phone line came to the single phone in Brady's office and sleeping quarters. The support duties of cooking and maintenance and guard duty would be handled by Dougie Lord and his six military policemen. Other housekeeping duties would be handled by the men on a rotation basis from the enlisted ranks. The food would be kept simple: meat three times a day with potatoes and rice and canned vegetables and fresh fruits. A complete dietary schedule had been worked out by trained people before they had left Johannesburg. The intent of the diet was to assist the men in being as conditioned as they could. An athletic dietician had been called in. He'd said, knowing nothing, "You train, gentlemen, on proteins. You play a game or fight a battle on starches." So they would train on a high-protein diet, building muscle and stamina.

And though it had been against the dietician's advice, there would be a daily allotment of two bottles of beer per man and a once-a-week allotment of a pint of liquor.

Brady and Cody Ravel and Carlton-Brooks were barracked in the headquarters shack. They each had a room to themselves, though Brady's bedroom adjoined the orderly room, which was considered his office as well as the dining area for the three officers.

Art Edge was barracked separately. He would have nothing to do until he and Cody began practicing for the actual operation. He had been put under strict orders to discuss nothing relating to the mission with anyone. Cody thought he was going to have a very boring time.

They were up that first morning at five. At half past, their breakfast was brought over to them, coffee and fried beef and bread. They ate on a little table in the center of the orderly room.

No one spoke until they'd finished eating. Brady was through first and he shoved back his plate and lit a cigarette, waiting for the other two to finish. Under his look, Carlton-Brooks began to eat faster, but Cody went on deliberately. He wasn't particularly hungry, but he saw what Brady was doing.

Finally, Brady barked at him, "Goddammit, Cody, com'on!"

Cody gave him a bland look. "Something wrong, Colonel?"

"You sonofabitch," Brady said. Then he looked down with distaste at the cigarette he was smoking. "Goddamn this African tobacco," he said. "I'd give fifty dollars for a carton of American cigarettes, no matter what brand."

Cody said, "It's the regulation brand, Colonel. We're all smoking the same thing."

Brady gave him a sour look and glanced down at his watch. He, as well as every man in the camp, was wearing a standard military hack watch, obtained from the United States by Weston. He saw that it was almost six o'clock. "All right," he growled.

Cody pushed his plate away.

Brady looked at Carlton-Brooks.

The major didn't look good: his eyes were red and watery, and his hand was obviously trembling as he took a sip of coffee. Because he'd been in charge of inspecting the duffel that the men had been issued, he'd managed to secrete six bottles of Scotch in his own. And after the long flight, he'd sat up in his room drinking the Scotch straight out of the bottle. He hadn't meant to do it, and he'd resolved that he was going to make use of this time in camp to get himself straightened out. He'd brought the Scotch because he knew what the liquor allotment was going to be and it had frightened him. He needed so much liquor each day to be able to function, and the allotment wouldn't be enough. So he'd brought the supplement, just enough, he'd told himself, to begin tapering off. And then he'd drunk up a substantial portion of his reserve in one night. He was disgusted with himself.

He could see the look Brady was giving him, and he was suddenly afraid that the colonel knew. He put the coffee cup down quickly to hide his trembling hand and lit a cigarette, trying to look relaxed.

But Brady said, "Major, you have been brought along on this operation as a training officer. Your function will be to regulate the training that I design and to carry out any orders I give or transmit through Major Ravel here. No one is going to have a brief on this mission with the exception of myself."

The adjutant glanced over at Cody. He didn't believe Brady was the only one that knew. He felt certain the pilot knew. But that didn't matter to him.

Which was what Brady was saying. He gave Carlton-Brooks a look and said with emphasis, "It could be dangerous knowing the details of this mission. Therefore, except for mealtimes and those occasions on my express orders, this office is off limits to yourself and every other man in this camp. I think you understand the reasons for that. And I want a twenty-four-hour guard posted outside that door, and I want this room secured at all times that I'm not occupying it. Is that clear."

"Certainly, sir," Carlton-Brooks said stiffly. "Does that include Major Ravel, sir?"

Brady didn't answer him. Instead, he gave him that thoughtful look and said, "Major, I'd be pleased if you'd on occasion show some judgment on your own initiative. You are supposedly an intelligent man. Make me aware of it."

"Very good, sir," Carlton-Brooks said.

A knock sounded at the door.

Carlton-Brooks said, "That would be Sergeant Major Lord, sir. He's reporting per your orders."

"Good. Let him in."

Dougie Lord marched in, his sergeant's baton under his

arm. He advanced to two paces from the breakfast table, and came to attention, slamming down his boots, one, two. "Sir!" he cried.

Brady looked at him curiously. "At ease, Sergeant," he said. He knew about Sergeant Lord. He knew that Carlton-Brooks had thought he was pulling something by running in the overage soldier. But that was all right with Brady. He'd taken the trouble to find out about Lord and the man suited his purposes.

"Sergeant, you will be under the direct orders of Major Carlton-Brooks here. And you and he, and the six men under your command, have the direct responsibility for the security of this camp. If any man gets outside or makes any contact outside, it's going to be trouble. Is that clear."

Lord came to attention, stamping his boots loudly. "Sir!" he said.

These old soldiers did have a style, Brady thought. Though it was a little loud in a small room.

"At ease," Brady said. "Are the men at breakfast?"

"Yes, sir!"

"Good. You report back to me when they've finished. We're to have a meeting at seven. You're dismissed, Sergeant."

Lord saluted with his baton, came to attention, and marched out of the room.

Brady said to the adjutant, mildly, using his given name for the first time, "Jack, tone him down a little, will you?"

Carlton-Brooks said, still stiffly, "He's trying very hard to please you, sir. He's an old soldier."

"I realize that. But just take a little of the edge off him. He's gonna deafen me slamming those boots down. We're in camp now and we've got a thorough training schedule in front of us, so we had better keep it as even as we can. Is that clear."

"Very, sir."

"You got that material set up for the meeting?"

"Yes, sir."

"All right. You're dismissed. Report to me at one o'clock and we'll go over the training schedule."

"Very good, sir."

Carlton-Brooks left.

Cody looked over at Brady and slowly shook his head. "Why don't you get off that guy's ass, Matt. You done got him so scared of you, he's afraid to piss without permission."

Brady looked thoughtful for a long moment. Then he gradually leaned back in his chair. He lit a cigarette. "I know it," he finally said. "And it's deliberate. I got a tough job to do, Cody." He looked over at the pilot. "And I got a tough bunch of men to do it with. This isn't the Army or the Marine Corps, in which I got the weight of the Congress and the will of God behind me. All I got is a little money and myself to hold these people together. I got to make 'em afraid of me. I got to make them fear that to fuck up with me is worse than a whipping from their daddy. I got to make them believe that not to answer an order instantly is worse than pissing in the collection plate. This is a tough bunch. A hard bunch." He gestured with his hand. "There's not a one of them sonofabitches doesn't think he ain't the meanest bastard ever walked through the valley. So I got to use every resource to invoke that fear, I can't do it on an individual basis."

He stopped and pulled on his cigarette for a moment.

Then he said, "One of the ways I got to do it is to take a weak bastard like Carlton-Brooks and just scare the living shit out of him. He's going to be around the men more than you and I. And they're going to smell it off him. They don't none of them know me; they never saw me before last night. So I got to get to 'em quick. And one of the ways is to use a guy like Carlton-Brooks to put out the odor. Pretty soon, they're all going to smell it and the word's going to get around, 'Better not fuck with the colonel. And if he says shit, then you squat. And if he says frog, then you god-damn well better jump.' " He looked over at Cody. "It ain't an easy job."

"No," Cody said, "it's not." He looked away, wondering how a man got so sure of himself that he could do the job that Brady had taken. It must be wonderful, he thought. Just slam ass wonderful. All that purpose. He said, "I'd hate to be sitting there, in your chair. All by myself."

"By myself?" Brady laughed. He picked up one of the table knives and flung it at the wall. It bounced away craz-ily. Then he looked over at Cody and laughed again. "What the hell you think I got you here for, cowboy? You're in it with me."

Dawn came as they walked out the door and down the white rock-lined walk. Out in front of the headquarters shack was a bare flagpole, set in the middle of a little circle of white rocks. The rope to raise the flag had long ago frayed and ruined, but, in the dry air, the flagpole was still as shiny and unmarked as when it had first been erected.

It was already hot. Inside the compound fence, there was not a single growing plant. Not a sprig of grass. It was all hot, baking red dust.

Cody said, "Jesus, what a hole."

But Brady said with satisfaction, "It's perfect. Ideal."

They paused just outside the mess hall door. Cody watched Brady mentally straightening. Even as Cody watched, his face got harder, his eyes flat and penetrating. He never slouched, but now he was even more erect. "All right," he said brusquely, "let's go in, Major."

Sergeant Major Lord was stationed at the door and he immediately leaped to attention as they came in. " 'TEHN-SHUN!" he roared.

The men came to their feet to the sound of chairs being pushed back. As Brady marched up the center aisle, Jack Carlton-Brooks fell in step two paces behind him. Cody drifted to the side and leaned up against the wall.

The men looked tired and drawn. They had finally bedded down at two A.M. and then had been routed out at six.

"At ease!" Carlton-Brooks said. And, "Be seated." He waited until they had settled down and said, "All right, gentlemen, let me have your attention. Some of you have had mercenary experience, some not. It is to be strictly understood that this expedition will be conducted at all times along precise military lines that all of you are already familiar with. All military courtesies will be rendered—with the exception of saluting. Your permanent party officers are myself, the colonel commanding, Captain Edge, second pilot, and at this time I should like to introduce the executive officer and chief pilot. At the back of the room is Major Ravel."

The men turned to look at him, and Cody slowly pushed away from the wall and stood erect. He could see Gerry Ruger staring at him curiously. A little further back in the room he saw John Peters.

"Your attention," Carlton-Brooks said. "As of this seating, you are all of equal rank. Squadleaders and officers will be picked at a time in the future. A very immediate time in the future, I might add. Now—" He consulted the clipboard he was holding.

"As to housekeeping. Security in this camp is directly under the charge of Sergeant Major Lord. Any breaches or suggestions should be directed toward him.

"At the conclusion of the colonel's remarks, you are to assemble on the parade ground. From there, you will be told off to draw additional uniforms and your other gear and weapons. At the back of this mess hall is a bulletin board. You will consult that as you leave. You will find your name posted to one of three strike groups, Able, Baker, Charlie. Henceforth, all training schedules will be posted on that board, and you will refer to it each morning. You may expect this first week to be given up largely to physical conditioning and weapons familiarization." He stopped and straightened slightly. "On this first day, I have the honor to wish you good luck and success on the mission that is to come. You may remain seated as the colonel addresses you."

Brady had been standing at the back. When Carlton-Brooks stepped aside, he didn't move for a long moment. Finally, he stepped forward, slowly. He had thrust his hands into his back pockets which made his chest bulge even further. He walked slowly down the first row of tables, looking intently into each face. Then he stopped and let his eyes rove slowly over the rest of the room. There was nothing in his face. After a moment, he walked back to the little raised platform and turned to face them.

He said, in that flat voice of his, the country accent giving it even more force, "We're having this meeting this morning to put you in the picture of what to expect and what I expect of you. And to answer your questions. Following this meeting you will have no further questions. The reason for that is I'm going to tell you everything you need to know and everything you *can* know. After that, you might as well save your breath because you're not going to get any answers. And I'm not going to like the questions." He stopped and let his eyes, once again, move over the room. "And believe me—you are going to come to be goddamn interested in what I like and dislike. Now—"

He turned and walked away several paces and then came back to the center of the platform. "You've been wondering for a long time what you were off on. Well, now I'm going to tell you."

He stopped and the men, almost unconsciously, leaned forward to hear the next words.

"This is a destroy mission," he said. "Completely unlike any you've ever done in any of your military careers. It will be of brief duration. You have been told to expect to be out three months. It may be a shorter time. We've got six objectives. Six enemy camps that we intend to destroy. My intentions are to take them three at a time with twenty-one-man combat teams assigned to the destruction of each. If that holds true then, each man here can expect to make two raids. Only two." He looked them over. "And for that, you're going to be damn well-paid. At a minimum, each man in this room ought to get at least five or six thousand dollars in base pay. In addition, if we're successful, totally successful, there'll be a ten-thousand-dollar bonus per man."

A murmur ran through the room. Sergeant Major Lord started to shout them into silence, but Brady held up his hand. "Let them think about it, Sergeant."

He walked up and down in front of them for half a minute. Then he said, "That's a lot of money. But I want a lot for my money. And I'll get it from you."

He waited, letting it sink in. Then he said, "You are about to enter the toughest physical and mission execution training you've ever been exposed to. I do not intend that this mission should fail for want of preparation. Besides the physical conditioning, you are going to know your objective, you are going to know your every move down to the last inch. When we move out of here, there will not be a single one of you who is not totally familiar and practiced, not only in your own job, but in the jobs of every man in your combat team. You will know your job and your objective and your enemy so well that you may well have a damn hard time trying to *forget* it in years to come."

There was a pointer lying on a table that had been set up for him and he picked it up.

"Now," he said, "we come to a point you better pay really good attention to. There may be some of you sitting out there who are beginning to wonder what you're doing here. Maybe some of you have been having a damn good time running round playing with the booze and the broads and the idea of all this hard work doesn't appeal to you. Maybe a few of you are starting to wonder just how you can get out of here and get back to civilization. Maybe a few of you have heard what a great life it is to be a mercenary, and you thought you'd come and try it just for the hell of it. Run, shoot, fuck, and loot. And maybe you're sitting there thinking this ain't nothing like you'd expected. And where's the door. Well . . ."

He leaned toward them holding the pointer out in front of him with both hands like a man with a bayoneted rifle. "I got some news for you. *Forget* it. You're here and you're staying." His voice was not harsh so much as it was direct and impersonal. "There're two ways out of this. One is when we successfully complete this mission and you arrive back in Johannesburg with fifteen thousand dollars in your pocket. The other is if you attempt a departure on your own initiative. That will result in being buried out there on that bald ass prairie. In that sand."

He stopped then and stepped back and lit a cigarette. After a puff or two, he came back to the front of the platform.

"But it's not all bad news," he said. "It is my full intention to complete this mission, successfully, and to arrive back in Johannesburg with all seventy of you in more or less the same condition you left. You may put absolute trust and faith in one element and that's me. I know how to do it. I know how to run this mission. I'm thirty-four years in the military and I've commanded every kind of combat there is to experience. I know my job. And I intend to see that you know yours. So you can stop and rest assured that you ain't in the hands of some fucking amateur. You do your job and you do it well, and we're all going to get along.

"And another point on the plus side. In this room are maybe the best seventy fighting men I ever saw. Within this room is maybe more combat and training experience than you could find in any other seventy men anywhere in the world. We've got commandos and combat rangers and Special Forces men from every army that's worth a shit. So you can depend on the man next to you. I know you're good. And I know you're tough. That's why you're here. That's why you're drawing the kind of money that you are. So I don't expect anything less than the best. All right, that's understood." He gave them another long look from his appraising eyes. "So let's move along. I'm going to give you a preliminary look at your enemy. Sergeant."

He stepped aside as Dougie Lord rushed forward to draw down a large projecting screen. Others of Lord's men drew the shutters to darken the room. The slide projector came on. Brady said, "I'm going to show you the work of your enemy, gentlemen."

There flashed on the screen a series of mutilated bodies: disemboweled, burned, disfigured, butchered, beaten to death. The pictures were of women and children as well as men.

Brady said, "Your enemy is a terrorist. A political insurgent who strikes mainly at the civilian population, seldom coming in direct contact with regular military forces. He operates from a series of bases in supposedly neutral territory."

The slides were flashing in a steady progression, thirty seconds to each slide.

Brady said, "He's Chinese communist armed and trained and led. Some of you who have participated in past mercenary campaigns in Africa have developed a contempt for the black rebel as a fighting man. Forget it. This soldier is a hell of a lot better than anything you've run on before. Any of you who view this as an exercise in target-shooting niggers in the bush had damn well better forget it. Such thinking will get you killed."

The screen went dark and Dougie Lord said, "That's the lot on that, sir."

"Run the next," Brady ordered.

It was photographs of the terrorist bases, furnished, as all the material was, by Neal Hall.

"This," Brady said, using his pointer, "is a preliminary look at your objective."

He said, "These larger buildings you see here are barracks. They will hold, at the time of our strike, between sixty and seventy men each. The construction is going to vary from camp to camp, but in the main, they are native built of board siding with thatched roofs. In each camp, you will find one, or possibly two, brick or concrete structures. These are occupied by the Chinese cadre and the permanent party members of the camp. The camp commander, political commissars, instructors. These will be hard-core objectives. At each camp, you will run into black Africans who are acting as instructors. These will be accomplished fighters. They will have received intensive military and motivational training in Cuba, mainland China, Russia, and the African states such as Ghana and Tanzania. Notice especially that these bases are in extremely remote areas."

An aerial photograph flicked on. Brady said, "You can tell that particularly from this overfly view. In most cases, there are no roads leading into the camps. The recruits and all supplies are brought in overland through the bush and depart the same way."

He stopped and looked at them, tapping the base of the pointer on the floor. "That is the same way we will arrive at these camps. Which, for us, is going to mean very long and hazardous approaches and difficult terrain while hand-carrying all equipment and weapons. You may begin to see, from this, the necessity of the conditioning."

The last slide clicked off. Brady put his pointer on the table. "Each of these camps," he said, "on our best information, will contain between one hundred and two hundred insurgents. You will be outnumbered anywhere from ten to twenty to one. You will now begin to understand the necessity of a well-coordinated, well-prepared operation. To sum up the general objective, we are going to routine this exercise until you can do it in your sleep. Then we are going to commit it with the greatest degree of violence modern arms and methods will permit. This is the simplest way I can put it. Your mission is total destruction, total annihilation. If a single enemy escapes from a camp that we attack, I will consider that you have failed." He straightened. "You have now had as broad a briefing as I can give you at this time. Are there any questions?"

He asked it as a test, a test of his will and of the men before him. He had made it clear that he would not welcome questions. Now he stood and waited. He had expected that there would have to be some sort of showdown this morning.

At the back, a hand went up. A voice came. "I have a question."

"State it," Brady said. He was looking at the man, who did not rise.

The man said, "Begging the colonel's pardon, I'd like to know where the fuck we are and where the fuck we're going." His accent was heavy cockney. He said, "I never been on any bloody expedition I didn't know sum'at about where I ruddy was. What if a bloke gets separated from his unit?"

A little murmur ran through the room and some of the men were nodding their heads. Brady let it die down before he asked, in a mild voice, "What's your name, trooper?"

"Wilkes," the man said, "George Wilkes."

Brady stepped down off the small rostrum and started up the aisle toward the man. As he walked, he did a quick mental review. He knew the background and all the pertinent data on every one of them. Now, he thought, Wilkes, George W., Royal Commandos, trained parachutist, trained underwater demolitions man. Thirty-one years old. Nine years conventional military service. A tough, capable soldier.

He arrived at the table. Wilkes was looking up at him in surprise, a twinge of fear starting to color his face.

Brady said in a low, driving voice, "On your feet, soldier." He waited until Wilkes had slowly stood up. Then he. pushed his face to within six inches of the soldier's and said, biting the words off murderously, "Soldier, the next time you speak to me or any other officer of this command, you will be in a position of ATTENTION! NOW HIT IT!"

Wilkes snapped, the color draining from his face.

Brady was leaning into him even closer. His voice was like a physical force, lashing and striking the soldier. "YOU BETTER HIT IT, MISTER! YOU BETTER FREEZE! YOU BETTER TURN TO STONE! DON'T YOU FLICK AN EYELASH! DON'T YOU EVEN BLINK!"

He stood there like that for a full moment, staring straight into Wilkes' unseeing eyes. A thin film of perspiration had broken out on the soldier's forehead. Without moving his eyes, the colonel said, "Sergeant Major Lord. Take special note of this man. If he makes the slightest fuckup, either in military courtesy or regulations, he goes straight to the sweatbox for one week on water only. And mister," he said, coming back to Wilkes, "if it's anything serious, I'll have you shot so fucking fast your soul will be in hell before your body hits the ground." He suddenly roared, "IS THAT CLEAR!"

"Sir!" Wilkes said. He was beginning to tremble.

"LOUDER, GODDAMMIT. I CAN'T HEAR YOU!"

"SIR!"

"LOUDER!"

"*SIR!*"

Finally, Brady stepped back. He gave Wilkes one last, thoughtful look and then turned away, leaving the soldier still in the rigid position of attention.

Back on the rostrum, he turned to the audience. In an ordinary voice, he said, "Now, I'll answer the soldier's question." He leaned forward slightly. "You don't have to worry about getting separated from your unit because you will not let yourself become separated. It is primary to this mission that the integrity of the combat team be maintained at all times. Is that clear.

"The only men," he said, "that you will not report back with will be dead men. And they will have been verified by at least two members of the team. And let me explain it so you'll understand. Any team that loses one of its members—leaves him behind wounded or allows him to be captured—will lose their bonuses! No matter how successful this mission is. That team will not participate in the bonuses. A loss of ten thousand dollars per man."

A murmur ran rapidly through the room, stopped immediately by Sergeant Lord's roar of "SILENCE IN THE RANKS!"

From the rostrum, Brady could see the men giving each other looks. He had reached them.

"One last point," he said. "You men have all come on this mission of your own free wills. The conditions were explained to you before you boarded the bus in Johannesburg. I, therefore, consider that every one of you has accepted my conditions. So," and he looked around the room, "you had better get ready to live with them."

He stepped off the rostrum and started for the door.

"Matt," Cody said, "I got to talk to you."

They were in the office. Brady was at his desk and Cody was sitting in a chair ten feet away.

Brady turned from his desk. He was wearing steel-rimmed glasses, the glasses incongruous on his hard face. He took them off and rubbed his eyes with a thumb and forefinger. "Speak," he said.

Cody looked down at the floor. "Look, Matt, I don't know about this business of pulling exec."

Brady gave him a look. "What are you talking about, cowboy?"

He said, still not looking up, "I'm not sure I want to be your executive officer, Matt."

"Why not?"

"Well, Matt, I hired on to fly the airplane. True, I accepted the responsibility for crucial information. And I can handle that. But I don't want a ground command. And I especially don't want a combat command."

There, he thought. It's out, at least.

Brady suddenly looked very tired. He shook his head slowly, his face much older.

"Why not? Why don't you want the job?"

"I just don't."

"That's no reason."

"It's the best I can give you."

Brady rubbed his hand across his face. "Look, let's table this for the moment. I don't want to talk about it right now."

"But I do. We got to talk about it right now. I got to get it straight with you."

Brady took his hand away from his face and looked at Cody for a long, thoughtful moment. "I'm going to play straight with you. This chair at the head of the class gets a little hard sometimes. A little uncomfortable. I got a lot of weight on me. I goddamn near got more on my plate than I can say grace over. And I've got to have me some help. I got to have me at least one man that I can count on one hundred percent. And you're it."

"No," Cody said.

"Bullshit, no."

"I ain't kidding, Matt. It don't got to be me. You got seventy combat soldiers in this camp and any one of them would be of more help than I can."

"No, you're wrong. There's seventy damn good combat troops here, but none of them are leadership material in your class. There's some can lead a squad and some that can lead a combat team. But that's not what we're talking about. I didn't pick you because I liked the way you combed your hair. I picked you because you're the best man for the job."

"You've got the wrong man," Cody said. He looked away. "I'm a pilot."

"Bullshit," Brady said sharply. "I've seen photostats of your service records. Maybe you never read your efficiency reports, but I did. You get A pluses for leadership and initiative. Especially in combat. So don't hand me that line, cowboy."

Cody got up and walked to the far wall with the little windows that were too high to see out. He lit a cigarette.

"All that don't mean shit, Matt," he said finally. "The point is, I won't do it. That's straight." He cut his hand through the air. "That's final."

Brady looked at him a long time. Finally, he picked up a pencil and tossed it across his desk. It hit and rolled off the edge. He said, "The pilot's got to know and the exec officer would have to know the details of this mission. But I got 'em both in one package, and if you think I'm going to waste that, you're out of your fucking mind."

"No," Cody said.

"Well, I'm a bastard." Brady leaned back in his chair, the swivel creaking. "Listen, what the hell is going on here? Have you suddenly gone crazy? What is all this about, anyway?"

"It doesn't matter."

"The hell it don't matter!" Brady's feet came to the floor with a thump. "You can tell me a hell of a lot of things, but don't tell me it don't matter. *I'll* decide that. Now, what the hell has put the goddamn burr under your tail?" His voice suddenly rose, harshly. "And I want answers, mister, not a picture of your goddamn back! You turn around here and answer me!"

"Okay," Cody said. "Okay, okay." He left the windows and came to stand in front of Brady. "I saw you up there today, Matt. I saw you handling those troops! I saw you convincing them that the most important thing they ever better do in their lives is to carry out this mission. Well, I can't do that! You understand? I don't give a shit if we get those bases or not!" He leaned across the desk, spacing his words for emphasis. "Did you hear me? Did it get through? I don't give a shit! And I fucking well don't want the responsibility. Now, you got that?"

He suddenly wheeled away and sat down in a chair in the corner. The hand holding his cigarette was trembling.

There was silence in the room for a long moment, and then Brady laughed. It was an ugly sound. "You little fucking frizztail."

"You better watch it, Matt," Cody said. He didn't look up.

"Watch it?" The chair creaked ominously. "I don't have to watch it, cowboy. *You* do!"

"Fuck you, Brady. I signed on to fly the airplane and that's it. That's *it*! You understand?"

Brady laughed again, but there was no humor in it. "You hide behind that airplane, don't you, Cody? You've got a little chickenshit talent, and you think that excuses you from paying your dues. You use it like a shield. You fly the airplane and then everybody's supposed to come by and shake your hand and kiss your ass and you get left out of the rest of the bullshit. Well," he said, letting the words drag out, "that old dog won't hunt, Major! Not in these woods."

"You can't make me do it, Brady." He still would not look up.

The colonel said, his voice deceptively mild, "You remember when we left Johannesburg, Major? You remember what you told me? You said, 'In this airplane, I'm boss.' Remember? Well, we're in my airplane now. This is my show and I'm going to run it. I may not get you there in one piece, but you're goddamn well coming along for the ride."

The chair creaked again.

"You got yourself a little stage fright, Major. Well, you probably will never have to go out in front of the footlights. But I ain't letting you go."

Cody kept his eyes on the floor, not saying anything.

"I don't give a shit whether you care if we get those bases or not. You'll still do your job for me. That part I guarantee you. I'm glad this came up now. I'm glad we got it all straightened out. Because it is straightened out. You'll do your job. Believe me, you will."

The chair creaked again.

"You wear a coat, Major, that's made out of confusion and self-pity. But about eight feet under all that bullshit is a ton of pride. Trust me, Major. I'll get down to that mother lode. I can't scare you and I can't con you. But I know who you are, better than you do."

He turned away then, back to his desk, and put on his glasses. "This interview is concluded, Major. I cannot force you to give me your best talents as my executive officer, but I will not excuse you from the obligation. You will be as combat ready as I am, and you will faithfully execute every order I transmit through you, and you will be as well oriented on the factors of this mission as I can make you. I learned as a young man that I could do whatever I had to do. You are no different. And I will treat you no different. This is a serious ball game, Major, and you'll hit whenever it comes your time to bat. Clear?"

Cody got up stiffly. "I heard what you said to the troops this morning. I assume it applies to me."

"You're goddamn right it does."

"Very good," Cody said. He turned away. "I'll see to the airplanes."

17

Forward Camp

The men were barracked by combat teams with Dougie Lord's six men divided among them. Schneider and Ruger and Peter Hawthorne found themselves on the same team. Hawthorne was a slim, transplanted Englisher who had been a friend of Schneider's and Ruger's since the Congo campaign. He had been an officer there, as well as in the British Army.

They came in that evening, after the first day's training, dead tired. They had run, they had marched, they had done the manual of arms and the only rest they'd got had been during the weapons familiarization course.

Now, they sat around talking, most of them still too tired to shower and clean up for evening mess. Hawthorne and Ruger were slumped on the floor. Schneider sat stolidly on his bed. The Mexican, Simon García, and a Canadian, Eric Hunter, were sitting nearby, listening. They were like many of the men who had never had mercenary experience, confused and uncertain about what to expect.

Ruger said tiredly, "I tell you, this is bloody fucking serious business."

Schneider said, "I told you so. Back in Johannesburg."

But then, Ruger laughed happily. "But, God, ain't it grand! It's a fucking bell ringer, chaps."

Hawthorne looked at him in amusement. "Ruger, what are you going to do when you get too old for this?"

"Die," Ruger said. "Just bloody die, lad."

They were quiet for a moment, and then Ruger said, again with a laugh, "Well, who's going to give us the opinion on the Iron Colonel? Surely it's in all our thoughts."

Schneider said thoughtfully, "He is a professional."

Ruger said, "Not much like the old days, eh Wilf?"

Schneider didn't answer, just shrugged.

The Canadian asked cautiously, "It is different, then? You chaps have done all these dos. Is this not the like of the others?"

Ruger laughed. "Sport, you've said it. This is not bloody like any of them."

"Is it better, then?"

Ruger said, "You tell him, Wilf. You kept the flaming diary in the Congo. Tell him about Kamina, our forward base. Tell him how fucking military and organized that was."

Schneider was a long moment in answering. Then he said, precisely and slowly, "We were mobbed up in Kamina in the Congo as a group of civilians completely unaccustomed and unprepared for the job we were supposed to do. After four weeks, we were still a mob of untrained civilians. Only disillusioned, broke, and tired of the many promises made to us and never kept. Every day we were there, another plane would arrive with more recruits. And almost as many men would get on the plane as got off, to return to Johannesburg. We wore uniforms when we left for Bukavu, but that was all we had in common with a regular army unit. We had been told by the recruiter, 'You will be trained by specialists in jungle warfare. You will be completely outfitted and equipped with the most modern weapons which any army in the world has.' What a laugh."

Schneider paused thoughtfully for a moment. "It is good to be here in a proper barracks with proper equipment and proper planning and preparation. What I remember best about the bivouac at Kamina was the filthy barracks. It was full of shit. It was decrepit and it was falling down. There were no proper sanitation facilities. There were no beds. We slept on the floor like pigs. There were no kitchen facilities. Our food was bought from neighboring tribesmen and it was swill. There was no training. There were no modern weapons. Once there came a report that the rebels were thirty kilometers away and advancing on us. You never saw such a panic. Many of the men tried to run away because we had no weapons to fight with. Only Sergeant Major Lord and his men had pistols. But they were for us. There was a group of Belgian soldiers encamped close by, but they had contempt for us. They would not admit us to their mess, nor would they even talk with us. But they were cowards. When the rumor of the rebels came, they ran away. That was what made us believe the rumor was true."

He stopped again, still sitting there stolidly on his bed. "Yes, this is much better. If I am to be a mercenary soldier, I prefer that it be done with the correct and serious approach that we are enjoying here. Yes, this is better."

There was a little silence when he finished, because he spoke so slowly that there had to be a pause to be sure he was through. When it had stretched out, Peter Hawthorne gave a bark of laughter. "Well," he said, "now you know. Any time you ask a Kraut a question you must be prepared for an answer."

"I find it instructive," the Canadian said.

Simon García said, "I don't think they should take away my cigarettes."

"That is my point," Schneider said. "It is clear that the professionals who are operating this expedition have given it a great deal of thought. If they have planned this mission down to the occasion of such matter as the cigarettes, then I think that they will also have given great thought to the combat element, that they will have planned that very well also."

Hawthorne said, "But, Wilf, do you think the money's as good? I rather fancied being a marauding band of free-lancers who bloody well took anything they could get their hands on. And no looting?"

Ruger broke in. "Oh, Jesus," he said. "Do you remember the bank, Wilf?" He rocked over backward, hugging himself at the memory. "Jesus, the bank at Bunda. We had this George Grover, see, in our bloody commando, who thinks he's a fucking genius with the old dynamite. So we take this town and we want to blow the bank safe. So bloody George, he knows how to do it, he says." Ruger threw his arms up. "Bloody fucking atomic explosion. The fucking dynamite goes off and the top of that bank goes and there's Belgian francs going into the clouds! We're fifty yards away and knocked over on our asses. BOOM! He blew money all over the fucking Congo. And old George, he says, standing there with his fucking glasses blown off his face, he says, 'Well, lads, maybe I used a bit much.' "

"I got ten thousand rand out of that bank," Schneider said candidly. "As did you. But, no, I don't think the money is not good. I earned thirty thousand rand. But I fought in the Congo for seven months. Here we are being asked to make two strikes. And for that we will receive fifteen thousand dollars."

"If we're successful," Hawthorne said.

It was at that moment that John Peters walked through the door. He was dusty and sweaty in his camouflage fatigues. He paused in the door and looked at them, his eyes, as always, mirrors.

Ruger said, "Ah, and here's John Peters, lads. Here's one that won't like it. Any of it. Hey, John?"

"You go to bloody hell, Ruger," Peters said. There was no emotion in his voice.

Ruger looked over at García and Hunter. "Our John here is a case. John's specialty is potting blokes in the back. Especially if they have sum' he wants. Such as money. What say you, John, about here? What are you going to do? No looting. None of the blokes got any money. You'll have to wait until we're back in Johannesburg before you can steal it."

Peters said, though now there was a touch of fury in his voice, "You sneer all you want, Gerry Ruger. But you're the bloody fool, not I. No swag, I don't fight. I don't double-time, and anybody thinks they can play John Peters this way has got another bloody think coming."

Ruger laughed. "Well, you just go tell them, John. Just go stick that little weasel face of yours up to the colonel and straighten him out. You do that, John. You go tell him how the cow ate the cabbage."

"Don't think I won't," Peters said. He ran his tongue over his thin lips. "And you'd bloody well better be careful yourself, mate."

"Not as long as I got you in front of me, Peters."

Peters wanted out. He had decided before the first day that this was not for him, and he felt a deep resentment that it had been done to him. He had even thought seriously about killing Brady, but he'd discarded that idea as being too risky. So, the only alternative was to get away and, for that, he'd need help. He had begun talking to the Belgian soldier, Lavel Horstmann, who was bunked next to him. Peters had recognized instinctively that Horstmann was not the soldier he appeared to be on paper. He was a coward. He had been in combat zones, but he'd always been very careful. And now Horstmann did not like the place he'd suddenly found himself. It was nothing like what he'd pictured a mercenary campaign would be. Besides, he missed his wife. He'd brought her with him to Johannesburg, and now she was back there by herself. He brooded about it.

Peters said to him, "The money's no good, lad. That bloody fucking colonel is cheating us. But I tell you, he don't do that to John Peters. I'm a fighting man, not a bleeding tin soldier."

They even got to the point of discussing how it might be done. Getting out of the camp and the long march would be hard enough, but the main difficulty lay in the fact that they'd arrive in a town without money or identification and no way to get to Johannesburg. Horstmann said he could cable his wife to wire them enough money to get back.

"We'll fix their wagons," Peters promised. "And we'll have the last joke. Our first month's pay is already sitting cozy in our banks, and we'll be bloody frigging gone and the rest of these saps will be back here sweating their asses off in this miserable hole. And me and you'll be sitting up cool in Drakes drinking beer and spending the bloody colonel's money. Bonuses! Hah, that's a laugh. 'If we're successful,'" he said, imitating Brady. "And who bloody decides? He does! That's who! And you think he'll fork over any more quid? Don't you believe it. But we'll fix their clocks. Proper!"

They were sitting in the office late in the evening. The relieving coolness that the baking plains gave an hour after sunset had come. A desk had been set up in the middle of the room for Cody. Brady's desk was behind and in a far corner. They were in clean fatigues after the hard day's training. The shutters had been turned out from the small windows, and there was a breeze blowing through. Inside, the room was bright from the force of the unshielded overhead light bulbs.

Cody was reading a draft of the operational plan that Brady had been drawing up. He frowned and put it down as he turned in his chair. "Matt, this is awkward as hell."

Brady stopped his work and looked up. "How so?" he asked mildly.

"We go in and knock off three of these dudes. Then we come out, wait a month and go in and get the last three."

"So?"

"So why the wait? Why don't we go get the next three a week later or a night later? We bring these troops back here for a month and we're liable to have mutiny on our hands."

Brady took his glasses off and put them on the desk. "We do it this way," he said, "because logistically it's sound. And psychologically sound. We need to throw the enemy off balance. Obviously, he can build other bases and import other instructors and soon be back in business. We hit him bam bam and he's going to think 'Well, that's it. That was the whole show.' And he's going on with business as usual. But *then*, you come back a couple of weeks later and kick the shit out of him again and you're going to get his attention. He's gonna get nervous and go looking over his shoulder, even with some time passing. Because he's not going to be sure you're not fixing to come get his ass again. And that's going to bother him and that's going to upset his plans. He's not going to be so quick to build those bases again and get on with his activities, because now he's not sure you're not laying over behind the next hill waiting to come in again. And that's going to give our people a little breathing spell. Enough time, maybe, to get a little constructive work done. And that's all we can do here.

"And logistically," he said, "it makes good military sense. You've got time to get your men out and rest them up and reorganize for any casualties you might have suffered. That's rough country, cowboy. Run around in there on consecutive nights, covering all those miles, and you might be asking more than the troops have brought with them."

"I see," Cody said slowly. Then he added, "No, I don't see. I understand the outstanding problems we're facing, and it appears to me that you're playing right into their hands. You go in and make a hit and you're going to have U.N. observers standing around waiting for you on the next trip. Then, what are you going to do?"

"Ah!" Brady said. He smiled in thin-lipped satisfaction. "That would be true except for the diversion in Angola. We expect to have enough brush fires going in Angola ain't nobody going to be paying much attention to anything we're doing here. And that's why we got time and why we can plan it like we want."

"Let's have a drink," Cody said.

"You want a drink?"

"Sure, don't you?"

"You realize," Brady said, "that we're doing rank has its privileges. The troops don't have any whiskey."

"So what," Cody said. "To quote you, 'Who the fuck says it has to be fair.' "

Brady pointed a finger. "You're getting goddamn smart, cowboy." He got up and went over to a filing cabinet and came out with a bottle of Scotch. Among dishes that had not been cleared away from their evening meal he found two glasses. "Ain't very clean," he said. "One of 'em's had milk in it. You take that one."

He poured them each an inch of Scotch, then plugged the bottle, and put it back in the cabinet.

They toasted each other from across the room. Brady said, "The fucking habit is catching, ain't it? These goddamn people over here can't take a drink without saying 'Cheers' and all that shit. And they can't take out a goddamn cigarette without offering the pack around the room. I smoke too much for that kind of stuff. I'd spend all my time offering people cigarettes if I did that."

They drank in silence for a moment, letting the whiskey come down into their stomachs. Cody could feel it relaxing him.

"Matt, what the fuck are we doing here?"

"Don't you know?"

"No. I don't know. Explain it to me."

"We're here because it's important."

Cody slammed his open palm down on the desk top. "Goddammit, that's my question. Why is it important? We're gonna make a fight for some people who want to hold onto some stuff that belongs to them. But there's another bunch of people say it belongs to them. Only we're going to go and kill some of those people. Now, you fucking well explain that to me. Is it important because we think the bunch we're going to fight for is right? Is that it? Is that what makes it important?"

Brady had a mouthful of smoke, and he let it out in a long, thin stream. As it blew out, he shook his head slowly from side to side. He said, "Nope. That ain't what it's all about and that ain't what's important. We're here because we got a commitment to ourselves."

"But that don't make any sense, Matt."

"What the fuck does? War is insane. Any form of war is insane. I'm just a dumb fucking country boy who happens to have war as his business, but I know it's insane. But then, there ain't a hell of a lot that human beings do that makes much sense of any kind." He turned in the swivel chair and put his feet up on the corner of his desk. "But I'll tell you this, cowboy, at least we're doing something. At least we got some action. We ain't sitting around mil-fucking-dewing in the boredom of a nonexistence."

"But, Matt," Cody said, "listen to me, will you? We're

talking about killing people. We're talking about going out and shooting people with guns."

"So what?" Brady said flatly. The talk was beginning to arouse him. He shot a hand out toward the window. "There's fucking politicians sitting around all over this world, sighing and mealy mouthing and shitting platitudes out their cocksucking mouths, and they kill more out of them goddamn carpet-floored offices than you and I'll ever kill in eighty lifetimes. And, cowboy, the folks they kill are just as dead." He leaned forward. "At least a soldier has got the honor and the grace to be shot back at. Is what we're doing important? You're fucking well right it's important."

Now he was aroused. He said, "Listen, them ain't choirboys we're going after. Them's folks been killing other folks. But that still ain't the reason. That's just the dressing."

"Then what is?"

"We got a commitment to action. And once you make the commitment that what you have chosen is right and purposeful, you should do it the best you can." He leaned back in his chair. "That, cowboy, is what it's all about. And if I'm wrong, then I've wasted a lifetime being wrong. But I figured out a long time ago there ain't no right and wrong, just different viewpoints. So, the only course a man has got is to get him a purpose and stick with it and do the best he can. The commitment to yourself to be proud of yourself. And, cowboy, I damn well am that. That's all I know."

Cody didn't say anything.

Brady suddenly laughed. "Quit asking so goddamn many questions. Quit trying to decide which end of the stick to get hold of. Just grab the sonofabitch and go to swinging. In the end, it ain't going to make any difference."

There came a knock at the door.

Cody looked up. "Come!" he said.

The guard, one of Dougie Lord's men, advanced into the room. "Sir!" he said.

"Speak."

"A delegation from the troops, requesting audience with the colonel commanding. Sir!"

Cody turned and looked over his shoulder at Brady. The colonel shrugged.

Cody asked, "What's the business of the delegation?"

"They would not state their business. Sir!"

Cody looked at Brady again. The colonel smiled thinly and pointed a finger at Cody. Cody said, "All right. Tell them they'll be received, but it'll be me that'll be seeing them. How many?"

"Five. Sir!"

"I'll see three. No more. And only one man talking."

"Sir." The sentry wheeled and marched out of the room. From behind, Brady said, "Very nice, Major."

The leader of the delegation was a big American paratrooper named Hawkins. The advance and position of the three men was slovenly. Cody leaned back in his chair and deliberately lit a cigarette. "Speak," he said. He did not give them the order to be at ease.

Hawkins said, a touch of sullenness in his voice, "We've come with a complaint. The men have got a request."

"And what's that?" Cody asked him dryly.

"Well, the training's too hard. This is a damn hot country and we think we ought to have a midafternoon break. The men think we ought to come in for a little rest during the hottest part of the afternoon."

"The men do? How many men is that?"

"All of 'em. Every sonofabitch in this camp. There's some other stuff, too, but we can start with this. We ain't members of any regular military organization and we got some rights."

Cody sat for a moment studying him, studying the

way he was standing, the way he was speaking. He said, with nothing in his voice, "Hawkins, it's been explained to you that the purpose of your training is to prepare you for the actual conditions you're going to run into. The strike we're going on is not going to have any mid-afternoon breaks in it. We're trying to get you used to the heat. That's what the training is designed for."

"Well," Hawkins said. "That's all right. But a lot of the men don't like it. And I can tell you I don't think they're going to stand for it."

"They're not?"

"No."

Cody said, still with nothing in his voice, "Well, why don't you just report back to them and tell them they'll have to stand for it."

"Listen," the paratrooper said. He completely broke attention and looked down at Cody. "Listen, we didn't come in here to see you, anyway. We came to see the colonel." He looked over at Brady. "We know our rights and we been sent to get them."

Cody said, "At ease, Hawkins. At ease." He said it for his own purposes of fairness. He got out of the chair, still saying it as he rounded the desk. "Stand at ease, soldier."

He came around the desk and Hawkins turned to face him; as his left foot was stepping forward, Cody hit the man in the face with his right fist with all the power of his shoulder driving behind it. Hawkins didn't fall straight down. He hit the man behind him, slumped off him, hit the desk in front, and then lay on his back on the floor. Cody reached down, grabbing the man by the lapels of his fatigues and tried to raise him. He was too heavy. He got him up to a sitting position and then hit him again. He went over backward, limply, his head hitting dully on the floor. The man didn't move, though his eyes were open. He was conscious.

Cody straightened slowly. He stood back against his desk, looking at the other two men. "Don't you move," he said. "Don't you flinch. You just stand there."

He waited then, breathing heavily, until Hawkins began to move. Then he said, his teeth clenched, "Get him up."

When he was erect, Cody said, "You been told you will respect the officers and purpose of this mission. You come in here again acting like tramps and I'll kick your ass right up between your eyeteeth. And soldier," he said, getting his face close to the big paratrooper's, "you think this was rank, or a cheap shot, you just come up to me tomorrow and I'll give you ten times more. And buddy," he reached out and took the soldier by the fatigue front and shook him, "it's been ordered military courtesies with the exception of saluting. You, I'm making an exception for. You will salute. You ever see me and you don't salute, I'll have your ass!"

Then he stepped back and said, "Get this ass out of here and I better not see any of you men in here in the *near* future!"

There was a long moment after they left. Cody sat down at his desk. He found that he was trembling.

After a long time, Brady said softly, "Oh, my. Oh, my."

Cody said, "Shut up, Matt. Don't say anything."

"I wasn't going to say anything," Brady said, "except I didn't know you could punch that hard."

Cody was silent.

Brady got out of his chair and went to the cabinet. "Let's have another drink." He got the bottle out and poured another inch into Cody's glass and then his own. There was a straight-backed chair against the wall and he brought it forward, set it down in front of Cody's desk, and straddled it backward.

They sat there like that for a long moment. Cody had his arms on the desk and wouldn't look up. He hadn't touched the glass of Scotch. The knuckles on his right hand were bleeding, but he hadn't paid them any attention.

Brady said, "You know I value you, don't you, boy?"

There was a long moment and then Cody said, "We're not going to talk whiskey talk, are we?"

A cut came in Brady's voice. "Major, you got a few idiosyncrasies. Some of 'em I'll put up with. That kind of talk ain't one of 'em. What the hell's the matter with you, anyway?"

Cody suddenly laughed and sat up in his chair. He shook his head. "Hell, I don't know. Nothing, I guess." He reached for the fresh Scotch and lifted it into the air. "Salud and cheers and all that shit," he said.

After they drank, Brady asked, "You don't feel guilty about hitting that soldier, do you?"

Cody looked at him in astonishment. "Hell, no!" he said. "And if he could have got up, I'd have hit him again."

"It was the wrong thing to do. If you felt you had to deal with him on a personal as well as a military level, you should have shot him."

"You're kidding."

Brady shook his head slowly. "No, I'm not. If you'd shot that bronco for insolence and insubordination, we'd of got some good out of it. That would have been in the military tradition and the troops would have understood it. As it is, Hawkins is going back to the barracks and tell the story, and there's going to be a bunch of those hard boys saying to themselves, 'Well, just let him try that on me and I'll break his ass for him.' Regulation punishment is military. A bullet is military. Your fist isn't. Never put your hands on a soldier."

Cody took it, listening steadily. After a long time, he said, "All right."

Brady was watching him carefully. He'd been afraid

he was going to say, "I told you I couldn't do this job." But he hadn't and that made the colonel feel better.

"Hell," Brady said, "it's late and we got to roll out at six. Let's knock this off and hit the sack."

But Cody didn't go to sleep right away. Instead, he lay on his bunk and smoked and stared up, the ceiling white enough to be seen even in the dark. He hadn't told Brady the strict truth. He did care if they got those bases, but maybe not for a reason the colonel would have understood. But, then, he didn't understand it either. Ruth Longhurst wasn't his woman and it damn sure wasn't his fight. So he shouldn't care. He leaned over and put his cigarette out in a saucer that served as an ashtray.

18

Longhaven Farm

They were having a meeting in the operations shack, Jim Leslie and all the farmers of the valley with the exception of Don Woodward, who was busy in Salisbury trying to sell out, and Percy Bice, who refused to come out on the roads after dark. They were sitting around informally, drinking beer. The meeting had been called by Leslie, and he leaned against the radio table and said, "Chaps, I've had some gen that I think you'd better prepare yourselves for. It comes from the army and it's just about what we've been expecting."

"Oh, shit," somebody said. "More good news." There was a bitter bite in his voice. "What have the bastards got now, the fucking atomic bomb?"

Leslie smiled, but his face was tired. "It's, of course, about Mozambique. Since they've gone down, it's turned loose a bloody lot more of the beggars for their good works, and it looks as if we're to inherit them." He looked at his beer bottle, swishing it softly around. "The army is confirming that there's a much bigger buildup at the terrorist bases, especially Chipedzia, than they've ever seen before. They've concluded it's Frelimoists coming over to lend a helping hand."

Bill Longhurst said tiredly from the corner, "That's no news."

Don Thompson said, "But, goddammit, there's still Angola. Not that I wish our Portuguese brethren any hard luck, but better them than us. It's a Frelimo operation in Angola," he added angrily. "Why the bloody hell don't they muck on over there!"

Jim Leslie smiled again. "Well, Don, I guess you could say it's because we're on the way. Or in the way." He took a drink of his beer and then wiped his mouth with his sleeve. "Of course, we're not getting the lot of them, just some on a lend-lease basis to show solidarity and all that muck."

Longhurst asked, "What's the latest from Angola, Jim? The news is so blasted splotchy."

Leslie looked over at him. "I don't know, Bill. But it doesn't sound good. Lisbon is making funny sounds again, and I just don't know how solid our European friends can be there. Nothing official. Just a feeling in the wind."

"Oh, fuck it!" Arnold Bienhorn, who farmed six miles down the road, said angrily. "*All* the bastards will pull out! Every damn one of them. Even those fuckers in Salisbury and the south. They sit up there and cheer and say, 'Good show, lads! Carry right on!' But it's not their bloody asses getting shot off. I feel like pulling out."

"Com'on now, Arnold," Longhurst said. "Cool off. Have another beer. It's no time for that kind of talk."

"Oh, yes," Bienhorn said bitterly, "I'm letting down the side and all that rot! Well, fuck it!"

They talked a little longer about how much time was left before the attacks began again and what the army was promising, and then the meeting broke up. Leslie and Bill Longhurst stood for a moment alone in the black, cool night.

"Pray for Angola, Bill," the D.C. said. "Pray that the

Europeans there can hold on. If that place goes, they've got us in the jaws of a pliers."

"Well," Longhurst said, "you can see how it is here. Woodward definitely gone and Bienhorn right on the edge and you know Percy. The only question about him is does he pull out before he goes around the bend. Will you come in and say hello to Ruth?"

"No," Leslie said. "It's late." His two askaris jumped in the back of his Land Rover as Bill and Jim approached. Longhurst let them out the gate and then trudged back to the house. He felt tired, and discouraged, and disgusted. He could even understand how Bienhorn felt. "And when that sort of talk begins making sense to me . . ." He let the mumbled words fade off and lit his way down the long hallway with a flashlight. Ruth, he could see, had already gone to bed.

He slipped in under the covers, feeling her warm thigh against his. The nights were much cooler now. A sure sign that the rains would come soon.

"What was that all about?" she asked out of the darkness.

"The meeting? Just the old stuff," he said. He adjusted his head beside hers on the pillow.

"Com'on, Bill. None of that now. Jim Leslie doesn't call special meetings just for the same old stuff. He's been visiting every farmer in the territory."

He was silent for a moment, then he said, a little note of helplessness in his voice, "Well, you know what time of year it is. What do you suppose it was about?" He wasn't going to tell her they expected it to be rougher this year than ever.

They were quiet together for a time and he thought she was dozing. Then she said, "Two of my sheep boys disappeared today."

"Oh, damn," Bill said wearily. "Now they're down to taking the pickanins. What do their people say?"

She shrugged beside him. " 'I don't know, Missy. Them wild boys, Missy. They run off, Missy. By 'n by you take these two boys here, Missy. They good boys. They tend your sheep, Missy.' Who knows what they say. And I'm missing a ram, one of my best Shorthorns."

"They probably ate him," he said. "A breeding ram for biltong."

"Shit!" she said loudly. She sat up in bed, the covers falling down to her waist. "Damn it!"

"Ah, love," he said quickly, groping for her in the dark. "Com'on now. It's only a couple of herd boys."

"I don't give a damn about the herd boys. I don't give a damn about any of it!" She turned to him quickly. "Bill, I want to see the children. I want to see some people. Let's go to Salisbury. Let's go and have an old-fashioned blowout. What say? Just for a few days. We'll get Don or someone to look in and leave the Bright Lights."

For a moment, he was tempted, feeling her desire rising in him. To break away; to be free for a few days; to get gloriously drunk and laugh and not have to carry a gun. But then he thought of all there was to do and how little time there was left to do it. And now, after what Jim Leslie had said, there'd be even less time. He felt a cold fear suddenly hit him in the stomach.

"Bill?" She shook his arm.

"Ah, love," he said. "We'll see the children at Christmastime."

"Christmas, hell!" she said fiercely. "Christmas is two bloody months away."

"Ruth, we can't." He faced her in the dark, barely able to make out the line of her head.

She heard the finality in his voice. Knew it was no good. "Oh, God, Bill," she said. "Let's do something. Let's go into Shamva and have a party. Let's resurrect the old club and get everyone from the village to go in and have a day of tennis and drink lemon squashes and have a dance that night. Something!"

"I'm afraid the old tennis court has fallen into a bit of disuse. Might be mined. Wouldn't that be a bloody joke! Chap serves and then BOOM!"

After a moment, she laughed with him and then lay close and put her arm across his chest.

"But you know," he said, thinking about it, "that might not be such a bad idea. It'd be taking a bloody risk, and we'd have to leave all the Bright Lights to look after the places. And it would have to be for one day. . . ."

She put her face into the hollow of his neck. "Oh, Christ, Bill, don't listen to me. It would be damned dangerous. And silly."

"Maybe not," he said, still thinking. After a moment, he said, "But we'll have to do it damn quick."

19

Forward Camp

The officer and noncom appointments had been made. Peter Hawthorne was given the rank of captain and made the leader of combat team Able. Both Ruger and Schneider were appointed lieutenants and given squads. A quiet, capable American named Sullivan was given command of the Baker team. The third combat team, Charlie, was given to a South African named James Schroder.

The awkward part of the mission came from the fact that three camps would be hit simultaneously, and Brady could be in company with only one. He would be going in with the combat team attacking the most important base at Chipedzia. There was a good possibility of radio contact with the other two teams, but radios in that terrain would be uncertain.

Brady had told Cody, "We got to have 'em trained like a roping horse. There's no room for error in this. We can plan it, but if they don't do it, we ain't got shit. And don't you ever forget we're going to hit a hundred, two hundred enemy troops with twenty-one men. They better be ready and they better know what to do and they better do it automatically."

They were in their tenth day of training and had moved outside. Brady had had rough models of the camps they'd be attacking set up outside the fences, out on the plain.

It was not really a life-sized model of the camp. They'd had neither the labor nor the materials for that. It was really a floor plan. Boxes had been set up to represent the corners of a barracks; two posts had been planted in the ground as the pole antenna of the radio station; rocks had been laid out to represent the concrete structures the Chinese cadre occupied. It would serve.

A wooden tower, twelve feet tall, had been constructed for Brady so that he could oversee the practice. He stood up there, with two runners posted down below, and watched. Cody stood with him, leaning on the wooden railing.

On a high point, fifteen yards to their left, Major Carlton-Brooks was stationed. Beside him was a runner. The operation concerned only the three squads of combat team Able. The other teams were, at that moment, on ten-mile marches with the full equipment that they would carry on the strikes.

On this tenth day, the water discipline had been instituted. Each man would subsist, during the day, on the liquids he could carry in two canteens. They were being given liquids with their morning meal and with lunch if they were in camp. But the water had been turned off until seven each evening. In a few days, the liquids would be discontinued at mealtimes, and a man would have to subsist all day long on what he could carry. As the final days neared, there would not even be the showers at night, and a man would have to make do for twenty-four hours with what was in his canteens.

It was a necessary fact of combat life. Fear and activity and combat made a man's mouth dry and made him want water. But he could preplan for it by gradually building up his tolerance to thirst. That was what the dieticians said, and the trainers who'd never gone into combat and had to spit when their fear and adrenaline had dried their mouths to cotton. But they had to try to plan every detail. And the learning of a water discipline and instilling it were as important as any other part of the training.

The leader of each squad was equipped with a backpack radio, an SCM 10-5. The radios had cost twelve hundred dollars apiece on the underground market. The radio and the power pack weighed eleven pounds and were strapped to the back of the leaders. The reception was through earphones and there was a boom mike, thin as a pencil, for transmission. A man would go into combat with both hands free and be able to transmit orders to his squad without doing any more than speaking.

Brady stopped on his tower. He had radio contact with his combat team leaders from the radio he was wearing. And he had the runners.

The troops were deployed on the plains surrounding the simulated camp. The camp was oblong, and two of the squads were arranged in an inverted V shape at its top. The other squad was in a skirmish line at the foot of the rectangle. The intent was that as the inverted V moved forward it would sweep what it didn't destroy into the advance of the trap line closing in from the other direction.

They were dressed as they would be for the actual attack, in camouflage fatigues and combat boots and steel helmets. Each man carried two canteens of water, a musette bag containing twenty clips for the AK-47s and grenades of several types.

It was almost sickeningly hot, and they had been at the drill for three hours. Every man had sweated until he had no more sweat to give. But it was so hot the sweat dried as fast as it came.

Ruger had command of the third squad, the trap squad

at the base of the triangle, and Schneider was leading one wing of the V.

They started forward, the men running at double-time, bent over, their rifles in front at the ready.

"Hold it!" Brady suddenly roared into his mike. Out on the plain, the squad leaders threw up their hands and the strike team came to a halt. They looked toward the tower.

"Goddammit," Brady said into his mike. "What's the matter with you people? Captain Hawthorne, goddammit, your number six and number seven men should already have been moving forward to disable that radio antenna. That is PRIMARY! Why are they trotting along with the rest of you like goddamn sheep? Now try it again and get it right!"

Hawthorne put his hand over his boom mike and looked down the line of men to Horstmann and Peters. "Goddamn you, John Peters," he said murderously, "get your arse in gear or I'll kick it sky-high!"

Peters said defiantly, "It's bloody hot and I'm tired." His thin mouth twisted. "You can all take it and shove it!"

"Move it!" Hawthorne shouted at him. He had purposely placed Peters and Horstmann where they were because that would put them out in front as they moved up to disable the radio antenna. No one wanted John Peters behind him.

Peters was mumbling as he walked back to his position.

"What did you say?" Hawthorne shouted at him.

"Nothing," Peters said sullenly. "Nothing for the likes of you."

On the tower, Cody said to Brady, "That's Peters. The one I was telling you about."

"I don't care if his name is Jesus Christ," Brady said, not really hearing. "He better get on the stick."

They did it again and again and again. A man suddenly fainted.

"Major!" Brady yelled at Carlton-Brooks. "Get that man out of the way!"

The troops stood on the plain, staring up at him.

"All right," he said into his mike, "let's do it again."

The sun was at its four o'clock position. They stood out there looking up at it. Then Hawthorne said to his command squad, "All right, chaps, here we go. And for God's sake, don't nobody fuck up." He could feel the radio on his back like a ton. He trudged tiredly back and raised his arm.

The plan of the attack was as classic as a cavalry charge. No heroics with sentries. No stealth. No maneuvering beyond the original approach. When the men were in position, the commander would say, "Go," and they would come sweeping through the camp, spraying everything that moved with the assault rifles.

The job of John Peters and Lavel Horstmann was to charge into the center of the camp, disable the radio antenna, and then rush forward ten yards, in front of the two large barracks that opposed each other, and hurl incendiary grenades onto their thatched roofs. That was to give light for the two wings of the V that would be converging right behind them. Then Peters was to rush to the concrete-block house and hurl grenades inside to kill the Chinese instructors.

John Peters could no longer support the rage that was building inside him. He was exhaustively tired. The water in his canteens was warm, and he hadn't been able to plan a way out of the camp.

He and Horstmann went, well enough, through their pantomime of cutting the radio antenna. But when it came time to run to the center of the camp and simulate throwing the incendiary grenades, Peters walked. He walked slowly. He walked, finally, in front of where the four boxes had been placed to illustrate the barracks. There he sat down. He sat down with his legs drawn up and hugged them with his arms and then rested his head on his knees.

The attack stopped.

Colonel Brady said evenly into his mike, "Bring that man to me."

No one moved for a moment and then Brady shouted down to the two runners stationed below him, "Goddammit! Bring that man to me!"

He went clambering down the ladder with Cody behind him.

Peters was done in. He was so tired he could barely walk. In the other days of training, he'd always found ways to slip through the hard work, catching a rest whenever he could. But today, out on the flat plain under the eye of the colonel, there'd been no chance.

"What's this man's name?" Brady asked coldly.

"Peters, sir," Dougie Lord said. He stepped forward and touched his sergeant's baton to his beret. "John Peters. Here, you," he said to Peters. "Come to attention."

Peters didn't move, just stood there with his head down.

Lord jabbed him hard in the shoulder with his baton. "ATTENTION!" he roared.

Peters raised his head. He did not like confrontations unless the odds were all on his side. And he would never have forced this one if he could have gone on with the practice.

Brady said to him in that cold voice, raised enough so that the other troops could hear, "Soldier, you will go until you fall out. If you pass out, that will be an acceptable excuse for quitting. That or death. But," he put his face close to Peters', "you better goddamn well be unconscious."

The heat was sapping Brady too. He stood there feeling how tired he was. He said to Peters, "This will cost you five hundred dollars." He turned to Carlton-Brooks. "See that five hundred dollars is deducted from this man's pay." Then, "Dismiss the men. That's enough for today."

He turned and walked away, toward the headquarters shack. Cody fell in beside him.

"You better watch that one, Matt."

"He's just another trooper to me."

That night, the soldier who'd passed out was found to be sick. Because the man was in his squad, Wilf Schneider came to report to Brady.

"He is burning with fever, sir," Schneider said.

"I'll come see," Brady said.

They roused Carlton-Brooks and then all of them, including Cody, went to the barracks. The soldier's name was Porterfield. He was a South African; a quiet, well-intentioned man whom most of the troops liked.

Brady put his hand on the man's head. It was dry and terribly hot.

"He has not come to," Schneider said respectfully, "since he was brought in."

The other men in the barracks were crowding around.

"Well," Brady said, "he's sick all right." He stood there a moment, thinking. Then he turned. "Sergeant Lord?"

"Sir!"

"Get some ice from the mess hall and pack this man in it. We've got to get that fever down."

"Sir!" Lord said. He left.

Brady said, "I don't know what else we can do for the time being."

There was, of course, no doctor or medical man in the camp. Brady, like several of the special forces men, had had basic medical training, but mostly in how to handle combat wounds. Neither he nor they knew much about exotic fevers. Now he said to Carlton-Brooks, "If we get the fever down, he may come out of it."

One of the men standing nearby muttered, "Might get a doctor."

Brady looked around sharply. But he said back to Carlton-Brooks, "Organize an around-the-clock detail to sit up with him. Give every man who sits up the equivalent amount of time off from drill tomorrow. I'm going to bed. Com'on Major Ravel."

When he was gone, one of the men said disgustedly, "Give every man the equivalent amount of time off from drill tomorrow. Great bloody Christ!"

Wilf Schneider said, "Shut up, you!"

But there were other murmurs. A man said, "'E needs a bloody doctor, not an ice house, for God's sake."

"No more of this," Schneider said.

And Hawthorne said, "That's it. You've heard Lieutenant Schneider. Now organize the sit up."

In the office, Cody said, "Christ, Matt, that guy's really sick."

"I know it," Brady said. He paused by the window, looking out.

"Well, hadn't we better do something?"

"I'm doing all I can. Got to get his fever down first."

"No, I mean, get a doctor in here. Or take him to one."

Brady looked at him. "Are you kidding?"

"Hell no, I'm not kidding. That man could die."

"He might well," Brady said thoughtfully.

"Then let's get him some medical attention."

Brady looked at him long and distantly.

"You're not telling me you're not going to get that man some help, are you?"

"What do you think?"

"I don't believe this," Cody said. "I slam ass don't believe it."

"Listen, Major," Brady said coldly and formally, "it's about time all of you, you and the rest of the men, got it straight in your minds that nothing is going to jeopardize the success of this mission. That man is a combat soldier who signed up knowing the risks he was taking. Whether he dies from a bullet or from a fever is immaterial." He was suddenly angry.

Cody looked at him a long moment. "I could never be like you, Matt."

Brady turned back to the window. "Nobody's asking you to."

Cody went out of the office to his own room.

Schneider lay tiredly and thought of his wife, Mary. He knew how terribly hard the separations were on her, but they were no less hard on him. The difference was that he did not let it affect him. In the dark, he whispered a little greeting and message to her. But he didn't believe she'd get it; he did it only for himself. Well, he thought, soon this would be over, and there would be another $15,000 for the bank account. That should be enough. Almost enough. And then, he suddenly thought, no matter if it's enough or not, we will sail away. He went to sleep with the promise on his mind that they would sail away the day he got back. He and Mary and the babies. Around the world, photographing the world. Even if you were a sensible German, you couldn't wait all your life to do what you wanted.

Carlton-Brooks was still awake, but for a different reason. Before the call had come to go with Brady, he'd managed to fall into a jumpy, nervous sleep. But now he was awake and he didn't know if he could support it the rest of the night. Even as cool as the room was, he was sweating.

He was out of whiskey. And he was in a panic. After the first night, he'd done well, rationing himself to where he was just able to maintain an even tempo. The good, hard work in the hot sun had helped so that he'd not had too many bad nights, not nights he couldn't handle. But then there had come last night when, for no visible reason, he'd decided to go off on a bender.

Oh, there'd been a reason and he knew what it was. It was that damn Colonel Brady, who stripped a man of all his dignity.

He cursed himself, lying there with the nerves jumping out of his skin. What a stupid move! He'd lain there the night before and drunk up *all* of his last two precious bottles of Scotch. And now there was no more. And the future stretched out like a black, nightmare-ridden eternity.

He didn't think he'd be able to stand it. He'd had the d.t.'s once before, and he was trembling now, expecting them again. The convulsions. The strange sounds. The god-awful, unexplainable fears. The fright. The agonies.

There was no more whiskey allotment. And tomorrow was the last day of the beer issue. There was only enough beer left for one more handout.

But he didn't want beer. He wanted the hard, driving, mood changing, nerve relaxing bite of whiskey.

"Oh, God," he said aloud in the night. "Oh, God."

He'd meant to use this bivouac to get himself straightened out. And all he'd done was get himself into trouble.

"Oh, God," he said again.

"Oh, God, what am I to do?"

He had the pistol. That was one way out. He lay there in the dark, considering it.

His mind took a turn to final humor. He could see himself going in to Brady and saying, "If you don't give me some whiskey, I'm going to shoot myself tonight."

And Brady would look at him a long time, his flat face thoughtful. Finally he'd say, "Well, if you miss, come around and see me tomorrow."

Oh, yes, that's what the bastard would think. Not even give me credit for being able to aim at my own brain.

But he felt better. And then he surprised himself by thinking about the pistol seriously. He was astonished and frightened because he knew he meant it. Well, he thought, at least that would be quiet nerves.

20

Forward Camp

Porterfield was no better the next day. He had come to at five in the morning, but he'd been feverish and violent. A man had run for Brady. With four men holding him down, they'd taken his temperature rectally and, even in the ice bath, it was still 104 degrees.

Brady had stood there, thinking.

Schneider said, "Perhaps we should sweat him, Colonel."

Brady shook his head. "No. That's an old wives' tale. We got to keep him in an ice bath."

They had no injections. And even if they'd had, they wouldn't know what to give. They held him, one man stroking his throat, and poured down him a compound of crushed aspirin and quinine tablets dissolved in water.

He seemed to go a little easier after that, but he was still thrashing around, his eyes shut and his jaw clenched.

In the afternoon, he went unconscious again. They tied his mouth open, running a handkerchief over his lower jaw and behind his neck, so that he wouldn't swallow his tongue. In shifts, a man sat with him, swabbing out his mouth with a wet rag so it wouldn't ulcerate.

That evening, a delegation formed to go to Brady. Schneider argued against it. Ruger and Hawthorne stood by silently. Schneider said, "You are wasting your time. We have accepted security and isolation as part of this mission. We are soldiers. Porterfield is a soldier. It is part of the same."

But they had gone anyway. Brady received them. Before they were allowed in, he turned to Cody, "Better watch this. It may get serious."

"All right," Cody said. He got up and went in his bedroom and got the 9 mm automatic they'd issued him. Then he came back in the room. He didn't sit down at his desk, for it was in front of Brady's. Instead, he took a chair in the corner.

The men came in. Brady had put no restriction on their numbers and there were seven of them.

He never let them speak.

As they came to attention, he said tiredly, "I know why you're here. And I know everything you want to say. And I'm not interested." He stopped and opened a desk drawer and took out the same model 9 mm automatic that Cody had. He cocked it and laid it on the desk. Then he said, looking up at them, "I'm sorry about Porterfield. And I'm going to do everything in my power to handle it. Here. But I won't bring in a doctor and I won't send him out. I will not jeopardize the security of this mission. You men better make up your minds to that." He stopped and slowly ran a hand over his short hair, from the back to the front.

"Depend on it," he said.

He did not move his hand toward the gun on his desk. But he said, "Now, you people get out of here. And pass the word. I'm fucking tired of these delegations."

They stood there for a moment, wanting to talk.

Cody suddenly got up and walked forward. "About-face," he said, his voice cold. "You've had your orders. Now get out of here."

They looked at him and then they turned and wheeled out of the room. It was a long moment before either one of them could speak.

Brady finally said, "Well done."

"Fuck you," Cody answered. He was sitting in the corner, smoking a cigarette.

"You don't have to agree with me, Major," Brady said, "but you have to do your job."

Cody looked directly at him, "Don't talk to me like that. I'll back you up, Matt, whether I agree with you or not."

Brady got up. "You want a drink?"

"No," Cody said.

"Yeah," Brady said, "but I know who does." He opened the door to the hall that led to the sleeping quarters and called, "Brooks! Major Brooks!"

After a long moment, the door to the adjutant's room opened, and he put his head out. "Sir?" he said weakly.

"Comb your hair," Brady told him. "And then report in here."

Back in the office, he went to the file cabinet and got out a new bottle of Scotch. As he opened it, he remarked, "Our Major is a drunk. I know he snuck some whiskey in here with him, and I think he's run out. And I think he's about to go off the deep end." He finished opening the bottle, then got two glasses and set them and the Scotch on his desk.

"But," he said, "I don't care whether he's a drunk or not. I don't care if he drowns in whiskey. All I want is for him to do his job. You follow me?"

"Yes," Cody said.

"Good."

The door opened and Carlton-Brooks came in. Brady

watched him as his eyes went directly to the bottle of whiskey.

"Sit down, Major," Brady said. "And have a drink." He picked up the bottle and held it poised over one of the glasses, looking questioningly at Carlton-Brooks. "You will have a drink, won't you?"

There was a thin film of sweat on the adjutant's forehead. He rubbed his mustache with one finger, staring fixedly at the whiskey.

"Uh, yes," he said. "Yes, sir. Why not."

"Why not indeed," Brady said. He poured the glass half full of Scotch, two inches deep. Then he poured a little in his own glass. "Sorry I can't offer you ice, but we're using all that for Porterfield."

"Shit," Cody said from the corner.

Brady looked over at him. "You say something, Cody?"

"I said shit, Colonel."

Brady looked down at his drink and smiled. "So you did," he said. "So you did."

Then he looked at Carlton-Brooks. "Be relaxed, Major," he said. "This is what, in the American army, we call a bull session. Just a bunch of the officers getting together and talking. Very informal." He set his drink, untasted, down on the desk and took his hand away from it. Carlton-Brooks was watching him intently. He'd taken his own drink up, but he couldn't touch it until Brady did. He set the drink back down on the table. His hand was trembling.

Brady asked, seeing it all, "How's it going, Major?"

"Fine, sir," the adjutant said with an effort. He was trying, with all his resolve, to sit straight in the chair and to appear relaxed.

"Think the training's going all right?"

"Yes," Carlton-Brooks said, "yes, sir." He crossed his legs. His right foot began to tremble so he changed positions, recrossing his legs. His eyes were burning. Oh God, he thought.

Brady put his fingers around his glass, started to lift it and then set it back down. He watched Carlton-Brooks' hand dart out toward his glass and then stop as he did. He smiled thinly. "We've got to work 'em. We got to work 'em hard."

"Yes sir," Carlton-Brooks said shakily. He did not know if he could support the moment much longer.

"Shit," Cody said. He suddenly got up. The revolver was tugging at his waistband. He left the office and walked down the hall to his room and pitched the gun on his bed. Then he went back in the office and went directly to the desk. There was an extra glass and he poured an inch of Scotch in it and then held it up like a toast.

"To the king," he said, looking at Brady.

The colonel laughed. "Sure," he said. He raised his own glass. "To the king."

Carlton-Brooks drank the whole of his drink in one pulling, sucking gulp. Over his glass, Cody watched him.

"Yes," Carlton-Brooks said, as he put his empty glass back on the table. Then he looked at them in embarrassment.

"Major," Cody said, looking at Brady, "this concludes tonight's bull session. You are free to return to your own quarters."

Carlton-Brooks got up. "Uh, yes," he said. "Thank you, sir."

Cody was still watching Brady. "But take this," he said. "As a memento of the occasion." Without taking his eyes off Brady, he reached out, found the top, capped the bottle, and then handed it to Carlton-Brooks.

"A token," Cody said, with his eyes still on Brady, "of our esteem."

"Thank you," Carlton-Brooks said. "Thank you very much, sir."

But at the door Brady stopped him. He said evenly, "Make it last, Major. Make it last."

Carlton-Brooks said with despair, "Yes, yes, thank you very much, sir." Then he was gone.

Cody said, "You like it, Brady. You like it too fucking much."

Matthew Brady turned and looked at him. "No," he said. "I don't. And you've got to believe that. I just do what I have to!"

"Shit," Cody said. "I'm going to check on Porterfield. If he's dead, I won't bother to wake you."

He went out the door.

21

South Africa

The call came the next day. The ring of the phone sounded astoundingly loud in the little whitewashed office. The orderly at the door took it and then went running for Brady.

It was Neal Hall. "Colonel, I've got to see you in Johannesburg, immediately."

"All right," Brady said. He looked at his watch. It was one o'clock. Then he looked up at Cody Ravel.

"How long to Johannesburg, Major?"

"Two hours," Cody said, "flight time."

"All right," Brady said into the phone. "We'll see you at six tonight. Where?"

"The Towers," Neal Hall said. "Your old suite. Same number."

"Fine." Brady put the phone down. He looked over at Cody. "We're going to Johannesburg. Get Carlton-Brooks in here."

They left an hour later, leaving Major Carlton-Brooks in charge of the camp. Edge had come out, glad for something to do, to preflight the airplane and have it ready.

"Wish I was going" had been his only comment.

"I don't blame you," Cody said, feeling the feverish rush to get away from the camp.

When he had the big airplane climbing steadily on course and the controls exact, Cody said, looking over at Brady, "I got a feeling that if enough people had known we were going, we'd have had company. Whether we wanted it or not."

Brady said, "This has got to be fast. I don't trust that goddamn Carlton-Brooks in charge."

"Well," Cody finally said, "he's all you got."

It was strange, even after such a short time, to be back in civilization. As they rode in from the airport, Cody stared out the window thinking back to the time, less than a month ago, when he'd made his first cab ride in.

Brady asked him, "What'd you say?"

"Nothing," Cody answered. Then he said, "Look, this meeting. Is there any need for me to be there? I got a little business of my own I'd like to tend to."

"Forget it," Brady said shortly. "You better know everything I do."

"All right," Cody said. But the thought of Flic had come to his mind.

They went directly up to the suite without asking at the desk.

Neal Hall opened the door immediately. He was obviously agitated.

"What the hell's going on, Neal?" Brady asked. They came into the middle of the room.

Hall just shook his head. "Fix yourself a drink first," he said, "if you want it. Whiskey's on the bar."

"No," Brady said. He sat down at the table. Cody followed him. "All right," Brady said, "what the hell's going on?"

"It's all gone cock awry," Hall said, looking tired.

"What's gone cock awry?"

"The lot of it," he said. He sounded disgusted and bitter and angry. He cut a hand through the air. "The operation, Angola, the lot."

Brady sat back in his chair. "All right. Let me have it slowly. In some kind of order."

"There'll be no operation in Angola," Hall said. He said it looking down at the table.

"What are you talking about? Are they pulling out the mercenary troops?"

"They never went! A bloody lot has happened since you went into bivouac. There's Portugal, which is complicated. There's been a political coup there and it's all changed. All of it. The settlers in Angola, the Europeans, are trying to reach a détente with the Frelimoists. They are talking now, not fighting. It's all over." He put his face between his two hands and stared down at the floor.

"No operation in Angola," Brady said. He looked out the balcony window.

"No," Hall said. "No cover. The political situation in the rest of the world is very bad. We have been denounced again in the United Nations, which is nothing new, but new resolutions have been voted. The pressure is intense. Our contacts in the South African government have asked us to leave as soon as possible. We have become a luxury they can no longer afford."

"Oh, shit," Brady said. He suddenly got up. "I guess I will have that drink. You want one, Cody?"

Cody shook his head.

When Brady was back, Hall said, "I shall give you one example of the pressure that is developing. A news team from a Swedish television station came to Salisbury. You know the mine outside of town, the gold mine. It's the custom there to give the African workers an hour break in the afternoon. They go up and sleep wherever they find themselves, under a tree, in the street. Wherever. The Swedish news team," he said with emphasis, "came in and filmed that pastoral scene, of a thousand workers sleeping an afternoon nap. And then," he said, and he began pounding his fist in his palm, "and then they went away and the commentary that goes with it is that here are innocent Africans *shot* down and *killed* by the imperialist government of *Rhodesia!*"

"Jesus," Brady said evenly.

"It's supposed to be a massacre. And it's been shown over half the *world!*"

Brady didn't say anything.

"So," Hall said, "you can begin to understand that it doesn't matter what we do. All they're looking for is an excuse. And they'll twist anything any way they can. In the United Nations," he said, "the black African bloc vote is very important. We're inconsequential. They'll trade us in a moment for help on other issues. All they're looking for is an excuse. It's all down to negotiations." He made a face. "Negotiations. What are we supposed to negotiate with? Our farms, our homes, our lives, the living we've built?" He suddenly got up. "I'm damned if I will."

"All right," Brady said evenly. "What are you telling me? Is it over? Is the operation off?"

The minister was at the balcony window. He was there a long moment looking out. Then he suddenly wheeled around. "No," he said. He raised his fist and walked to the table. "No."

Brady looked at him, waiting.

"No, I won't stand for it. No and no and no and no again." He put his clenched fist near Brady's face. "Matthew, give me one strike. I'm going against orders on this, but I can't stand it. I have been told to pull back. To cease and desist. But I cannot tolerate it. To take and take and take and never hit back. It's more than I can bear!"

He turned away and spoke with his back to them. "Give me this one strike. Three bases. There's only time for that. Nothing else would be permitted. But, God, go in and blow the bastards out of bed. Let them know we have some teeth too."

There was a long pause and Brady said, "We could use a little more time."

"There is no more time, Matthew. It has to be now or not at all." He turned and looked at the colonel. "I want particularly that big base at Chipedzia. That would be a rock right between their bloody teeth." He stopped and looked intently at Brady. "Do it for me, Matthew."

"All right," Brady said evenly.

"Do it for me now. It has to be now."

"All right," Brady said again.

"God." Hall turned away, running his hand over his head. "This will more than likely be my neck."

Brady got up without saying anything and got another drink. When he sat back down, he said, "All right. Tell me exactly how much time I've got."

"A week," Hall said. "At the most. And that means a week to get in, do the job, then clear out and dismiss your troops."

"Wow," Cody said, thinking about it.

The minister nodded. "I know what I'm asking. And how hard it will be. But it's going to take great effort on my part with my friends here in South Africa to get even that. I don't even know, yet, what I'll be able to think up to tell them."

Brady said, "All right, Neal. Now I've got to have the most up-to-date intelligence information you've got on the camps. This one at Chipedzia, especially. I want absolutely detailed information on troop strength."

Hall shook his head sadly. "I can't get it, Matt."

"What are you talking about? Bullshit, you can't get it. You've got to get it!"

"You don't understand, Matt. My minister has told me to cease and desist. There is no longer any mission. Therefore, there is no further reason for me to order out that type of information. It's outside my normal province. I'm in charge of internal security. If I went after the kind of information you want, it would be a dead tip-off."

"Ah, this is wonderful!" Brady said viciously. He got up and stalked to the balcony and threw his cigarette out. Coming back, he said, "Why, you're crazy! You talk like a man with a paper asshole. You fucking think I'd try to run an attack like this without up-to-date intelligence?"

Hall stood in the middle of the room, hearing him out. Then he said, quietly, "It gets worse, Matt."

"Worse?" Brady glared at him and spit viciously on the floor. "Worse? How the hell could it get worse? What, don't we get to use guns?"

"There's unconfirmed intelligence that, since they're not needed in Angola now, some of the Frelimo terrorists from Mozambique are going to be used against us from the bases in Zambia."

Brady just stared at him.

"It's unconfirmed, as I say, but you can imagine they're a better grade of troops than you could have normally expected."

Brady sat down. His face looked tired. "Christ, you don't ask much. As if there weren't already enough conditions on this mission, now we've got more. The people we're supposed to be working for don't want the job done. No intelligence. And now we got the Frelimoists *and* ZANU. Well, that's just dandy, Neal. You got more nerve than a fucking spinal cord to ask me to do this."

"Nerve?" Hall's face flamed and his voice turned angry. He drew himself up. "Nerve? Don't you talk to me about nerve, Matthew Brady! We've been operating on nothing *but* nerve in this godforsaken country for the last eight years! And there's some people sitting along that northern border might be called upon for a bit of nerve themselves." He slammed his hand down on the table. "I'm a soldier. I can't fight world opinion, I can't pussyfoot around with the politicians, I can't fight economic sanctions, but, by God, sir, I can fight my enemy if I can get him under a gun! Nerve? Don't you dare speak to me about nerve!" He was so angry his whole body was trembling. "I said I was a soldier. Are you?"

At length, Brady said, "Sit down, Neal. And cool off." Brady lit a cigarette, looking at the minister through the smoke.

No one said anything. Then Brady looked around at Cody. "What do you think, Major?"

"I think it's crazy," Cody said. "I think he's crazy."

"Think we ought to try it?"

Cody shrugged. "I don't give a shit. Why not?"

Brady laughed, a short bark. "Goddamn you, Neal. Now I must be the one that's crazy."

The minister was leaning forward anxiously. "It's got to be quick, Matt. The buildup from Mozambique is pushing. There's a reason for bringing in those seasoned troops, and my fear is that their first strike is going to be a big one."

Brady stood up. "All right, Neal. You got a game. But on your end, you better move heaven and earth to get me as much intelligence as possible." He looked long and hard at the minister. "Being a soldier doesn't mean you've got to be stupid."

"I will do everything I can."

"Do a little more."

At the door, Brady said, "Today is Tuesday. We'll go in Sunday morning." Then he half smiled and shook his head. "If I were you, I'd be out of town somewhere."

Cody shook hands with the minister. "How's that family we stayed with up there, the Longhursts, doing?"

"They're fine," Hall said.

"Listen—" Cody began. Then he stopped.

"What?"

"Nothing." He shook his head. "Just a thought."

22

Forward Camp

Porterfield was no better the next day, and there was a great deal of grumbling, but no one approached either Brady or Cody.

Brady told the men the news at noon the next day in the mess hall.

He was brief. "Plans have changed," he said, his voice tough. "We're going in much sooner than was anticipated. In the next few days. There will not be the training time we'd expected, so you will be worked long and hard in the little while we have left. Any of you not mentally ready for combat had better damn well get ready. And quick."

Cody could feel his own excitement beginning to rise.

He said to Brady, "Matt, what's going to be my job in the actual operation?"

Brady looked at him steadily. "What do you want your job to be?"

"I don't know."

"You'll stay with the airplanes and sweat us out. Does that suit you?"

"I don't know," Cody said again.

"It'll have to. I'm not going to risk my lead pilot in combat. Who'd bring us home?"

"I understand," Cody said. But he didn't know if he were feeling relief or disappointment.

Major Carlton-Brooks was feeling relief. He was not so much afraid of the combat as he was the time dragging on. Every day he'd seen that last bottle of Scotch diminishing inch by inch.

John Peters and Lavel Horstmann met in a corner of the barracks that evening after supper formation. "It's tonight," Peters told him in a low voice. "We've got to get out tonight, else they'll have us in their bloody game."

Lavel Horstmann had been thinking about it ever since noon. When Brady had made his announcement, the Belgian had felt his stomach do a twist. He'd suddenly envisioned himself charging into that camp, exposed and vulnerable. There was no safety in their few numbers. No way to be lost in the mass. A man would have to take chances, risk himself. Horstmann was suddenly very frightened. "Yes," he said. There was sweat on his face.

"We'll go tonight," Peters said. Then he cursed. "If they just weren't sitting up with that bloody Porterfield."

"We could lop him off," Horstmann said.

But Peters shook his head. "No. Too risky. We'll just get out on the sly."

They awoke Matthew Brady at five the next morning, Carlton-Brooks and Sergeant Major Lord.

"What?" he said, swinging around on his bed, dazedly. "Come in!"

Carlton-Brooks put his head inside the door. "May we see you, sir?" He was pale and his voice was trembling.

"What the hell?"

"In your office, sir. It's important."

Brady ran a hand over his face. "All right. But call Major Ravel. I'll be a minute."

"Very good, sir."

"Shit," he said, sitting around on the side of his bed and trying to see the time on the luminous dial of his watch. "What now?"

They were waiting for him when he arrived. Cody was wearing only his fatigue trousers, yawning and rubbing his hand over his face, but Carlton-Brooks and Lord were dressed. Lord was standing at attention in front of Brady's desk.

"All right," Brady said. He went around and sat down. "What the hell's this all about?"

There was a moment and then Carlton-Brooks said, from where he was standing behind the sergeant, "I'm afraid it's trouble, sir."

"I could figure that out, Major," Brady said dryly. "I didn't think you woke me up to tell me Lindberg had just landed."

"It's my fault, sir," Lord said. There was a quiver in his voice.

At four that morning, Horstmann and Peters had made their move. They'd broken into the mess hall and packed two musette bags with enough rations for a week, taking their own canteens and as many others as they could find. Peters had also appropriated a kitchen knife, but he hadn't let Horstmann see him slip it in his shirt. There was no use taking the AK-47s, not without ammunition. And there was no way to get into the grenades and other explosives.

In the night, Peters had hidden at the corner of a barracks while he told Horstmann to go first. "Just over the gate, lad," he'd said. "And I'll watch. Then you wait for me a quarter of a mile on. Due south, now. There's a good lad. Go on now."

He'd lain there, watching Horstmann go up and over the gate and drop down on the other side. If a challenge had come, he'd have gone back immediately to his own barracks, discarding his provisions and water.

But Horstmann had got away safely. Peters lay a few moments longer, watching, alert for any patrol that might be out. It remained quiet. He'd waited a little while more, then got up and sprinted for the high gate. It was hard work getting up the mesh wire with all the equipment pulling on his back. He'd climbed, his fingers gripping the wire hard, digging in with the toes of his combat boots. Then he was at the top, and he pulled himself up and swung a leg over. For a second, he sat there, breathing hard.

It was then that Dougie Lord had come charging out of the dark. "Halt!" he'd shouted. "Halt you!" He had his pistol drawn and he pointed it up at Peters.

Peters said, "Who's that?" Then he'd recognized Lord. "Oh," he said, contempt in his voice. "It's only you, Dougie Lord."

"John Peters! Come down! Instantly or I'll shoot! By God!"

But Peters had just looked down at him. "You won't shoot me," he'd said, the contempt plain in his voice. "This is John Peters." He'd started to swing a leg over. "And if you report me before I'm far away I'll come back and *kill* you."

"Stop!" Lord had shouted at him futilely, knowing already that he couldn't shoot. "Halt! I order you! Halt!"

But Peters had just gone on down the fence and vanished into the dark. And Lord had stood there, biting his lip, tears of frustration in his eyes.

Brady sat listening, his face impassive. When the report was over, Cody said tiredly, "Oh, shit! That tears it."

Carlton-Brooks said hoarsely, "We've got Peters, sir. But I'm afraid Horstmann has got away. Sergeant Lord came to me and we activated two of the trucks and sent four of the policemen out in them. They figured rightly that they'd go due south. They found Peters just up the road a mile."

"I'm so bloody sorry, sir," Lord said. A tear came out of his eye and rolled down his cheek. Brady looked at him in disgust and Carlton-Brooks said sharply, "Get hold of yourself, man!"

"But I couldn't shoot him!" Lord said, almost crying out loud. "I a'llus prided myself on being a tip-top soldier. And I couldn't bloody shoot him! I was afraid of him, from the Congo."

"Get him out of here," Brady said.

Then he looked at his watch. "About an hour to dawn. He'll have a two-hour start. We'll send the trucks out, but I think we got a better chance in the airplane. There's no use going until we can see. But let's get off right as soon as the sun's up."

"I'll go get ready," Cody said. He looked at Brady. "This is a bad break, Matt."

But Brady was looking thoughtful. "Maybe we can get some good out of it."

They took Hawthorne and another man from the Able team along in the airplane. Brady sat up front with Cody in the copilot's seat. The sun came up, hot and brilliant, on their right as they took off. Behind them, the trucks were going out the gate of the camp, trailing thin plumes of dust.

As they flew, Brady looked out the window at the treeless, featureless landscape. "Well," he said, "he can run, but he can't hide."

"Not down there."

"Joe Louis said that about the Billy Conn fight. The

old dancing master." Brady went back to looking out the side window, whistling tunelessly.

They could see for fifty miles in any direction. The air was clean and arid and dry, and the landscape below plain and bare. What few trees there were, were brown and leafless.

"You heading due south?" Brady asked.

"Right."

They flew on for another moment or two, the engines droning monotonously. Cody turned from the controls and glanced back through the passageway into the cabin. Hawthorne was sitting in the first row of seats with the other man from his command.

Brady said, "Ought to see him in a minute."

"Yes," Cody said. "He can't be far."

Brady looked out ahead. "Wonder what would make a man run off out into the desert like this?"

"Couldn't have been happy," Cody said. He put out his hand and set a prop forward a little.

"Didn't have a clue where they were. Yet they jumped the fences and were going to run ass off in the night. That's crazy."

"Scared, I guess," Cody said.

There was a long moment. Brady said, "You can't have soldiers like that."

"I guess they figured to wind up somewhere. I guess anything was better to them. We been training them pretty hard."

Brady had an AK-47 leaned up against the console between the two seats. He picked it up and cradled it in his lap.

"There he is," Cody said.

"Where?"

"Dead ahead. About a mile. See him?" He pointed out the windshield.

"Not yet."

"By that little rise. Now he's seen us. He's turning around and looking." Cody leaned forward and pulled both throttles back and began to lose altitude. He glanced at the altimeter, estimating they were about five hundred feet above the ground.

"Oh, yeah," Brady said. He unbuckled his seat belt and got up, balancing the AK-47 in one hand.

"Hey, wait. What do you want me to do? I can't land. Not here. You want me to hold over him for the trucks?"

Brady stopped in the passageway. "I want you to get this thing down as low and slow as you can get it and make a pass over him. If I miss the first time, make another one."

"What! Wait a minute; what are you going to do?"

But Brady was gone.

Cody reduced power further. Ahead, he could see the figure turn and start to run. Cody could tell he would be too high and too fast, so he threw the plane over in a steep bank and flew it through a 360 degree turn. As he came around, he saw his altitude was down and that his speed was dropping. He estimated them to be a hundred feet off the ground. The figure ahead was still running. Cody put the nose on him, depressing it as he cranked in thirty degrees of flaps.

Brady had motioned Hawthorne and his man to the back of the plane. There he pointed at the side cargo door. "Open it," he yelled. "Just pull that lever and swing it back."

They almost lost their balance as Cody heeled the plane over in the turn, but then they had it open and locked it back. There was a sudden rush of air and noise. They looked questioningly at Brady. He motioned them away and eased forward, catching hold of the side of the fuselage, and knelt down. He braced himself against the door, putting out his rifle and sighting just below the wing.

Cody saw the running figure come up rapidly, saw him turn and glance back. Then he heard the sudden roar from the rear of the plane and saw the puffs of dust dancing around Horstmann, saw him stumble, then flip and almost cartwheel.

"Oh, hell," he said involuntarily. He stared straight ahead out the windshield.

Then he felt something touch his shoulder. He looked back. It was the man from Hawthorne's team. His face was white. He said, his voice shaky even in the yell he used to get over the sound of the engines, "Colonel says to make another pass."

Cody nodded woodenly. He heeled the airplane over, bringing it sharply around. He saw the crumpled man ahead. He eased the plane over to the right so there'd be a clear field of fire out the left side of the airplane. As they passed over, he heard the sudden roar again, mixing in with the sound of the engines and the rush of the air. But he didn't look to see dust splattering around Horstmann, nor his body twitching.

In the back, Brady stood up, pulling the lever to extract a spent cartridge. The two soldiers were staring at him. He stepped close to them and yelled, "I just saved you and every man in your team ten thousand dollars. If that man had got away, that's what it would have cost you."

They stared back.

"Now close that door," Brady said. He went forward.

Only once did they speak on the flight back. That was when they saw the trucks approaching ahead. Brady said, "Buzz those trucks. And waggle your wings in the victory salute."

Cody said, "I'll buzz 'em to let them know to head back. But I'm fucked if I'll give any victory salute about shooting a man down."

Brady leaned close to his ear. "You got a lot to learn, cowboy."

They talked about it that night in quiet tones. There was no anger, no indignation, no move to form a delegation. They were too stunned for that. In an hour after they'd returned, every man knew the story. The guard watching John Peters had told him with relish. "Be glad we caught you, lad. This way you'll get a decent firing squad and a proper burial. Colonel just sent two men out to cover old Horstmann over with sand."

Hawthorne couldn't stop talking about it. "He just kneels down there, like it's a bloody fox hunt. And then, TA-TA-TA, pings him off. Just like that. Then cool as hell tells us we'd 'ave lost ten grand if he don't do it. Christ! Bloody Christ!"

It was Gerry Ruger who'd finally said, "Well, we would have, wouldn't we? All of us. Because Peters wanted to do a bunk. Horstmann knew the bloody rules."

He and Schneider had been sitting quietly through most of the talk. Now Schneider shrugged. "Does it matter? Would Horstmann have been better off brought back and shot by a firing squad?"

A man, an Italian named Cartinea, said, "Well, I don't care for it. It's barbaric. There's no need to shoot your own men."

The German looked at him coldly. "I myself am glad. I think now there is not a man in this force who does not believe the colonel is serious. If I'm to go into combat, I want orders obeyed so that we operate like a well-run machine."

Gerry Ruger said quietly, "I agree."

Cody asked, "What are you going to do with Peters, Matt?"

"Well, let's see. Tomorrow's Friday. I'm gonna shoot him. About six in the evening."

"With a firing squad?"

"No," Brady said. "I'll do it myself. It's my responsibility."

There was a long silence. A bug had got into the room, and it kept flying into the light bulb, making a banging noise.

Cody finally asked, "Why'd you do it, Matt? For the effect? For disciplinary purposes?"

"I did it because I had to."

"Com'on! You didn't have to kill him like that."

"You still don't quite get it, do you?" Brady asked him. "The second that soldier jumped that fence and began running, he was jeopardizing this mission. He had become the enemy. And it was my *job* to stop him, not rationalize his motives. He got on the other side and I killed him, Cody, for the simple reason that he'd become the enemy."

Cody didn't say anything. The bug kept banging away at the light bulb.

The training went on as usual the next morning.

Two men were selected from the seven held in reserve to take Peters' and Horstmann's places. Hawthorne went to Brady to say that Dougie Lord wanted to be one of the two.

Brady had said, "No way."

Then Hawthorne and Schneider had gone to Cody, and Cody had gone to Brady. "Give him a chance," Cody said. "He feels bad."

"No," Brady said again.

"You're going to have to argue with me about this one. Look, fuck it. I think the old man's still got it. And being a soldier is all he's got." He said brutally, "You're old. How'd you like to be out of chances? I trust him and I insist."

Brady looked at him strangely. "If you feel that strong about it."

"I do."

Porterfield died at ten that morning. They came running to tell Brady about it up on the tower as he was supervising a practice attack. He shrugged. "Bury him."

In two days, they had to routinize the execution of three separate attacks. In desperation, they'd made a crude setup of each camp, and Carlton-Brooks was overseeing one while Cody took the second and Brady the main attack on Chipedzia.

That morning, he'd told Cody bitterly, "You see we have no choice. We can make the assumption that Chipedzia will be the toughest objective, but you can't make assumptions in battle. We can't pull men out of the other combat teams to reinforce this one. We have to treat them equally, knowing full well that we shall meet twice the resistance at Chipedzia. But we have no up-to-date intelligence. Goddamn that Neal Hall, anyway. This is absurd!"

"Why can't we make assumptions?" Cody had asked him.

"Because you can't," Brady said, angry at the situation. "You make battle plans based on intelligence. We have none. As surely as I depleted men from one of the other teams, they would run into the heaviest concentration. So you cannot do that. That's criminal. That is unfair. That is inhumane. To a soldier. The criminal action in command is to send troops into a battle they can't win. Therefore, if you have to guess, you spread the guess evenly. That's your responsibility to your men."

In the hot sun and the exhaustion of the day, Dougie Lord ran every step of the way. The burning embarrassment of not being able to shoot, of feeling fear of Peters was still with him.

Once Hawthorne said, "Take it easy, Dougie. It's a long day."

"I'm all right, Captain," was all he'd answered. But he wouldn't get the answer about himself until there was the combat. This was just practice. And it didn't count.

They had finished lunch and were sitting there, drinking bitter coffee.

Cody said, "Matt, what are you going to do about John Peters?"

Brady looked at his watch. "I'm going to shoot him in five hours," he said matter-of-factly. "I told you that yesterday."

Carlton-Brooks' face twitched, but Cody was impassive. Cody said, "You are?"

"That's what I said, wasn't it?"

Cody leaned back in his chair and folded his arms. "Well, give us the details. I mean, exactly how."

Brady gave him a little glance. "I didn't know you were interested in that sort of thing, cowboy. Now, Major Brooks, here," he gestured across the table, "he's fascinated. Look at his face."

"Well, I've been thinking about it," Cody said. "And now I am interested." There was nothing in his voice exactly. "I want to know how you're going to do it."

Brady wiped his mouth with his shirt sleeve and lit a cigarette. He leaned over and spat on the floor. "With a gun," he said.

"No shit? Well, when's the trial? The court-martial?"

"Oh, we done had that. The jury was out when he was climbing that fence. When he fell on the wrong side, they found him guilty."

"I see. So now you're going to shoot him."

Carlton-Brooks cleared his throat. His voice was nervous. "I say, would anyone like more coffee?"

They paid him no attention.

"But exactly how, Matt? You going to assemble the troops and blindfold him and put him on his knees and shoot him in the back of the head? You going to use an automatic weapon? A pistol? One of the AK-47s or an FN? I mean, there could be a point of symbolism in this. Especially whether it's an AK-47 or an FN. What about it?"

Cody lounged back in his chair, tipping it back on its hind legs. It was impossible to tell what was in Brady's face. It could have been a smile.

"Well," the colonel said, "since you're so fucking interested, no, I ain't going to assemble the troops. I'm just going to go get him and march him out into the desert and shoot him."

"In the head? In the heart? In the belly?"

Brady looked at him, his face now turning flat.

"Then you going to bury him? Or what about cutting his head off and nailing it to the gate as a warning to everybody else?"

"That's not a bad idea," Brady said. He flicked cigarette ashes onto his plate.

Cody got up. "Major," he said to Carlton-Brooks, "will you please excuse us?"

"Of course, sir," the adjutant said. He scrambled to his feet and hurried out. Cody followed and made sure the door was closed. He came back to the table. "No," he said distinctly.

"No what, cowboy?"

"No, you're not going to shoot John Peters."

Brady laughed harshly, with no humor. "The hell I'm not."

Cody sat down, drawing his chair close to the table. "There is no point in it, Matt. Dammit. Not now."

"I said I would. That's the point. It's discipline."

"Discipline? Hell, man, we're going in, in two days. This whole goddamn operation will be over in a week. You let Porterfield die. Goddamn, how many examples do you need?"

"What is all this? How come you care so much about John Peters?"

Cody slapped his hand down on the table. "I don't give a *shit* about John Peters! He could get run over by a truck tomorrow and I wouldn't even notice!" He leaned forward. "But I do give a shit about myself. And if I let this happen, then there's something wrong with me."

Brady laughed, that same bad sound again. "I thought you were the original boy wonder who didn't care about nothing."

"Let's leave my character out of this for the time being. Look, I didn't like it about Horstmann, but I could understand a little. I liked it about Porterfield even less, but again, so okay. But there's not any fucking point to shooting Peters and you know it. Look, lock him up. Put him in solitary on bread and water. Deny him all pay and privileges. But don't shoot him."

"Oh?"

"No. I won't let you."

They stared at each other for a moment. Brady said, his voice going down low in his throat, "How do you plan to stop me, cowboy?"

Cody pushed his chair back from the table. "If you do, I won't fly the airplane."

There was a long silence. Brady spit on the floor again. "You trying to play cards with me, cowboy?"

"You heard what I said."

Brady nodded. His face looked almost good-humored. "You got a good hand. I admit it. But I got a better one."

Cody didn't say anything.

"You don't fly the airplane and I'll shoot you also. How's that?

Cody pushed his chair back further. Then he reached in the waistband of his fatigues and pulled out the 9 mm automatic. He cocked the hammer, holding the muzzle steady on Brady's face. "I got one of these too," Cody said. "And you try to shoot me, or have me shot, and I'm going to shoot a few folks on my own at the same time."

For a long time, Brady looked from Cody's face to the gun and then back to the pilot's face. At length, he got out a cigarette and lit it, pulling a kitchen match across the table top. The drag of the match on the wood made a grating sound in the silent room.

"Shit," Brady finally said.

With his thumb, Cody slowly let the hammer down and then put the pistol back in his belt. He sat back and folded his arms.

"Well, well, well," Brady said. "It's mighty nice to have my opinion of a man confirmed, but I'd have preferred less personal circumstances." He slowly shook his head and then let out a long breath. "Okay. I fold. But you get that little motherfucker in here. Right now. I want him to know who it was that saved his popcorn ass."

Cody got up. At the door, Brady said, "He won't thank you for it. All it'll make him think is that you're weak. I know his kind."

Cody turned. "I didn't do it for Peters, Matt," he said. "Get that through your head. And I don't care what he thinks." He opened the door and told the guard to have Peters brought over. "And Major Carlton-Brooks and Sergeant Major Lord."

When he turned back into the room, Brady was grinning at him cynically. "So this is the boy who two weeks ago didn't want to have a command. My, my, my. What has God wrought?"

"Oh, go to hell, Matt."

They brought Peters marching in. By then, Brady was at his desk and Cody was in a chair just behind him. Peters stopped two paces from the desk, snapped to attention, and said, "Sir!"

Brady looked at him with disgust. Carlton-Brooks and Dougie Lord were standing back by the door.

"At ease," Brady said in his flat voice.

Peters' feet stamped and his hands clamped together behind his back.

Christ, Brady thought, he's going to play the good soldier. He looked over at Cody, grinning cynically.

Peters was more frightened than he'd ever been in his life. His eyes were glazed. He ran a quick tongue over his dry lips. Usually he could say he was sorry; usually he could jolly his way out of a mess. Swear he was sorry and would try to do better. And they always bought it.

But he wasn't sure of that now. They'd told him over and over how the colonel had killed Horstmann. And they'd come by and told him the word was out: the colonel was going to have him shot. Immediately.

Standing there, he didn't like what he saw in Brady's face. A little tic began at the corner of Peters' eye.

Brady said levelly, "Peters, you deliberately and willfully broke the military code that was established for this organization. That code was explained to you in advance, and the consequences were explained to you. When you broke that code, you made yourself eligible for those consequences."

"Sir!" Peters said, breaking in. "Begging the colonel's pardon, sir. I realize that now, sir, and I've come to say I'm bloody sorry and that I'll take my punishment like I ought and be a better soldier for it."

"You can just can that shit," Brady said in a bored voice. "This is not a trial. Excuses or defenses won't be accepted. You tried yourself when you went over the fence. All you're here for is sentencing."

The tic at the corner of Peters' eye grew more pronounced. He could feel a pounding in his head. "I don't recognize the authority of this court," he said rapidly, shrilly.

Brady looked over at Cody. "Have the clerk of the court note the prisoner's objection," he said sarcastically.

"You've got no bloody authority!" Peters screamed shrilly. "This ain't no legal court. You ain't no bloody country. You ain't England!"

"Peters!" Brady said, coming back to the soldier. "Keep your goddamn voice down when you're addressing me." He stared hard at the soldier, noticing how he was trembling.

Peters swallowed rapidly. His eyes were fixed on the wall just behind Brady's head. The blood was thudding in his temple.

He had the knife. When they'd caught him, he'd managed to hide it between the cheeks of his buttocks, and they'd missed it in the perfunctory search they'd given him. Now he had it inside the loose blouse of his combat fatigues.

Brady said, "You talk about my authority. All right. I'm going to explain it to you. For your benefit and for the benefit of the rest of the men in this room. Some of them also don't understand it." He looked around at Cody and then glanced at Carlton-Brooks and Sergeant Lord.

"Men," Brady said, "make authority. Not courts or countries. Nationalism and patriotism are just bullshit words that mean everyone is in the same boat together. A matter of the common good. So I don't need a flag sitting behind my desk to have authority over you. It's enough that I represent the common interests of our cause. A cause you volunteered for." He looked around at Cody. "How's that, Major?"

Cody ignored the sarcasm. Instead, he leaned forward in his chair, watching Peters.

Brady was getting bored with the whole business. "Anyway," he said, coming back to Peters, "it doesn't matter if you understand or not. I don't much care. I sentence you to be shot at six o'clock this evening." Then he looked over at Cody, the sour smile back on his face. "However, because of *executive* clemency, that sentence will—"

The knife was suddenly in Peters' hand as he launched himself across the desk. He was screaming as his arm rose and as he drove the knife deep into Brady's chest.

The colonel was still looking at Cody when the knife hit him. He said, "Oh," and swung out his arm in reflex, hitting Peters, knocking him off the desk. Peters fell, tugging the knife free. Then he was up and his arm was rising.

In the back, Carlton-Brooks and Lord stood as if in shock. Carlton-Brooks whispered, "Oh, my God!"

Cody had not seen the knife, had not realized what was happening, until he saw it go into Brady's side. It was like slow motion. He was reaching for his pistol, but it seemed to take forever to get it out. Peters was coming forward again, the knife already starting on its downward thrust. Cody slumped out of the chair and onto his knees. He held the automatic thrust straight out in front of him with both hands. The muzzle was almost against Peters' chest. He fired and the impact of the bullet knocked the soldier across the room and into the wall and then to a heap on the floor.

Then time came back into motion, and Cody jumped to his feet and ran across and shot Peters again in the head.

It was quiet in the room. Cody whirled. Brady was sitting on the floor, both hands pressed to the side of his chest, his face tight against the pain.

Cody ran to Brady and laid him back. With both hands, he ripped open the front of the colonel's blouse. The knife had gone in on the left side, about midway up. Over Cody's shoulder Sergeant Major Lord said, "God!" and turned away. The knife had gone in between two ribs. The gash was an inch long and wide and ugly looking. Cody could see pink froth blowing out and hear the wind sucking back and forth as Brady breathed.

He tried to think what he should do first. It had been so long since he'd had the paramedical training in the special forces. "It's in the lung," he said to Brady. "I don't know how deep."

"Pressure," Brady said, grating the words out. "Tape it. Tight."

Cody looked up. Carlton-Brooks was still standing there, his face slack. "Get the medical chest," Cody yelled at him. "Goddamn you, MOVE."

Working swiftly, Cody tore open a big packet of gauze, found the sulfa powder and dusted the gauze and the wound. The sucking noise of the wind going back and forth through the wound sounded louder.

Brady watched him with the sulfa powder. "I wouldn't worry too much about infection, cowboy. Might not live that long." He tried to laugh.

"Shut up," Cody said. He slapped the gauze pad over the gash and then began tearing off long strips of two-inch-wide tape and smoothing them over the wound, adhering them halfway around Brady's hard chest.

While he worked, Cody's mind began to clear. There were certain things that had to be done. He'd need the airplane. He said to the military policeman, "Get me Captain Edge! On the double! No! Tell him to preflight

297

the number one DC-3, start the engines, and have it ready to go when we get there."

"Got to sit up," Brady said. He began to struggle.

Cody helped him, lifting him as gingerly as he could. Brady sat there like a Buddha, his legs crossed, holding tight against the pain. A little bubble of blood came out the corner of his mouth. He coughed, the noise rattling deep in his chest. He coughed again and then spit out a great wad of saliva and blood.

"Shit," he said. "Oh, shit."

"Take it easy, Matt," Cody said automatically. He tried to think. He'd need someone to tend to Brady while he flew the airplane. No, he thought, he'd need two men. He said to Carlton-Brooks, "Get me Schneider and Ruger. In here. On the double!" As the major ran out, he told Sergeant Lord, "And you get a truck and a driver and have it right at the door. With the motor running."

Brady was breathing easier now, with the hole taped shut, and the bad noise was gone. Cody rummaged in the medicine chest and came out with a morphine styrette. He started to open it, but Brady said, "No. Give me whiskey."

Cody said, "Matt, this is for shock."

"Whiskey do the same," Brady said. His face was white and there was sweat all over it. "Got to cut some of this blood out my throat."

Cody jumped up and ran to the filing cabinet. He came back with the bottle of Scotch, jerking at the cap. Brady was holding both hands to his chest, so Cody put the bottle to his mouth. Brady pulled hard three, four, five times and then signaled with his eyes. Cody lowered the bottle.

"Shit," Brady said, the word coming out of him like gravel. Then he coughed and spit again. "What a fuck-up," he said.

"Matt," Cody said, "I'm sorry. Jesus Christ, I'm sorry. It wouldn't have happened if I hadn't—"

"Never be sorry, cowboy," Brady said. Some of the color was coming back into his face with the whiskey. His voice sounded stronger. "Waste of time." Then he tried to laugh, but it ended in a grimace of pain. He said, "But the joke's on you on this." He coughed and then coughed again, and Cody wiped his mouth with a gauze pad. "Big joke on you."

"Take it easy, Matt, will you?"

"Not easy for you. Not now." He doubled over a little, grimacing, his breath coming in short gasps. "Whiskey," he grated out.

Cody held the bottle up to Brady's lips again. Brady took two swallows and then pulled his mouth away. A little of the whiskey ran out and down his chest. " 'Bout to vomit," he said. "Can't do that."

Cody squatted there, watching him intently. He felt bad, desperate, uncertain.

"Yeah," Brady said, breathing easier again. "Now you got it. Boy wonder didn't want a command. Didn't want no responsibility." He tried again to laugh. Cody put the bottle to Brady's lips again.

"Great stuff," Brady said, "whiskey."

"Matt, please quit trying to talk. We're getting you out of here in a minute. To help. You're going to be all right."

"No hospitals," Brady said. "Mission. Don't you forget it." He coughed. His face was going pale again. "We got a commitment. No, now you got a commitment. You in the head chair now, cowboy. And it's a hard motherfucker. Ain't no cushions to sit on in the head chair. Ain't that a joke. Ain't that a funny joke. The soft cowboy who thought he was so tough. And now he's going to have to—" He suddenly doubled up, squeezing himself tight with his hands. "Goddamn this," he said loudly.

Schneider and Ruger came running into the room.

They asked nothing, but they gave a quick glance at the heap that Peters made against the wall.

"We're taking him out," Cody said. "Make a chair carry with your arms and I'll get him in it."

They knelt on each side of Brady, locking their arms together almost at the floor. As gently as he could, Cody eased the colonel up and onto the seat their arms made. Brady was still holding his hands pressed to the left side of his chest, as if to hold the life in. Cody grabbed the bottle of Scotch and, supporting Brady with one hand, accompanied them out the door.

They sat in the tailgate of the truck with Schneider and Ruger supporting him on either side.

Carlton-Brooks was standing by. Cody said to him, "I'll be back in five hours. You hold them together. No explanations to the troops. I'll handle that."

"Yes, sir." Carlton-Brooks' pink face was flushed and sweating.

"I'm trusting you, Jack," Cody said.

The adjutant stood and watched as they drove off slowly. Then he walked back into the office. He looked at Peters, then at the floor where Brady had bled. He noticed the open file drawer and was going to shut it when he saw the two bottles of Scotch inside. For an instant, he stared at them. Then he shut the drawer. "Time enough for that later," he said aloud.

He went outside. "Guard!" he shouted.

A soldier came running up.

"Get that body out of there and then secure this office. No one is to enter. And I want that body disposed of in a hurry."

"Sir!" the guard said.

Brady and the two soldiers were far in the back, sitting three abreast in the little canvas seats. It would be easier to unload him from there when they landed.

"You're wasting gasoline," Brady told him with pain on his face.

"Fuck you," Cody had said.

Salisbury was out. Any place in Rhodesia was out, even though for one crazy instant Cody'd thought of taking Brady to Ruth. But then, they'd have to get him into the infirmary in Shamva, and he'd never have made that.

No hospitals, Brady had said.

So it had to be Johannesburg, the only place he had any contacts. He thought of Weston, but that was too risky. Too easy for someone to make the connection, too easy to blow Weston's cover.

He suddenly thought, I'm thinking like Brady. Mission. The mission.

There had really only been one alternative from the first, and he'd known it instinctively. Now, within radio range of Johannesburg he picked up the mike and thumbed the switch.

"Johannesburg approach. Douglas eight-two-five George."

"Johannesburg approach. Go ahead eight-two-five."

"Eight-two-five approximately one zero zero miles out. Inbound for a landing. Heading ninety-five degrees. Landing approximately thirty minutes. Have emergency medical on board. Request ambulance meeting. Request straight in vectoring."

"Understood, eight-two-five. Affirmative compliance. Radar contact niner five miles north Johannesburg International. Continue inbound. Straight in approach approved. Landing runway one niner."

Cody thumbed the mike. "Eight-two-five, request you telephone a Louisa Durier. Repeat, Louisa Durier. Repeat, Louisa Durier." He read off a card from his billfold. "Phone number four six two one eight zero. Imperative she meet this airplane at Johannesburg International. Will be taxiing direct to transit parking. Pilot Cody Ravel. Essential you transmit."

"Understood, eight-two-five. Affirmative compliance. Continue normal navigation."

And pray, Cody thought. It was a risk, but then what in this whole operation wasn't? Flic. He was taking Brady to Flic. It should have been funny, but it wasn't.

Schneider came forward.

Cody turned his head slightly. "How is he?"

"Not good, I think," the German said. "He is very weak."

"Tell him I said to hold on. Tell him I never lost a passenger yet, and he better not be the first."

Schneider bent down by Cody's ear. "He is very worried that you will take him to a hospital. He says that would jeopardize the mission. He keeps trying to talk about it."

"Goddammit," Cody said. "Tell him I'm not taking him to any fucking hospital! Tell him I know what I'm doing and for him to shut his mouth and obey orders."

Schneider said, "Yes sir, I will tell him that. I think that is what is worrying him." He hesitated a beat. "He kept insisting I come and tell you, you have to have a tough ass to sit in the head chair. Pardon me, sir."

Cody looked around. "Tell him I understand that. Tell him not to worry."

"I will tell him, sir. He will be glad to know that."

But do I know it, Cody thought. Do I really know it? He ran his hand through his hair.

The hell of it, he thought, is that I do know. And I know what it's going to feel like and what it's going to require, and I just hope to hell I can handle it.

Then they were booming in over the low brown hills and Cody was lining up the airplane for the final descent onto the silvery, shimmering runway. He cut power, pulled on flaps and then they were settling and he was taxiing for the transit parking.

They had let both the ambulance and the girl drive out onto the parking ramp. She was standing by her car, the wind blowing her dress. He didn't bother to turn the airplane, just drove it straight to them and killed the engines. Then he leaped out of the seat and jumped out.

The ambulance attendants were there with a roll-away stretcher. "What is it, sir?" one of them asked.

"Heart attack," Cody said. "Give him oxygen, nothing else."

Then he saw Flic running forward and he ran to meet her. He grabbed her shoulders as she came up.

"Look, this is my colonel. I can't send him to a hospital. Do you understand?" He could feel the thin silk of the dress under his hands.

"Yes—well. Yes, of course. It's important?"

"It's fucking important," he said fiercely. "Do you know a doctor you can trust? Absolutely. That won't talk."

"Yes," she said, looking dazed. "Yes."

"Absolutely?"

She hesitated only for a second. "One of my clients."

He was still gripping her fiercely by the shoulders. "Is he a surgeon?"

"Yes," she said. "I think so."

"Will he come immediately?"

Now she didn't hesitate. "If I call him."

"Then call him," Cody said, the hard driving urgency in his voice. "I'm going to tell this ambulance to take him to your house. That's where he'll have to be. And you get that doctor there as fast as he can move." He was looking down into her face. "He's got an hour to live if he doesn't get help. Do you understand?"

"Yes," she said, still a little dazed.

They were carrying Brady by, and Cody broke off to

go over to him. He was on his back, his face very white. They halted at the ambulance door. Cody said to the attendant, "Sit him up."

"What, sir?"

"I said, SIT HIM UP!"

"But you said a heart attack."

"Fuck what I said. In that ambulance, I want him sitting up." He suddenly thrust out the bottle of Scotch. "And give some of this on the ride in." Then he said. "No," and pulled the bottle back. He knelt down by the side of the stretcher. "Matt, how you doing?"

The voice was a gurgle. His face was much older. Cody slipped the bottle of Scotch down inside the sheet. "There's a little something for the trip." Then he took out the 9 mm automatic and cocked it so the ambulance attendants could see. He put it under the sheet, feeling for Brady's hand. He looked up at the attendants. "And here's something else for speed. If they don't get you there in fifteen minutes, shoot the bastards in the back of the head."

"Cowboy." Brady's voice was a whisper. Cody bent down. "See you in a few days. Kick the shit out of the bastards."

"Count on it," Cody said. Then he straightened. He motioned. "Get him in there. And you better set a new world's record." He gave them the address to Flic's house.

They had no questions, but began loading Brady immediately. "Don't worry, sir," one of them said. "We'll take care of him."

Cody turned around and took Flic by the shoulders and leaned down and kissed her briefly on the lips. "I've got to trust you on this. Can I?" He looked hard into her eyes.

"Yes," she said. "Of course."

"No," he said, "it's not of course. But it has to be.

There's a lot of lives at stake here. No Landon. No nothing. Just do as I've told you."

"All right," she said. She tried to put her arms around him, but he held her off at arm's length.

"Look, Louisa, you asked me for something."

"I remember," she said.

"Don't let me down on this and I won't let you down on that. I promise."

"I believe you," she said.

Then he let her cling to him for a moment before pushing her away. "Now get the doctor and get out of here. I'll be back in three or four days." He stared at her hard for an instant and then turned away.

"Let's go," he said to Schneider and Ruger. "Mount up."

23

Shamva

"Bill?"

"What, love?"

"Have you thought any more about those two Yanks that came up?"

They were driving home from the party in Shamva. It was late, almost dawn, and Bill drove carefully over the bumpy, rutted road. He'd had a lot of gin, but then so had everyone else. They were in convoy; all the farmers in the valley had come except Percy Bice. Even Arnold Bienhorn, though he'd worried about his wife who was three months pregnant. They had two cars of police from the barracks at Shamva escorting them. Bill was peering through the windshield. Only he and Ruth were in the Land Rover, and she was relaxed against the far door.

"What was that, love?"

"Those two Yanks."

The convoy was driving with lights out, and Bill was having trouble following the car ahead. They were fourth in line.

"What about them?" he asked, vaguely aware that he was drunker than he'd thought.

She laughed, "Oh, Bill."

She was a little drunk, too, he guessed. But that was good. That was damn fine.

"We had a good time, didn't we, love?"

"We had a grand time!" She laughed again with a good, easy sound.

"It was a good idea."

"Except Percy didn't think so."

They laughed hard at that, while he tried to see landmarks to know how much further they had to go.

"Good Christ, I'm going to have a head tomorrow!"

"Not like Don Thompson. Lord, did he put it away! You weren't there, but when we were dancing he asked me if I'd ever seen anyone drink a glass of gin standing on his head. So we went over and he got himself up against the wall. On his head . . ." She began to choke, laughing so hard. "Oh, God. Oh, God! It went up his nose! It got all over him! And then he began to strangle! And he fell over . . ."

Longhurst grinned. "That's why the bastard was soaked all down the front. I wish I'd seen that! Where was I, anyway?"

"Oh, you and Jim Leslie were off somewhere. Planning your bloody strategy, I suppose."

It took some of the laugh out of them. The reminder that tomorrow was coming.

"Goddammit," she said. Then, after a moment, she said, "No, goddamn that. We had the party and I'm satisfied."

"What's this about the Yanks? Was I right about you having eyes for that young officer?"

"Sure, Bill," she said. "He wanted to carry me right off. An old broken-down farm wife like me." He started to say something, but she said, "No," frowning, trying to remember what it was she'd been thinking before they'd got to talking about the party. "Oh, yes. I asked you if you'd wondered any more about them."

"Why should I do that?" And then, into the windshield, "Goddammit, Halley, hold it on the road, you old souse. You'll have the rest of us in the ditch."

"Oh, I don't know," she said. There was a touch of wistfulness in her voice. "It seemed strange them coming."

"They were just tourists, love. Just sight-seeing. They'll go back and make some bloody confidential report, and it'll go into a file somewhere and never be seen again."

"They just seemed different, somehow."

"Known many Yanks, love?"

"That's not what I mean. They were after something. The questions they asked. What they were interested in. Imagine them flying up here in a little plane like that. Why didn't the army send them down with an escort or some such? Give them a regular guided tour." The face of Cody Ravel flashed through her mind, and she could remember the feel of his hands on her shoulders and his face against hers. It was the way he'd acted that had puzzled her, but that wasn't something she could ask Bill about. He'd been angry, frustrated, she thought. Not at all the kind of man you'd have expected a general's aide to be. And going off in that little plane after the terrorists.

God, she thought to herself, I'm the one who's had too much gin. She shook her head hard, trying to clear away the thoughts that were there.

"No, love," Bill said. "There'll be no U.S. cavalry riding over the hills like in the cinema."

"I didn't mean—"

Bill suddenly said, "Oh, no! Oh, shit!"

A hundred yards ahead of them, about where the first car would be, there was a sudden, bright explosion. An instant later, there was a second, larger. Then came Boom! And then BOOM!

Bill jerked the Land Rover to the side of the road,

slewing it sideways. "Out! Out!" he screamed at Ruth, knocking the door open on his side.

But she'd already moved, throwing open her door and falling out into the darkness, hitting the hard, gravelly road, and then scrambling under the Rover. Bill was in next to her from the other side, and she heard the snick as he threw the safety off his FN. She'd forgotten hers, left it on the seat.

Ahead, they could hear firing. But from under the Rover, they could see only the occasional flash of automatic rifle fire.

"It's a mine and an ambush," he said. "They're up there. I've got to go up. It looked like the first two cars might have been blown." He was suddenly scrambling out, and she had a glimpse of his legs as he went running around the front. As quickly as she could, she ducked up and reached in and found her FN. Then she fell back under the car, the skin tearing on her knees and elbows as she scuttled sideways. She could feel her dress almost up over her hips. She lay there, peering out.

Bill ran low, weaving. He passed Halley's car and saw him and his wife crouching behind it. Then he was skidding beside Bienhorn. Just a few yards ahead, the police car was on its side, burning. Longhurst could smell the heavy fumes of cordite and burning rubber and the sharp bite of gunpowder. Bienhorn was half under his truck, behind a rear tire, firing out into the night. Longhurst flopped on his belly. He heard a staccato far up the hill in the darkness, seeing the flash before he heard the sound. He let off a long burst, firing half a clip. Then he rolled to his side, rolling a half dozen yards, and fired off the other half. As he rolled back, clawing out another clip from his coat, he could hear someone crying and moaning very near. He looked under the truck. He could just make out a dark form. But then there was another twinkle from up the shill and the sharp whine of bullets.

He fired steadily at the flash and backed in under the truck, shielding behind the tire opposite Bienhorn. The crying was louder.

"Bienhorn!" he said urgently over his shoulder. "Who's hurt? What's the situation?"

"Fuck it!" he heard the farmer say indistinctly through the firing. "Oh, fuck it, fuck it, fuck it!"

The others had come up, and they fired steadily into the night until there were no more flashes from the hills. Then they waited it out until the dawn came up a bright mist.

Bienhorn's face was a bloody mess. He'd been cut from the flying glass. He lay under the truck with his wife, holding her and crying. She'd been hit in the shoulder by a piece of flying metal, but she lay holding her stomach and moaning. The other women had come up, and they all lay under the truck and waited.

When it was good light, the men scouted both sides of the road. The ambushers had gone. In several places, they found scattered piles of AK-47 cartridges, but that was all.

Both the askari policemen in the lead car had been killed.

Bienhorn said, "They musta got an antipersonnel mine with their front wheel. Then they rolled on and hit one of the big ones."

Ruth said, "We're going to have to get Martha into the infirmary in Shamva. She's having a miscarriage, Bill." She stood there, her face dirty, her party dress destroyed. She'd burned one hand on the barrel of her FN. She looked up at him.

"Oh, God, love," he said. He felt helpless. There was nothing else to say. He put his arm around her, holding her as tight as he could.

24

Forward Camp

Cody had the men assembled in the dining hall at eight o'clock that night. All the way back on the flight he'd tried to think what he could tell them, but he still wasn't sure.

He stood on the platform a long time waiting for them to settle down. At last, Sergeant Lord stepped forward and shouted them to attention. They quieted, but Cody could still hear grumbling and whispering.

"I expect," Cody said, "that all of you already know what's happened. I expect there's two questions in your minds. One, why was Colonel Brady taken outside for medical help when Sergeant Porterfield was allowed to die. Two, what's going to happen to this mission now."

There were scattered, subdued mutters of, "Damn right," and, "Officers' privilege, like always," and "G'on, try and tell us about it."

Cody looked at Lord and the sergeant roared, "SILENCE!"

"I'll explain Porterfield first. To have taken him out of here would have risked the safety of this mission. He could have said something in his feverish state that would have given us away. And we weren't going to risk that. Colonel Brady is entirely different. This is *his* mission! His existence is absolutely vital to its success. And he was taken in absolute secrecy."

A soldier suddenly stood up. "Pardon me, sir. But that ain't the way we hear it. We hear you flew out of here with a dead man in your airplane. That there ain't no more Colonel Brady."

"Where'd you hear that, soldier?"

"It's what's they say, sir."

"Who's they?"

"You know, sir. It's just around. What the chaps are saying."

"I figured as much," Cody said levelly. He snapped out, "Lieutenant Ruger!"

"Sir!" Gerry Ruger came to his feet.

"Was Colonel Brady alive when we left him with the medical people?"

"Yes, sir."

"Was he in good shape?"

Ruger hesitated. He looked at Cody. "Well, he was wounded, sir."

"Was he dying?"

"No, sir," Ruger said strongly. "He was talking with you right up till they put him in the ambulance."

"Thank you, Lieutenant." Cody looked at the soldier who'd asked the question, "Well?"

"Thank you, sir," the man said. He sat back down.

Cody let his eyes sweep over the room. "Now this was just about what I'd expected would happen," he said in a hard voice. "A little something happens and you all get your bowels in an uproar and go running around like barracks lawyers. I bet I could damn near repeat word for word what kind of bullshit was being talked in all the little meetings you've been having. Well, you can just put a lid on that shit." He let his eyes meet theirs. "This mission will go ahead exactly as conceived and planned by Colonel Brady. The only difference is that I'll be acting for Colonel Brady. That's all."

That night he sat at his desk. Before him was the barrage of photos and organizational plans and battle plans that Brady had worked up. After a time, he sat back and ran his hand over his face and called for the orderly.

"Sir?" the man said, coming one step inside the door.

"Fetch the adjutant."

While he waited, he looked over at the phone. He wanted to call Flic to find out about the colonel, but he couldn't. The phone was for incoming calls only.

Carlton-Brooks came into the room.

Cody said, "You want a drink?"

"No, thank you, sir."

"You sure?"

"Quite. I'm all right."

Cody nodded. "I wanted to give you a briefing on what's going down. I'll talk to the men at breakfast formation and give them the word. They'll train until noon tomorrow, and then I want them to rest the balance of the day. Sleep if they can. We'll enplane tomorrow evening at six. The intent is to land at our jump-off point in the last minutes of light. We ought to be on the ground at eight thirty, just as it's coming dark. We'll rest there until midnight, then move out. We're facing basically a ten-mile march. We must accomplish the march in four hours, which is going some. The troops will be in position at four thirty, and at five all attacks will begin simultaneously. I will lead the main attack on the camp at Chipedzia. Two hours will be allowed for the attacks. Extraction will be the same way we went in. We'll pull out at noon."

"Very good, sir," Carlton-Brooks said. He coughed. "Sir?"

"What?"

"I was wondering. Of course, I'm not part of any team. I was wondering—"

"No," Cody said softly. He understood what Carlton-Brooks was feeling. We're going in at 5 A.M. It made your blood pump. He said, "No, you and your security people are going to remain here. The two airplanes will be overloaded as it is. Your job, while we're gone, will be to completely eradicate any signs of our presence in this camp. We'll return here on our way back from the mission only to refuel and pick you up."

"Very good, sir."

Cody yawned. "Now, let's both get a little sack time. We got a busy forty-eight hours in front of us."

The call from Neal Hall came at nine that next morning. It was for the purpose of giving Brady the latest updating on the intelligence information that was available.

Cody picked the phone up, but didn't speak.

The voice from the other end said, "Neal here. Matthew?"

"No," Cody said slowly. "This is Cody."

"Ah. Please put Matt on."

The line was weak and full of static.

Cody said, "I can't. He's not here."

"Then please fetch him."

"He's been hurt, injured. He's not at this location."

There was a silence from the other end. The only noise for a long moment was the faint whirr and crackle of static.

Hall said tiredly, sadly, "Oh, dear God. Are we simply to be mucked about forever?"

"He was stabbed," Cody said.

"Is it bad?"

"Very."

There was another long silence and then Hall said, "Well, that finishes it."

"No," Cody said.

"I don't quite understand."

"Yes, you do."

Now the silence was even longer. Finally, Hall said, "This is an undertaking of terrible importance and considerable latitude. A great deal of experience is required to lead this sort of thing. I don't quite think you have it, my boy."

"It doesn't matter," Cody said.

"I'm afraid it does. I'll have to think about this. I'm not sure I can agree."

"Suit yourself," Cody said. But it didn't matter whether the minister agreed or not.

"Is Matt in a hospital?"

"No. Of course not."

"Is there some way I can reach him. By phone."

"I think so," Cody said. He hesitated. "I have a number, but do you think it's all right to give it over this line?"

"We'll just have to take the chance, won't we?"

Cody gave him Flic's number. "Ask for Louisa and you'd better tell her it's from me or she won't talk to you."

Hall's voice took an edge. "Who is this woman, by the way?"

"A friend of mine."

"And how much does she know?"

"Nothing. Absolutely nothing."

There was a pause. Finally, Hall asked, "Why was it necessary you take him anywhere?"

"Hell, the man had a hole in his lung. He was stabbed, dammit. He was bleeding to death inside."

"So?"

"Oh, goddamn," Cody said in disgust. "Don't say that to me or I'll hang up this goddamn telephone."

"But weren't there better alternatives than this girl?"

"Such as?"

"Our friend in the wheelchair, for instance."

Cody was getting angry. "Don't say 'for instance' like I had a hell of a lot of alternatives. How'd you like me to have brought him down to your neighborhood and dumped him on your front step? Look, I made the best choice I could under the circumstances. And I didn't have a hell of a lot of time. I thought about the other man, but that would have meant taking him out in an ambulance, and a doctor coming out to treat a man with a stab wound in a set of combat fatigues. You people are so goddamn worried about security I figure I made the best choice with the least risk. And you can just stick it up your ass if you don't like it."

"All right, all right," Hall said. "Just calm down." There was a long pause. Cody sat there gripping the phone.

Hall said, his voice gone weary, "It's just that I'm so damned shocked by this. It's got me in a muddle."

"It ain't no goddamn picnic down here either."

"I've got to think this out."

"Suit yourself, but I've already told you what I'm going to do."

Hall said, carefully, "I'm afraid I'm going to have Matt's advice on that. Stand by. I'll call you back precisely at the stroke of one o'clock."

He gave the men their final briefing at noon, but even as he talked, his mind was on the call.

As he walked out of the hall, Carlton-Brooks was saying, "There will be an equipment draw at four P.M. by combat teams in alphabetical order. At five thirty, the

trucks will be in front of the headquarters shack where
we'll—"

Cody shut the door behind him and walked out into
the blinding sun. It was ten minutes to one. He walked
slowly to his office and sat down at the desk where the
phone was. He sat there watching it.

It rang with the strange, muted two-toned chiming
sound all African phones made. He picked it up.

"Hello," he said.

"Yes, Neal here." He sounded more weary than ever.

There was a short silence. The line was very clear.
Hall said, "Matthew's dead."

Cody stared at the wall just in front of him. There
was a long crack running through the plaster, and he
sat there trying to think what shape the crack reminded
him of.

"You understood me?"

"Yeah," Cody said. "I did." He kept looking at the
crack.

Hall said, "He died on the way in the ambulance. Ten
minutes after you left him."

Cody said, "It's a wonder he held on that long."

Hall said, "I have been giving a great deal of thought
to this." The minister's voice, though weary, was precise. "Since I can no longer ask Matt, I have to ask you.
Did he have confidence in you? To handle a job like
this?"

"He made me his executive officer, didn't he?"

"That could have been for many reasons."

"Then let me put it this way," Cody said, his voice
rough. "It doesn't make any difference. This operation
is going on. With or without your consent, Neal. I intend to carry out this job. About the only thing you could
do to stop it would be to call the other side and tell them
we're on our way."

Hall said carefully, "You forget. I hold the purse strings."

"Don't try that, Neal. That's no good."

"Why not?"

"You know damn good and well why not."

There was a brief pause and then Hall asked, "You feel that strongly about it?"

Cody gripped the phone, hugging it to his ear, putting the mouthpiece very near his lips. "Look, this mission was important to you people. Well it's important to me now too. I got a few personal reasons that I'm not going to explain. But all this is bullshit. I got the planes and the guns and the people, and I know where the targets are. Matt was a good teacher and I was a good student so you're going to get your strike, Neal. Depend on it."

"Well, well," Hall said. This time, his voice got louder and stronger. "Then let me give you a few facts, my cocksure young friend, and see if you're still so hot. We're already being hit in the north. Small patrols thus far, but the caliber of the attacker is much higher than in the past. This won't be shooting fish in a barrel, because the fish will be shooting back. From the best information I can get, it looks as if the buildup is going on. We now estimate that there's at least double the number at each camp as originally expected. And at the big one, the prize target, you can expect from three hundred to four hundred, and many of them are going to be our well-trained friends from Mozambique. Now, are you still so flaming eager? You can pull back now, return to Johannesburg, and your men will be paid off well for their time, without having fired a shot. And no one will blame you."

For just an instant, Cody had the vision of loading up and flying away from this godawful place, away from the fear and the uncertainty and the responsibility. The desire to do it was like an ache. But just for an instant.

Then he said, making his voice as flat as possible, "Scared, Neal?"

Something like a dry chuckle came over the phone. Hall said, "Hell, yes."

"So am I," Cody said, letting it burst out of him. "I'm scared shitless."

"All right, my boy," Hall said. There was a pause and then he went on. "All I can think of to say is good luck and God bless."

"Thanks, Neal."

"We'll be waiting for you when you get back."

"Adios," Cody said.

He hung up the phone and stared at the crack in the wall. "Oh, shit," he finally said. He rubbed a hand across his face.

25

Forward Camp

No one in the barracks was sleeping. Very few of them were even in their bunks. Down at the end, Dougie Lord, who'd moved in with the combat team he was now assigned to, was lying on his bunk with his eyes closed. But most of the rest of the men were congregated around the area occupied by Wilf Schneider and Gerry Ruger.

They were excited by the prospect of the coming combat. But because they were all very tough veterans, none of them wanted it to show. So they talked about other wars and other campaigns, carefully avoiding any mention of the coming strike.

Hawthorne said to Gerry Ruger, "Tell 'em about the game we played in the Congo, lad. Congo roulette."

"Ah," Ruger said, "now there was a game for a man. And about as bloody dangerous as anything you'll ever try. The odds were in your favor, but if the wrong number came up, Wap!, you'd had it."

"Well, how'd it go, Gerry?"

"What you did," Ruger said, leaning forward confidentially, "is you went out in the bush and ran down six of those bush black girls. Then you took 'em back to your tent and picked out one. See the way it went was that five of 'em give a great blow job, but the sixth is a cannibal."

The men laughed wryly, giving Ruger sour looks.

"Wilf," the Canadian, Eric Hunter, said, "what was that lot I heard you and Ruger talking about the other day, a truck you ambushed at some crossroads?"

Schneider sat up, swinging his legs around over the side of the bunk. "That was at Bunda," he said. "Very strange, almost frightening. We were encamped at the crossroads just at Bunda. It was late in the evening, almost dark. Someone shouted, 'A truck is coming.' The fools had driven right into our camp. James Schroder, who at that time was a very good man, jumped and fired a burst right through the windshield, killing the driver and his assistant. The truck rolled on a little further and then stopped. It was a big, enclosed affair with doors on the back. Like a proper van for moving furniture. We were lying all around it," Schneider said, "and we began firing into the back, just firing through the walls. And we began to hear a loud chant. 'Mulele mao.' 'Mulele mao.' 'Mulele mao.'" Schneider had his two hands held up about a foot apart. "You see the rebels were followers of Mulele, who was a very famous spirit medium. And they thought that if they chanted 'Mulele mao,' which means milk of Mulele, bullets would not hurt them. And we lay there firing and firing." He began to bring his hands closer together. "The chant was quite loud at first, but as we fired it began to lessen. Finally there was only one voice, 'Mulele mao.' Then there was silence."

"What was frightening about that?"

"Not frightening. No, that's not the proper word. It was eerie. It was eerie to hear it. It was so loud at first it seemed to boom all around us. And it was coming dark. It was as if it were in, how do you say it, stereophonic. It is very difficult to explain."

"What was in the truck?" Hunter asked him.

"Fifty-six rebel soldiers," Schneider said matter-of-factly. "When we opened the back of the truck, a fine mist of blood rose out into the air."

"Christ," Hunter said.

"But you know," Gerry Ruger said seriously, "he's right about that spiritualism rot. You bloody well can't explain it. When I was train guarding on that little line in South West Africa that the terrorists out of Tanzania were attacking, I had it happen to me. The terrorists had torn up a length of rail in a bad place, and me and the rest of the guards was deployed while the crew fixed it. I was out in front in a ditch beside the track. Then the blokes came out of the bush at us, just a bloody suicide charge, for there weren't that many of them. One of the chaps comes running right at me. Not really running, though, just sort of chugging along with his rifle at high port. So I potted him. Nothing happened. He just come trotting on. So I potted him again. Then again. Then again. By now, he was only about twenty yards off, and I could see the puffs of dust outen his blouse front where the bullets were hitting. I'll lay you I shot him ten times. And he just bloody comes trotting on. By now, I'm looking down at my rifle wondering if I've got it loaded with blanks. It's like one of those bloody nightmares where you shoot the bloody gun and the bullet comes rolling out of the barrel and falls on the floor. So anyway, the bugger just keeps coming, trotting with his rifle at high port. *And trots right on past me.* I look at his face and his eyes are glazed. Just bloody out of it. He goes on about another five yards, heading for the train engine, and then I guess he run out of blood or something, for he just all of a sudden falls down. But, bloody Christ!" Ruger shook his head. "Like the Kraut here says, you bloody well can't explain it."

Dougie Lord was trying, conscientiously, to sleep, but

he could hear the voices from the men at Schneider's bunk. He wanted to tell them they ought to be in bed, getting proper rest. But he'd lost that right when he hadn't been able to shoot Peters. Now, all he wanted was for the fight to hurry up and happen so that he could redeem himself.

It was four P.M. and the troops were coming out of the barracks and lining up before the equipment storage barracks to draw their ammunition and grenades.

Cody was out at the crude airstrip with Art Edge preflighting the two airplanes.

"Going to be close," he said to Edge. "The gasoline."

They were siphoning off fifteen gallons, letting it run into a five gallon bucket so that they could measure it, out of the left wing tank of the number two airplane.

"Got to cut it this fine?"

"Yes. Which means you'll have to watch your throttle settings and your lean ratio. I've done a half dozen weight and balance problems on both airplanes and it comes out the same for this short a runway. Half tanks the only way we can get these babies off the ground." The gasoline was running out slowly. As soon as the bucket was filled, they dumped it out. The smell of the gasoline was strong in the hot, still air.

After a time, Art asked, "Heard any word about the colonel?"

"Yes," Cody said. He didn't look up from his work.

"How's he getting along?"

"He's dead," Cody said briefly.

Edge was silent for a moment. At length, he said, "Well, I guess he knew that goes with the job sometimes."

"He knew," Cody said. He straightened. "By the way, I don't want the troops knowing about it."

"Right," Edge said.

"All right," Cody said into the mike to Edge, "I'm gonna give it a try." He was at the end of the runway, standing on the brakes.

"Give her hell," Edge said.

Cody pushed both throttles forward slowly. The airplane began to tremble as it strained forward. When both tachometers were reading 2600 rpm, Cody released the brakes, and the heavy airplane began lumbering forward. He had the control yolk pushed forward and he held it there, watching the air-speed indicator. At one hundred miles an hour, he applied gentle back pressure and the airplane lifted off, staggering, not really flying yet. The end of the runway was rushing toward them, but Cody pushed the wheel forward slightly, riding the ground effect from the air bubble underneath the wings, letting the air speed build, flying two feet off the ground. A low hill was rising. Cody watched it. He looked at the air-speed indicator. He had a hundred and twenty miles an hour just in time and he pulled back on the yolk, the airplane now flying, and they swept up and over the hill.

The radio crackled and Art Edge said, "Well, that proves it can be done. Here we go."

Cody continued climbing out, making a left turn and looking back to see Edge roaring down the runway, using exactly the same technique that he had. Then he was sweeping over the hill, and Cody turned back on course.

Into the mike, he said, "We'll hold five thousand for most of the trip. I'll buzz you just before I begin the descent to low level flight."

"Roger," Edge said.

Cody had brought Wilf Schneider forward to sit in the copilot's seat. He looked over at him. "Well, here we go."

"Yes," the German said slowly. "It should be very interesting."

26

Longhaven Farm—Strike

Bill Longhurst saw them as they passed. He was standing out in the back, near the door of the operations shack. They were passing a mile to the east of the farm, their motors loud.

"Hey, you chaps!" Longhurst called into the operations shack. One of the Bright Lights came out, and Bill pointed toward the airplanes. "What do you make of that?"

The planes were down low, a hundred feet off the ground, flying in tight formation. They came on, their engines roaring louder and louder as they neared.

"Why I don't know, Bill," the Bright Light said. "Think I ought to ring up Shamva?"

The farmer shook his head. "No, it's more than likely army business. And, anyway, they'll be over the border in five minutes. No time for our chaps to do anything."

They stood there watching until the two planes disappeared from view. After a moment, the sound of the engines was indistinct.

"Strange," the Bright Light said. "Could you see any markings on them?"

Longhurst shook his head. "No."

They stood there staring at the sky. The Bright Light was young, a shoe clerk in a department store. But he had been with the Longhursts before. He asked, after a moment, "How is Mr. Bienhorn's wife?"

"They lost the baby, you know," Bill said. He stared after the planes.

"I hear he's leaving."

"Perhaps," Bill said. "He's very upset right now, as you can imagine." He heaved his shoulders. "Well, I think I'll go in and see what Ruth's got organized for supper tonight. And you'll be a good chap, won't you, and watch for that new army unit that's due in. I think there's a hunt on tonight."

"Of course, Bill. But maybe it will be quiet. After all, it's been several days now."

"Yes. Perhaps."

Cody said into the mike, "Art, I've got the strip in sight. It's just to the left of that hill with the big rock up there. Runs right along beside it. I'm going to cut over to the left here a bit and set up a base leg and then take it straight in. It's gonna be dark in five minutes. You reduce power and fly some S turns to give us a little separation, but get in right behind me. And, Art, don't waste any runway. There ain't a hell of a lot of it and the rest is rocks. And even the runway is rough as hell."

"Roger," Edge said back.

The altitude required a very flat approach. It would make a full stall landing that much harder. A quarter of a mile from the end of the strip, he killed power and cranked in full flaps. He felt the controls begin to go mushy as a stall approached. But then they were at the end of the runway and he pulled back on the yolk and the air-plane settled.

"Hold on," he said to Schneider.

They hit hard, bounced into the air, settled, bounced again, less this time, then bounced again. Cody was praying they wouldn't blow a tire. Finally they were rolling, though still too fast.

"Help me on these toe brakes!" he yelled at Schneider. "On top of the rudder pedals."

He was pressing them as hard as he could, so hard the muscles in his calves were trembling. Ahead, the rocks and boulders were coming fast. At the last second, he kicked hard left rudder and the airplane swirled around and came to a stop.

"Wow," Cody said. He sat there a minute, sweat forming on his brow.

Schneider said seriously, "An excellent landing, Major Ravel."

"Wasn't it," Cody said. He unbuckled his seat belt. "Well, let's go see if anyone's left alive in the back."

Immediately after they were down, Cody called an officers' meeting inside the airplane. The only light was from the flashlights several of them were carrying. The blackout curtains were still over the windows.

"First," Cody said, "there will be no lights of any kind shown. That means no smoking. Not outside, nor in the airplanes. Not at any time during this night. I want each squad leader, sometime before we move out, to go over with each man exactly what he is supposed to do. Be goddamn sure he knows. You want trouble, you let one man fall down in his job and you're going to have it. Now you leaders of the base or trap squads, it is imperative that you do not advance into the kill zone. You must hold your line and let the targets of opportunity be driven up to you. Emphasize this to your men because I'm afraid that some of them might get a little eager and get too forward. The technique of this attack has been carefully worked out to contain all of the enemy and, at the same time, minimize the danger of our shooting into each other. *But positions have to be maintained.* Captain Hawthorne—" He looked for his face in the dark.

"Here, sir."

"I will be going in with your combat team. I—"

"Pardon me, colonel."

"The rank is still major," Cody said sharply.

"Oh. I thought with Colonel Brady—"

"Forget it," Cody said. "Now, what was your question."

"You say you'll be going in with us. But you are one of the pilots. And we only have the two."

"Don't worry about it," Cody said. "You can assure yourself, Captain, that I'm not going to expose myself to the firefight. I'm aware that I'm responsible for getting you people home. I'll take a position well outside the perimeter of fire, and I'll be there only if something breaks down or if any command decisions are needed. Other than that, I'm just along for the ride."

"Thank you, sir," Hawthorne said.

"Which brings me," Cody said, "to a hard point." He looked around the circle of faces, some indistinct in the reflection of the down-pointed flashlights. "And I mean this especially to team leaders of Baker and Charlie teams, because I can't be with you. When the fight is over, you may have wounded among your men. If you do, you're going to have to make an instant decision about their disposition. If they can travel, fine. They come back. If not, you're going to have to shoot them and then disfigure them beyond recognition. The criterion you'll apply will be whether they'll slow you down or not. If they will, you have no alternative. No one is going to carry anyone back. Some of them could be your friends. That makes absolutely no difference."

The team leader of Charlie, the South African, whistled softly. "That's hard, sir. Damn hard."

"Listen," Cody said sharply, "what the hell business you think you're in here, selling shoes?"

The man answered with quiet dignity, "I didn't say I couldn't do it, sir. I simply noted that it would be hard."

"We all understand that, Captain," Cody said. "To speak of it is pointless." He looked around the circles of faces again. "That's all I have. Are there any questions?"

No one said anything.

"Speak now," Cody said. "In a little while, it'll be too late."

One of them, in the dark Cody couldn't see which one, cleared his throat. "Pardon, sir."

"Speak."

"Some of the men have been asking," he said. "We understand we're going straight back to Johannesburg to be dispersed."

"Correct."

The man hesitated. "Just for the men to know. When do we get our money?"

"The money will be in your bank waiting for you. Every man will be paid for three months. Just as if this had gone the way we'd planned."

Another voice said, "Bonuses too?"

Cody looked in the direction of the speaker. "The bonuses will be paid on the success of this mission. And that hasn't been determined yet."

Wilf Schneider and Gerry Ruger were lying under the wing of the number one airplane.

Ruger put his arm up and looked at the luminous dial of his watch. "Ten thirty," he said. "An hour and a half to go."

"Quite right," Schneider said. "But that is not the important time. Five A.M. is the important time."

"How long you think it'll take, Wilf? The actual attack. The fighting."

"I have no idea. Not long, I think."

"Fifteen minutes is my guess," Ruger said. He fell silent for a moment. Then he said, "Fifteen minutes. For fifteen thousand dollars. That ain't bad, eh Wilf? Beats selling business forms or taking pictures."

They were on their backs, looking up. The outline of the wing partially obscured their vision, but they could see that the sky was clear and bright. There was almost a full moon. Schneider thought that it would be very helpful on their march. He wondered, in his meticulous way, if it had been planned for.

Ruger suddenly said, awkwardly, "Wilf, we been friends a long time. If I ask you something, will you tell me the truth?"

"Of course."

Ruger turned his head slightly toward his friend. "Are you scared?"

Schneider considered. "Not for myself. I am afraid to think of my Mary and my children alone without me. I would not like that. But for myself, no. I am not afraid of death. One cannot be afraid of something one knows nothing about. The great philosopher Socrates said that the fear of death was a pretense of knowledge. A man cannot know if it is bad or good, and to fear it is to assume it to be bad. That is ignorant."

Ruger said softly, "You're some Kraut."

Schneider said, "He made the statement just as he was to drink the cup of hemlock. The books say he was very calm. I have great admiration for a man who could think so clearly at such a moment of stress."

Ruger said, his voice strange in the night, "I'll tell you what I'm afraid of. I wish I could get it out of my bloody mind." He half-raised up, rolled over on an elbow.

"Yes?"

"I'm afraid of being wounded. I'm afraid of being wounded so I can't travel, and one of you chaps has to put a grenade between my teeth and blow my handsome face to smithereens." He tried a laugh, but it didn't work.

"They would shoot you first," Schneider said calmly. "You'd never know."

"I wouldn't like that so bloody much either," Ruger said. "A friend shooting me."

Schneider said, "I would much rather it be a friend, with good intentions in his heart to save me pain, than an enemy who meant me destruction."

Ruger sat up angrily. "Goddammit, do you always have to be so bloody practical?" He got up on his feet. "Christ!" he said disgustedly. He walked a few feet away, staring out into the dark.

They assembled quietly in the night. Art Edge stepped to Cody's side. "Good luck, Cody." He put out his hand and they shook. "Fair weather and tail winds all the way."

"Thanks, Art. You know what to do. If we're not back here by two P.M. tomorrow, destroy your airplane and get the hell out of here in mine. Go south."

"You'll be here," Edge said.

"I expect to be."

They moved out, a long column of men stepping carefully through the night and the rough country. Cody was in the lead, following the luminous dial of a compass. Hawthorne was just at his shoulder. Behind him, strung out combat team Able. And behind them were Baker and Charlie, the squad leaders at the front of each squad.

Cody was following a compass heading of three zero degrees. Its course would bring them to a point directly in line with the camp at Chipedzia. Two miles south of it, they would halt and the other two combat teams would split off left and right for their separate attacks.

In the dark, men stumbled. Occasionally one went down. There were no sounds except for the breathing and the noise of equipment.

After an hour, Cody felt himself begin to tire. It was not serious, but he could understand how serious it could become. He had underestimated the difficulties. The night and the rough terrain required a man to be constantly alert, stepping first this way and then that. It took it out of you. He slowed his pace and then stopped. Behind him, Peter Hawthorne put out a hand so that they wouldn't bump.

"Rest," Cody said over his shoulder in a whisper.

"Rest," Hawthorne said to the next man. "Pass it on."

Cody sank to the ground. The one good consolation was that the men were in better shape than he was. And as long as he could go on, they could go on further. He leaned back against a rise in the ground, back against the harness of the backpack radio he was carrying. It was twelve more pounds than anyone else had, except the squad leaders. At his belt were the two canteens of water along with a musette bag of rations for forty-eight hours. He had six fragmentation grenades hooked to his belt and in his pockets. Other men, according to their jobs, had thermite grenades and concussion grenades.

He looked back along the line, in the moonlight, seeing the men sinking to the ground. They had made a good march to that point. They were good men, he thought. Following him through the brush in an African country with no idea of where they were. No idea of principles.

He sat there, thinking about it.

How strange, he thought. That men would trust me like that. I say, "Move out," and they follow. I say, "Get in the airplane," and they do it. I say, "We got to destroy a target," and here they come. What for? For money? No, it's not for money. Not in the final analysis.

He wanted a cigarette, but he made himself quit thinking about that. That was out, like a lot of other things were out on this night. That was soft thinking. And all they wanted tonight was hard thinking. To go on and walk through the moonlight and the rough country and then blow the piss out of a bunch of bastards that were on the other side.

Get the bastards on the other side. After all the fine talk, after all the philosophizing, that was what it came down to. It didn't matter what you called it. A lot of fine folks had a lot of names for it. But out in the moonlight in rough country, there was only one way to describe it: Get the bastards on the other side. Because if they didn't, the bastards on the other side would get them and then it wouldn't matter about the money. Or any other reason they had for being there.

"Move out," Cody said quietly.

Hawthorne said to the next man, "Move out. Pass it on."

They walked, through the night and the rough country.

Cody stopped. "Officers' call," he said in a whisper. Behind him, Hawthorne said, "Word back. Send up team leaders and squad leaders."

In the night, they held a whispered conference. Cody took off his steel helmet and knelt on one knee. The others clustered around him. "All right, teams Baker and Charlie, this is your jumping-off place. Team leader Baker, your compass heading to your objective is zero three zero degrees. You've got about three miles to go. Team Charlie, your compass heading is two nine zero degrees. And you got about four miles to your objective. So you've got a little humping to do. Team Able, we'll simply continue on our course. Gentlemen, let's check our watches.

Make damn sure we've all got the same time." He looked down at the luminous dial, watching the sweep hand. "In thirty seconds," he said, "I'll have zero two zero five hours." He waited, watching the second hand. When it reached the top, he said, "Hack. Two zero five." He looked up, waiting for the few still adjusting their watches to finish.

"Okay, gentlemen. Simultaneous attacks at zero five hundred hours. Don't anybody get exposed before that. Be damn certain of it. Baker and Charlie, I'll try and reach you on these radios, but I'm uncertain if it'll work. We've got obstructing terrain in the way. But it doesn't matter. You know your job and you ought to be able to handle anything that comes up. Rendezvous back here at zero seven hundred hours. That means you've got barely an hour for your attack and the mopping up. So expedite. And be back here on time. I don't want to have to go looking for you. Team and squad leaders go ahead and put your head sets on now, but stay off the air unless it's absolutely necessary."

There were muffled sounds as they took off their steel helmets and adjusted the radio headsets with their earphones and boom mike. Cody put his own on, then set his steel helmet over it firmly. He pulled the boom mike down below his chin so he could talk normally. "Well, we better get hiking. Good luck, gentlemen, and kick the shit out of 'em."

27

The Camp at Chipedzia

And now there was nothing to do, but lie in the dark and wait. Cody glanced down at his watch. It was ten of five. In front of him, finally, was the camp at Chipedzia.

They were deployed in a perimeter twenty-five yards outside the rim of the camp. The approach had been relatively easy. If there were any guards, and intelligence had said there weren't, they hadn't been spotted. Cody was up on a little rocky knoll and had a fairly clear view of the camp through the dry bushes. Just in front of him was the concrete blockhouse at the north center end of the camp. In it, he knew, were barracked the Chinese instructor cadre. Farther on were the two large barracks, at each side of the camp and almost diametrically opposed. Intelligence had said they could hold up to one hundred men each. Then, farther on was a smaller barracks. All that was as it should be, as it had been in the photos. But there was now a fourth barracks, set catercorner at the far end, down where his trap squad was deployed. He studied it through his infrared field glasses. It was the same as the others except it looked new, raw. Even the thatching on the roof seemed fresh. He studied it a long time.

The center of the camp was clear except for several small instructional huts, open-sided pole affairs.

Cody rubbed his chin and studied the new barracks again. He couldn't see it very clearly, but he estimated it could contain up to fifty men. Like the others, it had board windows that were propped out with sticks.

He said softly into his mike, "Able dog three, this is Boss dog."

Ruger's voice came quietly back into his ears. "Able dog three here, Boss dog."

"You note the new barracks, your end?"

"Roger, Boss dog."

"When we move into the demarcation line, I want you to shift your squad down toward that barracks to be sure it's contained. I want your six and seven men on that end to take immediate offensive action against that target with frag grenades through those open windows. And see if you can't get an incendiary grenade on its roof."

"Roger. Understood."

He hesitated, then said, "Contain that barracks, Gerry. Whatever you do."

He ran a hand across his face and found that he was sweating, even in the coolness of the coming dawn. He could make a pretty good guess who was in that new barracks. And if they got loose, the show could be over before it got started.

The center part of the camp, what Cody thought of as the parade ground, was the kill zone. The attack was designed to drive the enemy into it so that he could be hit with maximum firepower. The inverted V, sweeping in from the top, would anchor its point on the block-house—once it was neutralized—while the wings enfolded from in back of the barracks. But now there was this new barracks, and it was too far down for the wing of the inverted V to reach. Ruger's squad would have to handle it.

He glanced down at his watch. It was five minutes to five, time to try to reach Baker and Charlie combat teams at the other two camps. He switched the radio dial to the long range frequency they'd preselected.

"Baker dog leader," he said into the mike, "this is Boss dog. Do you read? Baker dog leader, this is Boss dog. Do you read?"

He could hear a faint voice in the earphones, but he couldn't make out the words. It didn't matter. He said softly, "We're in position. Good luck."

Then he tried Charlie team. This time there was a better response. He could just make out the voice of Schroder, the South African.

"How's the situation there?"

"As expected, Major," Schroder said.

"All right. Two minutes. Good luck."

He switched back to the intercom frequency that the Able team leaders were tuned to. "Able dog, Boss dog. Two minutes. Move your men forward to the demarcation line."

The responses came back from Hawthorne and the squad leaders. Around him, he could hear the men of Schneider's squad, who had the left wing, wiggling forward. He came behind, staying three yards in the rear. They crawled until they were just at the edge of the camp clearing. Cody could feel his throat beginning to tighten, feel his breath getting hot. It was still very dark, but easier to see now that they were closer. Off to his right, the squat, ugly lines of the concrete blockhouses reared up. He looked at his watch, seeing the second hand sweeping around.

"Able leader, signal up your six and seven men."

"On station," Hawthorne said. "Ten seconds. I will give the go." There was a long, dazzling pause and then Hawthorne said, "Tallyho, chaps!"

Then Dougie Lord and the number six man, Strenge,

came racing into the middle of the compound. For a second, Cody couldn't see because Schneider's men had stood up and were starting forward.

Down at the end, Gerry Ruger had shifted himself to the end of his squad. He was crouched down on one knee, just a few feet from the new barracks. The openings of the line of windows looked black against the new wood. He pulled the pin on a fragmentation grenade, waiting. Down the line, other of his men were doing the same.

Lord and Strenge came swiftly. Lord ran to the double pole radio antenna, kneeling with a pair of wire cutters in his hand. Strenge was in the middle. Already he'd thrown a thermite grenade; it made a long sputtering arc in the night as it bled phosphorous sparks. He threw another one and then another one. The roofs were beginning to ignite.

Lord worked frantically, trying to find the ground wire for the antenna. It wasn't where it should have been. "Bloody bastards!" he muttered. Then he found it and cut it and turned and started running toward the blockhouse, pulling grenades from his belt as he did. He had a concussion grenade in one hand and a fragmentation grenade in the other. He could see that the door was partially ajar. It was going to be all right, he thought. He'd made it up all right.

He was less than ten yards away when the door suddenly opened, and a Chinese instructor, wearing only shorts, started out. The Chinese was yawning and rubbing his face, but through his fingers he suddenly saw Dougie Lord. For an instant, they stared at each other, transfixed. There was time for Lord to have thrown one of the grenades, but he didn't. He might have jerked his AK-47 around and shot the soldier, but he didn't. The Chinese reacted first, jumping back into the room and slamming the reinforced door.

The fires from the barracks roofs were beginning to erupt and the whole camp was coming as light as day.

Lord started forward again. When he was five yards from the blockhouse door, there was the sudden, sharp rattle from an automatic rifle out one of the front windows. Lord stopped, a stunned look on his face. Then he toppled forward. He tried to crawl, digging the toes of his boots in the dust, straining forward, his outstretched hand holding the concussion grenade. From the perimeter, the waiting men could hear the rattle of the automatic and see the back of his blouse jump and jerk.

"GO!" Cody yelled into his mike. "GO! GO! GO! NOW!"

Hawthorne was yelling, "ALL SQUADS! ALL SQUADS! GO! GO!"

Schneider's squad raced down behind the big barracks on their side, throwing grenades through the windows. At the end, they made a skirmish line and began to fire into the terrorists who were coming out the doors and windows.

Cody had moved up. They could not control the central kill zone because of the answering fire from the blockhouse. Already, that fire was holding Hawthorne's squad back. He yelled into his mike, "BYPASS THE BLOCKHOUSE, LEADER SQUAD. BYPASS THE SONOFABITCH AND STAY OUTSIDE THE PERIMETER. I'LL GET IT."

In his earphones, he heard Hawthorne scream, "Major, you bloody well stay out of it!"

But he was already running into the clearing, coming around the corner of the blockhouse. He could see Lord lying there with his hand stretched out, the concussion grenade still in his fist. He veered around the corner, hearing the staccato of the automatic weapon bursting out of the window just above him. He had to have that concussion grenade to blow the door open.

He dove toward Lord, came up short, and hurtled forward on his knees, grabbing at the grenade. Bullets kicked up dirt beside him. But he had the grenade and he flipped over on his back and went rolling over and over toward the door. The light was good now. The barracks' roofs were burning fiercely and, each time he rolled, he saw the white front of the blockhouse. They were firing out both windows at him, but the line of fire was always just a little behind.

He got to the door, hugging into it as close as he could. At the windows they were trying to get an angle to shoot him, but the depth of the casements was too great. They were hitting the edge of the concrete. Chips of plaster and cement were flying around him like snow. He jammed the concussion grenade between the doorknob and the frame, pulled the pin, then crawled under the window, his back pressed flat against the wall.

Dimly, almost unconsciously, he could hear the yells of the fight, hear the steady sounds of the automatic rifle fire and the distant and muffled explosions of other grenades.

Then the concussion grenade exploded and he whirled, half-dazed by the blast, and ran in a crouch for the door. It was blown away. He pulled the pin of a fragmentation grenade as he scuttled. White smoke billowed out the door. He pitched the grenade through the door as he dove by. He hit and rolled and came up on one knee, turning, his rifle at his hip, and began firing through the door.

The fragmentation grenade exploded and he threw in another. As it went off, he followed the blast through the door, his automatic rifle low, firing and firing.

In the smoke, a dim figure rose; Cody turned the rifle toward him. The firing made a terrible clatter off the stone walls. The figure went down. He turned, racing, moving, firing constantly. He saw a stab of flame and he shot at it until his gun stopped.

He fell to his face and rolled over on his back, clawing out another clip and slipping it into the rifle.

He was back up, firing in a 360 degree arc, the bullets whapping and ricocheting all over the room. He went to his face, conscious of the ricochets, but continued firing.

Leaving the rest of his trap squad in position to wait for targets of opportunity, Gerry Ruger ran swiftly down behind the barracks they were to contain. He pitched a grenade through each of the windows. The fuses were set for three seconds and, even before he'd reached the last window the first of the grenades was going off. He whirled, starting back, pausing to raise up and fire a quick burst through each window, careful to keep clear of the opening, for the grenades were going off in steady progression. By the sudden flash of their glow, he saw milling figures. He fired short bursts and then ran on. He was nearly to the last window when he saw something come flying out and land on the ground in front of him. He threw himself sideways, but it exploded even as he was in the air. Oh, shit, he thought. I've finally done it. The blast hit him like a hammer.

He was on his back, staring blankly up at the night, trying to think what had happened. He didn't hurt, he just felt confused. He tried to get up, but none of his limbs seemed to work. The edge of the barracks was just ahead and he pushed himself along with his heels. Then he felt a strange weakness. He touched his stomach and instantly drew his hand away. "Oh, shit," he said aloud.

The roofs of the main barracks were beginning to collapse from the fires. Hawthorne was holding his men back behind the perimeter of fire. Some of the terrorists began to come out, running frantically. Some of them were half-dressed and a few had weapons. Hawthorne was just to the left of the end door of the barracks. Four terrorists came bursting out, running straight for him and the safety of the bush. He cut them down in one continuous burst. Three more came out. He shot the first. His gun ran empty and he shifted it in his hands and clubbed the wild, screaming face in front of him. The third man ran by, seeming to not even notice Hawthorne. "Shoot that bastard!" he yelled. Beside him, his sergeant whirled and cut the man down just as he was disappearing into the bush.

The trap squad was taking fire from the new barracks. Sergeant Knowles, the second in command, looked wildly around for Ruger. "Where's the lieutenant?"

"They're coming!" a man shouted.

"Keep down, chaps. Fire now! Fire!"

Hawthorne said into his mike, "Able leader to Able two. What's your situation, Wilf?"

"We are holding outside," Schneider said. "I have one man hit, but we are putting heavy fire into this barracks and getting very little in return." He stopped talking. A terrorist had jumped out the window just to his right. He whirled and shot him.

"Move your men down further left, Able two," Hawthorne said. "We're getting fire from that new barracks down there. Able three, what's the situation?"

Lying on his back, Ruger heard the voice in his earphones, but his mike had somehow been knocked awry. He opened his mouth, trying to say something, but he couldn't seem to hear his own words.

"Able three, this is Able leader. Come in, Gerry. What the hell's the trouble?"

The roof of the barracks in front of Hawthorne suddenly collapsed, falling in a cascading roar of flying sparks. He could hear screams inside. But then terrorists came out, deploying in a line, firing wildly. The man beside Hawthorne suddenly said, "Oh, dammit!" and fell over. Hawthorne felt something pluck at his pants. He threw a grenade and then fell flat and was firing even before it went off.

"Where's Lieutenant Ruger?" Knowles was screaming. He didn't know whether to move the men back or not, and they were still getting fire from the new barracks. They had hit the roof with thermite grenades, but the thatching was too green to catch flame.

From the other small barracks, which were burning, twenty of the enemy poured out. They were across the parade ground from Schneider, but they ran in his direction. They had their hands in the air and weren't carrying weapons.

"Christ," the man next to Wilf said, "they think we'll take prisoners."

Schneider didn't answer, but fired steadily into the group.

Cody stood for a moment, dazed, in the middle of the blockhouse. He had stopped firing and some of the smoke had cleared, but it was still too dark for him to see. He stumbled over a limp form as he dove toward the door.

It felt incredibly cool outside after the heat and the smoke that he had created. He lay there, staring out at what he was seeing.

All of the buildings except the new barracks were now almost demolished by flames. Those terrorists who hadn't been killed inside had run to the middle of the camp and were milling back and forth. Some of them had weapons and were firing wildly into the night before them. A few had grenades. Occasionally, one would make a break for the bush, but he'd be cut down before he could even approach it. And all the time, the terrible fire from the concentrated automatic weapons was going into them, and they were falling by fives and tens.

Cody fed a fresh clip into his rifle. It was so hot he was careful not to touch the barrel. Then, dimly through the ringing in his ears, he heard Hawthorne's voice.

"Boss dog, Boss dog, this is Able leader. Boss dog, do you read, goddammit."

"Boss dog."

"Major, we're getting good return fire from the barracks down on the end and I can't raise Gerry Ruger. His squad looks pinned down, and we can't go in and clean this thing up with the field of fire they've got on us."

"All right," Cody said. "Stand by." He jumped and cut to his right, racing low, and then going to the ground as he hit the edge of the darkness. He could see the barracks at the far end. "All right," he said into his mike, "I know who those fuckers are. Schneider, get down there behind that damn place and get some grenades in through the windows. Thermite grenades if you've got any left. We'll smoke their asses out. And Hawthorne, send a runner down to trap squad and have them put up a grenade barrage, and you get concentrated fire on the front of the place to keep their attention off Schneider and his men. Let's do it. Now!"

He jumped up and ran behind the burning barracks to where he was directly across from the target. As he started to kneel, a black figure suddenly jumped up and swung at him with a bush knife. He ducked and it hit him on the steel helmet. He rolled to his side and then shot the man as he raised his arm again. He fell across Cody's legs. He kicked him free and then crawled forward and watched the attack.

Explosions suddenly went off all up and down the

front of the building as the trap squad hurled grenades. Then the windows lighted from the inside.

They'd be thermite grenades, Cody thought. They had some left. Good.

It didn't last long. In the end, two enemy soldiers ran out the front door and tried to make it to the bush. They were shot down within half a dozen steps.

There were scattered shots and then there came a kind of quiet. Over the earphones, Cody heard Hawthorne ordering, "All right, advance. Go in, go in."

They came into the light, slowly, like puppeteers coming on stage to take a bow, like men exposing themselves timidly from behind the terrible curtain of fire they'd been laying down.

Cody got slowly to his feet and walked forward. Now there was no sound. It was very quiet.

28

Longhaven Farm—Strike

To the east, it was coming dawn. The thatched roofs had burned to nothing. Now there were just the standing sides of the barracks, throwing up black, spark-filled smoke.

There were bodies everywhere. But the main concentration was in the middle of the compound. They lay there in heaps.

Cody stared at them numbly. They didn't look so very fierce now, not so very dangerous. Just clumps of organic matter, he thought. Well, Matt, he said to himself, it worked. Just like you planned it. We kicked the shit out of them. We got the bastards on the other side.

He looked at his watch, astonished to see that forty-five minutes had passed since Lord and Strenge had come trotting in to begin the attack. It had seemed more like five minutes.

The men were standing around watching him, their shoulders slumped tiredly. Wilf Schneider leaned against the bole of a tree, his rifle cradled in his arms. Peter Hawthorne stood near the center of the compound, looking at Cody.

Cody walked over to where Dougie Lord lay. He

leaned down and gently turned the little sergeant over. He'd been stitched across the chest by the automatic rifle fire. Lord's eyes were open. He still looked surprised.

Cody slowly straightened. He looked around the camp. He raised his voice, "ALL RIGHT, GODDAMMIT! IT AIN'T OVER. CAPTAIN HAWTHORNE, GET YOUR MEN MOVING! MAKE SURE OF ALL THE ENEMY WOUNDED AND SEE TO OUR OWN CASUALTIES! DO IT!"

They found Gerry Ruger a few moments later. He was still conscious. Cody knelt by his side, suddenly sickened by the sight of where the soldier's stomach and abdomen had once been. Wilf Schneider was there.

Ruger stared up, his hands by his side, not touching the wound.

Cody said, "Oh, God, I'm sorry, Gerry." He reached out awkwardly and patted the soldier's face. "I'm sorry as hell and we haven't got much time."

Ruger's breathing was rapid and shallow.

Cody was holding his pistol down and behind him. He patted Gerry's cheek again. "I'm damn sorry," he said, and brought the pistol up. His hand was trembling badly.

"No!" Ruger suddenly shouted. His voice was quick and urgent. "I want Wilf to do it!" He began to sob.

Cody got up. He looked down at Ruger's face for a second and then walked a few steps away.

The German knelt down. There were tears running down his cheeks, but he said in a normal voice, "Do you have any messages, Gerry?"

"I," Ruger said, then he convulsed. He clenched his eyes shut and put the knuckles of his fists to his mouth. "Do it quick!" he cried. "Oh, God, Wilf!"

Cody was standing with his back to them. He suddenly whirled around. "Wilf!" he shouted.

The German looked up. Even from there, he could see it in Cody's face. He got quickly to his feet and took

Cody by the shoulders, pushing him back. "No, Major," he said, the tears still running down his face. "He can't make it. He would die in the first mile. And he's in great pain."

"Ah, fuck it!" Cody said. He turned away, a giant band squeezing tight around his chest. Behind him, he heard a pistol shot. He started walking rapidly away. Ten seconds later, he heard the grenade explode.

All over the camp came the steady pop of individual shots as they killed the wounded terrorists.

Cody found Hawthorne. He grabbed him by the blouse front. "Hawthorne," he said fiercely, "you make damn sure we get every man back that's got any kind of chance at all. You hear me?"

"But—"

He shook the captain by his shirt front. "Dammit! Do as I tell you!"

Cody went over to the double pole antenna and tied the ground wire that Lord had cut. Then he hooked an alligator clamp onto the wire and tuned in the long distance frequency.

"Baker dog, this is Boss dog."

Sullivan's voice came through clear and loud. "Go ahead, Boss dog."

"What's the situation there?"

"We had it pretty easy, Boss dog. No surprises. Suffered two casualties. We're wrapping it up now. Do you want an enemy report?"

"No. Save that. Just get back with everyone you possibly can."

He told the same to Charlie leader. Schroder's voice sounded drawn. "We hit some bumps. Some of the buggers had bazookas and got holed up, and we had a bit of time getting them routed out. We might be a bit late to rendezvous. We're just getting mopped up here."

"Roger. We'll wait for you."

He stood later, watching.

At intervals, there were seven grenade explosions.

Later, Hawthorne came up to him to report. "Two hundred and twenty-six enemy dead, sir. I can get no sure information if any got away. We lost seven men and two are wounded, but they can travel. The dead are—"

"Save it," Cody said. "I don't want to know their names, Captain. Not now. That's for administration."

"Yes, sir," Hawthorne said.

"Are we ready to move out?"

"Yes, sir."

"Then let's get after it. We got a hell of a long trip home."

As they crossed the dry riverbed, walking now in Rhodesia, Cody looked up at the sky. Heavy black clouds were forming. Well, he thought, we made it. Though not by a hell of a lot.

It took them an hour longer to make the return trip. On the way, Eric Hunter, who'd been shot through the femoral artery, died. There was another grenade explosion.

That makes fourteen of us and a little over four hundred of them for the total operation, Cody thought, sitting slumped against a rock. A military logician would say that was brilliant warfare.

It was, he guessed. Right then, he was too tired to care.

They were thirty-five minutes overdue, but Art Edge was still waiting for them. He stood with Cody, by the wing of the number one airplane.

"You look all done in, Major."

"Yeah," Cody said. He took his steel helmet and slung it off into the brush. "Jesus Christ, Art," he said. He looked down at the ground. Standing there, slumping inwardly, he felt how tired and sore he was. He touched his neck and could feel encrusted blood. And his ribs hurt. And he'd burned one hand. There was a tear in the leg of his fatigues and through it he could see blood.

Edge said, "Looks like we're not quite going to have a load going back."

"Yeah," Cody said bitterly. "There's good in everything, isn't there, Art?"

"Look, Major, you're all whipped down. Why don't you give me a compass course and let me fly lead? All you'll have to do then is put it on automatic pilot and rest."

Cody shook his head. "No, Art, and it's not because I don't trust you. We're going to make a little detour. For personal reasons. Get the men loaded up."

Ruth was in the kitchen when she heard the thunderous sound of the big airplanes coming. She ran outside just as they swept over the house, a hundred feet off the ground.

"Bill!" she yelled. "Bill!"

He came out and they stood, shading their eyes, watching the planes diminish slowly to the south.

"What on earth?" Ruth said, when it was quiet enough to speak.

Bill shook his head. "I don't know, love. But that's the same two aircraft we saw yesterday. I'd bet a tractor on it. Coming back."

"And that firing from up north this morning. What do you suppose is going on?"

"I checked Army and they knew nothing about it." He shrugged his shoulders. "It's passing strange."

"I wonder," she said, then stopped.

"What?"

"Nothing."

"Well," he said, putting on his hat. "Wonders may occur, but there's still the new wheat to be seen to." He looked up at the sky, noting, with satisfaction, the heavy black clouds. "And it looks like we'll get our rain just when we need it."

"Rain," she said. "And what will it bring?" She crossed her arms, hugging herself.

"It'll bring water, love. To make the crops grow."

"And now you're glad."

"Hell, love," he said, "I'm a farmer first. Remember?"

29

Johannesburg

They landed back in Johannesburg at ten that night, coming into the little deserted airport they had left from. The buses were there to meet them, and Weston was there in a car with his chauffeur.

Cody stood and watched the men leaving the plane and boarding the buses. They moved like men in their sleep, stumbling with tiredness. On the way back, he'd announced over the plane intercom that full bonuses would be paid. There'd been a ragged cheer, but it had sounded mechanical. Smoking a cigarette, he watched them, knowing he'd never see any of them again. They would be taken to the armory, deprocessed and paid off. And then they would scatter.

He walked over to Weston's car and put his head in the window.

"Tallyho, Major," the cripple said softly.

Cody shook his head. "No. All the tallyhoing is over with. For me."

Weston said, "Neal is at my house. Waiting for you. He's already received some intelligence reports."

"All right," Cody said tiredly. "Let me see to this first."

He felt a hand touch his shoulder and looked around. Wilf Schneider and Peter Hawthorne were standing there.

Schneider said in his formal way, "I should like to congratulate you and thank you for a successful accomplishment." Then his voice changed. "And thank you for thinking of my friend Gerry."

Cody didn't say anything.

Hawthorne put out his hand. "A hell of a show, Major. But why in the name of Christ's church did you have to get into it? I saw you go running into that bloody blockhouse and I thought my heart would stop."

Cody smiled slowly and shook his head. "I don't know, Peter. I always thought I was the kind who didn't want to get involved. But I always seem to get into it somehow. You explain it to me sometime. I've given up."

Schneider said, "Nevertheless, we did it."

Cody looked at him, seeing his face distinctly in the dark. "What did we do, Wilf?"

The German said, "I don't know. But I know that we are here and we are alive."

Cody said, after a moment, "Yes, that's true."

It was a time later and they were lying in bed. It was morning and Cody had the paper Flic had brought him. He was reading about the protest that Zambia had lodged in the United Nations against Rhodesia. The representative from South Africa had arisen to ask proof be shown of the allegations of attacks on innocent villages. There had been none. In the end, a condemnation had been voted against Rhodesia. Cody lay there thinking what Neal Hall had said to him as he'd gripped his hand. "Good, lad," he'd said, his old voice strong and charged. "Good, lad. Fuck the bloody lot of them. Let them say what they want. You done it, lad, and they're lying over there licking their wounds. God bless you."

He thought of Ruth and of Bill and wondered how they were doing. He supposed he'd never see them again. He had hoped, as they'd passed over the farm, to catch a glimpse of Ruth, but it had all been just a blur.

He felt Flic's hand on his thigh, and he put the paper down.

"What are we going to do?" she asked him.

"I don't know," he answered. "I do know I'm going to stay still long enough to do some thinking for once. After that, I might know."

"Tell me something," she said.

He waited.

"Tell me why you brought your colonel to me?"

He looked across at the far wall. There was a mirror there and in it he could see them lying there together. He was stretched full out and she was curled by his side.

He said, "You want a straight answer?"

"Yes. I was very proud that you brought him to me. I'd like to know why, why you decided to trust me like that."

"You really don't want a straight answer, do you?"

"Yes, I do. Even if it's going to be bad."

"It's not so bad," he said. "First, there was no one else." He looked over at her. "And then, I believed that you wanted me to come back to you bad enough so that you weren't going to betray any trust I put in you. It was as simple as that."

"That's all right. I don't mind that answer."

He lay there staring up at the ceiling, thinking. It had been a week, but so much of it would come rushing back to overwhelm him sometimes.

She asked again, "What are we going to do?"

He suddenly sat up. "Goddammit, Louisa, I don't know."

In the mirror, he could see himself, see the lanyard

with the FN bullet hanging dark against his chest. He suddenly took it off and put it on the bedside stand.

"I can wait," she said. "We can stay here until you feel better. Why won't you talk to me about it?"

"Because I can't!" he said. "Dammit." He grimaced. "Try!"

"Look. It's not that I mind. It's just that you can't put your mouth on something like that. There're things that happen that words won't handle. I could describe some of it to you, but it wouldn't mean half the way it really was. I mean—" He stopped.

"Do you want a drink?"

He shook his head. "No. I don't want anything."

"Am I holding onto you?"

He turned and looked at her and half-laughed. "You know about how much good that would do."

"I must be crazy," she said. "You're going to make me unhappy as hell."

"You want to go up to Rhodesia? To live?"

"What would we do in Rhodesia?"

"I don't know. I'd fly for someone. You'd be with me."

"More shooting?" she asked him. "More shooting so that you grind your teeth at night and shake and sweat?"

He quickly looked around at her.

"Yes, you do. From the first night. Even after you've drunk so much you've passed out."

He suddenly got up and walked across the room to the window. It was raining outside, a steady, heavy downpour.

"The man told me once," he said, "that the only commitment a man had was to himself. Pick a purpose, he said, and commit yourself to it."

"Do you believe that?"

"Hell, no," he said. He came back and sat on the edge of the bed by her and lit a cigarette. He looked down at the glowing end. "He hated these foreign cigarettes, as he called them. He was always bitching about them."

"You thought a lot of him, didn't you? Your colonel."

"I don't know," he said. "He was very sure of himself. Never seemed to have any doubts. Didn't worry about what right or wrong was. But he was a mean bastard. He interrupted a lot of people's lives." He drew on his cigarette. "I imitated him for a few days. Played his part because he was already dead. But I didn't feel like it was me." He stopped.

She watched him, looking up at his face.

He said, "I hope what I did was important. One side thought it was. I did them some good."

He drew on his cigarette, still staring off. She put out a hand and laid it on his bare thigh.

"But the shooting—" he said. He stopped. "The killing—"

She waited, letting him talk.

"But no," he said. "No more shooting. Not for me. Not ever. No." He mashed his cigarette out in the ashtray. "Maybe someday I'll figure it out. What's important. And maybe I won't." He came around the bed and lay down beside her. "It's so simple," he said, "and yet it gets so fucking complicated. Every bastard wants something, and he's always got a damn good reason why he ought to have it."

"What do you want, Cody?"

He ignored the question. "Gerry was so afraid to die that he was in a hurry to find out what it would be like. Well, he managed that. And Wilf. I wonder if all Krauts are sensible. He got his money and now he's off sailing around the world. Dougie Lord! That's who I'd like to be like." He turned to her. "Stupid. Just blockheaded stupid so you don't have to think. If you outranked Lord and you told him black was white, he went color-blind. But he didn't have very fast reflexes. That's a mistake in somebody that follows blindly. The blind ought to have good reflexes."

She got up silently and left the room to make him a drink. When she returned, he was still laying on his back, still staring up at the ceiling, talking. "Bill and Ruth. They're sure. Hold onto the old home place. Hold on because it's ours. And did you know I hit a big paratrooper named Hawkins because he wasn't standing at attention? Now, does that make sense? If someone were to come into this room—why don't I hit you? You're not standing at attention."

"Here," she said.

He sat up and took the whiskey, drinking half of it in one pull. He paused and then drank the other half and handed back the glass.

"Matt. You know the only thing that worried Matt was what he was going to do next. I don't think he really minded getting it because, first, it was such a big joke on me and, second, because he didn't have anything else lined up. He told me one night, he said, 'Cowboy, the only thing that worries me about this campaign is where's the next one coming from.' How's that for insanity? But insanity, real insanity, is stacking them up in heaps. Do you know what heaps look like? Of course, I'm a big hero to Neal Hall. Rhodesia is mine, he said. Well, I don't blame him for knowing what he wanted."

"Cody, lie back."

He looked at her, finally focusing on her eyes. "Are you going to be bossy? What do you want, Louisa Durier? Tell us that. See if you can answer the easy questions."

"I want you to quit thinking about this for a while. I want you to relax and smile sometimes."

"Maybe I'll try that," he said. He held out his glass. "Fix me another drink. And make it a strong one."

She took the glass, but didn't move.

The phone began to ring. After a moment, Cody said,

"Either that's one of your customers or one of mine. Either way, tell them we've gone out of business."

"We don't have to answer it," she said.

"That's an idea." He lay his head back on the pillow. "Christ, I'm tired." He shut his eyes.